The Novel Exchange
..08 Main Street
..t Jefferson, N.Y. 11777

In the Panamanian city of Cristobal, Schleichner hesitated before stepping into the dark street. He frowned toward the limousine, unsure why it was moving without lights.

"Go on!" urged Hartman. "Go on!"

Schleichner finally turned to run.

The limousine struck Schleichner. He screamed; his body hit the windshield.

The assasins began to reverse away from the obstruction.

Unhurriedly, Hartman started his own car and drove carefully in the opposite direction.

It had been a sensible precaution, employing Schleichner; after thirty-five years, the Nazis were still very good at protecting themselves.

OTHER BOOKS BY JONATHAN EVANS
Available from Tor

Misfire
Takeover
The Sagomi Gambit

JONATHAN EVANS

THE SOLITARY MAN

A TOM DOHERTY ASSOCIATES BOOK

This is a work of fiction. All the characters and events portrayed in this book are fictional, and any resemblance to real people or incidents is purely coincidental.

Copyright © 1980 by Innslodge Publications Ltd., 1983 by Jonathan Evans

All rights reserved, including the right to reproduce this book or portions thereof in any form

A Tor Book

Published by Tom Doherty Associates, 8-10 W. 36th St., New York City, N.Y. 10018

First printing, November 1983

Book I is reprinted by arrangement with Coward, McCann & Geoghegan.

ISBN: 0-523-48082-2

CAN. ED.: 812-50-280-9

Printed in the United States of America

Distributed by Pinnacle Books, 1430 Broadway, New York, N.Y. 10018

For Anne Brown, with much love

No arts; no letters; no society; and which is worst of all, continual fear and danger of violent death; and the life of man, solitary, poor, nasty, brutish and short.

Thomas Hobbes, *Leviathan*

THE SOLITARY MAN

BOOK I

I

Cristobal has a deceptively respectable appearance, viewed from the port where the ships pause before entering the Panama Canal on their way from the Atlantic to the Pacific. Beyond the ocher- and yellow-washed buildings, French colonial with a suggestion of Beau Geste from the castellated balconies, it is an arm-grabbing, loosely lawed bazaar of a place. Inside the shops, robbery is disguised as good trading. Outside, it is ignored by the police. The shopkeepers consider themselves competitive. The muggers on the streets and alleys think they reflect the Panamanian irritation that it took the U.S. so long to recognize that this canal was not rightfully theirs.

There is a profusion of watch shops, selling the latest digital miracle from Tokyo, and the Indian traders blaze Bombay and Delhi silks from their open-fronted emporiums like fly-eating plants trapping prey with the brightness of their colors. Every street has its brothel, sometimes several. They have names like Eden and Paradise and Delight, but there are not enough local women to staff them. The government therefore engages on a six-month, medically guaranteed contract Colombian girls who work to raise the dowries for their white weddings in Bogota or Medellin or Barranquilla. The Catholic Church, practical as always, allows the arrangement to go uncriticized: the shame of not having a dowry is greater than the shame of having been a whore, and perhaps not surprisingly the training appears a useful basis for happy, contented marriages within the neighboring country.

Hartman supposed it was the nearest he would ever come to being in an American frontier town. He didn't want to come any closer. It made him nervous. The danger on the streets was greater after dark. Then the blackened alleys were full of movement and the pavement-jostling was more obvious, inviting challenge. Hugo Hartman never challenged.

He had rented a car, deciding it was necessary because it gave him some protection and, for tonight, some concealment as well. He'd locked it from the inside and sat low in the seat, a man who found it easy to be unobtrusive.

He wore suits with vests, to conceal the middle-aged thickness of his waist. The diabetes, which was not serious but merely a hazard of his age and easily controlled by pills, had nevertheless affected his eyes, making glasses necessary for any complicated work. He looked like a senior and rather self-satisfied clerk within window-shopping time of the retirement clock. This was misleading, but an appearance with which he was content: Hartman had never been self-satisfied and knew it would be difficult to retire, even though he wanted to, desperately.

Hartman, who had more reason than most men to know he was not brave, had been surprised at his response to the assignment. There had been fear, which had been natural enough: even an attempt to argue his way out of it in the air-conditioned calm of the CIA offices in the American Embassy in Paris. They had refused his objection, of course, arguing that someone who had spent two years in Bergen-Belsen was the obvious person for the final identification.

He'd expected to be terrified at his first sight of Fritz Lang: the numbing, unable-to-move-or-breathe type of horror that he had known so often in the camp. But it hadn't come; not fear anyway. There had been the stomach lurch of recognition, perhaps of apprehension, too, but that was all. It had taken Hartman several days to realize why, and he had grown annoyed at himself for confused thinking. Lang had been the commandant, the supreme arbiter over life and death, but removed from the inmates in the day-to-day running of the place. Lang hadn't been the man who had made Gerda his personal property, manipulating and goading and degrading her.

There was movement across the street, and Hartman squinted intently. Then he saw it was a whore and her client making their way toward a hotel, and relaxed. Would he get enough tonight to confirm the identity of the former Nazi? Not his doubt; Hartman didn't have any, not any longer. But he knew the CIA would demand more. The build of the man he had been sent to identify was heavier than he personally remembered from Belsen and from the dossier he had formulated after the war. And the face had been altered. But the ears were the same; Hartman often wondered why people bothering with the discomfort of plastic surgery always forgot how identifiable ears were. The man whose real-estate office Hartman was sitting opposite, and who now called himself José Lopez, had identical ears to the man in the faded SS picture of Friz Lang, which the Americans had given him at the briefing in Paris six weeks earlier.

It wouldn't have been enough on its own, of course. Hartman was a cautious man, in everything, and wanted as much as Washington further evidence than a vaguely matching stature and an apparent physical similarity. More, even, than the unexpected discovery that a small-town real-estate operator possessed a numbered Swiss bank account supplying him with a monthly income, which must exceed what he managed to earn promoting residential development in Cristobal. Hartman had been surprised how easy it had been to learn that; as surprised as his lack of fear at coming so close to Friz Lang.

A town as open and with as much moving population as Cristobal had obvious advantages for an on-the-run Nazi, but the corrupt environment also had inherent dangers. It had taken Hartman less than a week of observation to identify the regular mailman, two days to make his acquaintance, and just $500 to be given access, before delivery, to Lang's mail. The envelope with the Zurich postmark and the $400 bank draft had arrived two days after Hartman had established his interception. He'd copied the contents and replaced them in the envelope so quickly that the delivery to Lang's office was only five minutes later than normal.

Hartman shifted to ease the cramp and scrubbed his hand over the window to avoid it becoming misted up. So far it had been a very fortunate assignment; one of the luckiest he could recall. The information that had guided him to Lang had been provided by the CIA, a comparatively complete file which needed only his final confirmation. He'd stumbled across Werner Schleichner by accident. Not true, Hartman corrected himself. Not completely, anyway. He'd learned it by being thorough and because nearly all the first week of the assignment had been spent in mildewed, rat-running archives, until his weakened eyes had ached and his clothes had stunk from contact with the decayed paper of the naturalization applications that had been made to the Panamanian Ministry of the Interior.

There had been no record under Lang, and then he had remembered that the name of Lang's wife had been Siemens and decided to try the 'S' section. There had been no listing for the former camp commandant, but he'd found Werner Schleichner. He had recalled the man, just as he could remember every Nazi whose history had passed through his hands at the bureau formed in Vienna after the war. Schleichner was regarded as a relatively minor criminal, responsible only for the deaths of a hundred people at Dachau. But after what had happened to Hartman, no Nazi was unimportant.

He would have needed a guinea pig anyway, at some stage of the inquiry, and he thought of the medical-experimentation sections of the camp and savored the irony of employing Schleichner for the purpose. There had always been the risk of the two men knowing each other, even though Schleichner's detective agency was forty miles away at the other end of the canal in Panama. Schleichner might have been a corporal and Lang a commandant, and neither might ever have been attached to the same camp, but frequently links had been established after the war which had overlooked previous rank or position.

So Hartman had been circumspect at the first interview, intent for any indication from the man. There had been nothing: only proof of the lawlessness of the country in which Lang had chosen to hide himself. Perhaps nowhere but in South America would a man have accepted without question, as Schleichner had, that the way to prove a crime was to commit one. For $1,000, Schleichner had agreed to break into Lang's premises.

For a week, Hartman had watched Schleichner watching Lang. Not once had there been any sign of recognition between the former Nazis. But Hartman was convinced that Lang had identified the surveillance. It was going to be a useful test, seeing how the man reacted: a behavioral experiment of the sort with which Lang had once been so familiar.

Schleichner intended making the entry around midnight, when the streets began to get quiet, and Hartman strained through the darkness, trying to isolate Lang's one-roomed office from the others within the sleeping building. It was 11:55, so Schleichner must be inside. Would he obey the instructions explicitly? It was necessary that the man behave exactly as he had been told, in case Lang had put the place under guard. Tensed though he was, Hartman almost missed the movement when it came—it was little more than a shadow changing shape—and then Hartman identified the figure. Where was the envelope? Schleichner *had* to be carrying an envelope. Ten yards from Lang's office there was a bar that remained open later than all the rest. Colored bulbs were rainbowed over the entrance: some had blown, but in the uneven light that remained Hartman saw the manila shape in Schleichner's hand and nodded at the discipline that remained, even after so long.

The other watchers, whom Hartman had not isolated, must have seen the package at the same time and realized how close the man was to the mailbox. Their car started with a sudden, hurrying screech of tires, attracting Schleichner's attention. The man turned, at that stage no more than curious. Hartman couldn't see, but Schleichner was probably frowning toward the limousine, unsure why it was moving without lights.

"Go on!" urged Hartman, quietly, pumping his fist against the steering wheel. "Go on!"

Schleichner's hesitation seemed to last an interminable time. Then he began backing away and finally turned to run.

"The mailbox," implored Hartman. "Don't forget the mailbox."

Schleichner raced toward it, as if it were some sort of sanctuary where he would be safe. The car was very close now, traveling unnaturally fast for the narrow streets. As he fled in and out of the patches of light, head twisted for sight of those behind him, Schleichner created a bizarre kaleidoscope of terror. Schleichner reached the box seconds before the car got to him; the driver was pumping the horn, risking the attention in an effort to disorient the man before he had time to thrust the envelope through the slit.

The two events were practically simultaneous. The package went into the box as the car struck Schleichner. At the last moment, the Nazi screamed, more in fear than immediate pain, and tried to leap sideways to avoid the vehicle. The hood caught him at the base of the spine, arcing him backward so fast that Schleichner was lifted completely clear of the ground. His body thumped against the windshield and then appeared to be projected forward again. His arms were thrown out, in something like an embrace, and then he hit the display window of the watch emporium. Had the fender of the vehicle not hit it too, then it is unlikely that the force of Schleichner's body would have shattered the glass. The window caved inward, with a loud, cracking implosion, and at once the burglar alarms clanged out into the street.

The assassins' car began to reverse away from the obstruction of the window. Schleichner had landed in a crooked, upright sitting position and watches spilled all over him, so that he appeared like some obscene advertisement for the contents. There was a further brief hesitation as the occupants stared in at the watch-strewn body, to decide if there would be sufficient time to search it before the arrival of the police. Then they completed the reverse and accelerated away.

Unhurriedly, Hartman started his own car and drove carefully in the opposite direction. There would still be enough activity around the shop front when the box was emptied the following morning to prevent any interception by Lang's people. Neither would they have sufficient time to suborn the mailman as he had done. So the envelope was safe. Just as he was safe. It had been a sensible precaution, employing Schleichner; after thirty-five years, they were still very good at protecting themselves.

There was still no sign of the police when Hartman turned toward the waterfront. He paused at the intersection, glancing back; already a crowd had formed around the shop. By the time the police got there, a lot of watches would have been taken. Maybe even Schleichner's wallet. It was, after all, a very lawless place.

For a section head to travel all the way from Washington showed how important the CIA regarded the operation, and Peter Berman was aware of it. If only it could have been someone different from William Davidson. He was a neglected uncared-for man. His suits strained tightly around his bulging stomach, like a skin just about to split and be discarded. After every meal, most of which he ate messily, frequently spilling from his spoon or fork down the front of his already marked shirt, he picked his teeth, usually with a spent match. Berman thought he was disgusting and had decided that the man was a prick. Berman was a very ambitious man and regarded it as frightening that such a person controlled his future with the Agency. And Davidson did control it—jealously. Blocked from any further promotion and unable to accept the failed promise of his OSS career, Davidson apepared determined to go through the remainder of his operational life isolating others' mistakes to prove to his superiors how wrong they had been in not elevating him higher.

"I'm not at all sure it was the right decision to involve Hugo Hartman," said Davidson. "Not at all sure."

The man spoke as if he were addressing a large gathering and expected the words to be recorded for posterity.

"The information giving us the lead to Lang originated here in Paris," reminded Berman. "Hartman is attached to us and was actually imprisoned in Belsen. He was the obvious, logical choice."

"Should have been a CIA man. An American," insisted Davidson.

"Hartman is the best freelance we've got," said Berman, who had been the man's Control for five years. "Better than a lot of our own people."

"You're too impressed by him," protested Davidson. "Are you aware how we could use the information about Lang, if it all checks out?"

"Of course I am," said Berman irritably. Davidson was lapsing into his avuncular headmaster's pose. It was one of his favorites.

"Ivan Migal is head of the European Division of the

KGB,'' lectured Davidson as if he had not heard Berman's assurance. ''One of the three or four top men. If it can be proved, as our information suggests, that in the last stages of the war he worked clandestinely with Fritz Lang to get from Bergen-Belsen Russian prisoners-of-war whom the Soviet Union wanted to liquidate, we could throw so much shit into the fan that their service would smell for years!''

''I've had the whole operation outlined,'' said Berman patiently.

''You didn't tell Hartman of any Soviet involvement?'' demanded Davidson hurriedly.

''Of course not,'' said Berman, not bothering to disguise his attitude. ''His function is to identify Lang and then get the man to run. And we'll keep nicely in step to see which way he goes.''

''We hope,'' warned Davidson.

''Yes,'' agreed Berman. ''We hope.''

2

Hartman had for a long time been accustomed to his wife's mental condition, but on his last visit to Connecticut, on the way to Cristobal, there had been a physical deterioration in Gerda which had alarmed him. The telephone exchange almost immediately opposite the dock gate is American-maintained and therefore efficient; Hartman reached his son's clinic on the outskirts of Thomsonville with only a minimal delay. Thoughtlessly, he had not made it a person-to-person call, so it actually took longer to locate David than it had to establish the connection.

David stressed the irritation when he finally came on to the line. "What do you want?"

"How's your mother?"

"Ill," said David. "I thought you knew that."

Hartman sighed, no longer angered by the boy's attitude. There might be reason enough, but sometimes it seemed David enjoyed expressing the contempt.

"She seemed physically ill last time," he said, making the distinction.

"She is," confirmed David. "Since your visit, she's developed a pleurisy."

"How serious?"

"Everything is serious in someone as frail as she is."

"Is she still with you?"

"Of course. Why?"

"I thought she might have been moved to another hospital."

"We can care for physical as well as mental illness here," said his son.

"Perhaps I should come up."

"It won't do any good," said David positively. "It never has."

"No," agreed Hartman. She *had* known him once: there'd been the smile he'd recognized and the finger pressure to show him she had been aware of his presence.

"I'm very busy," said his son.

"I'll call you, as often as I can."

"I wish you wouldn't. I've got your Vienna address if there's any need to contact you."

"I'm moving around; you probably wouldn't get me there."

"All right," said David, indicating by his tone that the calls would be intrusive.

"How's Ruth?"

"She's well," said David, impatient with the forced politeness. "I really am very busy."

"I want to be there," said Hartman insistently. "I want to be there when . . ." He broke off, unable to finish.

" . . . when she dies," finished David. There was no sympathy in his voice.

"Yes."

"You'd better keep in touch," agreed the son.

Hartman halted outside the exchange, remaining in the protective shade of the building. Although not yet midday, the sun was already bleaching the color from everything around. From the pole on the administration building, the flag drooped listlessly, untouched by the wind. He made no move to leave the shade, his mind held by the conversation with his son.

It had seemed so sensible, all those years ago; so sensible and so logical and, in the early months, when she had appeared to respond to the different environment, so promising. It had been David who had suggested the transfer, arguing that Gerda would always associate Europe with horror, and that her best chance of recovery was to put her instead into the loving care of a son whose qualifications as a psychiatrist were as good as any who had so far examined her.

There had been friendship between him and David then; the proper father-and-son respect. And no thought of failure either. They'd planned her recuperation and the life they would lead, living close to each other in Connecticut. And even Hartman, who had known it to be impossible, though for other reasons, had been excited by it.

He had never seen the danger. And even if he had, he would still have taken the risk, in the hope that Gerda might have been brought back to reality; for that, any sacrifice would have been worth while. But she hadn't. There had been brief flashes of rationality, sometimes for as long as a month, which had given them the false expectation. But then had come the inevitable regression, each longer than that which had preceeded it, each more difficult to bring her from than the last.

He'd already lost a wife by the time Gerda got to America, and by taking her there, a son as well. From his treatment and his analysis of his mother, David had learned what she had had to do to keep alive an ineffectual, weak husband. Hartman had been making frequent visits then, sometimes three a month, and he had seen the attitude develop in the young man from disbelief to shocked contempt and finally to hatred. Irrationally, and illfitting a man trained to reason and logic, David didn't hate the Nazis for what had happened, but his father for wanting to live so badly that he had been prepared to allow the degradation.

Hartman shook off the thoughts, a physical movement like an animal discarding water from its coat. All the hurt had been caused and the recriminations uttered, so there was little point in yet another examination. He had an assignment to complete, and the memories were disruptive, threatening his efficiency. And nothing could be allowed to threaten that.

He moved into the sun, feeling the perspiration prick out at once upon his skin; he was glad it was such a short detour to the post office. He should have left off the vest. He went right, circling the block, and then back into the welcoming protection of the post office. He did not approach the desk dealing with the box-number deliveries, instead busying himself with a holiday postcard he seemed to have difficulty composing, enabling him to study the other people in the room, to decide if any particular observation were being kept. There was no way Lang could have learned of the general-delivery device, nor cause for him to guess it, but it was instinctive of Hartman to behave with such caution.

Satisfied at last, he went to the counter and produced the authorization certificate. The clerk smiled, went to the boxes rectangled behind him, and returned with the manila envelope that Hartman had last seen clutched in the hand of the fleeing Nazi. Hartman put it into the inside pocket of his jacket before turning, so that it would not have been visible to anyone beyond the counter.

It had probably been an unnecessary precaution, but Hartman had returned the rental car, in case the watchers outside Lang's office the previous night had recorded the numbers of all the vehicles in the street and tried to associate any of them with the burglary. There was a taxi waiting at the stand opposite. Hartman gave the address of the American administration office for the canal maintenance he had copied that morning from the telephone book. Only after he had ensured there were no following vehicles did he change his mind, canceling the destination and giving the name of his hotel.

It was a decaying, sun-cracked building, constructed by the French after the style of some of the waterfront buildings. The wicker chairs were splintered and threatened collapse, and rats and cockroaches moved in the quieter corners of the public rooms, untroubled by either the residents or the packs of emaciated, sharp-ribbed cats, which seemed burdened by the heat into a permanent dozing lethargy. The hotel had been built too early for air conditioning and the fans were locked in frozen immobility by some long-forgotten mechanical fault. Hartman, who had an inherent dislike of filth after three years in a concentration camp, detested the place. Since his arrival he had averaged three showers a day, and knew the skin rash that had developed upon his arms and around his stomach was caused by a nervous reaction, not by the amount of soap he was using upon himself.

He locked his bedroom door, then operated the handle to test if it was secure before taking the envelope from his pocket; it seemed remarkably thin. He moved to the bedside table, near the window, where there was more light. There were eight statements, properly stapled in order of arrival and showing that the $400 was dispatched from Zurich on the same day of every month; another set of local bank records recording, among ordinary payments, a $100 transfer on the eighth of every month to the Broadway and 57th Street branch of the Chase Manhattan Bank in New York; and five checkbook stubs recording local financial dealings. All the notations were in German. Hartman took the CIA file from his briefcase, searching through for photostats of Lang's wartime records. There was an unsteadiness which Hartman would have expected from age, but the documents in Lang's handwriting matched perfectly the inscriptions upon the check receipts; like ears, thought Hartman, handwriting was usually identifiable. There were copies of several land leases, which presumably Schleichner had thought appropriate for anyone investigating an embezzlement of resources, and Lang's membership certificate of some local real-estate association.

The last item was the most interesting. The Panamanian passport, now expired, must have been the first one issued to Lang under his phony name. It was dated 1952, and Hartman wondered where Lang had spent the intervening seven years after the war. He went carefully through it, page by page, learning the extent of Lang's travels. In 1956, he had visited Bonn, and again the following year. There were several visa stamps to South America, predominantly to Paraguay, and between 1957 and 1963 he had averaged three trips a year to America; New York was always recorded as the point of entry.

The scrap of paper fell from the passport as Hartman reached the last page. He bent to retrieve it, curiously. One edge was gummed, where it had been torn from an envelope flap. The word Eros had been written on it, in Lang's handwriting, followed by the figures 1980074. Hartman stared down at the familiar number, then took up the statements of the Bank of Panama and checked against the monthly $100 transfer to New York. It matched. Eros, he read again; the god of love. What connection was there between the god of love, $100 a month, and a former Nazi concentration-camp commandant? It didn't matter, as far as the present assignment was concerned: his instruction had merely been positively to identify Fritz Lang, nothing more.

Hartman waited for the heat to go out of the day before leaving the hotel again. He'd ordered the letterheaded paper from the printer on the same day as he had intercepted the first bank transfer from Zurich, and he examined it critically while the clerk was calculating his change. There had been no correspondence among the contents that Schleichner had taken from the safe, so it was unlikely that Lang would be familiar with the paper. Hartman, who had accounts at two Zurich banks and another in Geneva, knew it to be a good facsimile; good enough to convince Lang, anyway. There was more difficulty in obtaining the proper electric typewriter, and briefly Hartman feared the whole idea was going to collapse. There was a wide selection available, but they were directed toward the American market, and the first eight that he examined were all made with an English keyboard arrangement. It was not until the fifth shop that he found one with a European typeface, complete with umlaut key to provide the German punctuation that would be necessary for forgery.

It was dark when Hartman deposited his purchases at the hotel and set out for the last appointment of the day. He began regretting the decision to abandon the rental car and its protection. The bar in which he had arranged to meet Lang's mailman was at one corner of the market. The square appeared empty, the stalls and benches skeletal without canopies or contents, and it was only by looking very hard that he could see the shifting movement of people who regarded the space beneath a vegetable cart as home. Once, thought Hartman, he would also have thought of it as a home, and eaten the scraps that fell between the slats.

The conversation was instantly still at the entry of a stranger. Hartman had learned to conceal his fear, so there was no outward sign of the uncertainty he felt. He remained at the door, staring around. There was a remark, he didn't see from whom, answered by a sudden snigger. Hartman saw the man at a table by the window. Still he waited, for a sign of recognition. He didn't want the man frightened, having to acknowledge their association in front of his friends. The mailman smiled, thrusting his foot out beneath the table so that the empty chair moved back in invitation. The gesture was seen in the bar and the talk started again, slowly at first and then with less restraint; it was still quiet around their table, as people immediately adjacent attempted to eavesdrop.

"Didn't know whether you'd come," said the man. He was of mixed race. European-featured with a black skin.

"I said I would," reminded Hartman.

"There's been trouble," said the man.

"Trouble?"

"Inquiries about letters being opened."

It was a lie, Hartman knew: the beginning of the bargaining for a bigger bribe than before.

"You suspected?"

"I might be. Don't know yet."

"I want to look again, tomorrow." It was the day of the Zurich letter.

The man shook his head doubtfully. "It's getting too dangerous," he said. "I don't think I should risk it."

Should he finish the charade and frighten the man into agreement by threatening to expose him for what he had already done? Hartman looked around the bar; he was only there on sufferance, the sufferance of the man sitting opposite. The barman interpreted the gesture as an inquiry for a drink and approached the table.

"Beer," ordered Hartman, looking toward the mailman.

"Whisky," accepted the man, who had been drinking wine. "Imported Scotch."

"It's important to me," resumed Hartman.

"Too dangerous," repeated the man. "I could lose my job. Five hundred dollars isn't worth losing my job for."

It was probably more than the man earned in a year, thought Hartman. "Six hundred," he said.

The man laughed, a sneering sound. "You insult me."

"How much?"

"A thousand." He blinked, astonished at his own demand, and couldn't stop the quick, unsteady smile.

"It's a lot of money," protested Hartman.

The drinks came, and Hartman saw a lipstick smear on the rim of his glass; he pushed it aside. He wanted very much to get back to the hotel and shower.

"It's my career."

"I could manage seven fifty."

The man shook his head again, a weaker refusal this time. "There are inquiries, I tell you."

"Seven fifty," insisted Hartman.

"I'll have to think about it."

"I need to know. Now."

The man shrugged, as if he were making a concession he would later regret. "Eight hundred?" he tried hopefully.

"Seven fifty."

"If it weren't for my wife and the operations she has to have, I wouldn't do it."

"I understand," said Hartman, entering the game for the man's conscience.

"She's very sick."

"I'm sorry."

"You don't know what it's like, to have a sick wife."

"No," he agreed. He'd passed the time when remarks like that unbalanced him.

The man waited, still hopeful.

"Seven fifty," said Hartman.

The man humped his shoulders, a brief gesture of agreement.

"My hotel room," stipulated Hartman.

The gesture came again. Hartman looked around the bar. He was still the object of attention. The quality of the suit would have been noted, and the fact that his watch and signet ring were gold; probably the word had already gone out to the stall dwellers.

"Can you get me a taxi from here?" asked Hartman.

The mailman looked around the room and then back to Hartman.

"I should travel with you," he said, conscious of the need to protect an investment.

"Yes."

The man stayed very close to him when they left the bar, and Hartman realized it wasn't a theatrical precaution. A sullenness seemed to have settled in the room at the thought of a lost opportunity, and in the few seconds it took to cross to the taxi, Hartman saw that several figures had emerged from beneath the carts.

He remained for a long time under the shower back at the hotel, uncaring that the heat of the water burned the soreness upon his arms and waist. He'd seen a doctor about it, decided Hartman, when he got back to Vienna.

Hartman had bought some copying paper, as well as the letterheads, and rejected several attempts before drafting a letter which satisfied him. Even then it took another hour, because Hartman was an inexpert typist and had to abandon three half-completed letters because of mistyping; Swiss secretaries, like the banks that employ them, rarely make mistakes.

It was not a long letter, but Hartman was confident it would have the effect he wanted upon the former camp commandant.

"Dear Señor Lopez," he wrote, "I have been instructed to inform you that the funds from which we were authorized to remit the monthly sum of $400 (four hundred dollars) in your favor have been withdrawn and that you will be aware of the reason. Should there be an opportunity in the future, I assure you of our willingness to act upon your behalf."

Hartman scrawled a signature, identifying it as that of the vice-president in charge of overseas accounts. He read the copy several times, deciding it was an improvement upon the earlier, longer attempts, carefully folded it, and put it into his briefcase.

How long, he wondered, would it take Fritz Lang to run?

"Anything?"

"No," said Berman. He was concerned at the lack of contact from Hartman, but determined not to allow Davidson to take any advantage from it.

"I think we should consider moving our own people in."

"No!" said Berman urgently. "That could screw the whole thing. For God's sake, give Hugo a chance."

"He's had six weeks. How much does he want?"

"As long as it takes," came back Berman immediately. "He's thorough and he's good and he's accurate."

"But he's not an *American,*" said Davidson.

"No," agreed Berman, turning the qualification. "Which is exactly why we use him as we do. If Hugo gets caught, in Panama, he's a solitary Nazi-hunter trying to get his revenge for what happened in the war. And we're out, squeaky clean."

"A week," ordered Davidson, unimpressed with the argument. "If there's nothing in a week, I want more people sent in. Understood?"

"Understood," accepted Berman.

"*American,*" emphasized the section head.

3

Hartman was ready before the promised arrival of the bribed mailman. He moved the table nearer to the window, so that anyone standing at it would have his back completely to the room, and arranged the money in disorganized piles which would need concentration to count. He brought the table farther around, once, to provide the position he wanted and then rehearsed the imagined behavior of the man, checking to ensure that any movement from the bed would be unnoticed.

From the briefcase he took the letter he had forged the previous night, sliding it beneath the folded coverlet, then stood back near the door, surveying the preparations. The knock came anxiously, ahead of time, and the man hurried into the room when Hartman opened it, looking over his shoulder into the corridor as if expecting pursuit.

"It wasn't easy getting in here," protested the man.

"But you managed it," said Hartman. He had expected the final attempt to increase the price.

"It's dangerous. . . . I'm known in this town."

"The money is over there," said Hartman, sure of the effect.

The man's eyes visibly widened at the profusion of notes and his tongue came out from between his lips, as if he were experiencing a pleasant taste. Any further bargaining had gone out of his mind.

"The letters," insisted Hartman, holding out his hand.

"The mailman didn't move, held by the cash.

"Letters," repeated Hartman.

As it had been before, the mail was held together with coarse string; there were several circulars and about six envelopes. Hartman took the package, but didn't untie it.

"Count the money," he invited.

The man went slowly toward the table, stopping exactly as Hartman had anticipated he would, with his back to the room. He began to check the amount, hands moving very slowly, his lips twitching in time with the calculation. Hartman untied the letters with his eyes still upon the man, watching for any sudden shift of attention. The Panamanian was mesmerized by the cash.

Hartman bent away, looking for the Zurich postmark. It was the fourth letter, the quality of the paper heavier than the rest. Hartman tested the seal, a penknife blade beneath the flap to ease it open. It tore, twice, but not seriously in either place, and Hartman was confident it could be concealed when he stuck the flap down again. The draft and the statement were identical to those he had seen before. He hesitated, checking the man at the table once more, then pocketed the check and the statement and substituted the letter. It was done very quickly. There was sufficient adhesion without the glue he had bought, in case it had been necessary. He stuck the flap back, concentrating upon the tearing. It was completely hidden. It had all been remarkably simple. He remembered his thoughts outside Lang's office: a very fortunate assignment.

Hartman had retied the letters by the time the man turned back into the room; his jacket was bulged in several places, where he had bundled the money about himself.

"Thank you," said Hartman, offering the package.

"You didn't take anything? You just looked?"

"Just looked," assured Hartman.

"There *are* inquiries."

"You told me."

"It won't be easy again."

"We'll see," said Hartman. It was best to let the man believe there would be another time.

"I'm late."

"Then you'd better go."

"I'm at the bar, most nights," said the man hopefully.

"I'll remember."

"Rarely leave before ten."

"I know."

"Goodbye then."

"Wait." Hartman stopped him at the door and the man turned.

"Here," said Hartman.

"What is it?"

"Changed my mind," said Hartman. "We'll make it eight hundred."

Greedily the man reached out for the extra fifty dollars and Hartman looked at him sympathetically. He'd twitched and winced and been cowed like that once, Hartman recalled. And hoarded things about his body, just like the man was trying to conceal the money: food, mostly. There had always been the need for extra food. But money, sometimes. And even small pieces of jewelry that he had managed to steal when he was undressing the bodies or cleaning out the cattle trucks. On one occasion in the first weeks, before he had been made a trustee, Hartman had saved himself from an extermination line by giving a small diamond tiepin to the guard.

"Thank you," said the mailman fervently.

"You earned it," said Hartman. Poor bastard, he thought.

He locked the door behind the other man, automatically checking it was secure, then lifted the briefcase onto the bed and spread out over the coverlet the information he had obtained proving that José Lopez, Panamanian real-estate operator, was Fritz Lang, former Bergen-Belsen camp commandant. The checkbook stubs, compared with the man's handwriting, were the most positive evidence; and the early passport photograph, when the plastic surgery must have been very new and Lang's features could be distinguished more easily, under microscope magnification. The Swiss account was intriguing, but without any way of discovering the source to be what it obviously was, yet another tap into the vast pool of Nazi funds. It was not by itself sufficient.

Idly he flicked over the torn envelope flap upon which Eros and 1980074 were written and then picked up the local bank statements with the corresponding number. A side account, unknown to any Nazi paymaster with access to Zurich? The most likely explanation, decided Hartman. He picked up the expired passport again. There had been visits enough to New York, in the initial years of Lang's arrival in Panama. He would have still been nervous then, anxious to establish another escape route.

Hartman brought himself back to the scrap of paper and the local accounts. He wouldn't include them in the dossier to be compiled for Peter Berman. He'd proof enough, without it.

Because it was so early, he was able to reach the telephone exchange before it got really hot; he remembered the previous day's mistake, this time discarding the vest. Without it, he felt curiously half dressed, as if his trouser zipper might be undone. He selected the number at the Paris embassy by which Berman would know he was calling from a public exchange and avoid any indiscretion.

"Thank Christ you've called."

"What's the matter?"

"It's been six weeks."

"I had to be sure."

"I'm not criticizing. There has been local pressure."

"It's the man," reported Hartman. "I've definite, unquestionable proof."

Berman didn't respond immediately. Seven thousand miles from the sticky booth in which Hartman stood, Berman gazed through the embassy window over the orderly, winter-chilled streets of the French capital and felt the relief go through his body. He was going to enjoy the meeting with Davidson.

"Are you there?" demanded Hartman.

"Sorry," apologized Berman. "Just thinking. What have you done?"

"You instructed me to make him run," reminded Hartman.

"When will it be?"

"I don't know. I want you to be ready."

"Where?"

"I'd guess Switzerland."

"You'll check his departure?"

"Of course. There'll be enough time to get into position. But I think it would be wise to establish something in Zurich."

"All right," said Berman. "I'm very grateful for what you've done."

"It hasn't worked yet," warned Hartman.

"It's going to," said Berman confidently. "You've done a terrific job."

It was a comparatively easy surveillance to establish. There had always been the possibility that Lang would drive to Panama, but Hartman had guessed the train to be the more obvious choice and he was proved right. He had positioned himself in a bar with a view of Lang's office, just in case the man entered a vehicle, but shortly before the noon train he emerged and turned right, striding toward the harbor station. He carried an overnight bag. Sure of the man's destination, Hartman made no obvious attempt to follow, not bothering to purchase his ticket or board the train until just before departure and making no effort to locate Lang's compartment.

The carriages were very old and much traveled, straw and packing leaking from the seats; animal droppings mixed on the floor with discarded cigarette packets and food paper, and there was an odor of decay and dust.

Very soon they cleared the high-fenced protection erected alongside the canal by the American administration and entered the jungle. It encroached to the very edge of the track, vines cobwebbed between the trees to form a lattice among which the birds and monkeys fluttered and screeched. Once Hartman thought he saw a larger animal, but whatever it was moved too quickly for identification, leaving only shuddering tree fronds behind it. When the canal came into view again, it had lifted up through the first of the locks to the settled, middle section, widening out into broader lakes. Later, Hartman knew, it narrowed again before the locks which completed the adjustment between the differing levels of the Pacific and Atlantic oceans. Long-billed water birds stalked with majestic disdain among the reed grasses, and from the rail of a waiting vessel a man leaned, unaware of their passing, a fishing rod between his hands. The effort surprised Hartman, who illogically hadn't thought of there being fish in the canal. As if to prove him wrong, the man began hauling something in. He was too far away to see what it was.

All the windows were open, to trap whatever breeze was available, and mosquitoes and flies were blown constantly into his face; he sat with his hand before him, fanning himself for protection. He felt very damp and uncomfortable; it would be good to get back to the coolness of Europe. And to Rebecca. He hadn't allowed himself to think of Rebecca very much since he'd been away. But now the assignment was almost over; soon he would be going home. To the woman he loved.

Hartman was more alert at the Panama disembarkation, ready at the door when the train pulled in and one of the first to pass through the barrier. There was the customary crush at the taxi stand and Hartman failed to get the vehicle directly behind the Nazi. Fortunately there was a line of cars, and there were only fifty yards between them. Hartman chanced the airport, sitting forward upon his seat and gazing at the taxi ahead, tensed for any unexpected change of direction. Again he had guessed correctly.

Hartman was about twenty yards away as the German entered the airport terminal. Lang went to the Varig desk and Hartman stood back near the departure board, checking the convenient flights. One to New York, one to Buenos Aires, and another to Istanbul; the Istanbul flight stopped at Zurich. He located a closed booth to cut down the airport noise. Lang was moving too fast to use any other name than the one on his Panamanian passport, estimated Hartman. When Varig flight information answered him they confirmed that a J. Lopez was on the Istanbul aircraft, with a reservation as far as Zurich.

Hartman went to the post office section at the airport for his international connection with Peter Berman; despite the time difference in Europe, the CIA man was still on duty in the embassy compound.

"A full ten hours to get ourselves into position," said Berman enthusiastically.

"Yes."

"Like I said before, Hugo, a terrific job."

"Thank you."

"You'll bring the dossier in, on the way back to Vienna?"

"Yes."

"I'll be expecting you."

Hartman remained at the barrier, watching Lang board the European flight, then went to the Panam desk and worked through the schedules with the clerk. There was a midnight plane to Madrid which connected with an outward flight to France; it was as convenient as any direct routing to Vienna. Hartman selected the most comfortable taxi available, a Mercedes. The round trip to Cristobal to collect his luggage took four hours. He abandoned the electric typewriter in his room, sure it would quickly be converted into a gratuity for nonexistent service.

Because his diabetes demanded that he eat regularly, he went into the airport restaurant, dining from necessity rather than from enjoyment. Still with time to occupy, he telephoned David in Connecticut.

"The same as she was before, when you last called," said his son; there was some noise in the background, and Hartman assumed there was a party.

"No improvement, then?"

"If there had been, I would have told you."

"I should be in Vienna sometime tomorrow."

"I'll make a note. I must go now."

"I'm in South America," disclosed Hartman. "I could fly up if it was necessary."

There was no immediate response. David had his hand cupped over the telephone and was talking to somebody else.

"What?" demanded his son, coming back to him.

"I could come to Connecticut. Should I do that?"

"No." The rejection was very quick.

"There's no immediate danger, then?"

"There's not thought to be."

"I'll call tomorrow."

"Try not to clash with dinner."

"I'm sorry."

Should he contact Rebecca and tell her he was on his way home? She preferred him to, claiming she disliked surprises. There would be opportunity enough from Paris. He looked idly at the souvenir shops, unsure of a present for her. It was all rubbish, he decided: tourist stuff. It would be better to wait until he got back to Vienna. He was very eager to see her again. He waited, and inevitably it came, the guilt he always felt at loving another woman while Gerda lay comatose and unaware in a psychiatric clinic. Poor Gerda. And poor Rebecca, too. She'd been very understanding all these years; sometimes he got frightened she would find somebody else and leave him.

Davidson rarely went on any field operations, but he

had insisted upon accompanying Berman from Paris. They'd drawn people from Frankfurt and Rome as backup, giving themselves thirty operatives to cover the airport and alternate the surveillance to avoid detection by Lang. Berman could have had somebody else do it, but he had wanted to leave the car and Davidson's presence, so he had personally checked that the Varig flight was on time.

"Well?" demanded the section leader as Berman re-entered the vehicle.

"As scheduled." Berman, who showered twice a day and even used foot deodorants, became aware that Davidson suffered from body odor. He lowered the window.

"What do you propose?"

"Close surveillance, until there's any contact. If he comes from any bank with what appears to be documents, we hit them immediately."

Davidson nodded. "Jesus! Can you imagine the effect we could achieve with this in Moscow!"

"It'll be marvelous," agreed Berman. But Davidson would get all the credit, he guessed miserably. The bloody man was a positive impediment to his career.

One of the people Berman had placed inside the terminal to give a warning appeared at the doorway.

"It's landed," said Berman.

They both left the car and entered the arrival building. Berman checked the placing of his men, waiting for any comment from his superior.

"Looks O.K.," said Davidson. There was reluctance in his voice.

The formal, metal-voiced announcement was made over the public-address system and they watched the indicator-board symbols revolving to record the landing. They'd managed to get three men into the customs area, creating a chain of communications, so Berman expected to get warning well in advance of Lang's approach. After fifteen minutes, the first of the Varig passengers began appearing along the moving sidewalk that links the arrival piers to the main building.

"Any sign?" asked Davidson nervously; he would have seen it at the same moment as Berman.

"No," said the younger man.

"He's taking his time."

Berman refused to respond. About a hundred people had cleared when Berman saw one of his agents, riding the same sidewalk. He stared, waiting for an indication, but the man remained expressionless.

"What is it?" demanded Davidson as the agent approached.

"How do I know?" asked Berman irritably.

"He's not on the flight," reported the man, reaching them as Berman spoke.

"He was checked on," insisted Berman.

"He didn't arrive," recorded the man simply.

"Beaten you," said Davidson by his side. "The bastard has beaten you."

Berman turned sideways, astonished at the speed with which the section head was moving to avoid any responsibility.

"Because you didn't do it right," continued Davidson. "Because you insisted on using Hugo Hartman."

4

They had driven to the embassy in Berne in almost complete silence, the only conversation with Davidson sounding ominously like a rehearsal for the complaints the section head intended making when he returned to America. A communications room was made available to them at the embassy, and Davidson's first action was to call the headquarters at Langley and ask to speak personally to the Director. He was unavailable, but Davidson got the Deputy. It had been a disaster, Davidson reported; he was attempting to retrieve the situation, to locate Lang, but he didn't have much hope. It was entirely due to a local mistake about which he would be making a full report upon his return.

"Thanks," said Berman bitterly as Davidson replaced the telephone.

"Wasn't it a mistake?" insisted Davidson.

"I might have expected some support," protested the younger man.

"There should have been an operative aboard the plane. It was madness to let him fly alone."

Davidson was right, Berman accepted—which would make whatever criticism he later made at Langley very valid. Fuck it.

"Is there any way to contact Hartman?" asked Davidson.

"I don't think so."

"Jesus!" exploded Davidson. "Just what sort of operation were you running here?"

"He'll be at the embassy in Paris sometime tomorrow."

"Terrific! That gives Lang twenty-four hours to burrow himself away in whatever little hidey-hole he's prepared for all these years."

"We'll know soon where he disembarked. There were only three stops before Zurich," said Berman, who had left men at the airport to check with the airline.

"It'll be hopeless," predicted Davidson.

One of the men who had been with them at the airport entered with coffee, and both men stopped talking until he had left the room.

"You know why I came to Europe?" questioned Davidson suddenly.

Berman looked at him, waiting.

"Not just for the Lang thing," continued the section head. "For a suitability report. You're due for the promotion board."

"I know."

"Not going to look good now, is it?"

"No," said Berman.

"You screwed it, Peter."

Soon would come the attitude of patronizing disappointment, Berman knew.

"It was impossible to anticipate," he tried desperately.

"It's the oldest avoidance trick in the book!" rejected Davidson. "Openly take a ticket to somewhere and then get off en route; you're not even breaking any airline regulations!"

He *should* have put someone else in Panama to help Hartman in the end, Berman supposed; it seemed so obvious now.

"We might as well send everybody home," he said.

"No hurry," said Davidson. "Let's wait to see if we can find where he got off."

The more people around, the more chances of apportioning the mistakes, decided Berman. "All right," he said.

"What's Hartman got?"

"He talked of proof."

"What?"

"It wasn't a secure line; he couldn't say."

"Lang will cover every lead. It won't be any good."

"We won't know until we've seen Hugo," said Berman defiantly.

"*You've* seen Hugo," qualified Davidson.

Danger by association, Berman supposed. Davidson was very adept at political infighting. Perhaps it was something that was learned in Washington.

"He was still the man to send," defended Berman.

Davidson looked at the other man contemptuously, but said nothing. The telephone shrilled into the room and Berman reached anxiously for it, then stopped, deferentially. Davidson had been sitting, waiting for him to remember the seniority.

"Sorry," said Berman.

The section leader picked up the instrument and identified himself. He spoke without revealing anything of the conversation and there was no expression upon his face; probably another trick that was practiced at headquarters. Davidson didn't speak until after he had replaced the receiver.

"Well?" asked Berman impatiently.

"Mexico City," said Davidson shortly.

"Shit," said Berman. It meant the man had had the maximum opportunity to evade an attempt to pick him up.

"And he's booked again."

For the first time Berman became aware of the other man's demeanor, an attitude of uncertainty.

"I don't understand," said Davidson. "But the Varig computer records that Lang disembarked at Mexico City and two hours ago confirmed another flight"—he smiled up, toward the other man—"to Zurich!"

Davidson was moving at last, for another connection to Langley. "And this time we're going to be alongside," he said. Because it was an embassy circuit, the connection was immediate. While Davidson spoke, Berman paced the room, uncomfortable with the vague feeling of claustrophobia with the man who smelled.

"We can do it," said Davidson triumphantly from behind him.

Berman turned. "Good," he said.

"What's it mean?" demanded Davidson.

Berman studied the other man. Get everyone else's opinion first, then choose as your own the best suggestion, he thought.

"A check, to see if he were being followed?" suggested Berman.

"Possible," agreed Davidson. "Unlikely, I would have thought."

"What then?"

Davidson frowned, having to offer an opinion. "A meeting?" he said.

"With whom? And for what purpose?"

"If you'd had somebody aboard, we might have known the answer," came back Davidson quickly.

"It doesn't check out," said Berman. "If he's trying to run, then he'll be moving as quickly as possible. Why break a traceable journey for more than ten hours?"

"Because in Mexico City is someone whom Lang regards as important—important enough to seek advice from."

"We're in good shape," Berman decided suddenly.

"How?"

"Because we know about the stopover, in advance. We'll be able to trick him into saying whatever it was during any interrogation."

Davidson nodded. "Maybe," he said. Then he added: "You've been lucky."

"Lucky?"

"Our picking him up again so quickly. This wasn't looking at all good for you, thirty minutes ago."

"Very lucky," said Berman. He'd meant it as sarcasm,

but Davidson chose to misunderstand. "You'd better believe it," he said.

"If it's a group of Nazis in Mexico City, then we'll have gained by the way things happened," said Berman, considering a defense for Langley.

"I've already thought of that," assured Davidson. "We're putting the local man on the Varig flight and moving a team down from Washington."

To be marked as a credit for instant assessment and planning upon Davidson's records; the man was determined to make this a personal triumph.

"How much time do we have?" asked Berman.

Davidson checked his watch. "Five hours."

"I'm going to try a little sleep," said Berman. He didn't succeed. The cots in the embassy were uncomfortable and he had to share the accommodations with four others, whose sounds and movements constantly intruded, so that finally, instead of trying to ignore them, he lay listening in anticipation of them. It had been an appalling operation, Berman knew. Even the chance they appeared to have for recovery wouldn't affect Davidson's suitability report; the section head was riding the back of this one, seeing it as the guaranteed way of getting himself recognized and moved out of the cul-de-sac.

Berman rose before anyone else, determined to be first in the shower room; he was one of the few who had had the forethought to bring a clean shirt and underwear with him, in a shoulder grip. Davidson didn't appear to have attempted sleep; certainly he hadn't taken off his clothes. The suit was concertinaed around him and there was a sweat line, like a high-water mark, around his collar. Berman managed half an hour of the journey back to Zurich with the window open before Davidson complained, forcing him to close it and encase himself without any ventilation.

It was an early-morning flight, which meant that the airport was almost deserted and made observation easier. Davidson agreed with the emplacements as before, so there was no need for any further briefing.

"Good job we didn't send them back to Rome and Frankfurt," said Davidson.

"Yes," agreed Berman. Another criticism in the report, he recognized.

The grayness of dawn still clung around the airport and the mountains beyond; to the left the lake was hidden by mist, puffballed in uneven lumps like decorative icing on a cake.

"Dull-looking place," judged Davidson.

"Sometimes it's quite pretty."

"Don't like the Swiss; everything closes at eight for them to count their money."

"They're very good at it."

"Never seem to laugh very much."

"Counting money is a serious business."

The signal came from the doorway, as it had the previous night.

"Let's hope we have better luck this time!" said Berman, moving to get out of the vehicle.

"It'll be all right," said Davidson. "I organized it."

Berman felt more nervous than he would have expected; certainly worse than he had the first time. It had nothing to do with Lang, he accepted. It was the knowledge of how badly he'd failed.

"They've got him," muttered Berman, speaking softly for no reason; Lang was still more than 300 yards away, identified by the two CIA men who had positioned themselves directly behind him on the moving sidewalk.

"Inconspicuous son of a bitch," said Davidson.

"Perhaps the SS uniform and the swastika are in a safe-deposit box," said Berman.

"Perhaps they are," agreed Davidson seriously.

Berman sighed. Sarcasm was pointless.

The operation was perfectly coordinated. The CIA men tightened around Lang so that he was completely encircled, but in such a way that he would have been unaware of it among the crowd of Varig arrivals. There were operatives already waiting in cars, both in the parking lot and the road beyond, kept in contact with what was happening by a man in the uniform of an airport official, speaking into the handset identical to the radios the other personnel carried.

"Didn't I say it would work?" demanded Davidson.

"We'd better get the car."

Lang stopped on the pavement directly outside the exit, staring around intently, as if seeking something. Apparently unable to find it, he walked impatiently first one way and then the other, and then straightened in recognition, moving out between two waiting taxis and walking toward the shortterm parking lot.

"Someone here for him?" asked Davidson, his view blocked by another vehicle.

"Don't think so," said Berman, straining up. "It's a Mercedes . . . a red Mercedes."

Lang hesitated when he got near, examining the number. There was a brief smile. He threw the overnight bag into the back seat and very cautiously fastened the seatbelt before attempting to start it.

It was later estimated that the Mercedes had been packed with at least forty pounds of explosives. The blast completely obliterated it. The chassis, the only identifiable part that remained, arced thirty feet in the air and completely crushed another vehicle upon which it fell, fifteen yards away. Most of the terminal glass, some of it supposed to be shatter proof as an antiterrorist precaution, was blown in, and an airport cleaner whose carotid artery was severed bled to death before anyone realized the extend of his injuries. The CIA men who were walking as close as possible to Lang were killed outright, and two more who had anticipated his entering the Mercedes and begun to move their car into a trailing position were maimed, the driver permanently blinded by the inrush of the windshield glass and his companion deafened by the sound.

The gas tanks of two adjacent cars exploded at once and gasoline leaking from other tanks which split ignited. Before the fire brigade managed to extinguish it, the fire had destroyed twenty vehicles. One hundred people needed hospital treatment.

Berman turned hopelessly toward Davidson, realizing he couldn't hear what the man was saying. He understood, though, because it was only one word and Davidson was mouthing it, over and over again.

"Yes," said Berman, unable to hear his own voice either. "Fuck."

Until now Berman had reflected the fitness of a man who jogged every morning in the Bois de Boulogne and three days a week rowed in the Seine. Today he looked ill. He was whey-faced and could not stop the rapid, nervous blinking, which embarrassed him, so that he was constantly shading his eyes with his hands as if to hide himself. His eardrums were still affected by the explosion, and he kept straining forward to hear what Hartman was saying.

"Lang was set up," said Berman. Unable to judge the pitch of his own voice, the words switchbacked.

"Obviously," agreed Hartman.

"But by whom?"

Hartman shrugged. "What have you found in Mexico City?"

"Nothing," said Berman. "Not a bloody thing."

The American went back to the material that Hartman had brought back from Cristobal. He had already studied it for an hour.

"It *was* Lang," he said.

"Yes," agreed Hartman.

Berman tried to stare across the desk, but the blinking gave the expression of comic appearance.

"Is this *all* there was?" he asked pointedly.

"Just some local bank statements which meant nothing," said Hartman. There was no positive reason for withholding the information about the scrap of paper with Eros and the number written upon it; it was instinctive, like hoarding food and stealing from dead bodies in the camp. And it was New York, not Mexico City.

"Sure?" pressed Berman.

"What should there have been?"

"We thought . . ." started the CIA man, then stopped. "There should have been something about a wartime association," he resumed. "Something we could have used."

"Nothing," said Hartman, relieved. He was annoyed at himself now for not mentioning the jotting in the passport. But it was too late; to offer it at this stage would arouse the American's suspicion, and it was important to avoid that. So far neither side had ever become curious.

"Damn," said Berman. He cradled his head as if it were aching. "There's a section head looking over my shoulder," said Berman, more to himself than the other man. "It's been a disaster."

Berman was very ambitious, remembered Hartman. Once he'd even boasted of the hope of becoming Director, even though that was traditionally a political appointment.

"I'm sorry," said Hartman.

"It's not your fault," said Berman fairly. "I should have had a man aboard the plane when Lang left Panama."

"It sounded safe at the time. We knew his destination."

"Davidson doesn't think so."

"Davidson?"

"The section head. Says I fouled up. I could be dumped for this."

"Shouldn't you be in a hospital?" asked Hartman. "Resting, at least."

"No time," said Berman. "I've got to recover from this."

"There's nothing left in Panama," said Hartman positively. "Or in Zurich. It'll have to be Mexico City."

Berman nodded, then winced, as if the gesture caused him pain. "Davidson is going there. Christ, that bastard is going to screw me!"

"I'm returning to Vienna tonight."

"Sure," agreed Berman, looking back to the papers that had come from Lang's safe.

"It wouldn't be the end of the world, getting out of this business," said Hartman, trying to be encouraging.

Berman blinked up. "Not for you, maybe. But it's my *career.*"

"I've thought several times about quitting," said Hartman honestly. "I won't go on much longer."

Berman appeared not to hear him.

"I hope you feel better soon," said Hartman, rising.

Berman looked up from his desk again. Hartman felt very sorry for him.

"It'll take a long time to recover from this," said the American. "A very long time."

Hartman went straight from the embassy to the Ritz; he was enjoying the hotel, after the near-squalor in which he had lived for the past six weeks. He confirmed his flight to Vienna, and actually had the telephone in his hand to place the call to Rebecca and tell her of his homecoming when he changed his mind, asking instead for David's Connecticut number.

"I'm glad you called," said David, and for once there was none of the usual hostility in his voice.

"What's the matter?"

"Mother died this morning."

5

Their subdued suits had been pressed the night before and preserved in the cleaner's plastic covers, their shirts freshly laundered with 'extra starch' checked on the instruction sheet, and their shoes buffed to a painted gloss. Ruth, who believed in dressing for every occasion and always bought matching wraps and headbands for her six summer swimsuits, had purchased a complete outfit, even to the black stockings and veiled hat. Now, after the ceremoney, they sat stiffly in the funeral car, gift-wrapped in befitting grief.

At the moment of final farewell, Hartman had cried, in genuine sorry, uncaring of the attitude his son always showed toward him. David's feelings didn't hurt; not anymore. There had been a time when he'd tried to explain, to make the boy understand what it had been like. But the attempts had been many years ago. Boys, even grown-up boys with honor degrees in psychiatry from European as well as American universities, need fathers who are heroes.

By his side in the car, Hartman was aware of Ruth lifting the veil to put a handkerchief to her eyes. It was black-edged, he saw with surprise. She probably thought the gesture as necessary as the proper clothes. It must have been difficult finding a handkerchief like that.

"I'm sorry," said David.

"Sorry?"

"I really meant to get you here in time. It was quicker than any of us thought it would be."

"I understand." Even at the end he'd failed her, thought Hartman. He should have ignored David's rejection and flown up from Panama. It had been obvious she was dying when he'd seen her six weeks before.

"She had no resistance anymore," said David.

"She'd suffered so much."

"It was a nice service," said David.

"Yes," said Hartman. How could a funeral be nice? Easily, he thought. There could be proper sadness and proper dignity and proper words. Not like so much death he'd known.

"Your mother would have appreciated it," he added. It was the nearest he could come to praising his son's organization without David suspecting him of insincerity.

"I know," said the younger man. "It was always one of the factors."

"Factors?" asked Hartman, knowing the question was expected. He wondered if David strived for constant recrimination, or whether it came unthinkingly after so long.

"That contributed to her illness," explained David. "We could never erase the memory of the lines of naked people . . . the utter bestiality of factory destruction. . . ."

She had a lot to forget," said Hartman. It was a private remark, meant for no one else in the vehicle, but David took it.

"Yes," he said, turning to look directly at his father. "A lot to forget."

Between them Ruth attempted a diversion, bustling the new handbag on her lap and carefully slotting the handkerchief into a side pocket. It didn't seem damp.

"We've contacted the mason," she said hurriedly.

"Thank you," said Hartman. "I'll leave a blank check."

"There's no need," said David shortly.

"I know," said Hartman patiently. "I would still like to pay for it."

"As you wish," said his son. He paused, the hesitation obviously artificial. Then he quoted. "Much loved and grieved wife of Hugo Hartman."

"That's what I would like," agreed Hartman doggedly.

It would only be another hour, two at the most. He wouldn't respond. He wouldn't spoil Gerda's funeral day, as he'd spoiled everything else for her. Through the car window the Connecticut countryside was threadbare with melting snow, patched occasionally with proud green grass. Hardier flowers, crocuses he thought, flared from the unfenced gardens, like banners advertising the forthcoming spring. Gerda had liked flowers. At the camp, after her favoritism had been established, she'd risked daisies upon her windowsill. A preserve jar, he remembered; peaches. The label had been in French, the printing faded and difficult to read. It had come from a food hoard on one of the trains. Once Klaus Reinhart had given her a rose. But made him carry it to his wife, reducing the gesture to the bestiality of the naked lines outside. She had had to display it, though; everything depended upon pleasing Reinhart. Everything.

The car was climbing now. It was more difficult to see the houses, spaced farther apart and shielded from highway curiosity by landscaped trees rigid in their apparently careless arrangement. Hartman knew they were among the $250,000 houses, where successful psychiatrists like David lived.

The limousine swept into the driveway, past the clustered trees and the cropped lawn and the rolled tennis court. At the doorway there was an uneasy pause, David leaning into the car to talk to the undertaker and Ruth unsure whether it was expected of her to invite her father-in-law into the house. When he turned from the car, David seemed enclosed in the same uncertainty. Without issuing an invitation, he unlocked the door and entered the house. Ruth appeared confused, gesturing the older man to precede her with one hand and making half-halting movements with the other. She looked as if she were resolving some traffic congestion.

David had gone into the larger drawing room at the rear

of the house, not the one at the side that overlooked the tennis courts. From the panoramic windows, Hartman could see the swimming pool, still covered against the winter by its padded sheet.

"Drink?" said David. The cocktail cabinet was a huge globe, which parted in the middle to reveal the bottles and the glasses. The gin was in Nairobi, the Scotch in Tahiti.

"No, thank you," said Hartman.

"Don't think I'll bother either."

Ruth entered the room. She'd taken off the coat and gloves and veiled hat; the severely tailored suit, with its white-ruffled shirt beneath, looked like some sort of official uniform. For the briefest moment, Hartman felt the stomach movement that always came with any confrontation with uniforms, even customs officers or airport personnel and particularly policemen. The doctors at the camp brothels dressed like that; the ones entrusted with guaranteeing the officers against any infection, who checked the women daily and who didn't bother with treatment if any test proved positive, but merely thrust them into the waiting lines outside. It had been something Gerda had not been able to guard against in the beginning, when it had mattered. She had always been terrified of the black-tunicked women, and Hartman had inherited her apprehension.

"What's the matter?" asked Ruth, curious at the look upon his face.

"Nothing," apologized Hartman. "A sudden memory."

To cover the moment, he took his note book from his pocket and scribbled his name at the bottom of a Chase Manhattan Bank check.

"Here," he said, offering it to his son. "For the headstone."

David paused, unwilling to take it. Accepting the check meant he had to accept the inscription, Hartman realized.

It was a tribute David thought not just hypocritical, but an insult to his mother. It was difficult to recall that in David's conception, so soon after their release, he and Gerda had seen an attempt at normality that had been denied them from the first years of their married life. She had bloomed during pregnancy, as brightly as the flowers in the snow he'd seen coming back from the funeral. There had been no hint then of the mental collapse that was to come. Someone who had never used a hammer or a chisel or nails, he had fashioned a crib from an apple crate. And Gerda, who in spoiled prewar Vienna had only seen sewing from the seamstresses, who clustered sycophantically around her in the couturier houses of the Kärntner Strasse, had salvaged enough from a bed sheet to make a white dress with a matching bonnet.

David snatched the check from his father, the gesture overemphasized to show his protest. He went to the globe, opened it, and poured from the ready-mixed martini pitcher resting in St. Lucia. All the time he had the check crumpled in his hand. At last he stared at it, as if there would be something more written than just his father's name. Finally he cast it aside onto a coffee table, and Hartman suddenly knew his son would never cash it, but pay for the headstone himself and then await his father's argument when the check never cleared.

"She was very happy, you know," said the younger man, turning to his father.

"I'm glad," said Hartman.

"She had no memory at all of what it was like, in the end. In her mind she was living before, not after 1943."

"She was very happy, until 1943," remembered Hartman. "So very beautiful and so very happy."

"And brave," reminded David cruelly.

"Not then," corrected Hartman. "She had no need to be, then. The bravery came later. And then she was very brave."

As she had in the car, Ruth moved to intervene.

"You'll stay for dinner?" she said. She flushed and Hartman was undecided whether it was at the thought of the later rebuke from her husband for suggesting it or embarrassment at the very emptiness of the invitation.

"No, thank you," he said. "I have a plane to catch, back to Vienna."

"Are you sure?" she asked, the relief obvious.

"Quite sure."

"I don't suppose we will be seeing so much of you, now that Mother has gone," said David. It was a statement more than a question.

"No," said Hartman. "I don't suppose you will."

He looked at both of them, secure in their wealth and their safety and their future, and wondered if there would be any false demands to keep in touch. Neither spoke.

"Thank you for caring for her in the clinic as well as you did," said Hartman sincerely. "She was very proud of you. Her family knew Freud in Vienna."

"She was my mother. It was my pleasure," said David.

He purposely avoided 'duty,' using its absence to criticize his father.

"Of course," said Hartman. "Thank you, all the same."

The last time he had been to the clinic, David had been graying at the temples. Now his hair was black. Hartman supposed that dyeing it was necessary for the deputy director of the state's most prestigious psychiatric clinic, just as the nose operation had been important. It had gone wrong and the scar was visible. He had heard his son refer to it as a football injury.

He tried to imagine how David would have reacted to that midnight knock and the clatter of steel-shod boots and the bayonet prods and seeing his wife fondled and pawed. He would have fought, Hartman guessed. Just as he had attempted to do, until the rifle butt in the groin had brought him screaming to the ground.

Don't hurt me . . . please don't hurt me . . .

The words echoed in his head, the taunt more obscene than anything he had later witnessed in the 'satisfy or die' camp brothels, with the animals and sexual paraphernalia. His words, his plea, huddled on the floor of the last apartment, in which he and Gerda had hidden for three months, terrified of just such a moment as this. He'd looked up, mocked by their laughter, expecting to see in her eyes the contempt that had later come so easily to David. And seen instead the pity that had never left her expression, no matter what she had had to do to keep him alive.

"What time is your plane?" prompted David.

"Yes," said Hartman. "I must go."

He rose and stood facing both of them, not knowing how to say goodbye. And that was what it was, he accepted. Goodbye. The reason for his visits to Connecticut had gone. And as far as they were concerned, he was as dead as the poor, mentally crippled woman whom they'd buried three hours before.

"I'll visit the grave from time to time," he said.

"Yes," said David.

"Maybe I'll give you a call when I'm here."

"Yes."

"Thank you again."

"She was my mother."

"Perhaps you could send a photograph after the headstone has been erected?"

"I'll try."

"I'd apprecite it."

It was like a game, in which they had been allocated a certain number of words. Now each had run out, but was unsure which one had won.

"I'll be going, then," said Hartman.

"All right."

Hartman extended his hand and David looked at it, with the same curiosity with which he had earlier regarded the check. Hartman was conscious of Ruth's encouraging pressure against her husband's elbow. David reached out, limply taking his fingers, the merest token of physical contact. Hartman could not remember the last time he'd embraced his son.

"Goodbye, Ruth," he said.

She came forward and Hartman saw the stiffening of David's body at the thought they might kiss. Quickly he thrust out his hand again, wanting to spare her any later anger. But she had already been stretching forward, so the protection had been unnecessary.

They walked dutifully with him to the door and stood side by side but untouching as he got into the rental car. He turned the vehicle, then slowed, raising his hand in the final farewell gesture. Neither responded.

He knew the route perfectly, after so long. There had been interruptions, of course, when assignments had prevented it, but he supposed that over ten years he had averaged a visit every two months. Sixty Atlantic crossings and sixty car journeys through the bulbous New England hills, each time to spend an afternoon in complete silence holding the soft, unmoving hand of a woman who had rarely been aware of his presence.

There had been times, in the early months, when Hartman had hoped she might respond. The antagonism with his son hadn't yet arisen. So David, with his newly qualified enthusiasm, had rehearsed Hartman how to talk to Gerda about the life they would have together. Despite David's qualifications, Hartman thought he had known before his son how impossible it was, but he was prepared to go to any lengths, accept any suggestion to penetrate the mental barrier and make her well again. Occasionally she had appeared conscious of what he had said, turning as if aware of whom he was and smiling the faint, distant smile that sometimes came just before the struggle for words which always defeated her.

His journey took him through West Simsbury, so he had invented an imaginary house there, describing the rooms and the furnishings and the two-acre garden that was difficult to keep under control, and made empty plans for theater visits they would make to New York. There had been times when he'd become overanxious, almost angry, at her inability to comprehend, trying to urge some response by getting her to squeeze his hand if she understood, instead of trying to talk.

But the hand had remained unmoving and the eyes unfocused, and for several years there had not even been the distant smile. But he'd never thought of stopping the visits—not once. Loving hope, as he had regarded it? Or conscience calls, as David sneered, after their relationship had begun to collapse?

Hope, Hartman told himself. Obviously there had been conscience, too, for what happened in the camp. Just as there had been conscience when he had met Rebecca and realized he was falling in love. But he had always allowed for the startling recovery that David had insisted was psychologically possible.

What would he have done if she had got better? He couldn't have abandoned her, not again. But could he have abandoned Rebecca either? He didn't think so. He refused the questions, irritated at himself for having created them. It was hypothetical now; Gerda was dead. He would never have to make the choice.

Hartman reached the link to the Merritt Parkway and settled in the cruising lane, consciously within the speed limit. Hugo Hartman always obeyed the civil laws.

He'd said goodbye to a son as well as a wife, he thought suddenly. About Gerda the grief *had* been genuine. What about the boy? What feeling should he have for David? Certainly not the hatred that David appeared to feel for him. Dislike then, because of the boy's attitude? He didn't dislike him either. Or like him. The truth was a complete *absence* of feeling. He had loved David once. He'd cossetted him, hoped for him, and bored people with pictures, like proud fathers do, trying to find a similarity between himself and the boy to boast about. At school he'd dismissed the failures and encouraged even the minimal successes, and settled an allowance upon him when he'd passed the first of his university entrance exams. Indeed, Hartman supposed he had become a spy as much to support David's university courses as to pay for Gerda's psychiatric treatment. Spying—at least his sort of spying—paid well. So there had been money available when the training had ended and the opportunity arose for his son to buy into the Connecticut clinic.

He calculated the love between father and son had begun to falter within a year of Gerda's transfer to America. No, not falter. Been taken away from him, very gradually, as David had learned what had really happened in Belsen. Father and son had retreated from each other, one with sad, embarrassed regret, the other with amazement and disgust. Eventually Hartman had stopped retreating, although he couldn't date the moment. But David never had. He'd not just backed away from love; he'd gone on, into the opposite feeling.

It was not important. That was in the past now. It was the future that mattered. And Gerda's death meant his future would have to change dramatically. He smiled in anticipation: it would be so good to end it all.

He turned on to the Hutchinson River Parkway, knowing that soon he would see the beginning of the signs for Kennedy Airport. Instinctively he checked the time and realized there were still four hours before his flight. There was an argument against his going back at all. It would be far more sensible to go to La Guardia rather than Kennedy, catch the shuttle down to Washington, and sever his connections with the CIA. But Hartman had an orderly, analytical mind: it was one of the qualities that made him so good at what he did. He had begun first with the Soviet Union, and so it was right he should leave them first. And he had to quit, now that Gerda was dead. Visiting her had always been the explanation for his absences, to Washington and Moscow, whenever he had been away from Vienna upon an assignment for one when the other had wanted him.

It would be good to be free; to build a proper, conventional life with Rebecca. He felt the emotion come and swallowed against the tears. Dear Gerda. She had even made that possible. There was so many similarities between the two women; both utterly selfless, both concerned only for others and never for themselves. He loved them both, so much.

He connected with the Van Wyck Expressway, slowed by the volume of traffic as New York emptied itself of daytime people. Hartman decided he was a lucky man, getting the chance made possible by Rebecca: a chance for happiness. He frowned at the thought, examining it. So little happiness; difficult even to recall the moments. His marriage to Gerda, of course, even though he had been aware that had it not been for the Anschluss and what happened afterward, Ruben Weiss would never have considered his admission into the family. But the Jew-hunting in Austria was growing into a hysteria by the time Hartman stumbled out his proposal, and normal criteria, like normal behavior, had been abandoned. Hartman had known true happiness at the wedding, discreet though it had had to be in the hope of avoiding attention. So much, to avoid attention: the constant moving and shifting from houses and apartments, sometimes weeks and even, on one occasion, a month without seeing each other, each frightened that the other had been seized. There had been times together though—times when they had found a safe place in which to remain for a while, trying to shut out the brutal, evil world outside the apartment window.

There should have been happiness in their release, of course; an amazed euphoria that they had survived at all. But that wasn't the feeling Hartman remembered. By then he was encased in guilt, an impenetrable shell through which no other emotion could reach. And guilt, not happiness, had been his initial reaction when he realized what was happening between himself and Rebecca, his awareness that in his attraction to the woman there was a further betrayal of a wife blocked forever from reality and living inside herself, a small girl again, who played with dolls.

He would never lose that guilt, Hartman knew. It would always be with him, like a scar or a slight deformity which caused a limp of which he would always be conscious. But scars diminished and deformities became accepted.

One life had ended. Now it was time to begin another. How easy would it be? he wondered.

6

It was surprising, after the horrors to which he had been subjected there, but Hartman always felt more comfortable in Europe than in America. The American enjoyment of space unsettled him; in Texas or Kansas he felt alien, not through race or upbringing or heritage, but through size. The spread-apart towns seemed curiously out of proportion to the small populations that usually lived in them, and despite the orderliness that he normally admired, the mathematically crisscrossed streets and avenues seemed more clinical than convenient. In the new-added-to-the-old cities of Rome or Paris or Vienna he felt at ease; they fitted him, like one of his elegant, three-piece suits that had lost its newness and become shaped individually to his body.

Perhaps most surprising, it was in Vienna where he felt particularly at home. He enjoyed the Sacher torte and tea in the glassed salon of the Sacher, watching the customed, behatted matrons peck at their cakes and shrill their gossip like aging birds. He liked Demel's, imagining the atmosphere of a past era when the courtiers and the ambassadors from the Hofburg had swapped their secrets among the coffee cups. Or driving out with Rebecca, just after the first grape pressings and looking for the green bushes suspended outside the houses where they could stop and taste the sweet, fresh wine.

There was a feeling of permanence in the city; of civilized comfort.

It had seemed automatic to return with Gerda after the war; it was the only place they had known, and it never occurred to him to go anywhere else. There hadn't been any comfort or feeling of civilization then. In the first months, with the shortages and the deprivations and the

Four Power occupation there had even been some doubts. And then there had been his entrapment there. But he'd recognized soon enough that to blame Vienna for that was a juvenile effort to sift responsibility for his stupidity onto his surroundings. As he had adapted to the role that had been thrust upon him and then improved on it, the Austrian capital had increasingly become the right choice. Until David's establishment in America, it had even been the best place for Gerda's psychiatric care.

Always upon his return from an assignment, there came to Hartman within minutes of joining the city road from Schwechat Airport a feeling of familiarity, the comfort of entering a darkened room in which he had positioned all the furniture and therefore knew there wasn't a risk of stumbling into anything. Today the feeling was different. Stronger. An excitement, in fact. It was the decision, he knew; the awareness that at last he could arrange a settled, secure future for himself and the woman he loved. And who loved him. Perhaps he'd known something like it when he had passed the intermediary examinations for the accountancy degree for which he'd never been able to qualify. Ruben Weiss had accepted the proposal by then. And promised him a position in the firm; he would have thought that life held exciting prospects, just as it did now.

For the first time, Hartman became impatient with the subterfuge necessary to arrange a meeting with Oleg Karpov. It was a Tuesday, which dictated the approach; each day a different procedure was stipulated. From a legitimate import-export business on Felberstrasse, unaware of how they were being used, he obtained the number for a possible supplier of cold-weather motor oil. From them, he inquired after a mechanic qualified to service Leyland tractors, and on the third call, he embarked upon the formalized conversation which identified his true need and provided him with the way to his Russian

Control. Even then it was not Karpov to whom he spoke personally, but an intermediary who reestablished his identity with a further pattern of words and finally provided the address on Schüttelstrasse. It was not one of the houses they had used before. Normally Karpov preferred the old part of the city around St. Stephen's Cathedral. There the buildings were cluttered and bunched haphazardly together, ribboned with back alleys and side roads. The many exits and linking passages from terrace to terrace would have made an escape very easy.

The car went onto Franzenbrucken Strasse and Hartman looked expectantly to his left, easily able to see the giant wheel that dominated the Prater amusement park. He'd taken David there when he was a child. And Gerda, once, before the illness completely overcame her. She had been frightened by the noise and the bustling crowds and the uniforms, because the city had still been divided then between the Americans, the British, the French, and the Russians. He'd never suggested another visit.

The car went beneath the railway bridge and Hartman stopped it early, at Laufbergergasse. He paid, waited until the vehicle pulled away, and still remained at the pavement edge, checking for any surveillance before picking up his suitcase to complete the journey on foot. There was no snow, but a chilling wind scurried along the canal. Hartman pulled deeper into his overcoat, regretting the weight of the case.

It was a room on the sixth floor, at the back of the building. The Prater was very clear; at night, with lights, it was probably an attractive sight. Would the music that had disturbed Gerda be audible if they unlocked the windows?

Karpov bearhugged his greeting, with his usual extravagance. He was a large, barrel-chested man who enjoyed tweeds that added to the impression of his size. A devotee of the theater, he sometimes wore a cloak and affected a thick, drooping mustache, the tips of which reached his chin. On anyone else, it would have fashioned a permanently mournful expression; with Karpov, it provided a frame for an almost constant smile. The Russian was not smoking, but about him clung the smell of Gauloises. And whisky, too. Over the man's shoulder, Hartman saw the open bottle of Chivas Regal. One of the two glasses was already half filled.

"Welcome back, Hugo!" greeted the Russian.

Hartman disentangled himself, feeling the embarrassment he always knew with Karpov's exuberance. Unasked, the man filled the second glass and handed it to him. Hartman sipped, welcoming the sensation of warmth.

Karpov saw him shiver and grinned. "In Moscow, this weather would be considered warm."

"And drinking whisky at three o'clock in the afternoon as decadent," said Hartman.

"Bullshit," said Karpov, who admired Western swearing as much as all the other exports. "By now half the Presidium will be sleeping off their lunch and the other half will be screwing their secretaries."

"Sometimes I don't think you're a very good Communist," said Hartman.

The suggestion seemed to surprise Karpov. "I've never bothered about it," admitted the man.

Hartman saw the whisky cap had been thrown into the wastepaper basket: if he failed in other respects, Karpov drank like a Russian.

"Like the apartment?" asked Karpov.

Hartman stared around the room. It was anonymously furnished, with no personal identity. He could not have considered living there.

"Very practical," he said.

"Going to use it for my own seductions," said Karpov. He tried to leer, but couldn't sustain the expression, instead breaking out into a guffaw. "In Moscow it's easy.

You can always promise the girls visas, to make foreign trips . . ."

He laughed again. " . . . for me it's bloody difficult. How many girls do you think will take their drawers down for the chance to see Siberia or the wheat fields of the Ukraine?"

"Not many," said Hartman. He was aware of Karpov's curiosity at the suitcase.

"I came straight from the airport," he said in explanation.

Karpov nodded. "A sad visit," he said. The sympathy appeared genuine. "And a long one."

Karpov believed he had spent the entire time in Connecticut.

"She hadn't known anything for months—years even. Her psychiatrist told me she was happy in the end."

"David?" queried Karpov.

"Yes, David," agreed Hartman. He had forgotten the extent of the other man's knowledge of his personal life.

"Perhaps a happy release all the same."

"Perhaps."

Karpov looked at the case again.

"I didn't have the opportunity on this occasion," apologized Hartman.

"Of course not," said Karpov, adding to both their glasses. "I didn't expect that you would."

It was Karpov's ambition to possess a more extensive collection of American jazz records than anyone else in Moscow. Hartman knew he advertised through the various Russian embassies to all the Western jazz journals, particularly those with a large section devoted to sales. It was very common for Hartman to make purchases on his behalf at the conclusion of an assignment; there was an outstanding request for an early Brubeck, with Paul Desmond.

"Do you suspect some trouble then?" asked Karpov.

Beneath its whiskered canopy, the smile had been extinguished, and Hartman accepted that the social conversation was over.

"No," he said at once. "It was a private visit. And I was careful, as always."

"Yet you came directly from the airport?"

"Yes."

"So it must have been urgent?"

"I felt it was."

Karpov gestured to the bottle, but Hartman shook his head. The Russian added to his own glass.

"I'm an old man, Oleg," began the Austrian. "Too old."

Karpov shook his head, allowing the suggestion of a smile to return. "Nonsense. You're scarcely middle-aged."

"And tired," continued Hartman, disregarding the typical exaggeration. Like everything else, Karpov was well aware how old he was.

"It hasn't been an easy life. Not at the beginning, at least," conceded Karpov.

"And now I want rest. And a little happiness, before it's too late."

"You have a good life," reminded the Russian. "You're a rich man . . . very rich. There's nothing you lack."

"There is," insisted Hartman. "Something I want very much."

"What?"

"To stop. To live a proper existence."

For almost the first time Hartman could remember, Karpov looked sad. The expression had nothing to do with the drooping mustache. The huge head moved in reluctant shaking.

"That won't please us, Hugo."

"You tricked me," accused Hartman in sudden desperation. "After all these years, you owe me my release, for God's sake."

It *was* true. He had been tricked. But he'd been gullible, too, naively so. But everywhere in Europe, not just Vienna, was in confusion. And for two years he had cowed and cringed and reacted without thought, too terrified to question or doubt. The unthinking response had still been there, when he'd joined the bureau in a forlorn attempt at revenge by trying to identify the Nazis fleeing to their escape routes into Italy and Spain. So it had never occurred to him to query the honesty of the American. The man had not even appeared demanding; he had actually provided more information about escape networks than he had sought. Hartman had judged the suggestion that the very bureau had been infiltrated, so that their efforts to locate the mass murderers were being thwarted by pro-Nazis, reason enough to pass over the requested personnel files. It had seemed just as natural to gossip over coffee. And the man was sympathetic to Hartman's gradual story of Gerda's illness, commiserating that the drugs upon which she had come to depend were increasingly expensive from their only source, the black market. A loan, he had said. Repayable any time. It had been a month; thirty days exactly. Then Hartman had gazed horrified at pictures of himself accepting a bribe and learned the American was an officer of the KGB already formulating files on Zionists who might create problems in the as-yet-unformed Europe. And known immediately that he had escaped one prison for another, a concentration camp toady who had become a proven informer upon his own race. It was a revelation which need never be made public, his deceiver assured him. Providing he cooperated.

Karpov shrugged philosophically. "It wasn't me who tricked you," he denied. "And for years you've been treated very well."

"I've done enough."

"You've done brilliantly," praised the Russian. "That's the trouble. There isn't anyone else like you."

"That's ridiculous."

"No, Hugo. We have our own agents as good, of course. Some maybe better. But they're *Russian.* There are things we can't risk our people on, in case they are seized. But you're an Austrian. We could deny you and prevent any diplomatic incident."

Hartman blinked at the brutality. "At least you're honest."

"You know the reasoning well enough," said Karpov. "And I've always been honest, ever since we've been together."

"Yes," agreed Hartman. "You have."

"There's only one way you can leave us. You know that."

"Like the camps?"

"Death was the way out there," agreed Karpov.

"What if I refuse?" demanded Hartman in another surge of desperation. "You can't trust me on anything else. Not now that you know how I feel."

Karpov made a slow motion with his head, the sadness of someone hearing ill-considered words in an argument that will later be regretted.

"Yes, we can," he insisted quietly. "You don't dare expose any assignment, because you'd be exposing yourself for what you are by the same gesture. And if you refuse outright, then you know Moscow would have you killed. So it's either imprisonment or death. And you've always been terrified of either, haven't you?"

"Yes," admitted Hartman slowly.

Karpov spread his hands. "It's not me, you understand? If it were my decision, we'd go to the Three Hussars for a celebration meal, drink farewell champagne, and I'd thank you for all you've done. Those in Moscow don't see things the way I do."

Hartman studied the Russian, unsure of the truth. "You'll tell them of this conversation?" he asked.

Karpov turned down the corners of his mouth, accentuating another mournful expression. "Why should I?" he said. "They'd overact, as they always do. Summon you to Russia. Or send people here to lecture about loyalty. Best to say nothing."

"They might agree," said Hartman in vague hope.

"You don't really believe that, do you?"

"I suppose not."

"Trust me," urged Karpov. "I'll shield you from any assignment that looks too difficult; look after you. I'm your friend."

"I wanted to get out," said Hartman miserably. "To live normally. I've never known anything normal. Not once since 1943."

"Stop feeling sorry for yourself, Hugo."

"I've cause enough, for God's sake!"

"You're a fortunate man," disputed Karpov. "There are few who have succeeded as you have. Consider the benefits."

Hartman pushed his glass forward and Karpov refilled it, reaching with his other hand and patting the Austrian's wrist.

"It's a good life," he insisted. "When you get over Gerda's death, you'll think so too."

"They're not thinking of me for anything?"

"Not that I'm aware of."

"Perhaps it will be a long time." Again the echoing hope.

"Perhaps it won't," cautioned Karpov.

"Thank you," said Hartman. "For not telling Moscow, I mean."

"It's my job to make decisions like that," said Karpov.

And refuse agents retirement when they seek it? thought Hartman. How many other people did Karpov control in the city? Probably a lot. Vienna was the bridge between East and West.

"Does Rebecca know you're here?"

Hartman frowned briefly at the completeness of the other man's knowledge. "No," he said. "I came straight from the airport without calling her."

"She'll be pleased to see you."

"Yes." For a moment Hartman considered telling the Russian of his hopes for marriage, had he been allowed to quit. But then he decided against it. There was pleasure in having a secret of which Karpov was unaware. It wasn't the biggest, of course: miniscule by comparison. But still a secret: something else that gave him—a man who had never known independence—the feeling he had something of his own that the Russian could not manipulate.

"Why not take a holiday?" suggested Karpov brightly. "The snow is good in the mountains."

"I don't ski," said Hartman. "And Rebecca might find it difficult to close the shop."

"She's a successful woman."

"Yes."

"You must be proud?"

The suggestion surprised Hartman. Pride, like happiness and independence, was something with which he had had so little contact that he had consciously to think about it.

"Yes," he conceded. "I'm very proud of her. She's a fine woman."

"A lucky man," said Karpov, grinning widely with the satisfaction of having maneuvered the admission.

"A lucky man," accepted Hartman. What was it like to win arguments?

"Pity she can't know about me," said Karpov.

"Why?" asked Hartman sharply.

Karpov grinned again at the suspicion. "I was just going

to say you could have given her my love."

The Austrian stood, gazing over his Control's head toward the amusement park. The lights were already on, but it was not completely dark, and the glitter was subdued in the half-light, like a woman wearing rhinestones instead of proper jewelry.

"Take care," said Karpov.

"I always do."

"True," agreed Karpov. "You're one of the most careful men I've ever known. Probably why you're so good."

Hartman laughed bitterly. "Perhaps if I hadn't been, you'd have let me go."

"No," frowned the Russian, like a teacher disappointed at the difficulty of a pupil failing to comprehend a simple lesson. "I told you. You'd have been killed."

Rebecca had not been expecting anyone and she opened the door with the security chain still in place. She frowned through the narrow gap, the surprise and then irritation obvious.

"You didn't telephone," she complained. "You always telephone."

"There was something I had to do," said Hartman. "And then I forgot."

She became aware she was blocking his entry into her apartment. She released the chain and stood aside. He went in, putting the suitcase just inside the door and sighing at the luxury of familiar surroundings.

Although he and Rebecca were too old for sex to be the predominant part of their relationship, they had, of course, slept together. But quite often they just slept, needing the comfort rather than the relief of their bodies: a hand to hold in sudden awakening, or an embrace to be sure of in half-alseep uncertainty. But they had never, while Gerda was alive, discussed living together. Hartman, a subjective man, recognized it as a pointless propriety;

worse, a gesture more for his own conscience than for Rebecca's reputation. There were so many ways in which she had selflessly given since they had met. Now that Gerda had died, there was no longer the excuse. Until this moment, he hadn't considered the danger.

"I've nothing prepared," apologized the woman, following him into the room.

"I'm not hungry."

"Maybe a little sausage?"

"Later."

He turned to face her and Rebecca smiled, the shy, almost embarrassed expression he knew so well. He loved her very much, he realized.

"I missed you," he said honestly. "I missed you very much."

"I've been lonely, too," she said. "It's been a long time."

He reached out for her, and she came to him, still shyly, taking his hands and then offering her face to be kissed. She closed her eyes early, Hartman saw. It began softly, a friendly greeting for a return, but then Hartman gripped her tightly, remembering again the frustration of his meeting with Oleg Karpov, and the woman misunderstood, answering his passion.

"Was it too bad?" she asked. It took some time for Hartman to appreciate that she was referring to the funeral, so occupied was he by the Russian's refusal.

"No worse than I expected."

"David and Ruth don't understand what it was like," said Rebecca. "You shouldn't criticize them too much. And now it's all over."

She had so much forgiveness in her, thought Hartman. Far more than he had. But she would not like David and Ruth if she met them, he knew.

"Yes," he agreed. "So much is over."

Again he experienced the comfort of familiarity. He was

safe here, he thought. Nothing could touch him. That's how he and Gerda had felt for those few years of marriage before the arrest.

"Thank you for the flowers. You shouldn't have sent so many."

"I wanted you to know how much I missed you." Before going down to Panama, after seeing Gerda for the last time, Hartman had placed a weekly order with a florist in Connecticut.

"I'm sorry I didn't telephone," he said.

"I understand."

"I'm very glad to be back."

"I'm glad you're here," said Rebecca.

"How's business?"

"Fine."

Rebecca Habel had one of the most successful antique businesses in Vienna. Increasingly, as money had ceased to be so important, she had put her personal preferences above business profit and kept the choicest articles for herself, creating an exquisite home in which to live. Hartman had meant what he told Karpov; he was very proud of her.

"You've been drinking,' she accused. 'I can smell it."

"Only two."

"And when's the last time you ate?"

"On the plane . . . maybe four hours ago."

"Do you feel all right?"

He had always found it difficult to convince her that his diabetes was the mildest sort.

"I feel fine," he assured her.' 'Stop worrying."

"I do worry."

"I know," he said. "I'm flattered by it."

She took his coat, returning to the hallway, and while she was away he wandered about the room, still too unsettled by his encounter with Karpov to sit down. He'd planned to propose tonight, sure of her acceptance. There would have been champagne, and they would have laughed and maybe cried a little and made plans. And he would have stayed and they would have made love, not with the frenzy or needs of youth, but gently, properly. But not now. He'd failed by marrying her and attempting to live a lie already sometimes difficult to sustain. As close as they were, there had been occasions when he'd thought her curious that he should need to travel so much as a tax consultant for multinational oil companies, which was what she believed him to be.

Rebecca reentered the room and Hartman reached out for her again, wanting the contact. He led her to a French period settee, letting her sit before he did.

"I missed you," he said again.

She frowned, caught by his attitude. "What's the matter?"

"Nothing," he said. "Why?"

"You're different from how I expected you to be."

"It wasn't a very comfortable flight," he tried. "I'm tired. What's happened?"

"Nothing much''" she said. "I bought a beautiful icon. I think the man was a refugee from Poland, but he wouldn't say. I'll do well with it. And some new crocodile shoes."

She stretched out her feet for inspection and Hartman smiled down, enjoying her pleasure.

"Very'nice," he said.

Rebecca had been stripped of relatives in Dachau and released in 1945 wearing only a Red Cross coat and dress and cardboard shoes. Her interest in clothes was the most obvious effect of her deprivation, but like so many East European women accustomed either by experience or history to pogrom and revolution, she would have been capable of immediate flight, carrying upon her person sufficient convertible wealth to exist for six months. Maybe longer.

Rebecca could never be described as beautiful: not as

Gerda had been beautiful, wistfully frail, hair skeined around a face that makeup would have coarsened. "My virgin," Reinhart had called her proprietorially. And that's what she had been, despite everything that had happened. He supposed that was one of the secrets that kept her alive: invariably the other girls in the brothels had reflected the abuses, tried to make themselves into the whores they imagined the men wanted. But not Gerda. She had known the need; recognized its protection. She had emerged after two years as Reinhart's favorite as apparently unspoiled as when she had entered. It was only later he was to discover how hollowed she had been by what she had had to endure, more internally eroded than by the worst disease.

Rebecca's beauty was different. Indeed, there would have been some who would have even doubted an attraction. Broad face—Slavic almost—and prominently featured with the deep brown eyes and thick black hair of her race. Hartman loved her in another way. No less than Gerda. Just differently. With Rebecca there was the softness of understanding. But more, much more. Kindness. Sympathy. A willingness to give. Hartman shook his head, a personal rebuke. He knew the quality about Rebecca more important to him than anything else, yet his perpetual guilt prevented his openly admitting it and he despised himself for the self-deceit. Rebecca could forgive. She knew the terrors and the degradations and the humiliations. And so she forgave him his cowardice, as if by proxy, refusing to judge as everyone else would so readily have done.

"So now it's all over," she said. "Poor Gerda has been spared."

From anyone else it would have sounded insincere.

"It's a pleasant grave," said Hartman. "Near a tree. Beech, I think. In season it will flower."

He could have been describing a holiday snapshot.

Would David send the photographs he had asked for?

"I have some veal," Rebecca remembered. 'And there's cabbage."

"If you like."

"But no wine . . . you've had enough alcohol today."

"All right."

"You're sure there's nothing wrong? You seem distracted."

"I'm sorry."

"When are you going back to work?"

"I haven't decided yet. Not immediately."

"I'm very sorry about Gerda," said Rebecca, stretching sideways and taking his hand. "I know you loved her."

Hartman turned to look fully at her. "I love you" he said. He moved to speak again, then stopped. He wanted so much to say more.

7

Hartman had not positively set out to become a double agent. Like the gullibility that led to his Soviet entrapment, it showed a naiveté which his first experience should have guarded him against. The association with America had begun within a year of his Russian recruitment, while he was still attached to the anti-Nazi bureau. An innocent though he had been, he had by then realized the intelligence-gathering apparatus which was being assembled by the Four Powers attempting to divide Vienna between them. Bona fide Americans had shown interest in the bureau, the apparent purpose of their presence and inquiries failing to disguise their true function. The idea of approaching them had formed gradually, with no definite date or considered intention. If there were cause at all, then Hartman realistically accepted that in those early, ill-considered days it had been to provide an explanation; if he were discovered operating for the Soviet Union, he would have been able to prove a balancing association with America. No defense, he had recognized. But a plea of mitigation: an excuse at least.

But he had not been caught. Or even suspected. By some bizarre irony, Hugo Hartman, who had failed in everything else, discovered himself to be a perfect spy. From his timidity came his caution and from his caution came the attention to detail to which his orderly mind so easily became attuned. Everything about Hartman was ordinary. Middle height, middle build, undistinguished features, grayness hardly visibly in the sandy hair, he was the ideal unobserved observer. People were never aware of his entering a room, nor of his leaving. He became the sort of man who could apparently walk through snow or sand and never leave footprints.

The Russians, who had selected him, became the first to appreciate his potential. But Washington was close behind. Hartman had let himself appear offended at Karpov's assessment of his worth, but it had really been no revelation. He had known for years his value to both East and West, an operative whom each side could trust as if he were one of its own nationals, yet always someone who could be disowned if there were an arrest. In the beginning, it had been like entering a funfair hall of distorted mirrors and being unable to find a way out. But not for long; within another year, the image had become acceptable. His fragile confidence hardened with every operation; he became a professional. And then something more. The money helped. By then Gerda had been incapable of properly caring for David, so it was necessary to employ a nurse. And then there were the drugs and the nurses for Gerda and the payments for her increasingly regular visits to psychiatric clinics and hospitals.

As Hartman's expertise developed, the work he was given by both sides grew in importance. And correspondingly in danger. And so, therefore, did the fees he required. It was the way he fought back, imposing financial penalties upon them for their manipulation of his life; if he were to be a performing animal, he insisted upon the proper reward after each trick. Occasionally, in the early years, he had hesitated, anticipating protest, but none had ever come; he had rarely failed with anything with which he was entrusted, and, ironically, both Moscow and Washington seemed reassured by what they had to pay him, assessing the amounts as a fitting gauge for the high standard of work they were getting. Hartman had indulged himself with the American and Russian money. From his elegant, spacious apartment, it was possible to see the facade of St. Stephen's Cathedral, even the medieval measures set either side of the door against which the market traders had checked the length of their cloths and the roundness of their loaves.

Rebecca had helped him furnish the apartment and enjoyed it, even though in the early period of their relationship she knew she might well have been creating a home for another woman. But as the years passed and the doubts of Gerda ever leaving the sanatorium must have come to her, Rebecca had never suggested their living together. Hartman had encouraged the hesitation, whenever he had feared Rebecca might talk of it, allowing her to infer loyalty to his wife. Beneath the same roof, it would have been impossible to prevent her curiosity about his employment. Or properly to answer it.

Now there was no longer Gerda to provide the excuse either to Rebecca or those who employed him, and he didn't want one anymore. He wanted Rebecca, as his wife. Which meant he had to escape. He'd try again to persuade Karpov: the Russian's rejection had been instinctive, without thought. But first he'd end it with the CIA. He'd warned Berman, after all, the day following Lang's assassination in Zurich. And the American hadn't argued against it. There'd be a more sympathetic reaction from America, decided Hartman confidently. He remembered his thoughts on the way home from Gerda's funeral: the last chance for happiness. He couldn't lose it. Whatever it cost, he had to make it possible.

Rebecca reacted angrily when he told her he was going away again so soon, and it surprised him. Usually she accepted it as an unsettling necessity of the job she believed him to have.

"You said you weren't going to work again, not yet."

"A few days, that's all."

"You're not well."

"I feel fine," lied Hartman. The skin irritation was proving more difficult to clear up then he had expected.

"How long?"

"Maybe back tomorrow night."

"Promise?"

"I'll try."

It was the thought of breaking the promise to Rebecca, rather than the annoyance of a wasted journey, that first came to Hartman when he got to Paris and learned that Berman had been withdrawn to Washington for an indefinite period. It would be the Panama debacle, he supposed.

Rebecca was even angrier when he telephoned; it was understandable, he thought. One day he'd explain it to her, perhaps.

"You promised."

"Something to do with Gerda's estate," he said, ashamed at himself for the lie. If only he could tell her now. But she mustn't know. In her ignorance he saw her protection.

"Is it absolutely necessary?"

"If it weren't, I wouldn't go."

"Hurry back?"

"You know I will."

"I'm sorry," she apologized at last. "It just seemed such a long time before."

"It won't be, not on this occasion."

He managed a direct flight, getting to Washington's Hay Adams Hotel just before midnight local time. In Europe, it would be 5:00 A.M.., Hartman calculated. He felt exhausted, fatigue pulling at him; he *had* been right in what he'd told Karpov. He *was* too old. Hartman made another calculation: in the past two months, he had criss-crossed the Atlantic three times. And gone sideways to Panama. It must work out to nearly 30,000 miles; it was hardly surprising that he felt tired.

But despite the weariness he slept fitfully, his mind occupied with the possibility of Berman's annoyance at his unannounced arrival, and aware too that he had no guarded procedure to make contact with the man.

He rose early, unrested, and from the window of his hotel stood watching the capital gradually awaken. The cars came first. And then the pedestrians, overcoated and hatted against the cold. Hartman isolated two men crossing the park toward the White House, their breath clouding gray before them as they talked. Presidential employees perhaps. It seemed an animated conversation—almost an argument. He felt a surge of envy. Mundane jobs with mundane worries. How willingly he would have changed places with them, accepting all their problems in place of his own.

To occupy the time, he ordered breakfast in his room and then ignored it, bothering only with the coffee which he drank mechanically. At nine he took up the telephone book, smiling at the surprise he always knew at finding the CIA installation at Langley openly listed. In Moscow, even the existence of the Komitet Gosudarstvennoy Bezopasnosti was never admitted, and around its gray stone headquarters in Dzerzhinsky Square plainclothes KGB squads were on permanent duty, to question anyone showing the slightest interest in the building; to possess a camera guaranteed almost certain arrest.

Hartman was shunted from extension to extension until he finally located the European desk. At first, Berman's presence was denied, which was predictable with Hartman refusing to identify himself. Reluctantly, knowing the obstruction would continue unless he made a concession, Hartman gave his case number. Berman was on the line at once.

"This isn't secure, for God's sake. It's an outside line."

"I know," said Hartman.

"You're in Washington?"

"Yes."

"Why?"

"It's important."

"Something about the last thing?" The hope was obvious.

"I want to see you," said Hartman ambiguously. Berman would agree in his desperation. Hartman knew he would have to risk the later annoyance.

The American hesitated, trying to select a location where there would be some cover. "The Lincoln Memorial," he said. "An hour from now."

Feeling the need to be away from the confines of the hotel, Hartman set out early to walk to the monument. A disinterested sun was breaking sporadically through the clouds, but there was little warmth; puddles remained frozen, and the hedges and shrubs were aged by frost. After nearly two months in the tropical heat of Panama, he would be lucky to avoid a cold. It had been unthinking of him to come unannounced to Washington, Hartman decided, as unthinking as going to Paris without establishing Berman's presence there. It was time the carelessness stopped. He began consciously to concentrate upon his surroundings, embarking upon a circuitous route and fully employing the expertise he had perfected over three decades. He entered Georgetown, for once appreciating the grid system; in the regimented roads it would have been easy to isolate any pursuit. On Q Street he hailed a passing taxi, asked for Capitol Hill, and then went through the charade of changing his mind, paying it off still in motion, and alighting just after a light-controlled intersection, where he would have been sure of any following vehicle.

He was still at the memorial ahead of the time stipulated by Berman. He went inside, gazing up at the statue. Lincoln had opposed slavery, he remembered, although not as strongly as some historians liked to insist. He smiled at the irony; it made a fitting location for him to end his own bondage. He examined the other visitors, deciding they were all genuine tourists.

Berman, who was precise in everything, arrived exactly on time, coming toward the monument with the bouncy yet controlled strides of an exercise fanatic. Hartman wondered if he jogged here, as he did in Paris. In almost everything, Berman was the antithesis of Karpov. Based in a city where cooking was a religion, Berman supplemented every calorie-counted, garlic-free meal with vitamin extract. He neither smoke nor drank alcohol and always insisted upon the Perrier water being opened at his table, where he could be sure it was a fresh bottle and not one refilled and resealed.

Berman stood alongside, but Hartman did not speak, knowing the American would want to carry out the same check as he had done to assure himself of the innocence of the other visitors.

"There better be a damned good reason for this," said the American finally.

"There is."

"Lang?" Berman turned at the question and Hartman saw there was almost a pleading expression on his face.

"No."

"What do you mean, no!"

"That isn't what I came here for."

"What, then, for God's sake?"

"I'm getting out."

Berman continued to stare at the Austrian without comprehension. 'Getting out?' he said, as if the words had no meaning.

"Quitting."

Berman laughed, a short, nervous sound. "Oh, my God," he said again, disbelievingly.

"I mean it," insisted Hartman.

"I'm in trouble," said Berman, as if he were inviting a third party to adjudicate. "I'm in more trouble than I'm ever likely to be in my whole life. Davidson has got me skewered on a spit and he's roasting me a little every day, and you come all the way from Europe, breach every security procedure in the book, and calmly announce you don't want to work anymore. I don't believe it! I just don't believe it!"

"In Paris I told you I was thinking about it."

Berman shook his head, as if he couldn't recall the incident. Apparently feeling they had remained too long within the rotunda, Berman turned, leading the way outside.

"Davidson didn't find anything in Mexico City?" asked Hartman, following the American to an isolated bench.

Berman shook his head. "So now it's coverup time. I'm the favorite to be the sacrifice."

"I'm sorry. It's a pretty rotten life, isn't it?"

"I enjoy it," said Berman defensively.

"I don't," said Hartman. "That's why I'm giving it up."

"Don't be stupid, Hugo."

"I'm too old," said Hartman, setting out on the familiar argument. "It's not easy anymore. My nerve is going."

"I make the fitness reports," said Berman. "That's not my assessment."

"It doesn't matter," said Hartman, concealing the uncertainty. "I'm not going on anymore."

"Of course you are."

Hartman turned to the man beside him. "What do you mean?"

"I mean you can't quit, Hugo. That I won't let you."

"I don't *want* to go on. You must accept that."

"I won't accept it," said Berman reasonably, as if the discussion were academic.

"Bastard!"

"Don't be silly, Hugo. It isn't a personal thing."

"For me it is."

"It's just the effect of Gerda's death. I'm sorry about that, incidentally."

He was like a laboratory experiment, thought Hartman, permanently under some sort of microscope. It was strange how Karpov and Berman employed the same argument. Why strange? They were the same sort of people doing the same sort of job.

"I want to be free," he said, his voice breaking. He felt out, seizing the other man's arm. "Please," he begged. "Please let me go."

Berman, who had a dislike of physical contact, gently released himself.

"How do you think Davidson would read it?" he asked. "The entrapment of a Nazi in which you were closely involved fouls up, the guy is eliminated by someone or something we don't know anything about, and within a few weeks you say you want to get out. Wouldn't that be likely to cause a little suspicion?"

"I don't know what happened,' said Hartman immediately.

"I accept that, Davidson wouldn't."

Hartman decided it wasn't his protection that Berman was worried about; an operative quitting would add to the pressures under which the man was being put by the Agency.

"I'm no good, not anymore," said Hartman, uncaring of the desperation.

Berman reached out, allowing himself briefly to squeeze Hartman's shoulder. "You know the rules, just as I do."

"Rules?"

"Once you're in—once someone like you is in—there's only one way out. . . ."

Hartman remembered his earlier thoughts about slavery as he had stood before the statue of the American statesman. He closed his eyes, momentarily swept by a feeling of sickness and dizziness. He hadn't taken his pills or eaten properly.

"You all right?" asked Berman, concerned.

"Yes," said Hartman, opening his eyes again.

"I'll cover for you," offered Berman suddenly.

"Cover for me?"

"I'll have to file a report when I get back. I'll say we arranged it in Paris . . . that there was something important you wnated to tell me."

"I don't give a damn what you say," dismissed Hartman. He gripped his hands against the impotence.

"It's best not to make waves, not just now," said Berman. "And it will mean you can charge the air fare on your expenses."

Perhaps he should have waited until Berman returned to Paris. The decision would have been the same: Berman wouldn't allow himself to lose anyone, not now. The whole thing had been a ridiculous self-deception. He'd known Karpov wouldn't let him go and he had known Berman wouldn't let him go. He'd been posturing for his own conscience, so that he could tell himself he'd tried.

"You really shouldn't have come," repeated Berman. "There aren't many case officers who'd do what I'm doing."

Hartman was sure Berman's false report would be to spare himself from any further criticism, nothing more. The American, the precise man, looked at his watch. Hartman saw it was a heavy, digital affair, the sort that showed the time in the world's capitals as well as the second, minute, hour, and date. There was even a minute calculator built into the bottom. Berman would regard it as an essential timepiece.

"I must go now," said Berman. "There's an inquiry board in an hour."

"Of course."

"Let's keep a tighter rein, shall we?"

"All right."

"Don't forget to put the fare on your expenses."

"I won't."

Hartman was back at the Hay Adams before noon. Although he had no wish to do so, he forced himself to eat, knowing he had to maintain his blood-sugar balance. After he had eaten he confirmed his overnight plane reservation back to Vienna and then, as he had promised, telephoned Rebecca to warn her. There was none of the anger that had been obvious from Paris. She'd bought another icon and later that day a man was returning with some Venetian glass, she said. For supper the following night, they'd have wild boar and red cabbage.

Still with time to occupy before the flight, Hartman on impulse called the clearing section of the Chase Manhattan Bank, dictated the number of the check he had left for the stonework to Gerda's grave, and inquired if it had been cashed. It hadn't. It was possible the work had not started yet. But Hartman thought that was unlikely.

8

Rebecca slept with one hand across his chest; he could feel the edges of the rings pushing into his skin. They'd probably bruised his back, where she had gripped him earlier with a passion that had surprised him. She had detected the feeling and lost her shyness in the darkness of the bedroom.

"I'm pleased you're back," she had explained. "I wanted you to know how much I loved you."

He tried to ease her hand away, to lessen the chances of her discovering he was still awake. Had she guessed his difficulty in matching her emotion; of making love to her at all? He'd known she would expect it and so he had forced himself, drinking quickly when she had been out of the room in the hope that alcohol might help. He had a headache now, a constant discomfort behind his eyes and at the back of his neck.

The interviews with Karpov and Berman kept parading themselves in his mind; he could even recall the inflections of their voices.

There's only one way out, Hugo. . . . You're terrified of dying, aren't you, Hugo? . . .

Had they meant to mock? It seemed like mockery now. Maybe his recall was wrong; the tone of voice anyway.

Beside him Rebecca shifted, moving her hand away. She whimpered, but he couldn't recognize the words. He looked curiously toward her in the darkness. She rarely dreamed so obviously. He tried to make out her features, holding back from the need to reach out and trace them with his fingers. Would she be prepared to go on accepting separate establishments, now that Gerda was dead? For a while, he guessed; until sufficient time had passed for it not to cause any offense to Gerda's memory. And even then she might wait, expecting the approach from him. Dare he risk it? His fear was not so much of her discovering what he did, nervous as he was of it harming their relationship. She knew everything that had happened at the camp—of his cowardice. If she could love him still, with that knowledge, then she could adjust to learning that he was an agent, offensive though she might initially find it. His deeper reluctance was that she might become a victim. What if there *were* an arrest, the sudden scream of sirens and inrush of police? Would they ever accept that she could have remained entirely innocent? Wasn't protracted interrogation more likely, from anonymous, uniformed men? Stripped of clothes and the jewelry he knew she needed for her confidence, shapeless in prison coarseness and caged once more within a barred cell, questioned again and again until she made some innocent, thoughtless reply and convinced them further that she was lying. Involuntarily he shuddered, instantly worried the movement might have disturbed her. He wouldn't do it; couldn't do it. Was he prepared to lose her, then? It was a possibility that had to be considered. Wouldn't she see his refusal to marry and set up home as a rejection? Rebecca was a proud woman, with every reason to be so. She'd forgive him his weaknesses more readily than she would accept what she took to be his lack of interest.

The headache was worsening, the pain coming now in time with his heartbeat. Had he taken the prescribed number of pills the previous day for his diabetes? He couldn't remember. Aspirin might relieve the discomfort, but he would disturb her leaving the bed. He turned onto his side, away from her, so that their bodies didn't touch. He needed her, Hartman knew. The thought of being alone, of having no one, frightened him: it frightened him as much as the thought of death that he had so readily confessed to Karpov. Rebecca whimpered again, a strangely lost sound. And she needed him, he decided.

Outside, it was getting light; already shapes were beginning to form within the bedroom. He began to drift into a half-sleep, part of him consciously recognizing it as a dream, but unable to rouse himself from the terror of it. The windows were blocked by barbed wire, and there were dogs, Alsatians as they'd always used, slavering outside, baying to get through at them. Gerda was with him, as well as Rebecca. They were unclothed and ashamed of their nakedness, holding their hands before them in futile protection. The women weren't being kind to him, not anymore. They were screaming at him, demanding that he prove himself to be a man and show them the way out, but every time he opened a door, Karpov or Berman stood outside, thrusting him into the room again. And then it was neither Karpov nor Berman, but Klaus Reinhart, dressed as he'd always been in polished boots and the puffed trousers, with the Stalingrad medal and the Greek ribbon and the North African decoration clipped on his tunic, proof that he had shown his bravery elsewhere before the injury that had caused his SS assignment to the camp. Reinhart didn't have to push him, because he retreated automatically. And when he looked around Rebecca and Gerda weren't screaming anymore, but lying side by side in a bed, both smiling and reaching out, boasting their nakedness. Reinhart went to them, snapping his fingers for his clothes to be taken and neatly folded, for when he had finished.

He forced himself awake, grunting his fear. He was soaked in sweat, the bed damp around him. Rebecca was sitting up alongside him.

"Cover yourself up!" he demanded, the dream still very real.

"What?" she asked, confused.

"Nothing," he apologized. "I'm sorry. Bad dream."

She put on the lamp, though there was sufficient light in the room to see.

"Can I get you anything?"

"I have a headache."

Still naked, she got unselfconsciously from the bed and went into the bathroom for aspirin. He remained upright, watching her. She was very firm-bodied, he saw, suddenly excited.

"They won't get you," he blurted, as she returned with the aspirin and water.

She frowned at him. "What is it, darling?"

He shuddered again. "Bad dream," he repeated.

She had brought a hand towel from the bathroom, as well as the medicine. She sat on his side of the bed, drying the perspiration from his head and shoulders.

"Poor Hugo," she said gently.

"I didn't mean to awaken you."

"It's time to get up anyway."

"I want us to be happy, Rebecca."

"I know you do, darling."

"I'm going to try very hard to please you."

"You don't have to try very hard. You please me all the time."

She took a wrap from the bed on her way back to the bathroom. He listened to the noise of the shower; occasionally he could hear the song she was humming. It sounded melancholy. A lament.

By the time he had shaved, she had prepared breakfast in the window alcove from which they could look out upon Vienna. So many churches, he thought, a collection of religious relics. The Deutschordenskirche, far away on Singer Strasse. And the Michaeler Kirche much nearer. A steeple away to the right that he couldn't identify. Where was a God he could pray to and ask for guidance? There wasn't a God, he knew. He'd decided that years ago, in Belsen. By the side of his plate, next to the orange juice, were his pills. There was only one person who cared, Hartman knew: only one person whom he should worship.

"I wonder if the man will come back with the glass," she said, crumbling her roll. The customer with the Venetian crystal had failed to keep his appointment the previous day, and Hartman knew she was irritated.

"Perhaps there was a good reason for his not coming," he said.

"Like selling to someone else."

He smiled at her competitiveness. "He'll come back," he said encouragingly.

"Have you thought about seeing a doctor?" she asked suddenly.

"What?"

"You're not well," she said. "You haven't been since Gerda's funeral. I think you should see a doctor."

"There's nothing wrong," he said. "Maybe a little tired. . . ."

"There'll be no harm in an examination," she said, reaching across the table for his hand. "I don't want anything to happen to you."

"I'll think about it," he said.

"Soon?"

"All right."

They took the taxi first to the salon on Führichstrasse and then Hartman continued to his own apartment. After she had left the car, he traveled oblivious to what passed outside in the cart-width streets of the original city, immersed in thought. He'd always believed that dreams faded at the moment of awakening. Why was it then that his nightmare was still with him, the floating expression of Reinhart's face as vivid to him as it had been all those years ago, when he'd paid his nightly visits to Gerda? He awoke startled from his reverie, aware the car had stopped and that the driver was turning to stare curiously at him. Hartman paid, took from the trunk the suitcase with which he had returned from America, and slowly entered his apartment building. It was too old to have an elevator. He went gradually up the broad, sweeping staircase, pausing on each landing to recover his breath. He was too old, he thought again, much too old. The headache still lurked, like an ejected party guest awaiting the excuse to return.

It had become automatic to enter the apartment gazing down, because it was the method of initial contact from each side. He closed the door, secured the chain, and then remained with the suitcase at his feet, staring at the postcard. He couldn't tell which side it was from, and he was unwilling to commit himself to either by picking it up. At last, reluctantly, he moved, the groan as much that of despair as at the effort of bending. The home-furnishings catalogue he had wanted to inspect had arrived and was awaiting collection; it was a genuine card, from one of the better shops in the Kohlmarkt. So the Russians wanted him. Would Karpov keep his promise to protect him as much as possible?

Before commencing the intricate contact procedure, Hartman unpacked. He was a neat man, so it was natural for him to do so, but today it also provided a delay. How wonderful it would have been not to have responded. But he did. It took him twenty minutes to penetrate the protection with which Karpov surrounded himself, and when he was given the final location Hartman frowned, recognizing the Schüttelstrasse apartment again. Once more Hartman paid off the taxi some way from the address, continuing on foot and then in a roundabout route according to the instructions.

With his customary exuberance, Karpov hauled him into the apartment, clutching his hand in greeting and with his other arm around the Austrian's shoulders.

"Good to see you again, Hugo," said Karpov. "Good to see you."

Karpov stood away, wreathed in smiles and cigarette smoke, examining him as a proud father might look upon a son who had returned from some long absence.

"You're looking better," decided the Russian.

"I don't feel it."

Karpov ignored the contradiction. "What do you think?" he asked, indicating the apartment.

Hartman saw some prints had been added to the walls and a pot of trailing plants installed near the window, where they would have the benefit of some light. Near a door which Hartman presumed led to a bedroom there was an extensive stereo installation and alongside it racks of Karpov's record collection.

"Very nice," said Hartman doubtfully.

"There's a receptionist at the Sacher," confided Karpov. He cupped his hands before him, as if testing a weight. "Big tits. Coming tomorrow night."

"Good luck," said Hartman.

"Must get some mouthwash," said Karpov in private reminder. He smiled, broadly. "Just received a fresh shipment of beluga," he said. "We'll have it with some aquavit."

"I'm not hungry," refused Hartman.

"No one can refuse the best caviar," said the Russian.

A table had already been prepared. The caviar was in a silver dish encased in ice, and the aquavit bottle was frosted where it had been heavily chilled. There were two spoons and some coarse bread.

"No onion or hard-boiled eggs, as they have it in the West," said Karpov. "That's crap, for pansies. This is the only way to eat it. I think schnapps is better than vodka. More bite."

He spooned the caviar into his mouth, closing his eyes to savor the taste.

"Russia hasn't given the world much," said Karpov enthusiastically. "But if we've imparted a taste for this, then it should be grateful."

He uncorked the bottle and poured out the liquor. Hartman allowed himself a small portion of beluga and accepted the glass from Karpov.

"Success," toasted the Russian.

"To what?"

"Your assignment, of course," said Karpov. He moved the container toward Hartman, inviting him to help himself. Hartman did so, enjoying the flavor; it should impress the Sacher receptionist the following night.

"You promised me a rest," reminded Hartman.

Karpov moved his shoulders expansively, indicating the decision had been made by someone less sympathetic than himself. "I'm sorry," he said.

"What is it?"

"A traitor," said Karpov.

Hartman felt the Russian staring directly at him. He looked up, answering the look. Fortunately he had been eating, so the swallow appeared quite natural.

"Russian?" demanded Hartman. His voice sounded normal.

"He appears to have forgotten it," confirmed Karpov. He was heaping the beluga onto the bread, like an open sandwich. "This is supposed to be an aphrodisiac," he said. "I hope it works tomorrow."

"I've never been involved in anything like this before," said Hartman cautiously.

"It's America," said Karpov. "New York."

Again the Russian spoke looking straight at him, as if watching for some reaction. Hartman continued to eat and drink, finding the movement useful.

"Who?"

From a file conveniently at hand on a side table, Karpov took a photograph, offering it to the Austrian.

"Dimitri Poliev," he identified. "Second Secretary to our United Nations consulate."

"You have agents policing the United Nations," said Hartman.

"It's they who've become suspicious," agreed Karpov.

"So what's the need for me?"

"Because we want to know for sure. We don't want to move against the man without any justification."

"Your own agents," repeated Hartman.

Karpov shook his head, poking at the container in an effort to find the last traces of the caviar.

"We couldn't have Russians mounting any sort of investigation on American soil."

"It's hardly an investigation."

"It would still be too dangerous. It's got to be you."

The strings were being jerked and he was about to begin another puppet dance, thought Hartman bitterly. He felt a wash of resentment against the Russian.

"Fifty thousand dollars," he demanded. Hartman stared across the table to gauge the other man's reaction. It was ten thousand more than he'd ever asked before. What would he do if Karpov refused?

"Agreed," said Karpov immediately. He grinned, conscious of the Austrian's surprise.

"I told you before," said Karpov. "We prize you highly. Very highly indeed."

"In dollars," stipulated Hartman. He'd found a modicum of power and enjoyed playing with it, like a child recovering a favorite toy.

"Yes."

"Paid in advance."

"Of course."

He didn't have any supremacy, Hartman realized. Karpov was guiding him through the financial arrangements as he had in everything else.

"What do you want me to do?" he asked.

"Prove it. Or find sufficient doubt about the man that justifies an interrogation."

"And then?"

"We're putting in a squad," said Karpov. "Your contact will be the embassy in Washington. There'll be no direct link between you."

To protect their own people in case he were caught, realized Hartman. Another transatlantic flight. It was becoming ridiculous. He felt engulfed in an aching lassitude.

"Why not somebody else?" he asked.

"There isn't anybody else."

"I'm very tired."

"It shouldn't be difficult."

"It always is."

"There's something more," said Karpov. He turned to the file again, coming back with a magazine clipping. He pushed it across the table, smiling expectantly. "What about that!" he said.

It was an advertisement offering four early pressings of some Charlie Mingus recordings with Charlie Parker.

"I've already replied," said Karpov. "I don't care what they cost. I must have them."

"All right," said Hartman wearily.

"Do you know how rare they are?" demanded Karpov, unable to understand Hartman's lack of interest.

"No," said Hartman.

"They're unique," insisted Karpov, as if he were trying to instill some enthusiasm into the other man.

"I'll get them for you," promised Hartman, pocketing the advertisement. "What about the money?"

From the file, Karpov extracted the tight piles of dollar notes, neat and secure in their bank wrappers, enjoying the look on Hartman's face.

"Count it," he invited.

Hartman did, very carefully. "Fifty thousand," he agreed, looking up. There had been more available, in anticipation of an even higher figure. He was no different from the greedy mailman in the Panama hotel room, he thought.

Karpov stretched across the table with the familiar arm-patting gesture.

"What do I have to do to convince you?" he said. "We're only interested in keeping you happy."

His headache had returned, Hartman realized; it was worse than before.

Karpov stood close to the window, waiting for Hartman to reach the street below. He identified the Austrian, and nodded with admiration at the ease with which the man assimilated himself along the passersby.

Karpov's suitcase was already packed and waiting in the bedroom, his fur-lined coat and hat laid alongside in readiness. He left the apartment building through the rear exit, normally used by the delivery men, and the waiting chauffeur got from the car, took his bag, and then opened the rear door for him to enter.

They took the ring road to miss any congestion and reached Schwechat in under an hour. The plane to Amsterdam was not delayed, for which Karpov was grateful. He boarded, wondering whether all the sideways movements were absolutely necessary; he knew he was undetected. The Moscow visit was as unnecessary: Migal was a worrisome old woman. He took three of the miniature bottles of wine with his in-flight meal and had sufficient time on the ground at Amsterdam to enjoy two cognacs. He was traveling on a French passport, so there was no recognition or special attention aboard the Aeroflot flight to Moscow, and the cabin staff was too well trained to evince any curiosity at his immediate clearance at Sheremetyevo, with the Zil parked and waiting the moment he left the aircraft.

It was two years since Karpov had been home. Despite the warmth from the heater, he shivered in the back of the car; he had forgotten how bone-chillingly cold it became in Moscow. Little wonder everyone appeared so miserable.

The road was cleaned and dry, the snow frozen into guarding walls on either side.

"It's cold," Karpov said to the driver, trying his Russian like a student.

"It's been colder," dismissed the man.

"I'd forgotten what it could be like."

The man made no response. Miserable wanker, thought Karpov. The city began to form, a black interruption on the skyline and then the more definite shapes of buildings. Babushkas were hunched over their snow-clearing shovels and brooms, in gossiping groups, plump in their layers of protective clothing. Within the city, the cluster of traffic slowed them; inevitably the biggest obstruction was caused by a broken-down bus. Double-decker, Karpov saw, when they finally got past; the sort that Stalin had never permitted, definite in his peasant's conviction that they would not negotiate a turn without toppling over.

They went directly to Dzerzhinsky Square, the official car recognized, and moved through the usual checks.

"Thank you," said Karpov politely to the driver. Again the man didn't reply. Karpov realized he had forgotten the surliness, as well as the cold.

Ivan Migal, head of the European Division of the KGB, was waiting expectantly in his office. In the corner, a samovar gurgled, like an old man's dyspeptic stomach. The central heating was high and Migal wore a thin suit. Karpov knew he would become discomforted in his heavy European clothing. It was very Russian; one extreme to the other.

"Comrade Colonel," greeted Migal.

"Comrade General," responded Karpov.

"A good journey?"

"Pleasant enough."

"I'm grateful for your coming."

Karpov hesitated at the humility. False, he judged.

Migal had never been a humble man.

"You described it as important," he reminded.

"Consultation from time to time is always important, don't you think?" said Migal. He was a small, fussily assured man who favored the hard, detachable collars and style of eyeglasses that Lenin had worn, imagining a resemblance. It invited ridicule, which made it a strange affectation for someone regarded within the Kremlin hierarchy as a survivor. Migal had been a protégé of Stalin, whom he had served with unswerving loyalty, but with the caution necessary to evade the purges with which the megalomaniac had maintained his undisputed power. That in itself had come to be admired long before Stalin's death, but it was not until after 1953 that Migal's reputation had become firmly established. He had been accepted first by Bulganin and then, even more readily, by Khrushchev. It was rumored that Migal had been considered by the Russian leader at one time for overall dictatorship of the KGB. Karpov often wondered if the man were as unassailable as everyone seemed to believe.

"Very important," agreed Karpov.

"You've briefed Hartman?"

"This morning."

"How did he respond?"

"The death of his wife seems to have upset him, predictable though it was," said Karpov.

"The natural culmination of guilt?" suggested Migal.

"Perhaps," agreed Karpov.

"What about the other woman?"

"He's in love with her," said Karpov.

"Could it affect his work?"

"It might make him more reluctant than he used to be," conceded Karpov.

"How much did he want?"

"Fifty thousand." Karpov was aware of the surprise upon Migal's face.

"He's becoming very demanding," said Migal.

"I think he wanted me to refuse," said Karpov.

"He would still have had to do what we asked."

"He knew that. To insist upon a high payment allows him some independence."

"He's a good man," said Migal.

"The best."

"How's Vienna?" asked Migal.

"Very civilized," said Karpov. The whole journey had been a complete waste of time, he thought. And he'd also had to postpone the meeting with the Sacher receptionist.

"Still collecting your jazz records?"

Karpov paused, seeking criticism in the question. "Yes," he said. "It's quite extensive now."

"Going straight back?"

"Thought I might visit my wife. I haven't seen her for two years."

Migal nodded. "I don't think you should be away from Vienna for too long."

Then why withdraw me? thought Karpov. "I thought I'd go back tomorrow."

"That'll be fine," agreed Migal.

The KGB chief went reflectively to the samovar after Karpov had left, preparing himself another cup of tea. He'd have gauged it, from Karpov's responses and attitude, if the man had had any awareness of what had happened on Stalin's orders during the war. So Hartman didn't know from his time in Belsen of the deal involving the Russian prisoners. It was a relief.

The affair with Fritz Lang had unsettled Migal, making him aware of how vulnerable he could still be. If the Nazi hadn't disembarked at Mexico City and made contact through the embassy to find out why his $400 retainer had been stopped, there was no way he could have prevented the man's capture by the CIA. And the Americans had intended to seize Lang and then attempt to expose him for what he had been ordered to do toward the end of the war. He was certain of that; the agents whom Migal had installed in advance of Lang's arrival in Zurich, along with the booby-trapped car, had identified at least fifteen American operatives. One of his people had actualy got so close as to get cut by the flying glass.

Migal shuddered, confronted by a sudden thought. It was the nearest he had come to disaster for many years. He should have had Lang killed long ago. It had been a very careless oversight. He would have to ensure he didn't make such a mistake again.

Karpov would believe his recall ridiculous; it didn't matter. It had been important to judge the man's demeanor, to decide if Hartman had confided in him. It was good to know that Hartman was unaware of what had happened in Belsen. The Austrian was far too useful to be killed. Migal would have regarded it as a waste.

9

It had been a bad evening, one of the worst Hartman could ever remember spending with Rebecca. She had refused to eat in a restaurant and the meal she had prepared had been indifferent. He had praised it, of course, but she had refused the flattery, dismissing it as rubbish.

"I'm sorry," he said, knowing the reason for her irritation.

"You were in America only a few days ago."

"I didn't know then that this would come up."

She flushed: embarrassment, he guessed. "I've no right to be demanding," he said.

"You've *every* right," he assured her.

"I just expected to see more of you after . . . after everything."

"I wanted that too," he said.

"Is it necessary for you to work so hard?"

"I've managed a reputation over the years," he said. "People keep coming to me."

"You could refuse," she said innocently.

"It isn't as easy as that," he said. Dear God, he thought, how I wish it were.

"Why not?"

Hartman hesitated, unsure how to guide her from any further curiosity about what he did.

"I'm a specialist," he said. "Few people possess the technical knowledge that I do about international regulations governing oil. So I seem to be the natural choice. It's rather flattering."

"There must be *thousands* of accountants specializing in oil," she insisted.

"Yes," said Hartman. "It sometimes surprises me." He knew there was perspiration upon his face; he took his napkin to his lips, extending the gesture to wipe it away.

"Have you ever thought of retiring?"

"Yes," he admitted.' 'Very seriously."

"You could, couldn't you? I mean, you're a rich man."

"I shall soon," he said unconvincingly.

She was looking at him very intently. "You do mean it, don't you?" she asked. The doubt was obvious in her voice.

"I want to try," he said. "But it isn't easy. I've built up quite a network of contacts. It's very difficult to just end, like that." He snapped his fingers.

"I'm sorry I behaved as I did," she apologized unexpectedly.

"That's all right."

"No, it's not. You've a lot on your mind . . . it was selfish of me. Unforgivable."

"I don't want anything to spoil us, Rebecca," he said, matching her seriousness.

"Neither do I."

"Perhaps one day you'll know how difficult things are for me." Should he confess now? And hope she would respond as he expected, with her usual forgiveness. She was looking at him across the table, smiling softly, offering to make up their quarrel. What if she didn't react as he anticipated? What if her forgiveness had all been used up, and she realized instead how he had deceived her for all these years? The risk was too great. He'd live any lie to keep Rebecca.

"What does that mean?' she asked.

He laughed, a dismissive sound. "Too melodramatic a use of words," he evaded.

"How long do you expect to be away?"

"I don't know," he said. "Not long, I hope."

"A week?" she suggested hopefully.

"Perhaps," he said. "Maybe a little longer. I won't know until I get there and discover what the problem is."

"Hurry back."

"Of course."

"Will you stay tonight?"

"I'd like to."

"I'd like it, too."

This time he went to bed without the apprehension of failure, and Rebecca was anxious to show her regret for causing the unpleasantness. Afterward she settled with her head against his shoulder, her hair wetly across his chest.

"I *do* love you," she said with an odd fervor.

"I know you do."

"I want you to know that."

"I do," he said.

"Keep safe in America."

"Of course."

"And come back as soon as you can."

"You know I will."

She went to sleep long before Hartman. He lay awkwardly, with the need to support her, feeling a numbness move into his shoulder but unwilling to disturb her. Karpov *had* kept his promise, Hartman thought. The Russian had promised him an easy assignment, and trying to determine whether or not Poliev had succumbed to the CIA shouldn't be too difficult. Perhaps it really wouldn't take more than a week. Then again, it might. The Russian security people hadn't been successful. Rebecca shifted, making it easier for him to free himself of her weight. Tonight's conversation should be a warning, he recognized; it would not be long before she became more curious. And in their argument he had detected a hint of something else. Soon she would begin to question the need for them to live apart. Hartman was frightened of sleep, remembering the nightmare of Gerda and Rebecca and Reinhart, but when it finally came he slept dreamlessly, awakening only when Rebecca moved to get up.

The tension of the previous night had left them, but

they breakfasted with less conversation than usual, Rebecca saddened by his depature, and Hartman aware of her feelings and subdued by them. As usual, he shared her car to the salon.

"Be careful," she repeated outside the shop.

"I promise."

"And come back soon."

"I promise that, too."

"Telephone?"

"If I can." Hartman was aware of the driver's bored attention from the front of the vehicle.

"I love you," said Rebecca, leaning across to be kissed.

"I love you too."

Hartman saw her into the building, then gave his own address. At the apartment he told the driver to wait, while he collected his luggage and then continued on to Schwechat. Hartman always traveled first class, because it was easier. There was no line at the check-in and he accepted the hospitality hostess's invitation to the VIP lounge. There was a courtesy telephone, and he considered calling Rebecca and then decided against it. There was nothing for them to say, so the only outcome would be to make her more depressed. During the flight Hartman ate only what he considered necessary for his diabetes and drank nothing; he was beginning an assignment, and when he worked he rarely bothered with alcohol.

Hartman's introduction to New York had been through the postwar films in which gleaming yellow cabs traveled unlittered streets and all the policemen had Irish accents. He'd never forgotten the surprised disappointment of his first arrival, and it always came again when he returned. The driver of the taxi he got at Kennedy Airport sat encased against attack behind a wire-reinforced glass cage, with a tiny flap through which the sign requested payment with the exact money. The rear fender was crushed and rusted from some long-ago collision, and through the split seam of the doorway a rainstorm of the previous day had formed a puddle which swilled back and forth across the rubber floor as the vehicle negotiated bends and obstructions.

As always, the Van Wyck Expressway was clotted with traffic, and roadworks near the Triboro Bridge increased the congestion. They stop-started toward a Manhattan skyline clouded with purplish-brown smog, past the debris of abandoned cars which had been cannibalized of wheels and other detachable parts, and now slumped, hoods and trunks open, like hungry metal cuckoos. It took two hours to reach Manhattan. The most obvious sign of the city's near bankruptcy was the road-surface neglect. They bumped and jarred over splits and potholes in the road, the underside of the vehicle sometimes grinding into contact. As the driver entered 61st Street, crossing toward Fifth Avenue and the Hotel Pierre, they became jammed alongside one of the subway ventilation grids, and the steam swirled around and leaked in through the gap which had earlier admitted the rain; it smelled very much like the Panamanian train that had carried him from Cristobal. There might be an enervating electricity about the place, Hartman thought, but the spark was dulled by a dirty bulb.

Hartman entered the hotel gratefully, patiently waiting his turn at the diminutive registration desk. The clerk apologized that it had not been possible to allocate him a room overlooking Central Park, and Hartman felt too tired and uninterested to argue; he wasn't in New York for the view anyway. He was on the twenty-first floor overlooking a concrete courtyard, which was difficult to see so far below, and with what he assumed was another wing or section of the hotel facing him. He unpacked, hung the 'Do Not Disturb' notice on the door, and went immediately to bed. If he managed sleep, he would be able to get over his jet lag in one day.

"I find it difficult to understand sometimes," said Ruth.

David looked up from his book. "What?"

"You and your father."

"What's to understand?"

The woman made a movement with her hands, as if she were molding something. "The *degree* of feeling between you."

"There's reason enough," insisted David, returning to his book to indicate the conversation was over.

"He hardly had any choice over what happened at the camp, did he?"

Her husband looked up irritably. "I don't want to talk about it."

"Did he?" repeated Ruth.

"I said there was reason enough."

She frowned, trying to understand. "What?"

David started to close the book, as if he intended talking after all, then changed his mind and opened it again.

"He allowed something to happen," he said badly. "Something horrifying."

"To your mother?"

"Yes."

"Why won't you tell me?"

"Maybe one day."

"Why not now?"

"Because I'm not ready."

10

The United Nations building was the obvious place at which to start. Hartman awoke early, still disoriented by the European time difference, so he got to the UN headquarters an hour before the allocation of tickets for the General Assembly meeting; there were still people ahead of him. He remained patiently in line, idly studying the sculpture in the auditorium. He was aware how tightly the Russians controlled the movements of their people, busing them morning and night from the official residencies in Riverdale to the General Assembly Building or the Soviet office building on 57th Street. Any CIA contact would therefore have had initially to have been made in this building; it couldn't have been easy. He wondered if it were still done here or whether they had managed to establish some other meeting place.

There was the usual thrust when the tickets became available, but Hartman maintained his place and managed to get a seat in the public gallery. The debate was on Africa. Hartman gazed down into the vast chamber, squinting to see the identification plaques. Predictably it was the African delegations who gathered first, anxious to record their presence. The Soviet diplomats were among the last to settle in their seats.

Hartman needed his glasses and even then had difficulty at first in isolating Dimitri Poliev. He was in the second row, and several times, while Hartman watched, the man leaned forward to prompt the Soviet spokesman or respond to some query. The British delegate was at the podium, and Poliev was conspicuous as the only Russian confident enough of his English not to bother with translation earphones.

It was an uninspired debate, country after country

reiterating its established position on apartheid. Hartman listened without interest. Poliev was a very active member of the delegation, constantly attentive to the senior officials. The Austrian left the gallery well ahead of the luncheon adjournment, anxious to reach the recognized meeting place of the diplomats ahead of any mass exodus from the chamber. From the green-tinted windows of the North Lounge, he could see the barge boats linked like hinged crocodiles on their slow way toward the dockside in Queens.

The representatives began drifting in, and Hartman positioned himself with a view of the approach corridor. Without office accommodation within the building, it was the corridors in which the Russians customarily held their tactical discussions, pacing back and forth oblivious of anyone around them, heads bent against eavesdropping. Today they seemed to consider there was no need for any debate preparation. They came directly into the lounge. Poliev was maintaining a respectful distance behind the diplomats he had been appointed to advise. He seemed younger than he had appeared in the picture that Karpov had given him. Hartman decided it was probably the glasses that had aged him in the official portrait. They were rimless, but in person seemed less prominent. The Russian was a fresh-faced, eager-looking man, discreetly but carefully dressed. Hartman guessed the clothes had come from Fifth Avenue, not Gorky Street.

Poliev detached himself from the main group almost as soon as they entered the lounge, going right toward the reading room. Hartman allowed two other people to enter in front of him, then followed. Poliev was at a reading stand, consulting an index. As Hartman entered, he went to a shelf and took out a slim volume, carrying it to one of the tables. Hartman picked up a pamphlet at random and sat four spaces away, the magazine held in front of him so there was no discernible movement when he looked over the top to keep Poliev in view. The Russian had a notebook before him and appeared to be making notes. He remained at the table for almost ten minutes before snapping the notebook closed with a gesture of finality. Hartman stirred attentively as Poliev moved to replace the book, wondering if it would be so simple. The gap remained where the reference volume had originally been, but Poliev moved two books along, putting it back in a different position. Hartman did not attempt to follow the Russian, going instead to the bookshelf. Poliev had been studying an official UN report on the oil-production forecast in Nigeria; it was applicable to the Assembly debate. Hartman left only long enough to establish that Poliev had joined the other Russians at a table; the notebook was open beside him and he gave the appearance of talking with the aid of his notes. When Hartman returned to the reading area, the Nigerian survey had been moved from the place in which the Russian had put it, back to its original position. Hartman gazed around the room. There were at least thirty people there.

Hartman watched the debate throughout the afternoon and then moved to the ground floor when it ended, watching Poliev enter the bus with the rest of the Russians being returned to their homes. Poliev certainly didn't intend any clandestine meetings tonight.

Had the displacement of the book been a signaling device? wondered Hartman on his way back to the Pierre. It had appeared an innocent-enough gesture. Which was why it would have been so unchallengeable: even the subject was applicable to the discussion, increasing the acceptability of it. But it remained a piece of CIA tradecraft: Hartman had on two occasions even been instructed to employ a similar procedure himself.

Hartman went directly to the dining room to compensate for his missed lunch. He ate sparingly but properly, aware of his diet, and again refused alcohol. He took his pills with water. He did not hurry, his next move clearly formulated in his mind. Because the call was outgoing and therefore traceable through the hotel switchboard, he changed some dollars into coins and telephoned the Soviet Embassy in Washington from one of the booths in the lobby. There was a delay while he was identified, and when he was finally connected to the extension he demanded, Hartman was peremptory, knowing the instructions would have come from Moscow and that therefore the diplomat would be nervous of him; so few people were that it gave him a small satisfaction, unnecessary and even immature though he recognized the behavior to be. He dictated his room number for the reply, then reentered the elevator for the comfort of the twenty-first floor. The response came within an hour, and Hartman nodded to himself in the empty room, impressed with the speed.

Russian diplomats in Western countries exist under two sets of restrictions. The first and most obvious is that imposed by the host nation and usually limits their movements to within a certain radius of the city, a matching retaliation for similar impositions on Western embassies in Moscow. The second is operated by the Russians themselves. Embassy personnel, from the ambassador downward, have to record their movements and provide, at least a week in advance, a list of any social functions they anticipate attending and name who approved their acceptance. It was this second record, of Poliev's intended movements, that Hartman wanted.

The following evening there was a reception for a Nigerian government party on a visit to America and Hartman thought again of the reading-room choice. The night after that, he had logged his intention to attend a performance at the Metropolitan Opera House at Lincoln Center. Hartman stopped the diplomat at the other end of the line, not wanting to work more than three days ahead.

He told the embassy official he wanted contact early the following day with a list of every event Poliev had attended during the previous two months.

A productive day? Or nothing? It was impossible to decide. With the reception the following night, the oil-production figures could have been a rather boring but nevertheless polite preparation for some cocktail-party conversation—the sort of attention to detail that a diligent diplomat might bother with, anxious to impress a Third World minister. But why ignore the obvious space and put the book back in a different position? For the moment it was insoluble, Hartman decided. Perhaps the information he'd asked for from the embassy would help.

Ruth remained a little apart and behind David, conscious of the moment and not wanting to embarrass him. He stood for a long time, his lips moving very slightly in prayer. At last he looked up, studying the words the headstone before removing his head covering and stepping back to where she waited.

"It looks very nice," said Ruth.

"I'm pleased," agreed David. "They've stressed it for any further subsidence, so nothing should crack."

"He'd be very upset," she said.

"It was hypocrisy," insisted David.

The inscription on Gerda's grave read:

Gerda Hartman
wife of Hugo Hartman
and deeply grieved mother of David

"He was her husband," pointed out Ruth.

"She could hardly have known it."

"Can't you find any pity for him?" she asked, distressed at his vehemence.

"It's difficult," said David. He turned away from his mother's grave, and Ruth started to follow him from the cemetery.

"It must have been very frightening," she said. She shivered, unable to stop herself. "I don't know how I'd have reacted in the circumstances. I don't think I'd have been brave."

"He never tried."

"Do you think he'll come here again?"

"I hope not," said David. "I tried to make it clear he wouldn't be welcome."

"Your mother loved him," reminded Ruth as they got into the car.

David hesitated at the driver's door. "That was the one thing I could never understand," he said.

11

In the same way that a master craftsman emerges from his apprenticeship and then improves the teaching for his own style, so Hartman, over the years, had developed into an agent unlike any other operated by the Soviet Union or America. Very early he had determined upon the obvious protection of never involving himself with the side for which he was not at that moment working. If his paymasters were the Russians, then it was to them he gave complete allegiance; if the assignment were proposed by the Americans, he disdained all contact with Moscow. Each gained, of course, by his association with the other, but it was an accrued benefit; from the master craftsman, the customer of the moment buys the experience of everything that has gone before. It was because he knew the systems of both and had the sort of mind to recognize it that Hartman knew the benefits—and the danger—of patterns. Both the Komitet Gosudarstvennoy Bezopasnosti and the Central Intelligence Agency were vast bureaucracies and, despite the misplaced belief that they operated on individual brilliance, they were basically run by clerks who insisted upon paperwork and forms and files. Neither appeared to realize the outcome. Inevitably and often unconsciously, the demand for regularity and conformity permeated down to field operatives. It created the greatest risk to detection and was therefore a vulnerability Hartman was constantly aware of and on guard against.

The conversation with the Washington embassy had begun disappointingly. It was when he was halfway through the bored recitation of Poliev's movements log for the previous two months that Hartman recognized the CIA's mistake and shook his head at the stupidity of it. Hartman waited for the flare of satisfaction, the self-awareness that he'd proved himself. But nothing came, not as it usually did when he realized he was likely to succeed on a mission. He knew it was depression at the uncertainty of his future with Rebecca.

The diplomat in Washington came to the end of the list, allowing the irritation to show in his voice at the apparently meaningless chore. He'd make sure the man learned how important it had been, Hartman decided.

"Anything else?"

"This is more than sufficient," thanked Hartman. He sat back, gazing at the list before him. With so little trouble it could have been made undetectable. Six weeks before, Poliev had attended the New York City Opera. The following week, a performance of Shakespeare's *As You Like It* at the Vivian Beaumont Theater. A month ago, it had been a concert at Avery Fisher Hall. After the weekly interval, he'd gone to another at Alice Tully Hall. And tomorrow he was going to another part of Lincoln Center, the Metropolitan Opera House. Tomorrow was a Wednesday. All the other visits had been on a Wednesday.

"A pattern," Hartman muttered to himself. Lincoln Center was an odd coincidence, he thought, remembering where he'd met Berman in Washington less than a month before.

Hartman left the Pierre by the Fifth Avenue exit, pausing outside the door. The smog had lifted, admitting the winter sun. It was a bright, winter-crisp day. He'd walk through Central Park, he decided; there was no hurry, now that he was sure.

He skirted the zoo, wondering if the rock outcrops were natural or artificially made to achieve the rugged appearance. The roadways were thick with joggers, trying to run away from obesity or ill health or both; they made an eccentric fashion show of track suits and sweat suits and long shorts and short shorts and even, near the boating lake, a bespectacled man trotting inside an oilskin bicycle cape so big that it looked like a mobile tent. There seemed to be an understanding with the drivers of the flower-bedecked horse buggies; runners to the road edge, carriages in the middle. The coachmen provided an independent display in opera hats and Confederate uniforms and dracula cloaks; it was like a fancy-dress parade in a mental asylum, thought Hartman. He preferred the quieter public places of Vienna, even the Augarten, disfigured by the antiaircraft tower that was a reminder of the war and which defied demolition. His favorite was the Lainzer Tiergarten, with its deer and wild boars and horses. He'd taken Gerda to the Tiergarten, on one of the first occasions they had been allowed to walk out without a chaperone. He'd tried to kiss her, and she had become embarrassed, blushing and pushing him away, complaining that they would be seen.

The park was wider than he had estimated, and he was breathing heavily by the time he got to 72nd Street. He was able to identify the buildings that formed the center by the time he got to Amsterdam Avenue: the opera house was the third one, he knew. He went in through the side, coming out onto the fountained piazza and gazing up at the high-domed windows. They looked cathedrallike. The opera was *La Bohème*, not one of his favorites. But he wasn't attending for the music. The studious, anxious-to-please girl at the ticket desk looked mildly curious at his request for seats at every level.

'Not the best,'' she apologized. ''The booking has been heavy.''

''They'll do,'' Hartman assured her. Back out on Columbus Avenue, Hartman halted uncertainly. It was just midday. The opera was not until the following night. How should he occupy the intervening thirty-six hours? There was Connecticut and Gerda's grave, he supposed. But if he left now, it would be dark when he arrived. And there was no possibility of his being invited to stay overnight with Ruth and David. He could set out early the following day. But a delay might arise, which he couldn't anticipate. And he couldn't risk a late arrival at the opera house. What then? Without any obvious, understandable reason he began thinking of Panama and Fritz Lang and the worried Peter Berman, convinced that his career was destroyed. A vague impression began forming itself in his mind, a memory that wouldn't quite come. It was associated with Berman, but he couldn't decide how. Something to do with the man's desperation to survive the Panama debacle? The first question prompted another. How desperate was he? Desperate enough to offer anything, in return for help? Inexplicable, for the moment, he recalled the New York bank deposits. And then he recognized the cause; always the transfer from Lang's account had been on the eighth of every month. Perhaps, subconsciously, it was the date which had started the whole thought process: today was the eighth.

He remembered the urgency of Berman's question when the man had thought he'd come to Washington with something additional on Fritz Lang. He hadn't, on that occasion. But if he could find out more about the account with the 1980074 deposit number and the connection with the god of love, then he might have something. He might have something important enough to make a deal, his freedom for Berman's future. It was worth a try: anything, no matter how remote the chances of success, was justified if it brought any nearer the possibility of his happiness with Rebecca. There would still be the original withholding to disguise, but an explanation would be easy enough, to satisfy someone as anxious as the American.

He'd given the Broadway and 57th Street address of the bank to the taxi driver and settled back into the seat before he realized he had no clearly formulated intention of what to do. Pose it as a credit-worthiness inquiry? He didn't know the acknowledged procedure and in any case they would demand some sort of identification. He remembered his own account at the same bank, but at their Wall Street branch. He took the checkbook out, gazing down at it; the last payment was for Gerda's headstone. The idea came as the taxi arrived, and for a moment Hartman sat there considering it. Not flawless, but just possible with what he already knew. He entered as unobtrusively as always, looking for the area that exists in most American banks occupied by counsellors and deposit advisors. It was to the left; three people, one a woman. Before approaching he went to one of the writing booths and against his own account wrote out a check for the $100 that would normally have been dispatched from Panama, leaving the payee section blank and not signing it. Then he approached one of the desks, smiling hopefully. The woman responded and he accepted her offer.

"I feel remarkably silly," he began apologetically. "But I wonder if you can help me over a small matter concerning one of your customers?"

The bank official regarded him curiously.

"I am a business colleague of Señor Lopez in Panama. Normally every month a money order for $100 is transferred here from his account in the Bank of Panama. Because I was visiting New York, he asked me personally to make the payment . . ." Hartman stopped, smiling this time with vague embarrassment and producing the check he had recently half-completed. ". . . I've mislaid the depositor's name, so I can't complete it," he said.

Still the woman remained curious. "I'll need to know some more . . ."

"That's the stupidity of it," anticipated Hartman. "I can remember everything else. The account number here is 1980074. The consignee from Panama is Señor Lopez. It's the Cristobal branch and the number is 38279."

At last she relaxed, confronted with the sort of details she understood. She spoke into the internal telephone and shortly a guard approached with a file. Hartman appeared very relaxed in the chair, giving no indication of the excitement he felt. She frowned up. "The order has been made as usual," she said.

Hartman gave a matching expression. "Señor Lopez was most insistent. I'd better complete the transaction and leave it for him to resolve back in Panama."

The girl looked doubtful, and Hartman passed the check across to her. She hesitated, then took up a pen, scribbling the name in the space available.

"I haven't signed it," reminded Hartman.

She paused again, then returned the slip of paper. Albert Richman, he read.

"Albert Richman!" he said, snapping his fingers at the imagined recollection. "Of course! It was so stupid of me to forget."

"A very old customer," said the woman, the file still before her.

"Since the 'fifties, Señor Lopez told me," guessed Hartman, remembering the date of the Nazi's first passport and the entry stamps into New York.

The woman nodded. "An unfortunate man."

"Unfortunate?"

"Badly crippled. We've always believed the Panamanian payment was some sort of disability pension."

Still Hartman remained unmoving, but the excitement started again. Not another sanctuary, established by Lopez: someone else. There *would* be information enough to trade with Berman.

"Señor Lopez didn't tell me," said Hartman, eager to continue the conversation. "This month there'll be a double payment."

"He'd welcome it," said the woman. "He appears to rely on it."

"A pleasant surprise, then."

The woman looked at the clock somewhere behind Hartman and the Austrian chanced another guess. "A man of habit?"

She nodded. "Always around three o'clock. I think he's on his way to work."

The luck he had thought about in Panama was still with him, decided Hartman. "I've kept you long enough," he said, moving to stand.

"I'll need your name," stopped the woman. "For the records."

"Lang," said Hartman. "Fritz Lang." It was fortunate there was no identity printed on the check.

He watched until the woman had completed the entry, then gave the Cristobal address of the dead Nazi.

"Thank you," he said sincerely, rising at last.

"You're welcome," said the woman.

One-thirty, noted Hartman, outside the bank. Ninety minutes to wait. On the next block he saw the neon of a short-order resturant and moved toward it. He shuffled along the lunchtime line by the dispensing counter and then waited, tray in hand, until there was a vacancy at one of the window stools. It was almost impossible to see the bank, he realized when he finally sat down. Identification would be difficult, he decided objectively. He couldn't re-enter the bank and risk suspicion from the counsellor from whom he'd learned so much, and even if he did, the chances of his isolating Albert Richman were no greater than if he remained outside: the man would go to a different section of the bank to make a withdrawal. He would attempt pursuit of anyone as obviously disabled as the woman had indicated, but even if he failed to learn anything further, he still had enough to negotiate his release from the CIA. He could hardly have been in a more convenient location, he thought, smiling at the irony: the KGB financing a visit to America where he could quit being an operative of the CIA!

He lingered as long as possible on the stool, but was still back on Broadway thirty minutes before Richman's habitual arrival. He strolled casually first on the same side of the street as the bank, then crossed and patroled the opposite pavement. There were sufficient people to conceal the observation from becoming obvious. Even a few parked cars adding to the protection.

Hartman was near a vehicle when he saw the man and much later wondered if he would not have physically collapsed had it not been there for him to reach out for its support. The terror swamped him, freezing him against the protection of the stationary vehicle like a sudden and complete paralysis. He found it difficult to breathe, as if a band had been drawn about his chest, and the blood throbbed through his head loudly, so the sensation was of hearing rather than feeling a heartbeat.

The man moved with a stiff-kneed awkwardness, hand braced against his thigh for support: the right leg, remembered Hartman. An assault on the tank near Stalingrad. There'd been a medal for it, to go with all the others. The last, because it was for the injury that had caused his transfer from the front line to Belsen.

Hartman tried to concentrate, to call upon the experience he had developed over the past thirty-three years, but the thoughts refused to coalesce, impressions and memories flurrying through his mind like leaves in autumn.

There was only one positive awareness, repeating itself to him like a chant, over and over again. He'd found Klaus Reinhart.

Davidson paced his office, a theatrical performance, and

Peter Berman refused to respond to it, sitting apparently relaxed by the desk and gazing out the window. Outside the trees were bare. Branches twitched as they were blown by the wind coming up through the Potomac Valley. Davidson stopped the promenading, irritated it hadn't affected the other man, and picked up from the desk the report in which Berman had attempted to cover the true purpose of Hartman's visit to Washington.

"It's bullshit," he said. "Pure bullshit."

Davidson was bluffing, Berman knew. The last inquiry session into the Zurich disaster hadn't been as forceful in apportioning responsibility as the section head had expected, and he was nervous the Director wasn't regarding it seriously enough.

"It was well intentioned," defended Berman. "The man thought he had something important. When he discovered I was off station, he came here. Stupid, I agree. But well intentioned, like I said."

"What was it?" demanded Davidson.

"The NATO leak," said Berman, the alibi assured. They had spent a month investigating the suggestion that defense secrets were getting from the Brussels headquarters and proved it untrue.

"He came to Washington for that!" said Davidson, knowing there was no effective challenge he could make to the story but not believing it either.

"It would have been important enough, if it had been true."

"But it wasn't."

"Hugo didn't know that."

"He was still wrong to come here."

"I told him so," said Berman. "He won't do it again."

"He's too experienced to make a mistake like that," insisted Davidson.

"What do you mean?" asked Berman. He would have to defend his story, to avoid any further trouble at the inquiry board. He guessed Davidson was going to waste a lot of time.

"He'd be dangerous if he wasn't loyal," said Davidson in his lecturing voice, as if he were revealing a great truth. "He found Lang, after all."

"You mean he told the Russians!"

"Why not?"

"He didn't know of the Soviet involvement."

"How do you know he gave us everything he found in Panama?"

Berman gave the first shift of unease. Hadn't it been too much of a coincidence, the demand to quit so soon after the Panama affair?

"He's loyal," insisted Berman, hoping the doubt wasn't obvious in his voice.

"I'd like to prove it."

"How?"

"Why not run a check on him? It wouldn't take more than a week."

How much of the credit would Davidson allow him if they brought in a culprit for the fiasco? Very little, decided Berman. But it would still be better than being made the only scapegoat.

"Why not?" he accepted.

"Let's put a priority on it," urged Davidson.

"All right."

"I hope I'm wrong, Peter."

It was patronizing time, recognized the younger man: Davidson always used his first name when he began being patronizing.

"Sorry?"

"You're in enough trouble as it is . . ." explained Davidson. He made a measuring gesture, bringing his hand up to the level of his eyes. " . . . in it up to here. It wouldn't look good if it were found you'd been running a double."

"I don't believe Hugo is a double."

"You agreed quickly enough to a check."

"Because it was sensible," defended Berman. "I *would* have expected Hugo to get more documents than he did."

"This true?" asked Davidson again, returning to Berman's account of Hartman's Washington visit.

"Yes," said Berman. He was trapped into supporting the lie now.

"It had better be, Peter. You're in the shit already. If I found out you were holding something back, I'd personally see to it that you regretted it for the rest of your life."

"I know you would," said Davidson.

"So?"

"It's the truth."

12

It was a very easy pursuit. Hartman let Reinhart get a long way ahead, with far too many people between them to permit any suspicion, conscious always of the man's head-bobbing progress. Only when Reinhart halted for the downtown bus did Hartman become apprehensive, closing up and slotting himself into the line with only five other passengers separating them. So close, he realized. The man of whom he had lived literally in mortal terror was so close, maybe ten yards away. Hartman became aware of his own bravery, surprised at it. He was nervous, certainly, his stomach a turmoil of uncertainty. But the initial fear had gone, the helpless paralysis he had always known in Reinhart's presence. Would it last, this unexpected courage? Or would he collapse, as he'd always collapsed before? He squeezed his eyes, trying to conjure the image of Rebecca. He'd lost Gerda; he couldn't lose Rebecca through the same sort of cowardice. Reinhart was his escape, his chance at least. He didn't know how, because his thoughts were still uneven, but instinctively he was aware there would never be another opportunity.

The bus came, crowded as always, and Hartman strained forward, concerned he might be too far behind; he was the next to last allowed on. Reinhart was strap-hanging halfway down, dully regarding the passing street outside. There was a pressed-down, defeated attitude about the man, a resigned weariness. He'd seen it before, remembered Hartman; far more pronounced than in Reinhart. It had often come to the lines of naked people as they edged forward, realizing in those last few moments that there was no longer any hope. Hartman saw there had been some attempt at face alteration, but not as extensive as Lang had undergone. Just a shaving of the aquiline, nostril-flared nose and some thickening of the cheeks, to which age had further added, so that the jowls sagged. A wide-brimmed, strangely dated fedora prevented Hartman seeing if the Nazi retained his hair. Reinhart had always worried about his appearance, and even now there was an attempt at neatness with the over used, shabby clothes. The shoes were worn and low-heeled, but polished, and an attempt had been made at a crease in the trousers, shiny with perpetual wear. The usefulness of the jacket had been extended with leather cuffs and elbow patches, and the shirt looked clean, though the collar was tufted and frayed.

Hartman was tensed for Reinhart's disembarkation. It came within a few stops, and Hartman let several other passengers intrude between them before following. Although it was not yet dark, Times Square was awake and fervently anxious for business. The sidewalks were crowded with people, like the approaches to a sports stadium just before the main event. Neon flared and jumped everywhere, so many flashing signs and strident, glittering promises that it was difficult to read any of them. To Hartman, setting up his safe-distance pursuit again, it looked like the place where rainbows came to die. It was a very short journey and, when he saw Reinhart turn, Hartman hurried forward, concerned he might miss the doorway toward which the German was heading. And then, almost swamped by those around it, he saw the sign and smiled as the final link in the chain that stretched from Panama became clear. The 'E' of Eros was threatening to short out, flickering on and off undecidedly. There seemed no formal hotel entrance, just a single doorway with a stairway immediately beyond, presumably leading up to some reception desk on the second floor. Across the front of the building was a jarring on-off neon sign in the form of a huge arrow, up and down which red and green lights appeared to travel, to indicate the ground-floor shop advertising adult books and nonstop sex films imported from Denmark. Next to it was a sex shop, the windows apparently covered against the underage eyes of passersby, but in fact decorated, on closer examination, with cunnilingus erotica.

Was this where Reinhart lived, wondered Hartman, in a short-term hotel among the pimps and the whores who were already on the streets for the early-evening trade? Until Gerda, Reinhart had always had the insatiable need for the camp brothel; it was the sort of environment in which he would have sought to bury himself. Certainly Fritz Lang had regarded it as the contact point.

A prostitute approached, smiling hopefully: short skirt, boots to her thighs, and breasts jiggling beneath the thin sweater. Hartman moved away before she could reach him. There was no cause to remain any longer. The need was to think, to plan. He would have to be very careful, anticipating every possible mistake. Little that had happened to him since his release from Belsen was as important as this.

He was impatient to get back to the quiet of his hotel room. Once there, he slumped into the chair, sweat pricking out on his forehead with the effort to get some coherence into his thoughts. At first, they wouldn't come. The only image was Reinhart, always Reinhart. Reinhart at the arrival sidings, death to the left, temporary reprieve to the right; Reinhart at the undressing sheds, hidden valuables to one side, clothes to the other; Reinhart at the medical-experimentation selection, riding crop gently against the cheek for a sentence of unanesthetized agony; Reinhart at the barracks inspection: 'Don't let him look at me; please Jehovah or God or whatever Your name is, let him look at someone else'; Reinhart choosing the women, squeezing their breasts, touching their faces, sniggering at their fear; Reinhart mocking him, forcing him actually to wear one of his own uniforms and salute, like a good Nazi, for the games he used to make him play; Reinhart at the brothel, every night at the brothel; Reinhart with Gerda. Always Reinhart with Gerda, parading her, showing her off. Reinhart's Gerda. "Do you love me, little virgin? Say you love me. Say you love your Klaus."

The shaking started suddenly, as if his nerves were being touched by electric prods. Hartman let the spasm run its course, biting at his lip against the thought that it might be the cowardice that had been so long coming. Please don't let it happen. God. Don't let me lose this opportunity. Let it be latent fear, clearing itself like the last few sores of an infection. Please let me be brave, just once.

It stopped finally, but Hartman sat tentatively, like an injured man unsure the drugged pain won't return. No more shaking came.

He was in a position of power, he realized suddenly. For the first time in his harassed, humiliated, manipulated life, he was the one with supremacy. And there could be no one whom he wanted more at his mercy. Hartman's hatred of Reinhart was far deeper than any fear. It occupied every part of him, an obsession more fixed than the worst paranoia. It didn't stop with what had happened at the camp. Reinhart was the focus for every misfortune that had occurred afterward. Because Reinhart had cowed him, he'd been trapped by the Russians; because Reinhart had warped any judgment he might have had, he had offered himself stupidly to the Americans; because of Reinhart's legacy, neither would allow him his freedom. Always Reinhart. The specter of his life.

Hartman knew he had enough to deal with Berman. More than enough. But would the American let him go, never again summoning him with one of those early-morning postcards? *Could* he even make the decision? He was the Control, certainly, but with little influence, it seemed, after Panama and Zurich. He might already have been removed from Paris or relegated to some minor, unimportant role within the embassy. And if he reached any sort of agreement, with Berman or whoever else might have been appointed in his place, would he ever be sure they'd keep their word? Hartman knew his worth, the purpose for which he was maintained by both the American and the Soviet governments: Karpov had actually admitted it, with his customary bluntness. He was the disposable man, the person with whom either side could deny any association if there were ever an arrest. What chance did he have, expecting sympathetic treatment from the CIA? None, he accepted realistically. They might promise, to learn his side of the bargain. But there was no such thing as an unbreakable undertaking in the world in which Hartman lived.

What then? The awareness of his helplessness, yet again, punctured the euphoria in which he had entered the hotel room and the pendulum swung, sweeping him to despair. He couldn't go to the police and expose Reinhart as a Nazi war criminal either. Any file would automatically go to Langley and his name would be inscribed upon it. And what explanation could he make to any CIA inquiry about his presence in Manhattan when they believed him to be in Vienna? To expose Reinhart risked exposing himself. The specter had played another trick, dancing before him in mockery.

Hartman felt the wetness against his face and realized he was crying. Ther had to be a way; there had to be some escape!

Once you're in—once someone like you is in—there's only one way out. . . .

Berman's cynicism came back, like a taunt. No worse than Karpov's.

There's only one way you can leave us. You know that.

Hartman sniggered suddenly, his breath catching with the tears so that it came out as a sob. He blew his nose hard and laughed again as the idea began to formulate. As it hardened, he began to fill with an excitement that he had never known before. It was as if he were being inflated from within, so that his skin became tight and sensitive to the touch.

They'd shown him, these cynical men who pretended to be friends and were ready to disown him at the first sign of trouble. There *was* a release—a way to freedom—not just from the Americans, but from the Russians as well.

He'd kill himself.

He'd provide the evidence and the proof and the body of Klaus Reinhart. He sniggered again. Reinhart, who had taken so much away, could give him something back. He could give him the chance of happiness he sought with Rebecca.

How difficult would it be to commit the perfect murder and switch identities? He shook his head, irritated at the question. It wasn't a consideration. He'd overcome any obstacle, any problem.

What about Rebecca? Probably the most difficult part. She couldn't be told, not until it was all over. And then he would have to risk the shock. She'd be frightened at first; bewildered, certainly. He would be asking her to abandon an identity and assume another without any warning. But she loved him. That would make it all possible. There was enough money in Switzerland, in accounts that neither Moscow nor Washington knew about, to guarantee absolute luxury wherever they chose. She'd come to accept it, after the initial confusion.

He was going to be free after so long! Free. To be normal. If the excitement didn't dissipate soon, he felt he would burst. He fought against the emotion, recognizing its danger. He didn't have freedom yet, just the opportunity. If he were going to make it more, he would have to perform as he had never performed before. So there was no place for excitement or hysteria or plans beyond the immediate moment.

Could he kill a man, even a man who deserved death as much as Klaus Reinhart? Hartman had been responsible for deaths several times; he'd known the danger to which he had been exposing Schleichner, as recently as Panama. But he'd never taken a life with his own hands: always there had been someone else to be the executioner. He closed his eyes, able so easily to see again the camp and the sheds and the naked lines and Gerda, with her pathetic preserve jar of flowers in a room in which Reinhart had kept her, liked a caged animal, to perform any trick he might demand.

Yes, thought Hartman positively. He could kill Reinhart; he believed he could kill him very easily.

Peter Berman read the report again, aware of the apprehension building up within him. There had to be some mistake: they'd misunderstood the cable or hadn't taken it seriously enough. He drafted another, increasing the priority so they'd get up off their asses and do what they were told. It was ridiculous, claiming that Hartman had disappeared—bloody ridiculous. He stood, aware he was late for the inquiry session. He wouldn't tell Davidson, not yet. There was no point. There had to be a simple explanation for Hartman's absence from Vienna.

13

The additional bank deposit was to be the first pressure, the initial pinprick of uncertainty with which Hartman intended to goad Reinhart, as the Nazi had once goaded by fear so long ago. It was very difficult for Hartman to make the move, to lift the receiver that would connect him to the voice from which he had always cringed and flinched. Rebecca, he kept repeating to himself. Rebecca. He had to do it, for Rebecca. He clutched at her name like a talisman, a symbol to force his cowardice away, snatching out for the telephone, needing both hands to hold it against his head. Hartman could hear a radio blaring as the connection was made to the Eros; whoever it was seemed to prefer to shout rather than to reduce the volume. He identified himself as an official from the Chase Manhattan, but realized the man hadn't heard. It didn't matter.

"Albert Richman?" echoed the voice, as Hartman talked on. "Not here at this time of the day."

There was a curious relief, through Hartman's nervousness, at the awareness of a delay in reaching Reinhart. "I thought he lived there."

There was a laugh at the naiveté. "He's the night clerk. On duty at five."

A setback, recognized Hartman. Certainly the bank deposit was a lost weapon for the time being. But not a disaster. "What time does he finish?"

"Twelve, of course," said the voice impatiently. "Any message?"

Hartman hesitated. "Just tell him there was a call."

"Any name?" asked the man, confirming he hadn't heard Hartman at the beginning of the conversation.

"No," said Hartman. "No name."

Just sufficient, judged Hartman, replacing the receiver. An unexplained call that would create the nagging doubt in a man permanently tensed against discovery, as Reinhart would be. Hartman was irritated with himself, knowing he was glad that Reinhart had not been there and that there had been a postponement of his coming close to the man. Coward, he accused himself. Coward. He grabbed again for the talisman. "Rebecca," he said aloud. "Rebecca."

Hartman was later getting to the General Assembly Building than he had been on the first day and he failed to get a gallery ticket. He waited until the luncheon adjournment, and went again to the North Lounge. This time Poliev did not appear. He stayed through the lunch period, but Poliev did not join the Soviet delegation, and Hartman decided there was no point in waiting until the evening to see if the man would be on the homeward bus; he knew Poliev's movements for that night.

Unsure of the opportunities there would be to contact Rebecca during what he intended to do in the next few days, Hartman ordered winter roses telegraphed to her in Vienna. This was the last time they would be apart, he realized: no more flowers from faraway places, no more fading international telephone calls.

He ate early, needing to be one of the first arrivals at Lincoln Center. The Metropolitan Opera House has a vast foyer, which made his identification of Poliev difficult, and as curtain time drew closer Hartman felt the stirrings of unease that he might have missed the Russian's arrival. The crowd was at its thickest, during the last fifteen-minute flurry, when Hartman saw the man. Relief flushed through him and with it annoyance: he should have expected Poliev to choose such a moment, a time when the crush of people gave him the maximum protection.

Hartman hurried forward almost too quickly in his anxiety. He had his various tickets separated between his fingers, ready for whatever part of the building Poliev approached it. It was the circle, up the broad sweep of stairs. Hartman feigned misunderstanding, going to the doorway through which Poliev entered, but which did not accord with his ticket number. The throng of people helped him, pushing him forward from behind. Rather than redirect him, the overworked usher allowed him to pass through to find his seat inside the auditorium. It gave Hartman the opportunity to watch Poliev until he got to his place before trying to find his own seat. The ticket clerk might have apologized for it, but for Hartman's purpose it was ideal. He was on the aisle, with a perfect view of the Russian.

On one side there was a couple already in their places when Poliev arrived, but the single seat to his left was empty. Poliev behaved quite normally, consulting his program notes and staring around with vague interest and shifting to settle himself more comfortably. A man took the unoccupied seat as the lights dimmed, one of the last arrivals. It would have been proper, had the Americans checked Poliev for Soviet surveillance, Hartman recognized professionally.

From where he sat, it was possible for Hartman to watch through opera glasses and appear to be looking at the stage, which was how he identified the contact. The singing and movement were coming to the climax of the tavern scene when there was the slightest shift from Poliev. The arm nearest his companion lifted. Both men sat with their programs in their laps, a shield against whatever passed between them.

Poliev remained seated during the intermission, but the man left almost as soon as the lights came up. Hartman hurried after him, anticipating the handover which the CIA always operated and wanting to be close when it occurred. He had thought they might choose the bar, where the crowd would hide the encounter. Instead Poliev's companion hesitated in the outside foyer, located the man he wanted near the balcony, and strolled toward him. More good fortune, recognized Hartman; it would have been difficult to photograph in the bar.

He was only about five feet away when the courier who was to leave with what Poliev had handed over indicated the program in the approaching man's hand, apparently to check some point of the performance. Poliev's contact surrendered it immediately, hand-waving a charade that the man could keep it. Under cover of his own program, Hartman managed three exposures on the miniature Minox camera: one of them both full face. With thanks for the gift, the man went to the balcony rail and made the pretense of reading. Poliev's neighbour strolled further along, reacting at once to the warning bell and moving back toward his correct entry door. Hartman did not bother to return to the auditorium, waiting instead to see what the courier would do. The man had heard the bell too, but didn't try to go back to the opera. He went down the stairs, the program secure in his pocket now, paused to select his exit, and hurried toward it. There was a car waiting, Hartman saw. Very professional and very patterned.

Everyone had returned inside by the time Hartman came away from the balcony rail. He wouldn't be allowed back in; it didn't matter. He went down the same stairway as the courier, retrieved his coat, and went out into the piazza. It had become very cold. Hartman wondered if the fountains might freeze over. He found a drugstore on Columbus Avenue and paid an extra four dollars to have the film developed by the following day.

It was ten o'clock when Hartman got back to the Pierre, and he decided there was time to speak to Rebecca after all. The connection to Vienna was quick, and from her voice Hartman knew she had received the flowers.

"You're very thoughtful," she said.

"I didn't phone last night. I'm sorry."

"I guessed you were busy. How's the job going?"

"Very well, I think."

"You should be home soon, then?"

"I hope so."

The enjoyment of hearing from him was noticeable in her voice and he warmed to it. The man had returned with the Venetian glass and she had already sold it, with a one hundred percent profit. To celebrate, she had ordered a suit she'd seen in the Kärntner Strasse put aside until his return, so that he could be the judge of whether or not she should buy it.

"I miss you," she blurted out suddenly.

"I'm missing you."

"Call tomorrow?"

"It might be difficult. I'll try."

"I love you."

"I love you."

He checked the time, anxious to be in place before Reinhart left the Eros.

"I must go," he said.

"Why?"

"I've still got some work to do."

"It's late at night in New York," she protested.

"I'm trying to finish quickly, so I can get home to you," he said.

"You're doing too much," she said, unconvinced.

"Maybe soon I'll be able to stop."

"I wish I could believe it."

The excitement came again as the taxi approached the Eros, but controlled this time. And no fear, not like the feeling he had known that morning, hunched before the telephone. He'd be able to curb it if it came again. Just as he was curbing the anticipation of trapping the man. He was going to make it work. Nothing could endanger that. He was going to get his happiness. With Rebecca.

Times Square was far more crowded than it had been the previous day. Theater crowds added to the crush, people spilled from the pavement into the street, and there was a cacophony of car horns as drivers tried to clear a path. Darker than when he had first been there, the neon popped and glittered more obviously now, clown-facing some of the people walking by and making him blink. Whores, male and female, simpered and smiled from almost every doorway, and there was a line at the bookshop alongside the Eros. The 'E' had finally gone out completely. Hartman let himself be carried along, seeking a spot to stand and watch the hotel entrance from which he could avoid being accosted. Halfway along the side street there was a shuttered, darkened building in the doorway of which a drunk was slumped, a wavering line of urine marked out across the pavement like an umbilical cord. Hartman pulled inside, face twisted at the smell. Once the bundle at his feet snuffled and moved, and Hartman jerked back, afraid the man was coming awake and might claw upward, seeking his support. Soon after, a girl approached offering herself, accepting his refusal with a philosophical shrug. Hartman guessed her to be about sixteen, despite the makeup. From the direction of Seventh Avenue patrolled a carefully uniformed policeman. The trousers were pressed, the shoes the plastic type which always shone, and his cap was purposefully arranged upon his head. He took no notice of everything around him and everything took no notice of him. Deep within Hartman moved the apprehension at the sight of a uniform: in the distance, there was the urgent sound of a siren. Hartman was unsure whether it was police or ambulance.

Midnight passed and Reinhart did not appear. Hartman shifted, concerned. Had Reinhart panicked at the unexplained call? Run, because a man who had called himself Fritz Lang had personally desposited another $100 into his account? He should have stayed the previous night; forced himself to think more clearly and realize the risk.

Reinhart appeared at the doorway and Hartman's anxiety leaked away. The Nazi paused, as if unaware which way to go. Immediately opposite the Eros was a bar; distantly there was the sound of a jukebox. Reinhart looked toward it, then emerged onto the pavement and began moving toward Eighth Avenue. Another whore was approaching him as Hartman moved out to follow.

Reinhart moved clumsily from shadow to shadow, hand stressed against his thigh in the peculiar rolling walk that had triggered Hartman's recognition. Twenty yards behind, Hartman concentrated into the pursuit every scrap of expertise he had accumulated in the previous thirty-three years, frequently edging into the same concealment as Reinhart had used minutes earlier. Twice, before they reached Eighth Avenue, the German turned, gazing intently at the street behind. Each time Hartman anticipated the check before it was completed, pulling himself once into a doorway and the second time near some stacked refuse. In the darkness he smiled, aware of the other man's perpetual fear. He would want to utilize that fear soon. Hartman was sure he would know how to do it; he regarded himself as an expert in the emotion.

Eighth Avenue was better lit than 42nd Street, and Hartman let the distance between them increase. On 41st Street, Reinhart turned west, struggling toward the Hudson River docks. Hartman settled comfortably behind, smiling again as he recalled his earlier reflections about the pattern mentality of the CIA and the KGB. Obviously unconsciously, Reinhart had developed a regular check. Every fifty yards, judged Hartman. When he came from the concealment into which he had pulled himself, ahead of the German's turn, he began to count. Almost right, he thought, when the man swivelled again. It had been forty-eight paces.

It was hard to be definite from the distance he was

having to keep and the impression might have been distorted by the limp, but Hartman began recognizing the similarity in build between himself and the German for which Reinhart had once mocked him in those uniform parades. Hartman estimated that he was maybe a few pounds heavier than the other man, but it would be insufficient to cause any curiosity. And the broken leg wouldn't matter, if everything worked as he hoped it would; as it *had* to.

They walked for a long time, practically to the West Side Highway, coming to an area where office and apartment buildings merged with the beginning of the larger dock buildings. It seemed colder, with a stronger wind off the river. Hartman closed the gap between them, guessing Reinhart wasn't going to continue much further, and making the mistake of his own criticism about reliance upon patterns. He had expected Reinhart's backward look at the established interval, so that when the man turned after twenty paces, having reached where he lived, it almost caught the Austrian. He saved himself only because he was alert, aware seconds before it came of the man's attitude of familiarity as he reached home. All he could do was to hold himself unmoving in the black protection of a wall. He stood stiff against any challenge or indication from the other man that he had been seen, not allowing himself even to breathe. Reinhart stood for several moments staring intently up the street, then disappeared.

Knowing it could be a trap, with Reinhart waiting in the concealment of an alley, but with no alternative, Hartman hurried forward, eyes locked to the spot where the German had last stood. It was a peculiar building, something the high-rise planners appeared to have changed their minds about. It was small, only three stories high, dwarfed by skyscrapers on either side. At street level it was a flower shop. As Hartman stood in the shadows of the taller buildings, a light went on in a top room. Top right, he noted.

Briefly a figure appeared at the window, making sure for the last time.

He'd succeeded, thought Hartman, not attempting now any control over the satisfaction he felt. He knew where Reinhart lived and where Reinhart worked and where he banked and by what name he was called. It was going very well; almost too well.

Back at the Pierre, he remained for a long time in the bathroom after washing himself, examining his face in the mirror. The hair might be the biggest risk, although in the camp Reinhart had been as fair as he was. It depended whether it had retained its color. They'd both been blue-eyed, recalled Hartman, remembering the pitiless stare. And the features he was not concerned about. Still he stayed at the mirror, staring at his reflection. He *looked* ill, Hartman decided, the first thought how convenient that was for the people he would be trying to convince rather than any concern over his health.

There were lines etched around his eyes and the skin below was pouched with tiredness. The absence of too much gray hair that he had earlier noted meant that he looked younger than he was, but his face was sallow and too full, despite the doctor's insistence upon the importance of diet. When he began the new life with Rebecca, he would be stricter with himself: the proper food at the proper times. And exercise. He was going to allow nothing, nothing at all, to interfere with that happiness. He looked toward the telephone, guessing the time change with Vienna; Rebecca would probably still be awake. He wanted to tell her, like a child boasting of a present ahead of its birthday. Not that way, he rejected. There was too much to explain, too much forgiveness to seek. When he told Rebecca, it would have to be to her face, where he could reach out to touch her and try to make her understand. She would, he was confident. They were going to be happy together.

14

Hartman forced himself to confront fully what he intended to do, knowing he had to purge himself of the terror that had gripped him at the thought of making telephone contact with Reinhart. So far he had maintained a distance from the Nazi; pursued the man while he was unaware, from which there could have been no danger. But there would come the moment when he had to make himself the bait, to enter the hotel in which Reinhart would be waiting, knowing he had been found. And knowing, too, the identity of his pursuer. That would be important. In the end, Reinhart would have to think he could win. Could he do that? Could he maintain the pretense a few feet from someone who had once had such power over him? He shuddered, chilled by the thought. He wouldn't know, not until the moment came. He'd never been brave, Hartman accepted. Never. He didn't know the way to be, the conviction or the strength that had to come to make it possible. He was like a blind man, unaware of the ability to read.

But he was going to do it. He was going to do it for Rebecca; and Gerda, too. She would have wanted him to have this second chance, just as she had wanted him to live. He would be avenging her for the sacrifices she had made.

He planned his day carefully, recognizing it as the beginning of the subterfuge by which he wanted several people to be deceived. From the Soviet Embassy in Washington he demanded a further list of Poliev's movements, by which Moscow would infer he was continuing the investigation, and then called his son's home.

Ruth was surprised, hesitant and stumbling in her replies. The main purpose of his visit would be to see the grave, Hartman explained, but if David was available in the afternoon, he would appreciate a moment of his time. Ruth said she thought it unlikely that he would be back from the clinic, and her reluctance increased when Hartman suggested calling upon him there, rather than at the house. They agreed on two o'clock, which Hartman estimated gave him enough time for any delay.

The visit arranged, he waited until the morning activity in the corridor outside his room subsided, then moved out cautiously. He found what he wanted, a maid's closet around a corner not quite hidden from his own room, but about fifteen feet from it. Farther than he had hoped. Realistically he accepted he was lucky to find such a place at all.

He rented a car, hurrying the vehicle through the midmorning traffic congestion, impatient for Connecticut. As he drove, he let his mind run over what he had done, seeking omissions or flaws. All right, as far as it went, he decided. The greatest uncertainty was whether Reinhart would react as he wanted him to, and whether the terror would stay away to let him do it.

There were few men he knew better; in the camp, he had been able to gauge his mood by a look, understand any demand from the merest gesture. But that had been more than three decades ago. Reinhart would inevitably have changed and be more difficult to anticipate. There was only one thing of which he could be sure: Reinhart would have lived thirty-five years in fear.

He reached the turnpike and for once risked taking the car beyond the speed limit. David would be the first test, the rehearsal for everything that was to follow.

Hartman had meant the promise he had made at Gerda's funeral, to return for occasional visits to the grave. But if he were to succeed with a new life, it was another promise he couldn't keep. He entered the cemetery slowly, knowing it would be the last visit and wanting to commit everything to memory. He smiled sadly, seeing from a distance the new whiteness of the headstone. The overhanging tree *was* beech; it would be beautiful in a few months time. To the right, a group of mourners came to the end of the formalities, paused by the still-open grave, and then began to disperse along the path. Two women were crying as they passed him. Hartman stopped, standing to one side to allow the people by.

He began squinting, trying to read the inscription when he was some way off, then stood at the bottom of the grave, his lips moving slightly as he recited the words. He supposed he should feel anger, but the only thing that came was sadness, a sudden wash of grief that brought wetness to his eyes, as when he had last stood there.

Would it never end, the taking away of things from him? He stopped the self-pity almost as soon as it had begun. It was going to stop, because he was going to make it stop. For once he was going to be brave and everything was going to work out as he intended. The altered inscription made one thing easier; if David could cheat him with that, it removed any guilt he might have felt about deceiving David as he intended.

"I know you'll understand, darling," he said softly. "You always understood."

He'd forgotten flowers. He bent, rearranging those that remained from the funeral, picking out some that had died. He stayed bent, pulling away a few leaves and broken twigs that had been blown over the newly pebbled surround. He fought against the tears, feeling the loss more now than he had at the funeral.

"Goodbye, Gerda," he said, rising. "Goodbye, my darling."

Men were working, keeping David's grounds to their landscaped perfection. One was collecting leaves, driving a small tractor with a spined scoop in front, and another was raking the tennis courts. As Hartman got near the house, he saw David's car parked outside; obviously his son preferred to keep him away from the clinic.

The door opened before Hartman had time to ring the bell. His son made no attempt to disguise the anger.

"I had a full day at the clinic," he said in immediate protest. "It's damned inconvenient."

"It won't take long . . . I told Ruth I'd go there."

"It's better here," said David quickly. He stood aside for his father to enter the house.

"What is it?" he asked when the older man was inside.

"I was coming to the grave . . . I thought you might help . . ." Hartman hoped the indecision was properly pitched, and that David was aware of it.

"Help?" At last there was curiosity mixed with the hostility.

"I don't feel well," complained Hartman.

David allowed another sigh of irritation. "You'd better come into the study," he said. "Ruth is out."

Hartman didn't believe him, but he had no immediate wish to see her. He followed his son into a fully equipped medical room. Through the window he saw that the covering had been taken from the swimming pool. A man was bent over the filtering system.

"I thought you were going back to Vienna?" challenged David.

"I went . . . then I decided to come back again. . . ." Hartman gave a movement of helplessness, as if it were difficult to convey the reason. "I wanted to see the grave again. . . ."

"I'm a psychiatrist, not a medical doctor," remarked his son.

"It's not physical pain that I'm suffering."

"What then?"

"I've been very depressed since your mother's death."

"I'm hardly surprised."

"Why?" asked Hartman, in apparent innocence. He

wanted his son to remember the interview, and he didn't think the boy could cause him any further pain.

"I would have thought guilt might have entered into it."

"I suppose you're right," agreed Hartman. He sat hunched in the chair, as if he were trying to make himself smaller. "It seems her death has brought it all back. . . . I was a coward, such a coward."

"Yes," said David, brutally. "You were."

"I wish it could have been me who died, rather than her," said Hartman.

David was regarding him intently now: professionally.

"What do you mean?" he asked.

Again Hartman gave the helpless shrug. "With her gone, there doesn't seem much point in my working anymore . . . in doing anything anymore. . . ."

"You sleeping?"

"Hardly at all."

"Emotion?"

"What?"

"Crying, things like that."

Hartman appeared embarrassed. "I seem to cry all the time."

"No physical pain?"

"None."

"Hasn't the crying lessened, as the time since the funeral passed?"

"It's got worse," said Hartman.

"It's an understandable depression, remembering the circumstances," insisted David.

"I want to be cremated," said Hartman sharply.

"What?" frowned his son.

"If anything were to happen to me, ever, you'd be consulted as the next of kin. I don't want to be buried with your mother . . . it doesn't seem right . . . I'm not worthy . . . not worthy at all. I want to be cremated."

Of the entire meeting, it was vital that David remembered this. The thought of Reinhart being interred in the same grave as Gerda was too obscene to contemplate.

"No," agreed David immediately. "It doesn't seem right.

"You'll remember, then?"

David didn't reply, instead sitting at his desk with his head slightly tilted, an attitude of concentration.

"It's not being morbid," said Hartman. "These things need to be discussed."

"Yes."

"Can you help me—some pills or something?"

"Tranquilizers might make it easier for you to sleep."

"Anything," pleaded Hartman. "If I don't get some sleep soon, I'll go mad."

"How soon are you going back to Vienna?"

"I don't know," said Hartman uncertainly. "Quite soon, I expect."

"Go to your own doctor there. I'll prescribe some Valium, but take the bottle with you, so he'll know what drugs you've been on."

"I'm very grateful."

David looked up from the prescription pad. "It's my professional pledge to help anyone," he said.

"Thank you all the same. I went to the grave before I came here."

David remained looking at him, waiting.

"It's a nice headstone," said Hartman.

"Yes."

"You seem to have forgotten what I asked you to have inscribed upon it," said the older man.

"I didn't forget."

"Why, David?"

"It wasn't right," said his son, picking up their previous conversation. "Any more than it seems right for you to be buried in the same resting place."

He wouldn't forget, Hartman realized. The boy's

attitude would ensure that. Hartman remembered the last few moments in the cemetery and the tears came easily. He brought a handkerchief to his face.

"You paid for it yourself?"

"You knew I would."

"I'm not proud of myself," said Hartman, his voice muffled behind the cloth.

"It would be very hard for you to be," said David, unrelenting.

"Can't you forgive?"

"No," said the younger man. "There's something I can never forgive."

He completed the prescription and handed it across the desk. Hartman leaned forward anxiously to take it.

'You might as well have this,' said David, taking something from his desk drawer.

It was the blank check. Hartman's first impression was to tear it up. Instead, he folded it and put it into his pocket.

"I'm sorry I broke into your afternoon appointments," apologized Hartman.

Reminded, David looked impatiently at his desk cloak. "If I hurry I can pick up most of them."

"I won't detain you, then."

David rose, ending the meeting. "Those pills will only help you rest," he said, indicating the prescription. "With the reasons I know you have for the depression, I'd recommend your getting psychiatric help when you get home."

"You think there might be some disturbance?"

"I've never known a case history where it was more likely."

Hartman paused, wondering if he had achieved enough. "You wouldn't consider treating me?" he asked. "You know so much already, after all."

"No," said David quickly, shaking his head. "I wouldn't treat you."

His son had enjoyed the rejection, Hartman knew. It was a pity he would never be able to let the boy know the function for which he was being manipulated.

"I'm very busy," encouraged David.

Hartman followed his son into the hallway. From along the corridor, in what Hartman presumed was the direction of the kitchen, came the sound of activity. Probably Ruth, he thought. He didn't think they employed any internal household staff.

"Thank you," he said at the doorway.

"You could have got the same from any physician in New York. You didn't have to come all the way up here."

"But I couldn't have seen Gerda's grave."

"No," agreed David. "You couldn't have done that."

David followed his father into the driveway, entering his own car. For the first half-mile, the two vehicles were in convoy. When David turned off, there was no signal or indication of farewell. Hartman laughed aloud. He felt pity for his son and triumph in what he had managed. It had gone far better than he had expected.

Hartman tried to reach Manhattan before the evening rush hour and failed. The traffic began on the Bronx River Parkway, and by the time he got onto Bruckner Boulevard the jam stretched for more than half a mile. He sat irritably at the wheel with many things to do. It was quite dark by the time he got to Franklin Delano Roosevelt Drive, and as quickly as he could he turned off onto a cross street, seeking an easier flow of traffic. On Columbus Avenue, he collected the pictures of Poliev's contact at the opera and waited for the prescription for Valium to be filled. He abandoned the rented car opposite a fire hydrant, knowing that the towing charge would be added automatically to the bill and provide another small indication of odd behavior from a man suffering mental pressure.

By eight, he was back near the Hudson River. It was colder than it had been the previous night, thought Hartman. Or was it apprehension? He wondered what he would find inside Reinhart's room.

15

Lights were still on in the florist's shop and there was far more activity in the street, despite half of it being occupied by dock warehousing. A man apparently checking the residents' list, Hartman eased the steel picklock into the outer door, feeling the perspiration break out at the slowness with which the tumblers clicked into place. There were five residents in the dwarfed building, and Albert Richman occupied apartment five.

The door opened and Hartman was inside in seconds. He stopped just beyond the entrance, judging the occupants and the area too poor to have any burglar arrangement which responded to any unauthorized key, but being careful as always. There were sounds from above—a baby crying distantly and some music—but otherwise it remained quiet.

The pause had given him time to adjust to the darkness. A stairway rose immediately before him, alongside the ground-floor shop. He located the light switch but ignored it, ascending hurriedly. There was a door at the top, blocking off the tiny first landing. Again Hartman hesitated behind it, listening for anything on the other side. The music was clearer; Glenn Miller, he thought. He wondered if Karpov would consider it for his collection. Probably it didn't qualify as jazz.

He pushed through, seeking access to the next floor. There was no door this time, just an opening and some stairs beyond. He crossed the landing, gaining the protection of the farther stairwell.

At the top he turned right, knowing the location of Reinhart's room from the previous night's observation. This was the moment when the risk of discovery was greatest from the two other doors which opened out onto the building. From behind one there was complete silence; from the other, the subdued mumble of conversation. Two people, he guessed.

He crossed the gap as lightly as possible, soft-footed against any creaking boards. Outside Reinhart's room he waited, so that he could openly knock if one of the other doors were opened in sudden inquiry. The mumbled talk continued uninterrupted.

Reinhart had two locks. Both were more complicated than that leading from the street. Hartman started on the mortice first, assessing it easier. He worked listening for two sounds, that of the lock gradually giving and then for any movement from the surrounding rooms. It was a new lock and stiff, even though it was well oiled. The grease crept out along the picklock, making it slippery in his hands. He felt it give at last. Hartman stayed tight against the door, releasing his breath. It was not just the oil making the probe difficult to hold; he was sweating heavily now.

He was about to start on the second lock when there was a sudden blare of sound. He turned, hand raised to knock upon Reinhart's door as an apparently genuine visitor. It was from the landing below; definitely Glenn Miller. The music lessened as the door was closed again. There was the echo of footsteps, but they receded too, going down the first stairs into the street. Hartman had to dry his hands before he could begin again. Once he thought he had arranged all the securing bars into place, but the door remained unyielding to his touch and he realized that he had worked too hurriedly, missing one. Forcing himself to slow down, he started again, located the tumbler, and slipped it back.

It was his experience that saved him, years of undetected entering and leaving rooms occupied by people who did not want to be intruded upon. He didn't thrust through the door, as he had from the street. Instead he opened it slightly, allowing little more than a two-inch gap sufficient for his hand to get through. Because it was the most difficult and therefore the most likely placing for any precaution, he stretched upward to the top of the door, but the gap was free of any obstruction. Reinhart's leg, he remembered; it would be hard for the man to hold himself at any height.

He brushed the wire halfway down the door. He stopped, testing the tension to see how much wider he could make the opening. It was very tight. Holding the door with his left hand, he groped his right farther into the room, until the edge was cutting into his wrist.

It was a basic booby trap, the trip wire secured to the rear of the door and then run through a slide ring screwed into the adjacent wall. To open the door would force the wire through the ring, tightening it to trigger whatever lay beyond. Hartman couldn't unfasten the wire at the point where it was attached to the door, so he changed hands, able to feel the slide ring better with his left. It was hinged, like a clasp on a necklace. He depressed the opening, let the wire fall through, and opened the door wide enough to enter.

Again he stopped with his back to the closed door, trying to establish his surroundings. The room took vague shape around him in the opaque light from the uncurtained window; with some unknown trap within feet of him, he would have to risk the light. The illumination was low, but he still had to blink against it in the first few seconds of brightness; the windows would have to remain uncovered until he isolated the device. He saw it instantly, relaxing at its crudity. There were no second trips, so he walked around it, covering the windows, and then back to the table. The wire would have pulled away a snap trigger, detonating a cluster of explosives held together by electrical tape. Leaning closer, he saw the glint of metal and then reached out gently, feeling the points with his finger. Also taped against the explosive were darts, which would have been driven out at rifle-barrel force by the explosion. Did Reinhart always leave his room so protected? Or had it been his reaction to learning that there had been a mysterious call to the Eros?

He left the booby trap, turning to the rest of the room. The bed, unmade, was against one corner, a bookshelf at the head. At the foot there was a small portable television set. The table on which the bomb lay was obviously where Reinhart ate. A greasy plate still lay there, two empty beer cans beside it. There was a curtained alcove, with just a suit, raincoat, and a spare pair of shoes in it. Next to it, another curtain shielded a miniscule shower area. A washbasin was crowded in there as well. On the far side of the room, and with no drapes for separation, was a break into the wall beyond which was a hotplate and a small refrigerator. About everything there was a sense of apathetic decay. Hartman was reminded of the listless attitude in which the man had held himself on the bus.

Hartman began with the alcove. At the awareness of touching something that Reinhart wore, he momentarily held back, then grabbed out against the revulsion. There was a half-empty cigarette packet and some lottery tickets in the breast pocket of the suit, and three pens lined up in an inside pocket. The raincoat contained nothing. He did not leave the alcove, but felt around seeking any hidden compartments. The hatchway was unconcealed; he'd just missed it during his first examination. He opened it, hauling out the cardboard suitcase. Just a few shirts, nearly all frayed at collar and cuffs, and a pair of summer slacks. He felt inside the tiny cupboard, tapping for an echo which would have shown up the hollow space. There was nothing. He searched the shower and kitchen areas as thoroughly, though their size and openness made any concealment unlikely. Finally he concentrated on the main room. He worked methodically, upturning chairs to examine the undersides, where things might be taped and hidden, squeezing cushions for any hard objects, stooping to see beneath the table. He went through the books page by page, then shook them from the spine to dislodge any inserted paper, and not only examined the television but unscrewed its back and base to see inside.

He stared for several minutes at the bed, memorizing the dishevelment, then stripped it blanket by blanket and sheet by sheet, feeling at the pillows and then heaving the mattress off, examining it from every angle and then pushing against it, to detect anything inside.

It was a sprung, divan base. He felt against it, from the top; then, straining at the effort, hauled it to its side, so he could see the underneath.

The opening had been made in the bottom right-hand corner, a zipper stitched neatly into the fabric so that it could be closed and would have been quite undetectable to anyone stooping to look underneath. Hartman approached it carefully, unsure of another device to protect such a place of obvious concealment. Nothing appeared to be attached to the zipper clasp. Gently, a tooth at a time, he prised open the covering. The base interior had been hollowed out and a wooden box inserted to create a lining. So sure had Reinhart been of his hiding place—and perhaps his booby trap—that he had not bothered with a lock. The lid was secured by two push bolts. Still Hartman was careful, studying them before sliding them back. The lid was chained, so that it dropped to form a tiny table. Hartman did not reach in, but examined first the placing of the contents. Needing more space than that available from the lid, he carried everything to the table, put it down, and then remained staring at it. A shrine, he thought: a lovingly preserved place of worship for a creed and a time of which Reinhart was still a disciple.

Hesitantly, knowing the revulsion that he'd earlier experienced at the thought of touching the man's clothing,

Hartman felt out, prodding through the relics, memorabilia that Reinhart must have collected of the time even before he had been old enough to join the party.

The Luger was the largest and most obvious, one clip already in the grip, a spare alongside. Preserved in a plastic envelope but yellowed and tattered, the original advertisement in the anti-Semitic *Münchener Beobachter* for Hitler's 1919 formation meeting in the Munich Hofbräuhaus of the German Workers' National Socialist Party. Reinhart's own, later, party card, with a picture—maybe just seventeen, unformed face and bright, staring eyes—the Gothic script of the Nationalsozialistische Deutsche Arbeiterpartei harsh and frightening. A faded, page-bent copy of *Mein Kampf*. An SS badge, presumably Reinhart's. His identification card: the man older now, the features formed, a new fervency about the expression."

A wallet remained, and when Hartman opened it the shock shuddered through him. It wasn't a wallet, not for money anyway. The pictures were neatly assembled: chronologically, he supposed.

Reinhart, as he had been in the party card picture, stiffly at attention in his Brown Shirt uniform; Reinhart with an elderly couple, probably his parents, smiling proudly at the photographer.

Hartman turned the pages, wincing at the progression. Reinhart in the third row of a rally, perhaps his induction ceremony into the SS, with the figure of Hitler quite visible on the rostrum; Hilter around the planning table at the Reich Chancellery; Hitler and Speer at the Berghof; Hitler and Eva Braun relaxing in a chair, again at the Berghof, the location carefully lettered in stiff, formalized script below the print; Hitler and SS Adjutant Otto Hunsche.

Hartman moved another page, and despair moaned from him at the recognition. The sheds and the control towers and the wire and the faces, cheeks hollowed, eyes protruding and unnaturally large from emaciation. The tears came unchecked, his vision blurred. His block, third on the left; the place where the trustees lived, partitioned for their own protection from those against whom they had turned. From the window, he had been able to see the brothel. He picked up the wallet, holding it closer, identifying the block again. Third window from the top. Gerda's room. The special place; Reinhart's place.

"My darling," he moaned. "Oh, my poor darling."

Tears run into his mouth, salty. He sniffled against them. He found his handkerchief, pressing it to his face, biting at the cloth to stop any sound, his shoulders jerking with his grief.

It came as an odd unconsciousness, the closing of his mind to reality or awareness, but without any physical weakness, so that he didn't collapse. He started awake, recognizing his surroundings and frightened of the time he had remained gazing down without sight at the photographs of Belsen. Distantly the noises from the building came to him; from a faraway street, a frequent police siren sounded. Or maybe it was a fire truck. He couldn't tell. There always seemed to be such sounds on the streets of Manhattan. He looked at his watch. He must have stood there for almost twenty minutes. He moved at last, feeling an ache where he had held himself so rigidly.

He carried the memorabilia back to the divan, setting it out upon the lowered lid, then repacking it exactly as it had been arranged when he first opened it. He ensured the bolt claps were laid in the direction in which he had found them and guaranteed the zipper was completely fastened. He bgan to leave evidence of his entry with the bed, remaking it so the covering was slightly different from how it had been before he stripped it.

He had replaced each book in the shelf in the position from which he had removed it. Now he changed two. He loosened the screws from the back of the television set so there was a miniscule but obvious gap. It worked from an indoor aerial and he moved one of the arms, widening the distance between them. He repacked the suitcase by putting the trousers above the shirts, unlike their position when he searched it. He put the cigarette packet into a different pocket of the suit and left the curtain separating it from the room with a six-inch space from the wall.

He made no other changes, but when he opened the curtains onto the street he left one covering more of the window than had been visible when he entered. The room in darkness again, he listened against the doorway for any sound outside. The mumbled conversation seemed to have stopped. He barely opened the door, confirming the impression. Quickly, he held it wide, using the weak illumination from the landing light. With the steel probe with which he had entered, he scored scratches on both locks. He stooped for the trip wire and carefully reassembled the booby trap, lightly fingering the cord to ensure the tension was correct. Reinhart had to suspect nothing until he got inside.

At the Pierre, Hartman took his diabetic pills, then read the instructions on the Valium that David had prescribed. He took out the four recommended tablets and flushed them down the toilet, then briefly studied the snatched photographs of the men who had dealt with Poliev at the Metropolitan Opera House.

Tomorrow he had to attempt some sort of identification.

16

It was his natural, instinctive thoroughness which made Hartman want to name the man who had sat next to Poliev for the performance of *La Bohème*, but, anxious to increase the pressure on Reinhart, he decided to impose a time limit on the inquiry. He had enough, if the information were not immediately available.

He got to the UN as it opened, making his way familiarly to the North Lounge and entering the reading room in which he had first come to suspect the Russian diplomat. The Nigerian oil-production pamphlet was where he had last seen it. He chose the official publication section, frowning at the volume of material. Every committee or member country or delegate seemed to believe the world wanted their printed views. He need only concentrate upon America, Hartman knew. He settled down to the repetitive, painstaking check, examining every picture. He found it, after an hour, and sat back, shaking his head in amazement. Patterns created to the point of madness, he thought. He continued for a further hour and found three more publications containing photographs of the man next to whom Poliev had sat. In one caption, he was named as Richard Brewer and described as a special assistant on the staff of the United States delegation.

He had enough to incrimate the Soviet diplomat, Hartman decided. What would happen to Poliev? There was an obvious answer. It couldn't be helped. The man had been handled carelessly, so the CIA deserved to lose an informant. And Poliev deserved to lose his freedom. More likely it would be his life, realized the Austrian. The man's own fault, just the same.

Hartman noted the dates and file numbers of the UN publications, and purchased them all from the stand outside the reading room. He returned at once to the reading room; to the file he was creating, he added the pictures taken at the opera house and the written report he had brought with him from the Pierre. He sealed the package and addressed it to the Soviet Embassy within the UN buildings, wondering fleetingly if Poliev would come into contact with the material that was going to result in his own arrest.

Hartman descended to the customarily thronged main hall, judging the moment when a tourist group entered. He mixed with it and deposited the package for UN delegation collection. Hartman left the building at once, seeking a street telephone booth. He found one on First Avenue and got an untroubled connection to the Soviet Embassy in the capital. Again enjoying the unaccustomed authority, he gave instructions that were curt and demanding: a courier from the UN delegation should collect immediately what was waiting on the ground floor and take it directly to Washington on the shuttle; he wanted Moscow informed at once.

It was just after noon when he got to the Eros. Already there was some hopeful activity from a few prostitutes in the street and the neon flared, defiant of the daylight destroying the effect. At the doorway, Hartman paused, waiting for the feeling. There was distaste that he always felt at squalor, but no worse than in Panama. And uncertainty. But no fear. If there is a God who has given me this second chance, then make me strong enough to succeed, prayed Hartman.

It was a short flight of steps, the walls on either side greasy with the continued passage of people. At the top, a landing widened out into a small lobby, with a small counter to the left. The clerk was secure behind the sort of wire-reinforced glass that had protected the driver of the taxi which had brought Hartman from Kennedy Airport. The only access to the clerk was through a small, rounded opening, the sort of hatchway used by theater cashiers. A cage suited the clerk. He was a sharp-featured, shrunken man, with quick, darting movements, like a small animal. There was some attempt at propriety in that he wore a suit, collar, and tie, but his clothes were as stained and greasy as the stair walls, and as he shuffled forward Hartman saw he was wearing tennis shoes.

"Yeah?"

"I'd like a room."

The man looked beyond him expectantly, then frowned back.

"For yourself?" The question was hostile, and Hartman realized the man was examining his clothes, fearing officialdom.

"Yes."

"We gotta current license for the fire regulations."

"I'm sure you have," said Hartman.

"Single room?" asked the man disbelievingly.

"Yes."

"How long for?"

"Maybe two nights."

"That your only luggage?" the man asked, nodding to the briefcase that Hartman had prepared before leaving the Pierre.

The Austrian nodded.

"Gotta pay in advance. Cash."

There was about everything an instutional smell, a combination of urine, kerosene, and stale air air trapped behind never-opened windows. Far worse than in Cristobal.

"All right."

"Twenty-five dollars." In the man's voice was the greedy hope of the mailman in Panama: would he still be waiting every night in the bar by the market? Hartman counted out the money.

"Nice room," assured the clerk, friendly now. "Front top. There's a bath."

Hartman picked up his bag and began mounting the second flight of stairs. The only light was from a single, unshaded bulb on the top landing and once he stumbled in the semidarkness. The smell of urine and bodies was stronger, and abruptly his mind was thrown back to the wooden barracks filled with row upon row of racks in which skeletal people lay, the distance between the bed above so narrow it was impossible to turn over. He shuddered, halted by the memory. He felt the acid of vomit at the back of his throat and swallowed anxiously. He could not move until the sensation had receded; it was several minutes before he started climbing again.

At the top of the stairs, the corridor led away to the left. From behind one door came the disjointed words of a controlled argument, like a dispute in a bazaar. From another came the groans of what he presumed to be ecstasy: it didn't sound very genuine. He checked the door number against the key, took breath like a man about to plunge into a cold sea, and then opened the door. The initial impression was one of impermanence. The curtains were almost gauzelike, making shadows of the buildings beyond. The green and red of the neon sign pursued themselves in a technicolor race against the wall near the clothes closet, the edges of which were so marked by cigarette burns that it practically appeared a pattern. There was a small table, for some indefinable use, and an easy chair, greased like everything else and squashily wet to the touch when he pressed down against the seat. The bedclothes were as flimsy as the curtains. What purported to be blankets were made from cotton, and when Hartman pulled them back he saw the sheets were dirty and stained from previous passing occupants. Beneath one pillow was a half-smoked cigarette, obviously hoarded and forgotten in a moment of passion. As he pulled the other aside, a cockroach lingered stubbornly, then slowly made for the edge of the bed as if challenging an attack.

The bath of which the clerk had been so proud was separated from the main room by another diaphanous piece of cloth. The bath was rimed with dirt, and there were rust marks where the taps dripped continuously. The top left-hand corner of the mirror over the basin was broken away and the rest was discolored, giving a reflection like staring into a wind-stirred pond. There was no drinking glass in the toothbrush container, and the basin was as stained as the bath. From the debris around the plug, it seemed someone had recently cut his hair, using the basin as a receptacle. Hartman leaned sideways, flushing the lavatory without lifting the seat. The smell remained as foul as ever.

Hartman opened his briefcase, checking the contents, anxious to be away from the room as soon as possible. The Israeli passport in his real name was uppermost, the first thing at hand. He winced down at the photograph of Gerda. He wanted Reinhart to find it, but he didn't want it defouled by contact with the man.

"Sorry, my darling," he said. "So sorry."

It had always been necessary to apologize.

He gazed around, unsure where to place it, deciding finally on the table. He arranged it in careful alignment with the edge.

The clerk was at the hatch when he got down to the lobby.

"Looking for a little action?" he inquired confidently. Two women lounged in the entrance, looking up.

"No."

"Lot going on around here."

"You're not here at night, are you?"

"Day man," said the clerk, confirming his seniority. "Albert does the evening."

"I see," said Hartman. He hoped a single booking was unusual enough to get the conversation repeated.

"Gonna be late?"

"No," said Hartman. "Back quite soon."

Hartman had delayed obtaining any sort of weapon until the very last moment, still unwilling positively to consider physical violence until it was absolutely necessary. And now it was, if he were to go through with the attempt to lure Reinhart into a situation where he could commit the perfect murder. He found the garage-supply store along 42nd Street, the materials laid out for self-selection. He hefted several tire levers, wanting weight with compactness, and finally chose one that gave him a six-inch projection beyond the handle. He entered the Pierre feeling self-conscious, aware of the weight pulling at his jacket.

In his room he concealed it in the largest of his suitcases, which he locked against any discovery by a chambermaid. At the bureau he set out paper, envelopes, and pen like a student about to embark upon an examination. And like a student, he didn't know how to begin.

To whom it may concern? But it would concern no one, apart from Karpov and Berman, and they would learn it another way. He hoped. Certainly not David and Ruth. Rebecca? Yes, of course Rebecca. But no one here knew of their relationship; that's why it would work.

It would have to be David. How irritated the boy would be, having so soon after the first occasion to spend a day, maybe two, going through the tiresome routine associated with death. Definitely David, determined Hartman. He would be impatient at identification, anxious to get away.

"Dear David," he wrote. "You have found it difficult, with every reason, to forgive me these last few years. So although I ask for it, I know I cannot expect your forgiveness for what I do now. For too long you have found me despicable."

Hartman paused, reading through the opening sentences with a pen against his teeth.

"I know it is impossible," he took up, "to conceive the

feeling I had for your mother. I loved her more dearly than I will ever love anyone. And she loved me. I know that is also difficult for you to believe; more difficult than to forgive, perhaps. But it is true.''

Hartman stopped again, putting his hand across his eyes. At least there would be some truth in the letter.

He resumed: ''It is the fear of every man, confronted with danger or the threat of pain, that he will not be a man, but a coward. I faced that moment. And became the coward. For more than thirty years I have lived with that knowledge, the worst cancer a man can have. Your mother, who loved me, was brave for both of us. She saved my life and gave her own, not physically, not for a long time, but in a way far worse than death.''

Hartman sat back, reading the whole letter through. He would have to guard against it becoming an apologia.

He took up the pen again. ''You are a psychiatrist, supposed to know the ways of men's minds. Perhaps, if you can for a moment forget the dislike with which you have held me for so long, you will be able to understand the guilt I have felt for the life that was destroyed because of me. While she was alive, there was point in my being alive. Although more in your care than mine and more in your protection than mine, I still felt responsible: having failed her once, I was not going to fail her again. But now she is dead. There is no longer any reason for my staying alive.''

It was becoming longer than he had anticipated. And more truthful.

He moved to end it. ''I know it is argued that no man who is sane can kill himself. I am depressed, certainly. And have always been burdened by guilt. But there is no imbalance in my mind, I hope my death will cause you less inconvenience than I did when I was alive. I ask again for your forgiveness. Keep Ruth safe, safer than I did your mother.''

Just as he had had difficulty in beginning the letter, now Hartman could find no way to sign himself off. Once David had called him Father; once even Dada. But for so long now there had been no endearment between them; his son never addressed him as anything. Impatiently, knowing the boy would probably never bother to read the conclusion anyway, he ended: "Your father."

He read it through several times, trying to resolve the uncertainties. There wasn't the desperation he had intended. But perhaps it was the better for it. To anyone making any investigation, it aroused questions. After a protracted interview, David would be even more anxious to get away from the mortuary.

Only at the last moment did he hold back from folding it; people don't fold suicide notes they intend leaving behind. Intead he opened the suitcase in which he had locked the tire lever and lay the letter flat inside. He remained with the case open, staring at the heavy metal bar. He took off the paper wrapping, testing its weight as he had in the store. Please don't let my courage fail me at the last moment, he thought.

He timed the call to Connecticut for when David would be at home, but wanting Ruth to be aware of his supposed depression.

"What is it?" she demanded, recognizing his voice.

"I saw David yesterday . . . about not feeling well."

"I know."

"Can I speak to him again. Is he there?"

Hartman held the telephone tightly against his ear, detecting the mumble of conversation beyond the hand she had placed over the mouthpiece. He'd managed to sound anxious, he knew.

"Yes?" David's voice was curt and hostile.

"I'm still not getting any sleep."

"There are doctors in Manhattan, for God's sake!"

"Help me, David."

"What do you want?"

"Can I take more of the pills? . . . I must get some rest."

"No," refused the younger man immediately. "Four is the maximum of the strength I've prescribed."

"What can I do?"

"See a doctor there," repeated David. "When are you going back to Austria?"

"I don't know. Can't I come to see you?"

"I'm very busy," rejected David.

"The clinic, not your home."

"It's impossible."

"I'm not well, David."

"Find a doctor where you are. There's nothing more I can do."

"Please!"

"Tell him to call me if he wants my opinion."

"You won't let me come up there?"

"There isn't any point."

"I'm not *well*," insisted Hartman.

"There are millions far worse," said his son.

There was no purpose in prolonging it further; he'd managed what he wanted to achieve.

"Goodbye, then," he said.

"I'd appreciate your not calling me again."

"I won't bother you," promised Hartman. He wondered if his son would remember that remark later.

Davidson kept him standing, like a schoolmaster addressing a habitually miscreant pupil. Berman stood by the desk, staring just over the man's head, awaiting the attack.

"So I was right?" demanded the section head.

"I didn't say that," corrected Berman.

"What, then?"

"We can't seem to locate him in Vienna," said

Berman. He kept opening and closing his hands, as if he were squeezing some apparatus to strengthen his arms. He appeared unaware of the nervousness.

"He's run," insisted Davidson.

"He could simply be on a trip."

"To the Soviet Union," finished Davidson.

"I don't think we should overreact, not yet."

"Have you been straight about this?" asked Davidson suddenly.

Berman paused. Was it better to continue the lie or start trying to assemble whatever scrap of defense was left to him? He'd had people positioned for a week, and there'd been no sign of Hugo.

"There was something else," he said reluctantly.

"Something else?" Davidson's voice was brittle.

"Something else we talked about when he came to Washington."

"What?" Davidson snapped back the question, moving very slightly toward the left-hand side of his desk. Berman wondered if he had activated a tape recorder; there was a session of the inquiry board tomorrow.

"He said he wanted to quit. That he was very tired and didn't want to operate anymore."

Davidson sighed. "Oh, Peter!"

"I said it was impossible," said Berman hurriedly.

"And then let him go without instituting any sort of surveillance?"

"He's loyal," said Berman defensively.

Davidson laughed, a sneering sound. There *was* a tape recorder, Berman knew.

"He's gone over, Peter. You might as well accept it. He's gone over, and your career is in ruins. I warned you not to lie to me. I warned you."

"There's probably a very reasonable explanation,' said Berman desperately.

"Then what is it, Peter? When are we going to know what it is?"

"I've put out an all-stations call."

"What priority?"

"Alert."

"Do you realize the danger a disaffected agent can create?"

"Yes," admitted Berman.

"It doesn't look good, Peter."

"I know." The use of his first name was intentional, going beyond the usual patronizing. Davidson wanted to illustrate proper concern to those who would later hear the transcript.

"Have you called for an analysis of everything with which Hartman was involved, to assess the possible danger?"

"No," conceded Berman. Shit, he thought.

"Don't you think you should?"

"I'll get on it right away."

"I don't like this, Peter."

"Neither do I. I'm sorry."

"I want him found soon, Peter."

For Christ's sake stop calling me by name, thought Berman. "I'm doing my best," he said, not seeing the opening he was providing for the other man.

"The last time you attempted to do your best, you told me a lie," reminded Davidson.

"He came for the NATO leak!" There was desperation in his voice that would seem even worse on the playback.

"What was it first? The NATO leak? Or the demand to quit?"

"The NATO leak," insisted Berman.

"That might be put to the test later," warned Davidson.

"The NATO leak," repeated Berman.

"You know I've got to go higher with this?"

"Yes," said Berman miserably. There had been a time when he had seen himself as Director. He believed he'd actually boasted about the expecation to Hugo.

"You made an error of judgment, Peter."

"That's still to be proven."

"Let's make it soon, Peter. Let's get something very soon."

"I hope to."

"So do I, Peter. I hope it very much."

Five thousand miles away, in his Viennese apartment, Karpov sat studying his records, trying for music that would suit his uncertain mood. He chose Bix Beiderbecke; there was a harshness in the man's trumpet-playing and there was a harshness in what Karpov was doing. Hugo Hartman was his oldest agent, and the cable from Moscow that awaited collection by the embassy courier abandoned him, as one put aside a suit of clothes that had gone out of fashion. He let the strident chords sweep over him, for once not devoting his full attention to the technique.

With an operative as valued as Hartman, Karpov had set up a protection system many years before. So the Russian had known within a day of the CIA inquiries.

The American approach had been covert, of course; so casual that the concierge at the apartment building did not consider it anything unusual, nothing more than men with an already unsuccessful delivery inquiring the whereabouts of a customer they didn't want to disappoint. But Karpov recognized it. So he had Hartman's favorite restaurants checked. And learned of the inquiries that had been made there, and put Rebecca Habel under observation, and identified the American watchers.

If they were seeking his whereabouts in Austria, it meant he was undetected in New York. But judging from the scope of the inquiry, it wouldn't take long to locate him there. Karpov sighed, a sound of great sadness. He'd felt for Hugo more than was usual for a Control and his operatives. He'd respected the man for his ability. There was the concentration camp, of course: the episode would remain with Hartman until he died. But Karpov refused to judge. He knew of men holding their country's highest award for gallantry no braver than Hugo; courage was often nothing more than cowardice, misunderstood.

The investigation meant that Hugo would have to be discarded before there was any embarrassment. It was fortunate that the Poliev inquiry had been completed. Successfully, as always. Hartman was usually successful.

The doorbell rang and he rose, expectantly, sloughing off his depression. The Sacher receptionist was costing him a fortune in caviar. It was worth it, though.

17

Hartman had tried to prevent it coming: gripped his hands and held his body taut, trying to drive it away. But it hadn't worked. The trembling vibrated through his body and he was smeared with sweat. Rebecca, he kept repeating to himself. Rebecca. He had to do it. For Rebecca. He bathed his face in water, gazing into the mirror of the hotel bathroom. The skin was sagged and waxen: a frightened face. "Rebecca," he said once more, needing the talisman of her name. It took two hands to lift the receiver. The first time he misdialed and had to start all over again, and when the first ringing sounded in his ear he whimpered and clamped his mouth tightly shut over his teeth, to stop it coming again.

"Yes?"

He couldn't speak. Hartman's mouth moved, fishlike, but nothing would come.

"Yes?"

"*Guten Abend*," The German greeting strained out. Rebecca. If he didn't do it, he wouldn't have Rebecca.

"I don't understand. What did you say?"

"Klaus. Is that Klaus?"

"You've got the wrong number. This is the Eros Hotel." He didn't attempt to put down the telephone.

"Listen, Klaus, listen very carefully. Kommandante Lang told me to call you, a warning. Someone is making inquiries . . ."

The urgency was easy in his nervousness. So far Reinhart had refused to respond in German.

"This is the Eros Hotel."

"It's a private thing, a Jew who was once at the camp," Hartman hurried on. "He came to Panama, robbed Kommandante Lang's office. There were some details of your bank transfer . . ."

"Who is this?"

German at last! Triumph surged through Hartman, stronger even than his fear.

"Schleichner," said Hartman easily. "Werner Schleichner. I wasn't with you at Belsen. It's not important. Listen carefully. He got away from Cristobal before we could get him; we're sure he's working alone, and we want to stop him. He may come to the hotel. So be careful."

"Where are you?"

"I can't come to you today. I'll make contact soon. But take care. And remember. We want him stopped."

"Can I call Kommandante Lang?"

"He's gone to Zurich. The money was stopped."

"I think my room was entered," offered Reinhart.

"What!" Hartman pitched the surprise perfectly.

"My room. I think someone was there. Nothing's missing . . . important, I mean."

"Don't you take precautions?"

"Of course. That's why I wasn't sure. It would not have been easy."

He'd be sure now, Hartman thought. Now the fear would be coming in a solid, gut-churning knot.

"Be very careful."

"I'm going to be."

Hartman put the telephone down abruptly, as if it had suddenly become too heavy to support, or contaminated from its link with the Nazi. He'd done it! He'd opened the trap and Reinhart had responded, as he had hoped the man would. It still wasn't the worst part, where the most danger would be. Now he had to go back to the hotel, to become the open bait. And let Reinhart think he could still save himself.

It was a little past nine o'clock when he got to the Eros. There was a familiarity about the street now, as if he had known it for a long time. There was an altercation going on outside the bar, two men circling each other like nervous chickens, with the customary reluctance actually to start fighting. The jukebox blared louder than usual through the open door. Two girls were idly looking on, laughing. The 'E' in Eros had been repaired, and now it was brighter than the other letters. He was accosted once, shrugging the woman off without looking at her.

His eyes were held by the doorway through which he would have to pass. Reinhart would be at the top of those stairs; Reinhart, who had always controlled him and manipulated him and made him perform, whenever he'd gestured. Slowly, forcing the movement, he began to climb toward the rectangle of dull light at the top. Nearer, he saw there was only one bulb at night. Flies and moths were glued to it. There was scarcely any illumination at all behind the minute counter, just a shade enclosing a lamp on the far table. Hartman heard rather than saw a presence, the movement slow and unwilling.

Hartman could see the leather-tipped sleeves but not the man's face. Would Reinhart be feeling the first stirrings of recognition now, remembering the coward and knowing he could escape?

"I'm staying here."

Reinhart didn't say anything.

"Twenty-eight," said Hartman.

The hand came through the arched hatchway. It was dotted with liver spots and the nails were bitten until the cuticles were puffed and red. Reinhart hadn't bitten his nails in Belsen. He hadn't been frightened then.

"Goodnight," said Hartman, moving toward the second stairway. There was a grunt from inside the cage. It was very animal like.

The shaking came back as Hartman got to the room. He stopped inside, pressed back against the door with his eyes closed, hands clenched to suppress it. Rebecca; he couldn't fail Rebecca. It went finally. He approached the briefcase, looking for the signs. It was slightly at an angle from the edge against which he had positioned it. Gently he opened the flaps: Gerda's photograph was on top and the passport beneath. He'd left it the other way. Hartman felt another spurt of satisfaction. So Reinhart *did* know! He'd entered the room, as Hartman had hoped he would after the call. He put the passport and the picture inside his jacket, tensing at the sound of movement on the stairs. He heard the forced conversation of a whore and her client, and relaxed. Around him the hotel shifted and creaked: it was the time when business was most active, and the traffic on the stairs was heavy. Usually they moved without talk, either too accustomed or too shy. Once he heard a girl say, "Don't worry, it'll be all right." Several times there were artificial giggles of surprise at some preliminary begun before they reached the room.

Would Reinhart have brought the Luger? Hartman's apprehension was immediate. Wouldn't that have been the natural reaction from a nervous man suspecting his sanctuary had been penetrated? Hartman was very hot. Sweat bubbled against his face and ran wet against his body. He felt trapped in the room, impatient to get out. Had he stayed long enough? There was more sound from the stairs, and Hartman crouched against the door, straining for a voice. Sufficient. Reinhart had identified him, which was what he had wanted to achieve. There was no need for anything more; not here, anyway. His wet hands slipped on the handle and he groaned in frustration, hauling the door open. He emerged on to the ill-lit landing in a stumble. It was empty. From behind a closed door, someone moaned: a man, he guessed. He had actually started down the stairs before he realized from the blackness at the bottom that Reinhart must be ascending. The man was moving without any sound, his back against the wall to accommodate his limp. The German became aware of Hartman as Hartman became aware of him. Both stopped. Hartman recovered first. His initial thought was that he was a perfect target, bad though the lighting was, silhouetted in the rectangle of the stair head. The second was that Reinhart was supposed to think he would be unaware of any danger.

"Got to go out in a hurry," Hartman called down. He began descending again, feeling the steps jar against his feet as he reduced the possibility of Reinhart missing him if the man had the gun in his hand. Reinhart remained where he was, blocking any escape. Hartman felt out for the rail, about to pause: his legs felt without sufficient strength to hold him.

A prostitute saved him. The girl and her client, subdued by their recent activity, emerged from somewhere behind Hartman, unspeaking but making enough noise for Reinhart to hear them. The black mass before Hartman appeared to shift uncertainly, and then to retreat as Reinhart became aware of the need for shadows. Despite his disability, Reinhart moved quickly clear of the lower landing before Hartman had reached it to make any identification. By the time Hartman got to the reception hatch, the interior gloom was as it had been before, the man's outline difficult to isolate.

"Important meeting," said Hartman, returning the key. "Almost forgot."

"Coming back?" The voice was guttural, heavily overlaid with a German accent.

"Uncertain. Maybe not tonight."

Hartman got to the street breathless and trembling again, like a man who has known the initial terror of drowning suddenly discovering land beneath his feet.

He remained at the entrance, needing to stand still, to recover. He'd have to remember Reinhart's difficulty in walking. He turned left unhurriedly, toward Eighth Avenue. Near the intersection, he checked expertly. Thirty years behind, a head jerked and bobbed in ungainly pursuit. Hartman continued up Eighth Avenue, waiting for a cluster of vacant taxis, and when he stopped one he leaned in at the door for a prolonged conversation with the driver before getting in.

He was unsure whether he could spare the time, but Hartman stopped at the reception desk at the Pierre to make another preparation.

"I'm not feeling well," he said.

The receptionist smiled the smile of professional sympathy. "There's a hotel doctor, if you'd like . . ."

Hartman shook his head abruptly. "I just need some rest," he protested. "Can you see I'm not disturbed?"

The man frowned. "There's a notice in your room, Mr. Hartman," he reminded.

"Can you tell the switchboard I don't want any calls?"

The man nodded. "I'll see to it."

"Nothing until the morning," emphasized Hartman.

"I understand."

It didn't take long once he reached his room. He snatched the metal bar from the suitcase, pausing momentarily at the sight of his suicide letter, then slammed the lid back. The door took him longest, because it had to appear an accident. He secured the catch up, so that it opened from pressure against the outside handle, stiffening at the whine of the elevator; surely Reinhart couldn't have obtained the room number so quickly. It went beyond his floor, and he sighed with relief.

The maid's closet was locked, but it gave almost at once to his picklock. Hartman pushed carefully inside, wrinkling his nose at the odor of polish and disinfectant. There were brooms and mops against one wall, and he moved them farther back so that he would not risk colliding with them. He stumbled over something, bending to pick up a vacuum-cleaner hose. He wedged it back where he had put the brooms.

Hartman turned, pulling the door behind him to within a quarter of an inch, glad there was an internal handle with which he could close it altogether if some resident came along the corridor. He needed a toilet quite badly. He bit at the edge of his lip, annoyed at the stupidity of it at such a moment. He shifted with discomfort. It would be impossible to go back to the room. Perhaps there was a bucket somewhere in the darkened closet: it would make a noise and mean he had to take his attention, however briefly, from the doorway. His watch did not have a luminous dial, so he was unable to see the time. He began to inch out with his feet, trying to detect a container of some sort; something fell over with a soft, plastic sound and he stopped, bringing his legs tightly together.

The elevator whined again, a distant but distinct sound, and Hartman pressed against the door crack. The tire lever felt heavy and difficult to hold, because his hand was sweating. Quickly Hartman took a handkerchief, wrapping it around one end to pad the handle. The elevator passed to another floor.

When movement came it surprised him, actually making him jump because he had expected it from the direction of the elevator. It was from the other way, from one of the rooms. The man and woman were arguing in the formalized, uninterested way of a long-collapsed marriage, each side listing grievances as if a balance had to be struck. They weren't even bothering to raise their voices.

"How was I to know Bergdorf Goodman didn't take American Express?" protested the woman.

"You could have asked, before you went into their goddamned beauty parlor."

"There's a sign in the store window," she insisted.

"To say you can use it for a credit rating for one of their own cards. I had to leave a meeting to pay for that hairdo, for Christ's sake!"

'Do you think I did it on purpose?'

The man's reply was lost as he got near the exit. Because he expected the sound of the elevator in response to the arguing couple's summons, Hartman almost missed the approach. He was actually feeling out again, with his hand this time, for a bucket or even a bowl when he sensed rather than saw something and then pulled against the narrow crack, concentrating on his room. It came again, discernible this time, a figure moving slowly and quite silently, the body rocking on a permanently straightened leg. He'd pulled the last remaining string and made his puppet dance, thought Hartman.

Reinhart stood outside the room listening. Then he came on, around the bend so that he could stare down the half-concealed corridor; he appeared to be looking directly into the gap from which Hartman was observing him. The German didn't hurry, examining the passageway. At last he went back toward the door to Hartman's room, pressing against it to hear any conversation going on. Hartman saw him feel out for the handle, testing it, and knew he had to move. There was the briefest moment of swallowing hesitation, then he eased the door back, actually holding his breath in case its sound alerted the man.

There was about twelve feet between them. The gap began to close, and Hartman saw that Reinhart hadn't attempted to open the door but was standing, head to one side, as if he could hear talking inside. Then he saw the man's hand shift to his jacket and realized that the door had given.

Reinhart became conscious of Hartman at the very moment he tried to go through the opening. He had started to push, then halted, staring around. For the first time in thirty-five years, Hugo Hartman was face to face with Klaus Reinhart, a man who had subjugated him so completely by fear that he had become an automaton, programmed to respond practically without any spoken order. It would have been difficult to measure as a unit of time, yet the moment seemed to extend from seconds into minutes and from minutes into something longer. Hartman had hoped it had gone, as badly as he had once known it; scoured from him by what had happened afterward or buried too deep ever to be resurrected beyond that which he had already experienced. But it came almost as if there had not been a gap of three decades: the terror that he had always known in the man's presence, a numbness that spread from his very core to permeate out through his body, holding him in its paralysis. He saw the flare in Reinhart's eyes, the spark of awareness, and the man's hand started moving again, the one already deep in his jacket pocket.

"No!"

The anguish burst from Hartman, not in a shout but in a desperate moan. He lashed out with the metal bar, sweeping wildly toward Reinhart. The German was still half-turned and off balance, with one hand trapped inside his coat. The lever caught him across the chest, and Hartman was vaguely aware of the crack of the man's collarbone. Reinhart cried out, stumbling backward into the lobby of the room under the force of the attack. Hartman struck out again, clumsily because he was restricted by the narrowness of the entrance area. The second blow caught Reinhart in the face, splitting his cheek. He recovered in the middle of the room, turning completely, with the gun half clear of his pocket. His right arm was useless because of the shattered shoulder, and he began feeling across his body with his left hand.

"No!"

This time it was more a scream, a cry of determination. Hartman clubbed out again and Reinhart tried to avoid the bar, bringing up his left arm in a warding-off action. It was too late; it stopped a lot of the force, but did not prevent the tire lever from cracking against the side of his head. He groaned, staggering at the beginning of unconsciousness, and Hartman hit out again in frantic swiping flurries.

". . . loved you . . . Gerda loved you . . ."

He heard his voice, but didn't recognize it as his own. ". . . didn't love me . . . loved you . . . always loved you . . ."

He stopped hitting the man, suddenly, as if the power motivating him had been turned off. The secret—his hidden knowledge, concealed deep inside. Something that even David had not been able to discover. But it was true. He knew it to be true, even though he had never afterward challenged Gerda, not wanting the pain of her reply or to hurt her with the admission. There hadn't been love at first, of course. At first she had terrified, as they all were. But gradually it had evolved. Initially relief, then gratitude, then love. A hideous aberration in a hideous life. Why an aberration? Why try to excuse it as a mistake? Reinhart might have been guilty of mindless cruelty to everyone else, but to Gerda he was kind. Always kind. And protective. A strong, protective man, with medals to attest his courage. Was it surprising that Gerda, who had never known strength or courage and very little kindness from her husband, should come to love a man who showed them all?

And his life had been a gift from Reinhart to Gerda, like the chocolates and the food and the perfume and the silk dresses.

He became aware that the door leading out to the corridor was wide open. And that he'd shouted. He ran to it, anxious for any approach, and even after he had closed it he stood in the tiny lobby, intent for any sound.

It was the realization of how Reinhart was lying that took him away. He slipped the bolt, hurrying back to the unconscious Nazi. He was bleeding from several lacerations. Hartman bent uncertainly, then took off his jacket and put it beneath the man to prevent any stains from reaching the carpet.

The touch of Reinhart's body repulsed Hartman, making him gag. He pulled back on his knees; he couldn't fail now, not having got this far. Rebecca, he thought. Rebecca. Reinhart groaned, spurring him into movement. It came very easily, the ability to undress lifeless bodies. He sniggered at the irony of doing it to his teacher, biting against the hysteria.

Mustn't collapse yet; still a lot to do, before he would be able to feel any relief. He worked methodically, chanting the procedure in his mind. "Always from the bottom up . . . left to right . . . right to left . . . roll here . . . roll there . . ."

He stopped at another sweep of near-sickness. Even the underclothes would have to come off. He snatched for them, grimacing at the whiteness of the man's body. He must have existed for a long time beyond the touch of any sunlight.

Hartman transferred some of Reinhart's clothing beneath the man's head, needing his jacket. He went through it quickly, establishing the contents. His passport, credit cards, driver's license, Austrian identity card, return air ticket, the unused check David had returned, the diminished Valium bottle, a picture of Gerda and David, and then another of David with Ruth, with the Connecticut address inscribed on the reverse, and finally the photograph he had left in his briefcase at the Eros for Reinhart's identification.

Hartman stripped naked and, without bothering with alternative clothing, began to dress Reinhart. It was more difficult than undressing the man, because he had never been trained to do it. He was concentrating now, concerned with details. The underclothes were no problem; he hadn't expected them to be. The shirtsleeves were too long, but Hartman decided that wouldn't matter any more than the jacket being too large by about half a size. The trousers would have sagged, too, had Reinhart ever attempted to stand in them. Oddly, the shoes were too small, so that Hartman had to force the man's listless feet into them. Not perfect, he recognized. But satisfactory. Once he had had to wear Reinhart's clothes for a purpose, and now Reinhart had to wear his. He stared intently at the man's face. The features didn't matter. Reinhart was grayer than he was. But David would hardly notice. Certainly not sufficient difference to cause any doubt. He turned the man's hand; it was fortunate that Reinhart had adopted the cover he had and not attempted some manual job that would have created callouses. To complete the transfer, Hartman strapped his watch on Reinhart's wrist and slipped the signet ring onto the little finger of the man's left hand.

Reinhart groaned again, moving slightly this time.

Remaining unclothed for a purpose, Hartman doused all the lights in the room, hurrying to the curtained windows. He strained the drapes back and then the net curtaining beyond. There were several lighted windows overlooking the inner courtyard, but all were curtained. He thrust the window as wide as it would go, groping back into the darkness for the body. Reinhart was awkward to lift. Hartman dragged him, hands cupped beneath his arms, until he was almost at the windowsill, then heaved him into a sitting position against the wall, so that he could wedge himself beneath the man and hoist him upward, fireman fashion. Only his hands against the lapels prevented the man toppling backward and plunging down to explode into an unidentifiable pulp against the concrete courtyard twenty-one stories below. Hartman remained there, unable to release his hold. He could never explain it, not now. He'd gone too far. Had Reinhart moved? It had seemed so. Still he couldn't let go, his fingers aching with the effort of supporting the body. Gerda, remembered Hartman. Reinhart had taken Gerda from him. He couldn't let it happen again. He couldn't lose Rebecca. Not Rebecca; his last chance at happiness.

He let go.

For a moment, Reinhart's body remained there, slumped in an apparent balance, and then, slowly, it vanished backward. Hartman stayed unmoving, unable to bring himself to look. Wind blew through the open window, making him shiver in his nakedness. A murderer, he thought. I am a murderer. Was that any different from being an executioner by proxy? And was anyone a murderer who took the life of a man whose murders could not be counted?

His coldness broke the reverie. He jerked the curtains over the window, needing to illuminate the room again. He went first to the bathroom, examining himself in the full-length mirror. No bloodstains. No difference at all, in fact. He'd killed a man with his own hands and he looked the same as he always did.

Suddenly the need for the toilet returned. He laughed, with humor not hysteria. He'd committed murder, and his greatest need afterward was to relieve himself. He washed, hurrying in case the body was discovered earlier than he expected. There wasn't a great risk, he knew. Not until the tradesmen's arrival in the morning. He dressed in a suit he took from the wardrobe, gazing down at Reinhart's discarded clothing. From the bathroom he got a laundry bag and went through the Nazi's pockets as he folded the suit away. There was nothing at all to establish any identity: just three dollars and some coin in the trousers, two keys, which Hartman presumed to be to the booby-trapped apartment, a comb, and a pen. In the right-hand jacket pocket was the Luger, complete with the spare clip. Hartman put that into his own jacket, balancing it with the tire lever, not risking the weight in the plastic bag. He straightened, motionless in the middle of the room, anxious to forget nothing. The recollection came to him, annoyance burning into his face at the nearness of a mistake. He took the suicide note from the suitcase, placed it carefully on the bureau, and smiled at the completeness of everything. At the door, he carefully slipped the 'Do Not Disturb' notice over the handle.

At the ground floor he turned left from the elevator, but didn't use the Fifth Avenue exit, instead going through the bar and gaining the street that way. He crossed at the lights, judging the Plaza opposite the best place to get a taxi. At the park he saw the trash bin and thrust the plastic bag deeply into it.

There was a taxi available, as he had hoped. It was past

midnight by the time the vehicle was moving over the Triboro Bridge. He was a careful driver, keeping to the inside lane, and Hartman saw his opportunity. Quickly he wound down the window and tossed the Luger and the lever into the East River far below.

"What's the matter?" demanded the driver.

"Wanted some air," said Hartman, rewinding the window. He'd go first to Canada, only an hour away, he decided. Somehow it seemed safer than incarcerating himself for several hours in any aircraft bound for Europe. Rebecca would have to be given at least two days. Maybe longer.

Hugo Hartman was dead. The thought came unexpectedly, exciting him. He'd taken the only way out that Karpov and Berman would allow. And it had worked. He was free!

"Been some trouble up here today," said the taxi driver, jerking his head in the direction in which they were traveling.

"What?"

"Heard on the radio that the Russians tried to repatriate one of their diplomats from the United Nations."

Hartman remained silent.

"Man's wife said he was being kidnapped—that they'd kill him. She asked for asylum."

"What happened?"

"According to the news, the poor bastard was gone before anyone could do anything. Wouldn't like to be taken back to Russia to be killed."

"No," agreed Hartman. "Neither would I."

18

By coincidence, the meetings in Washington and Moscow took place within hours of each other, both emergency sessions because the affair was regarded as so important. Because it had happened in America, making information easier, the encounter in Washington was first. It was very hostile.

"I think we were very lucky, Peter," said the section head.

"Yes," agreed Berman. So the record was on.

"It could have gone very badly for us . . . worse than Zurich, even."

"I realize that."

"We're quite sure there's nothing else—that the suicide note was the only thing he left?"

"Quite sure," said Berman. "We've had access to everything."

"Very lucky," repeated the other man.

"I said we could trust Hugo," insisted Berman, anxious for any sort of defense. There was little point, he knew, defeated.

"It was a gamble, Peter. A gamble that wasn't necessary."

"I couldn't have let him go!"

"But you did!" said Davidson, turning the argument. "You let him go out and kill himself."

"That's not what I meant."

"I know what you meant, Peter. No one will suggest you should have let Hugo retire. But everyone will say you should have guarded against what he did."

"He didn't incriminate us."

"We weren't to know that. We weren't to know he wouldn't leave a letter saying he was killing himself because we wouldn't release him. Can you imagine the effect that would have had!"

"But he didn't," said Berman defiantly.

"You weren't careful enough, Peter."

"I know that now. Did you see the son?"

"I was in the room during one of the meetings. I didn't involve myself in any of the questioning, obviously.

"There hadn't been any conversation between them, about what he did?"

"I'm certain of it," assured Berman. "There were a lot of reasons why Hugo killed himself."

"I know the history of the man," reminded Davidson, allowing his irritation to show. "I thought he might have said something, the boy being his only relative."

"I didn't get the impression that they were very close."

"What do you mean?"

"He seemed anxious to settle everything and get away. And he didn't seem upset."

"Shock," judged Davidson. "It's bound to be a shock, losing both parents so quickly."

"Yes," agreed Berman, "Probably that."

"Hugo was a good man," said Davidson, performing for the tape.

"The best," agreed Berman. The other man appeared to have forgotten very quickly his suspicions of Hartman's defection.

"It'll be difficult to replace him."

"With the sort of background and experience he had, almost impossible."

"Richardson is going to find it difficult,' said Davidson.

"Richardson?" demanded the younger man.

"Hank Richardson. Used to be in Beirut. We've decided to give him Paris."

"I see."

"I fought for you, Peter."

"I'm sure."

"But there was really no defense, was there?"

"I could demand a meeting with someone higher up . . . the Director even," said Berman.

"It's *their* decision, Peter. Not mine. They've decided you failed . . . failed badly."

"What do I get?"

"Administration, here at Langley."

"A clerk!"

"It's pensionable, Peter. Index-linked."

"Son of a bitch."

"Let's not get messy, Peter."

"I was right," shouted Berman, for the benefit of whatever transcript was later made. "I said Hugo wouldn't let us down. And I was right."

"There are different ways of being right," lectured Davidson. "The correct way. And the incorrect way. Yours was the incorrect way, Peter."

Karpov was not irritated by his recall to Moscow this time, recognizing the importance of the meeting with Ivan Migal. It had meant another canceled arrangement with the girl from the Sacher, but he wasn't too distressed about that either. She was a very active girl, and Karpov was beginning to feel the strain.

"Poliev has admitted it all," said Migal.

"It would have been difficult to deny," said Karpov, who had seen Hartman's report. "Hugo did a damned good job."

"Would you have ever thought he might do something like this?"

"He was depressed, certainly, after his wife's death."

"It's still surprising." Migal was relieved after all at Hartman's death. Even though there had been no way of the man knowing the arrangement he had come to with

Fritz Lang, the fact that Hartman had been in Belsen had always created an uncertainty. Migal didn't like uncertainties.

"Poor Hugo," said Karpov. "He had a shitty life. He was convinced he was a coward."

"Was he?"

"I thought he was very brave."

"There's likely to be a protest from America about Poliev," said Migal.

"He's a Russian national," pointed out Karpov.

"Oh, certainly," agreed Migal. "It'll blow over. They're just going through the motions, because it happened to be on American soil. We're not worried."

Had Hugo got his Charlie Mingus records? wondered Karpov. He'd probably never know.

"It's been a bad month for you," sympathized Ruth. She wore her black suit again. The black-bordered handkerchief was unused but ready in her hand.

"I'm all right."

"Was it too bad?"

"I've seen dead bodies before."

"But like that . . . all smashed." The woman shuddered, irritated with herself for having started the conversation.

"It wasn't very pleasant," he conceded. "Fortunately there was a lot of documentation. I didn't have to rely on the body, or look at it even."

"I know what he had done—what sort of man he was—but I'm sad you couldn't have been friends," said Ruth.

"I couldn't forgive him when he was alive," said David. He looked at her and the woman saw he was very near to tears. "He wasn't my father, Ruth," he blurted.

She frowned, bewildered. "But . . ."

"If she hadn't had to save him, it might have happened. . . ." David was speaking to himself, almost unaware of his wife.

"Who?"

He frowned at her, an expression of deep pain. "Someone who made himself very close to my mother."

"How did you find out?"

"The analysis . . . found out everything when I was trying to treat her."

"Why did you let him be buried with her? He didn't think he was worthy, after all."

David smiled sadly. "It's too late," he said. "Because he'll never know. . . ."

He started to cry and she reached out for him.

"I'm so sorry . . . so very sorry for the way I treated him," he sobbed. "It really wasn't his fault . . . not his fault at all."

"He's with her now, David," said the woman. "They're together at last. That's all he ever wanted, to be with her."

"Yes."

"And it was proper that you should change the headstone to the inscription he wanted."

"He'll never know that either."

19

Hartman flustered around the room, unsure of the emotion he felt. It was difficult to identify, because anything like it had been so long ago. The wedding day, he recalled at last. Before he had set out for the discreet marriage to Gerda, he had gone around the apartment he had prepared, just as he was worrying around the hotel suite, anxious that everything should be right to please her.

Rebecca liked roses, and so there were two long-stemmed arrangements in red, another in white. He went to one in which he had already replaced the flowers, making some minor adjustments. And then on to the ice bucket, needlessly twisting the champagne. Was it right, near the window? Yes, he decided. They could sit there and look out over Zurich's lake, after he had told her everything. She'd need time to think; a view would allow her some distraction. When it was all over, they could sit there and plan. There were a lot of plans to be made.

She had been bewildered by his contact from Toronto. Not by the telephone call, but by the instructions, addressing her in a tone he had rarely used before, almost hectoring, allowing her no arguments. Finally there had been the cheap blackmail: "If you love me, you'll do it." It was an indication of the strain coming through, after all that had happened. But there was no way that she could have known that; not yet. He'd apologize today. As he would do many things today.

The reassurance was as unnecessary as touching the flowers or the wine, but he took his hand again to his jacket pocket, feeling the shape of the box. A much bigger, more expensive engagement ring that he'd given Gerda. But then he had not had the money available, as he had now. He took it from his pocket, unsnapping the lid. The diamond flared at him from its high-shanked, emerald-surrounded setting. Three carats, the jeweler had guaranteed: a very special ring. Perhaps large and ostentatious, but he knew it was the sort of thing that Rebecca liked. He remembered, too, the cause of her need. He'd give it to her very early, before he explained everything. She'd need its security, to do what he intended asking her. She would have to know she was safe.

Hartman wondered if she would be upset by his not meeting her at the airport. She'd seemed surprised on the telephone. But he knew he was right. There would have been immediate demands in the arrival lounge, and then further insistence in the car bringing them to the town. And she would have become irritated at his refusal, so the explanation would have finally started on the wrong note. The setting had to be perfect. He increased the spacing between some of the white roses and twisted the champagne again.

Although he'd confirmed the aircraft's landing, knew the time it took to get from the airport, and had been checking his watch almost minute by minute, Hartman still jumped at her knock. He did not move at once, instead gazing around for the last time, then inhaled deeply, preparing himself. The knock came again. She stood uncertainly in the corridor, half-turned as if she expected it to be the wrong room. She didn't answer his smile.

"Rebecca!" he said, reaching out for her.

She stayed in the corridor. "What's happened?" she demanded, worried.

"Come in."

She entered the suite with apparent reluctance, staring around as if she expected other people to be there. Hartman saw that she only had one moderate-size case. There appeared to be more jewelry than normal. The East European creed: in times of uncertainty, prepare to run at the first opportunity with as much as you can carry.

"What's happened?" she asked again, gesturing vaguely into the room. "Why are you registered under a different name . . . why . . . ?"

He held up his hand, stopping her, then took her shoulders and pulled her to him. She remained unresponsive to his kiss.

"I love you," said Hartman.

She softened at the words, brushing her lips across his face in apology.

"I'm frightened," she said. "It's . . . it's stupid. . . ."

Leaving her case just inside the door, he led Rebecca toward the window and seated her in the chair with the best view of the lake and the mountains beyond; the sun was almost setting, capping the snowfields with a gold filigree.

She said nothing while he opened the wine. She accepted the glass, still silent.

"To us," he toasted.

She sipped, her eyes never leaving his. Confronted with her confusion, Hartman felt unbalanced by it. He'd rehearsed the meeting, but now he couldn't remember his lines. He thrust into his pocket, bringing out the ring. He held out the box toward her.

She put her glass down on a side table, accepting it, but still stared at him, not looking inside.

"Open it," he urged.

"What is it?"

"For you."

Her face moved at the sight of the ring, an impression difficult to gauge.

"It's beautiful," she said. Her eyes were wet when she looked up at him.

"For you," repeated Hartman. "I want it to be your engagement ring."

When she made no response, he said, "Maybe a ceremony might be difficult . . . you'll understand why, later. But I want us to be married, Rebecca. To live together."

She looked back to the ring. "I love you, Hugo," she said, as if there were the need to convince him.

"I want you to," he said urgently, seeing the opening. "I want you to love me very much, because it's going to be difficult for you to accept what I have to tell you."

There was a window seat, for the best view of the lake, and Hartman edged upon it but looked back into the room. He was only a few feet from Rebecca and by leaning forward could reach out for her hands.

"I'm not a tax consultant," he began. "I trained a long time ago, but never qualified. I have no special knowledge about international oil legislation. . . ."

Rebecca was expressionless, the glass beside her on the table and the ring in her lap. Her hand was still against it but unmoving. Once the sun caught the diamond and it sparkled briefly. Hartman was reminded of a firefly. He gulped at his drink, needing the pause. He wouldn't make a full confession, he decided. There would be to much, as it was. The Russians, he determined. She was a European and understood the Russians better, knowing their extremes.

"It happened after the camps," he said. "Almost immediately after the camps. . . ."

He reached out for her hand and she allowed it to be taken. It remained passive in his; just like Gerda's had.

"I didn't mean it to," he said defensively. "I was tricked. Gerda was ill, by then. Needed treatment. David was a baby, hardly a year old. . . ."

The words took him back into the past. He spoke haltingly as the recollections came, but the explanation was easier. He didn't look into her face, but at the ring. Several times he drank, but not for any pause this time, merely because his throat and mouth were dry from the length of the account. He told her in detail of the entrapment, of his reluctance, of the Russian blackmail, of the assignments he'd been forced to go on, and of how, increasingly, his prestige had grown with Moscow. He looked up once, at a movement from her, just in time to see her taking her hand from her eyes. Sadness, he realized gratefully; she felt sadness for him, not contempt.

He started again, knowing an unexpected embarrassment as he talked of his meeting with her and of the guilt he had felt at the growing, awareness of his feelings.

"Then Gerda died," he said. For the first time there was some response from her. She tightened her grip against his hand suddenly, not a gesture of reassurance for him but more one of pain within herself.

"I wanted to be free," he went on. "Free to live a proper, sensible life. With you."

Her hand moved at fresh emotion, then stayed against her face as he told of his meeting with Karpov and of the Russian's refusal.

"He said there was only one way out," recalled Hartman. "And that was to die."

She gripped his fingers again, and when he looked up he saw that her head was forward, bent toward her lap.

"And so I have," he added, regretting that it sounded theatrical.

It was several minutes before she stared up, appreciating what he had said. She was crying freely, tears smearing her cheeks.

"What?" she asked with difficulty.

Hartman paused to refill his glass, then recounted the New York assignment without any hesitation. Only when he came to Klaus Reinhart did he falter, knowing that in an account difficult for her to comprehend he was approaching the point when she would learn he had taken a man's life. He digressed, talking again of the camp and of Reinhart's part in it and what the man had done to Gerda.

"He was the most evil man it's possible to imagine," he insisted, anxious to convince her. "I found him . . . by some incredibly lucky coincidence. I found him after thirty-five years, hiding in a filthy New York hotel. . . ."

She'd stopped crying, Hartman saw. Now she was regarding him curiously.

"I've perfectly faked my own death, Rebecca," he said. "I've arranged it so that the KGB will think I've committed suicide."

She began moving her head from side to side, in an effort to understand. This was the moment, Hartman realized: the moment when she might be revulsed by what he was saying and be driven away from him forever.

"Klaus Reinhart," he blurted out, wanting to get the account over. "I killed him, Rebecca. But it isn't murder, not like killing anyone else would have been murder. I positively identified him, so there could have been no mistake. He *was* the man: the man responsible for the death of hundreds—thousands even. Not just Gerda's humiliation. There isn't a court in the world that wouldn't have imposed the same sentence upon him."

"Why are you telling me this?"

Rebecca's voice was dry and fragile, like someone who has been ill talking after a period of unconsciousness. Hartman smiled at her sympathetically, reaching across with his other hand to stroke her wrist.

"I know it won't be easy," he admitted. "I am asking you to give up everything—all you've worked for since you left Dachau. I can't go back to Vienna, because Karpov would find me there. But I'm a rich man, a very rich man. I want us to move away from Austria, go anywhere in the world you like. And set up home together. It'll be a false name, I know. But it won't matter. There will no risk of discovery. I want to live with you and protect you and love you and make you happy for the rest of your life."

He saw her wince at what he was saying and hurried on,

carried by his own nervous enthusiasm. "It will mean disposing of your shop, of course. We can do that through a lawyer, without the need for you to be present in Vienna. The Russians know about you, so it would be too dangerous to return . . ."

"Stop it!"

Hartman halted, hearing the pain in her voice, then immediately tried to placate any fears. "Trust me, darling," he pleaded. "I know the shock, the horror even. I know what I'm asking you to do. Believe me, I know. But it's our chance, Rebecca. My chance. I want so very much to be normal. Please don't refuse me."

She jerked upright, then appeared to become aware of the ring. She stared down, as if seeing it for the first time, then placed it on the table near her champagne glass. She started to walk, and again Hartman was reminded of an invalid. Her steps were hesitant, as if she were unsure of falling.

"You must know something," she said, her back to him. "You must know it and remember it. Whatever happens, you must remember it. . . ."

She turned, staring at him to reinforce the memory.

"I love you," she said. "I love you as I've never loved anyone else . . . could love anyone else. My only wish is to spend the rest of my life with you . . ."

"Then—"

"Let me speak," she insisted. She moved, aimless steps in front of the window. Hartman said nothing, gazing up at her hopefully.

"Why do you think we met?" she asked suddenly. She had been walking back toward him, and he looked up at the question. She was near tears again, Hartman saw.

"A chance meeting at the Sacher . . ." shrugged Hartman, smiling at the recollection. She could not be anything but confused; it would be better to let her talk herself out.

Rebecca shook her head, a gesture of enormous sadness. "That wasn't a chance meeting, my darling."

"But what else . . . ?" started Hartman and then stopped, beginning to realize. He felt a sweep of unconsciousness and reached out for the seat edge to remain upright. No, he thought. Please, no.

Rebecca continued relentlessly, purging herself. "I came to the Sacher that day with orders to meet you. To become your friend and then your lover . . ."

"I don't want to hear!" protested the man. "Stop it!"

"I want you to know," insisted Rebecca. "You *must* know. I'm Russian, Hugo." She shook her head. "It would probably be difficult now to find any proof, but that's what I am. Russian."

"*Why*?" The question wailed from him.

"Moscow valued you. They valued you so very highly that they wanted someone as close to you as possible, to warn them immediately if there seemed any doubts."

"I can't . . ." started Hartman, but Rebecca talked on, not allowing any interruption. She was very near to him now, looking down, so close that her tears actually fell against his legs.

"*I'm* your Control, Hugo . . . the real Control. Karpov is the link with Moscow—my superior."

"Not true," mumbled Hartman. "I don't believe it can be true."

She put out her hands, touching his face, and he flinched away.

"I love you," said Rebecca. "I love you so much that I've actually thought of killing myself, rather than go on with it. But I'm not brave enough. And it wouldn't help you, because it wouldn't end with my death."

Two words got through to him from all the rest. Having held away from her touch, he now groped up, taking her hand. "Love me?" he asked. His voice was pleading.

"So very much," she said. "Completely."

His confused emotions swung back. He felt a surge of excitement. "Then it doesn't matter," he said urgently. "What happened in the past doesn't matter. We can still run . . . they don't know . . ."

She put her fingers against his lips, stopping him. "Didn't you think it strange how I could understand your feelings for Gerda, even though you loved me?"

Hartman blinked in fresh uncertainty. "What do you mean?"

"Didn't you ever wonder why I didn't make demands on you, like any other mistress would have done?"

"Why?" he said, straining to understand the new point.

"You must believe me, Hugo. You must believe that there is nothing in this world that I would rather do than run away at this very moment and try to hide, hopeless though it might be."

He jerked up, bringing her to him. "Then let's *do* it!"

She pulled away from him, very gently. "I've got a husband," she announced flatly.

Hartman shook his head, unable to speak.

"I haven't seen him, not for fifteen years," said the woman. "I don't expect to see him ever again, despite all the promises. He's in prison camp—somewhere I don't even know. But whether he lives or dies depends on how successful I am in maintaining you as a good agent. . . ."

Hartman began to cry now, hurriedly scrubbing his hand across his face, embarrassed that she should see him weep.

"I don't love him, Hugo. Although I say so in the monthly letters we're allowed. Not as much as I love you. But I can't abandon him. Any more than you could abandon Gerda."

He stared at her, his vision blurred.

"Can I abandon him, Hugo?" Now it was Rebecca who was pleading.

Hartman swallowed, trying for control. "No," he said shortly.

"Can you forgive me?"

"I don't know," he said honestly.

"Will you try?"

"I don't know that either," he said.

She winced, looking away. He was still holding her, and he could feel her shaking.

"Do they know I'm here?" he demanded.

She trapped her lip between her teeth at the question, slowly shaking her head. Then she said, "I haven't told them."

"So I could run, by myself."

"Yes," she said.

"If they couldn't trace my return to Europe, it couldn't be regarded as your fault," said Hartman anxiously. "They couldn't carry out any threat against your husband."

There was another hesitation before she replied. "I suppose not," she said. "Not if they didn't discover you'd come back for me."

Silence built up in the room. Outside, it had become quite dark, lights pricking out on the hills and mountains. It was Hartman who broke it, as if he were speaking to himself. "By myself," he said.

"I'd understand if you went."

"By myself," repeated Hartman, still distantly.

"I don't think they'd find out," said Rebecca.

"But they might."

"Yes," she agreed. "They might."

"Then he'd die?"

"That's always been the threat."

"Maybe you, too?"

Rebecca shrugged, a gesture of defeat. "Maybe," she said.

They stared at each other. It was Rebecca who spoke. "I've never said anything."

"Said anything?"

"About the other trips—the other trips when I've known you haven't been working for the Soviet Union."

Hartman sighed, a very deep sigh that seemed to deflate him, so that he physically became smaller. "There's a Lufthansa flight to Vienna at eight," he said. "We'll have to hurry."

BOOK II

1

Only the Director and his deputy occupy the seventh floor of the CIA headquarters at Langley, with its private dining room and the bathroom which didn't work when President Kennedy tried to use it during the opening ceremony in 1962. Directorate heads are on the sixth floor, and it was here that the conference was held, chaired by the Director of Operations, Henry Patterson. Because Fritz Lang had been identified in Panama, the head of the Latin American subdivision, Oscar Mills, was present. And as the former Nazi had been assassinated in Zurich, Gerard Jefferson, Director of the Western Europe section, was summoned as well.

William Davidson sat at the bottom of the table, sagged and crumpled in his chair, recognizing this as his last chance.

"This shouldn't take long," said Patterson briskly. He'd read all the reports and considered the evidence against Peter Berman, and he had already decided it was a failed operation best relegated to the archives, where all mistakes should go to be forgotten. He removed his eyeglasses and began polishing them, anxious to move on to other matters.

"I think there's still something left," insisted Davidson. He knew there wouldn't be another operation to get him out of the promotional cul-de-sac.

"Like what?" asked Mills. He was the sort of person whom Davidson hated most, younger by at least ten years, polished-faced and Ivy League, an Eastern establishment entrant whom Davidson knew regarded him as one of the relics from the wartime agency, someone to be treated with patronizing courtesy but not taken seriously.

Davidson produced photographs from the dossier in

front of him, offering them to the other men. "The regular camera reconnaissance of the Soviet Embassy in Mexico City got Lang going into the building. And then coming out." Davidson separated the pictures. "When he went in, he was carrying an attaché case. When he came out, he wasn't."

"We've all seen the pictures," said Jefferson. Neither he nor anyone else moved to take them from Davidson.

"The original report in Paris said Ivan Migal was involved with Soviet prisoner repatriation from the Nazi before the end of the war. And here's Fritz Lang, commandant of a concentration camp in which Soviet prisoners were known to have been housed, going in and out of a Russian embassy just twenty-four hours before he was assassinated in Europe," persisted Davidson.

"The Paris report was only émigré gossip," said Mills stubbornly. He'd already discerned the attitude of the Operations Director and was moving to support it.

Davidson went back to his dossier again. "Here's Hartman's report," he said. "There's no doubt it was Fritz Lang he found. And no doubt that Lang was at the embassy. We've moved on less . . . far less."

"To say what?" demanded Patterson.

"It's a link between the Nazis and the Russians, for God's sake!" Davidson hadn't meant to lose his temper. He snapped his mouth closed.

"The war was a long time ago," said Jefferson.

"Not for some," insisted Davidson.

"If there'd been any way of getting hold of that attaché case, then I accept we'd probably have had a damned good operation." Patterson paused pointedly. "But we let it slip through our fingers, didn't we?"

Davidson looked away at the criticism. "I regret the mistakes as much as anyone," he said. "But I still think there's enough to do something."

Mills shook his head. "With a provable, unarguable

association with Migal, someone we could name and of whom we could have produced photographs, then I agree. But all we've got here is some amorphous connection, a Nazi going in and out of a Russian embassy. The Soviets are as good at media manipulation as we are; they could even turn it into a story for their benefit, rather than for their detraction."

It was a waste of time, thought Davidson. The meeting had to be held, to show that procedure had been followed, but the sons of bitches had already made up their minds. He'd lost.

"Was there any indication that Hartman might kill himself?" asked Mills.

Davidson looked warily toward the younger man. "None," he said. "It's hardly surprising, considering what had happened to him, but he appeared all right to our people when there was last contact."

"Pity," said Patterson reflectively. Wanting for the record to show how well he'd considered all the evidence, he added, "Hartman was a damned good operator."

"It was unfortunate he was told to finish in Panama and not follow through to Europe,' said Mills relentlessly. 'Then we might have found out what was in the attaché case."

Davidson went to answer, but Patterson spoke first. "We'll file it," he decided. "Some you win, some you lose."

"No further action?" queried Davidson, still clutching at hope.

"No further action," confirmed Patterson.

Hugo Hartman had tried to prevent the barrier—or her realizing there was one, at least. But he couldn't avoid the feeling, illogical though he recognized it to be. She'd had the chance to expose him. And not just in his effort to escape but on the occasions when she'd correctly guessed he was working for the Americans. But Rebecca hadn't. She had protected him, just as Gerda had protected him. So she loved him. She must—completely—to take the risks she had. Which made the resentment ridiculous. But he couldn't help it. He'd considered Rebecca the one honest, real person in the dishonest, unreal life he led. To learn otherwise—that it had always been otherwise—was more than shocked hurt: it was betrayal. Immediately he confronted the counterargument. Wasn't that exactly what he'd expected her to accept? More even; he'd expected her to accept the lie of all their previous time together, and then abandon everything to run with him. Hypocrite, he thought. He was a bloody hypocrite as well as a coward.

"What did you tell Karpov?" he said.

Rebecca looked across the balcony table of her apartment, wine glass between both hands. "That somehow the Americans got on to you at the United Nations. That you realized it. and that, having found Reinhart, you decided on the way to get out."

"Sure he accepted it?"

"You can never be sure of anything with Karpov," said the woman. "But I think so."

Hartman pushed away his scarcely touched meal. "I wonder when he'll want to see me."

"He gave no indication." Rebecca paused and then said, "There's something else."

Hartman looked up nervously.

"When we were talking, I suddenly realized that they might decide to retire you after all, because of the CIA risk. That it wasn't just a physical danger, to my husband. That there was a danger to us as well. If they retire you, there wouldn't be any further reason for their keeping me in Vienna."

Hartman swallowed against the feeling welling up inside him. "Of course," he said. "I hadn't thought it through, but of course."

"So I told him you were all right . . . that there wasn't any reason for not keeping you operational."

Only one way out. Only one way for someone like you, Hugo.

"Rebecca!" he said. "I know you as Rebecca."

She looked at him, momentarily bewildered, then understood. "It's my given name," she said. "And I'm Jewish. But it's not Habel."

"What, then?"

"Gusadarov."

"You knew all about Gerda," he said. "Tell me about him."

Rebecca looked down into her glass, as if the memory were difficult. "His name is Boris," she said. "Boris Gusadarov. He's an engineer. Or was. A Ukraninian—part of the nationalist movement. An important part, which was why he was arrested and tried." She looked up wistfully. "Anti-Soviet activity, prejudicial to the state," she quoted. "I guess he was very brave . . . most people would say stupid, I suppose. He actually went to Moscow, to make the protest there. He might have had a chance, of survival at least, if he'd had the time to cultivate the Western journalists, so that his arrest would have made bad publicity. But the authorities were too clever. They picked him up within a month of his arrival."

"How long has he been in prison?"

"Fifteen years . . . almost sixteen," she said. "I'm not really sure where he is. There are so many camps."

"Dear God!" said Hartman. He'd only been in Belsen for a fraction of that time. "He must be strong," he said. "Strong and brave."

"I never thought of him as that," said Rebecca. "Determined, certainly. But never particularly strong or brave, until he went to Moscow."

"He'd have to be," said Hartman positively.

"I suppose so."

"What about you?" asked Hartman. "Are you part of their service?" He wanted to know everything, never to be tricked again.

Rebecca shook her head. "There was some training, after they decided how to use me, but I didn't join voluntarily. Boris was always the pressure: the reason."

"From Karpov?"

She shook her head again. "It's inherent for him to apply pressure, I suppose. But the ultimatum was made in Moscow by the Division Director, Migal."

"Karpov has been good to me," said Hartman. "As good as it's possible for him to be."

Rebecca considered the remark and said, "I suppose he has to me, really."

"He doesn't behave like a Russian."

"He's not supposed to, is he?" she said realistically. "He's highly regarded in Moscow. Certainly he's got a lot of responsibility, in Germany as well as Austria. I think he's even got assets in France."

Hartman hadn't known the extent of Karpov's territory. He'd run an appalling risk of discovery, working for the Americans; thank God at least that part was over. "He'd have to highly regarded, if he's Control of an area like that," he agreed.

"I meant what I said in Zurich," said Rebecca suddenly.

"What about?" asked Hartman, momentarily not understanding.

"Loving you."

Hartman looked at her but said nothing.

"Are you going home tonight?" she asked.

"I hadn't thought about it."

She waited, as if expecting him to say something more.

When he didn't speak, she said, "Isn't it a bit silly?"

"Silly?"

"Maybe there was a reason for keeping two homes when Gerda was alive. And more than just because of Gerda. I didn't want it, any more than you did, because of what I was doing. But now you know. You know everything."

She waited again and, when there was still no response, she said eagerly, "It could be your apartment. I wouldn't mind."

"We'll see," he said at last, aware of the hurt that showed at once in her face. Why the hell was he being so stupid! There was no need to avoid it, not now.

"I understand," she said quietly.

"No!" said Hartman quickly, anxious to recover. "It would be dangerous, at this moment. I don't want to endanger you if Moscow doesn't acept what we've told them—if they suspect I was trying to run. Let's wait until we're sure."

Rebecca looked down to her hand, appearing to see for the first time the ring Hartman had given her in Zurich for reassurance. She took it off and offered it to him across the table.

"What's the matter?" he asked.

"I don't want it," she said. "Not yet."

"When?"

"When you're sure," she said. "I'll wear it when you're sure."

"I *do* love you," said Hartman desperately. "Let's just give ourselves time."

She smiled at him sadly. "I wonder how much of that we've got, my darling."

2

The Moscow headquarters of the KGB is made up of two buildings. Before the 1917 revolution the ocher-colored original formed the offices of the All-Russian Insurance Company. Into it, after the transfer of Lenin's government in 1918 from Petrograd, Feliks Dzerzhinsky moved his fledgling intelligence organization. Now the square in front is named after him, and his goateed statue dominates it. In a land officially without religion, it is a shrine to an organization part of whose function is to eradicate religion and shrines.

Tradition—like religion, sneered at as a Western affectation—dictates that the Director and his immediate heads of directorates occupy this building. Their subordinates are relegated to the uneven extension, added during World War II by inmates of Stalin's labor complexes and German prisoner-of-war camps.

Ivan Migal, as Director of the European Division which forms only part of the First Chief Directorate of the KGB, had his offices in the secondary section. Standing at his window overlooking Dzerzhinsky Square in the late afternoon, as he was doing now, Migal could clearly define from the projected shadows the jagged division between the original and the later building. It was an unbroken line, marked only by the height of the differing stories, but Migal reflected that unless he resolved the problem—and resolved it quickly—the gap between the two buildings might for him be the distance between Kiev and Odessa.

Migal had existed on the periphery but nevertheless among the elite upper echelon of the Soviet hierarchy for forty years by testing every footstep before imposing his full weight. Such caution was the core of his survival. For forty years he had been content to see the stars ascend from behind, burst past in a momentary flare of acceptance, and then burn themselves out by either overambition or error to end up in the execution cells of Lubyanka, at the rear of the building in which he now stood, or in the labor camps spread like an infectious rash across the Soviet Union. In almost every case, Migal had been able to chart their downfall; in some, he'd even conspired in it. So he knew how it was done. He knew about the vast computerized personnel records, so detailed a whole building was needed to house them on Machovoya Ulitza. And how, once the decision was made to purge, those records were retrieved and combed for anything incriminating, no matter how small or inconsequential, the prosecutors working like archeologists painstakingly recreating an ancient vase from shattered shards.

Ivan Migal had been careful about records, from the moment of his wartime recruitment in Georgia. No failed operation bore his authorization; no project later to become an embarrassment because of a policy change showed him the originator. Except one: the solitary operation of which he considered himself as much a victim as the thousands of Soviet prisoners who had been exterminated. Lavrenti Beria had been the Director then, building the Soviet intelligence organization to a level that never existed before or since, a tyrant as ruthless as Stalin, whom he was determined to succeed. Beria had sought an opportunity in the decision of Stalin to reimprison or slaughter the tens of thousands of Russian troops who had surrendered or been captured during World War II and whom Stalin believed to have become anti-Soviet agents.

But it hadn't become the embarrassment or advantage Beria had intended.

Western governments cynically cooperated in the prisoner return immediately after the cessation of hostilities, making exposure politically impractical at the time. And Beria had himself been purged before the opportunity came again.

But the operation had begun before the officially declared peace. An operation from which Beria had carefully distanced himself.

And the only one from which Migal had not been able to do the same.

Upon Beria's direct and unavoidable instructions, Migal had been placed in damning, provable administrative control. They were purged and disgraced now, so it didn't matter that the conception and implementation came from Stalin and Beria. Or that Migal had not personally forged the unofficial links with the enemy to get Russians from Belsen and Buchenwald and Treblinka and Dachau, taking them from one hell to another. Indeed, it would have been better if that had been his role, because those carefully kept records didn't contain the names of the unimportant, dispensable emissaries. Just the functional heads, the men who had arranged the transporation and compiled lists and documented the fate of those who had returned.

There had been dozens of files; dozens that he'd patiently retrieved with bogus operational reasons from the storage systems and from which he had erased his name. But the dozens could be hundreds. In those last chaotic months of 1945 it had been impossible to keep accurate figures—estimates even—of each prisoner recovery. Nazis seeking friends were pushing POW's eastward by the trainload, and each consignment needed some sort of bureaucratic documentation.

And Fritz Lang had been a Nazi most fervently seeking friends.

Migal turned abruptly away from the shadows showing the separation he intended to cross, confronting the most appalling mistake in his carefully managed career. It was inconceivable that he could have been so stupid! Hadn't he paid Lang blackmail money for thirty-five years? And weren't blackmailers predictable?

Except that, just once, it hadn't seemed predictable. It had seemed the opportunity for which he had waited so long. Lang panicked and desperate, ready to make any deal. And the Soviet Embassy in Mexico—an embassy he had to confine to making only a surface examination, for obvious reasons—confirming that Lang was carrying what appeared to be originals of wartime documents.

Migal stared down at the faded, tattered files that the terrified Lang had desposited at the embassy, in return for Migal's promise of protection and sanctuary when he arrived in Zurich. They *were* wartime records. And they contained two prisoner operations of which Migal had been unaware and which listed his identity, an identity already removed from the Moscow index.

Migal had actually believed he was finally safe, having finally eradicated the one embarrassment that would have prevented his promotion into the original headquarters that Feliks Dzerzhinsky had once occupied.

Until the letter had arrived from the Swiss bank through which he had channeled Lang's money, the one conduit between them. There was no panic here: Lang had obviously written it years before, certain of his continued security. Lang wrote that he trusted Migal. And trusted his protection, the protection he was sure would be invoked if ever a threat had to be confronted. Which was why, in the event of anything ever happening to him, he had made copies of all the documentation with instructions that they should be dispatched after a certain period of time after his death or unexplained absence to wartime friends who might have need of similar protection.

Lang's original documentation was not the only dossier on Migal's desk. There were several more, carefully created and maintained files on every Nazi Migal had been able to trace who had a provable association with Lang.

Like Klaus Reinhart.

Migal didn't believe in coincidence, any more than he really believed in the doctrine of Karl Marx or that Lenin was anything other than a political opportunist whose system had evolved into a tyranny worse than that of any of the czars.

The apparant use by Hugo Hartman of Klaus Reinhart—someone who could not have been more closely involved with Lang—in faking a suicide was too much of a coincidence; much too much. Because, according to Karpov's initial message from Vienna, Hartman had acted on account of CIA detection. And Migal knew, from the observation at the Zurich assassination, that Lang had been walking into a CIA trap.

Dozens could be hundreds, he thought again. It would only need one, in the hands of the American service, to bring him down. And Migal didn't intend being brought down. He intended to cross the divide, from one building to another, and be promoted to the control of an entire directorate. And he didn't intend it to end there, either.

Ivan Migal wanted the directorship of the entire organization; that was what he'd always wanted. And what he was determined to get.

Because of what he did—officially and otherwise—there was frequent communication between Gunther Gesler's law practice in Bonn and Swiss banks. But it was never unexpected, which was why the package from Geneva unsettled him. Even after so long, Gesler never took chances. After locking the office door and putting his calls on hold, he examined the parcel minutely, because it was big enough to be a bomb. It was an hour before he was satisfied and unwrapped it. It was a bomb, although not the sort he had feared.

3

The *urkas*—the professional criminals who preyed upon the political prisoners—didn't bother Boris Gusadarov anymore.

They'd tried, of course. It was the understood and accepted way of what was considered life in the camps, at Potma and Krasnoyarsk and Novosibirsk and Tomsk and Irkutsk and Taishet and Chita and Sverdlovsk and Chelyabinsk and Magnitogorsk and Perm and Verchnevralsk. Gusadarov knew, because he'd been through all of them. But he hadn't accepted the system of terrorism within terrorism.

He'd never known the name of the convicted murderer who'd robbed him of the quilted jacket within minutes of his arrival and strip search at the transit camp at Potma. Any more than the man had known his: names weren't important in the camps. He'd just marked whom he suspected, waiting for the occasion when the man wore it, proving his guilt. It was only a day, because the *urkas* were arrogant, unused to opposition.

Gusadarov had killed him.

He'd been surprised how easy it was, to kill another man. He had the strength of outside living then, not the harder, brutalized sort he'd developed since, the strength of animal survival. He'd waited, near the separate *urkas*' barracks, watching for the man to leave unaccompanied, protected by the jacket against the snowstorm for the visit to the latrine. Gusadarov had attacked from behind, knowing he was no match for a professional killer, kneeing the breath from the man and then strangling him before he could recover.

Gusadarov had left the body on the barrack steps and proclaimed his own guilt openly the following day, by wearing the jacket.

It was a direct challenge, one they had to confront. It had come in Camp 19 at Chelyabinsk. They moved against him as a gang then, as they usually did, intending a mass homosexual rape, forcing him to become a male prostitute.

But they'd been too confident, because anyone fighting back was so unusual. They'd come at him in the kitchen, where he'd been assigned as a cleaner. And where there was boiling water.

He'd caught three with the cauldron. One later died from the severity of the scalding, and the other two were scarred for life. The two who had been missed by the water had at least been halted by it, halted sufficiently for him to get the meat cleaver from the man who later claimed to have seen and heard nothing. Gusadarov had severed the left arm of the first, just above the wrist. And crushed the face of the fifth man so badly that he was permanently disfigured.

Gusadarov accepted that he had been lucky—if that were a word appropriate in the conditions in which he existed—but the two instances established the reputation which moved and grew with him through the telegraph system of the camps. It even worked beyond the *urkas* to the guards. For years now he hadn't been treated as harshly as he might have been: there was usually a whole piece of meat or fish in the midday soup, rotting though it frequently was.

The *urkas* feared him, in their gypsylike tradition, because they said he was mad. But Gusadarov wasn't mad. He was a single-minded man of absolute determination. And that determination was to do anything, irrespective of how bestial or subhuman, to survive imprisonment. And be set free.

It wouldn't have been easy—possible even—without a focus for that determination. But he'd had one, before being told of the psychological need by a trustee whom he'd met in the first weeks of his sentence, who had existed for twenty years by clutching to a belief and refusing to lose it.

That had been the word the old man had used; clutch. Gusadarov knew it didn't apply in his case. "Clutch" indicated desperation, and there was nothing desperate in the focus of Gusadarov's reason for surviving.

Rebecca loved him. That's why he'd become an animal. To survive to be with her again. To be with Rebecca.

4

Hartman was surprised by the choice of meeting place selected by Karpov because until now the Russian had always insisted upon the privacy of a safehouse. And depressed by it, too, because the Prater inevitably reminded him of his failed visit there with Gerda. He entered the park and turned into the amusement section, losing himself automatically in the surging crowd. It was very loud, sideshow sounds and children's cries and barkers' demands for attention. He remembered how Gerda had clutched at his arm, frightened by it all, by then all her courage used up. At least she was beyond fear now. Hartman was sorry he would never again be able to visit Gerda's resting place.

The Ferris wheel dominated the attractions, a spinning circle of light. Hartman walked along the designated route, knowing the contact had to come from the Russian. As an exercise for his own benefit, he tried to isolate the observation he knew he would be under, to guarantee he was alone, but couldn't. Hartman had traversed three lines, and when it came he admired the other man's tradecraft. Hartman considered himself an absolute professional, able to anticipate any approach, but Karpov arrived alongside him without his being aware of the man until the very last moment. Karpov had a wurst in a roll and there was mustard on his chin.

"Years since I went to a fair," said Karpov. "Isn't it fantastic!"

"I suppose so."

"It's good sausage," said Karpov, offering it sideways. "Want some?"

"No, thank you."

The two men allowed themselves to be carried by the crowd, Karpov staring around with little-boy enjoyment.

They arrived at a rifle range and Karpov said, "I want to shoot! I challenge you to a contest."

"I've never done it," said Hartman. How many times had he wished he had a gun and the ability to use it? And more than the ability. The courage.

"I'll win you a prize, then," promised the Russian. He handed Hartman the half-eaten roll and took up a rifle. Inexpert though he was, Hartman recognized the ease with which Karpov handled the weapon. Karpov fired the first shot, missed, and straightened, turning to the Austrian.

"They've fixed the fucking things," he complained. "Sights are all cockeyed, and there's a bias to the left." He grinned. "We'll teach the bastards."

Karpov used the first allocation of shots to discover the imbalance of the weapon and then paid again. In the next session he punctured the bulls-eye with every shot, attaining the maximum score. It won him a doll with yellow hair and a purple dress. Karpov handed it to Hartman and retrieved his sausage. "A present for Rebecca," he said.

The Russian envied the other man his relationship with Rebecca. All right, so there was deception in Hartman not knowing who Rebecca really was, but there was no deceit in the actual relationship. It was something settled and established—comfortable. His own screwing sessions were nothing more than exercise, sexual gymnastics. And after so long apart from Irena, he was married to her in name only. There was nothing Karpov regretted about his time in the West except its effect upon his marriage.

Hartman stood holding the gaudy toy, feeling ridiculous. At least now he'd be able to explain how it happened. "It's not the sort of thing she's used to," he said.

"Exactly," said Karpov. "That's the way to keep a romance going: constant surprise." Karpov hesitated, looking directly at the Austrian. "New York was a surprise," he said, echoing the word.

Remembering that this was supposed to be the first time

Karpov had heard an account of his supposed CIA detection, Hartman went carefully through the account he had rehearsed with Rebecca and which he knew she had already recounted to the Russian. Karpov walked slowly, head bent slightly forward over his chest, his interest in the fair gone.

"You think they picked you up at the United Nations?"

"That would have been the obvious place. I suppose they had a watch on Poliev. It would have made sense."

"Then they would have known of your identification of Reinhart," seized Karpov at once.

For the first time Hartman was glad of the crowd jostling around him, because he was able to turn as if to avoid someone coming in the other direction and disguise any reaction. "No" he said. "I became aware of their observation at Lincoln Center, before I discovered Reinhart."

"That was an amazing coincidence," said Karpov. "Quite amazing." The Russian looked directly at the other man. He'd never imagined Hartman capable of killing someone. But then he didn't look capable of doing the job he performed so well.

"Yes," said Hartman. Now that he had given his explanation, he had to say as little as possible. And lie as little as possible, too, in case one falsehood clashed with another.

"How can you be sure you lost them?"

"They were careless enough to let me identify them in the first place, they really weren't very good at all." Hartman was sweating, the habitual vest tight and constricting around his body. He wanted to wipe his face, but didn't.

"If you lost them, why the identity switch?" persisted Karpov.

Rebecca had to be wrong in imagining Karpov had believed her! "I didn't know what sort of file they would have created, before Lincoln Center. When I found Reinhart, it seemed the perfect solution."

"Amazing," repeated Karpov. He let a gap into the conversation. "I never thought you could kill, Hugo," he said, uttering his earlier thought.

"Only Reinhart," said Hartman. "I could only ever have killed Reinhart."

Karpov became aware of the other man's sweating. The emotion of a memory, he decided: the memory of a hated man.

"The Americans seem to believe it was you who died," said Karpov.

"How do you know?" demanded Hartman.

"They mounted surveillance here in Vienna."

"What!" Fear engulfed Hartman. He half-stopped and was then thrust forward by the movement of the crowd, so that he stumbled against the boardwalk.

Karpov felt out, squeezing the Austrian's arm. "Don't worry," he said. "It's all right."

"Tell me what happened."

"You're valuable to us, Hugo. You know that. So we take precautions. While you were in New York, we discovered that the Americans had your apartment under observation."

"Then . . ." started Hartman, but Karpov wouldn't let him speak. "I said it's all right," repeated the Russian. "They began a surveillance and then they lifted it. We've been very careful, believe me. There's been nothing, not for weeks. The suicide completely fooled them."

Disjointed thoughts swirled through Hartman's head. Why had the Americans put a watch on him in Vienna? It could have only been because of Lang, and officially he'd finished that assignment before the Zurich killing. One thought was replaced by another, and Hartman turned to look at Karpov. "So you knew," he said. "You knew the Americans were on to me." It provided confirmation for everything he had said about New York! So Rebecca had been right, without knowing why.

"Yes," said Karpov. "We knew." The Russian took his arm, leading him along a smaller walkway and away from the fair. "I thought I'd lost you, Hugo, I really thought I'd lost you. I was upset."

Hartman realized he had no need for apprehension, not because of Karpov at least. Confident now, he said, "You'd have abandoned me, of course."

Karpov seemed suddenly aware of the half-eaten sausage in its chewed roll. Disgustedly, he discarded it into a wastebin. "I didn't want to," he said honestly. "I had to. You know that."

Pressing his advantage, Hartman said, "America will be difficult for me from now on."

"I suppose it will," agreed Karpov.

"But that's all," said Hartman, introducing his own qualification. Rebecca was all he had, and he couldn't risk losing her, whatever the cost.

"I'm glad it's worked out so well, Hugo" said Karpov as they made their way toward the exit.

"So am I," said Hartman.

Karpov looked at the purple-dressed doll that Hartman was still holding. "You couldn't ever explain that properly to Rebecca, could you?" he commented. "You've both got too much taste."

"It wouldn't be easy," admitted Hartman.

"I'm still screwing the Sacher receptionist," said the Russian. "Why don't I take it to her: it's her kind of thing."

Willingly Hartman surrendered the doll. "I thought you shot very well," he said.

Karpov grinned. "Never know when you might need it," he said. "I'm a survivor, like you."

Rebecca recognized his excitement and let him talk, holding back from any interruption although his conversation jumped, leaving gaps she couldn't understand.

"So we're all right!" concluded Hartman. "The American surveillance here actually confirmed the story we created about New York."

Rebecca nodded. "We still don't know what they were here for," she said guardedly.

"It doesn't matter,' said Hartman. "They're not here anymore. It means that Moscow believes me and that nothing is going to happen to stop us being together."

"That's important," she agreed. "Our being together."

His excitement went away, replaced by seriousness. "There isn't anything else," he said. "All we've got is each other."

5

Gunter Gesler had enjoyed a good war. He knew it was popular in the new Germany to disdain any war as good—to regard the expression as obscene—but his had been good. He'd enjoyed it, too. Every minute of it. Without the war, Gesler knew, he would have probably ended as a small-town Bavarian lawyer, like his father before him, a toady to the mayor, his wife vying for social status with the doctor's wife, his biggest concern a paltry overdraft or a minimal mortgage.

The war had given Gunther Gesler opportunity, and he'd taken it, with the two-handed enthusiasm of the most fervent Nazi, finding no difficulty then with the philosophy of racial superiority, any more than he did now.

To belong to the SS had meant to be elite among the elitists, one of the chosen. Gesler had realized that from the very beginning and never abused the chances, like some had. He'd given everything to an organization capable of giving him everything, working with a dedication that had taken him to the rank of colonel. He had the ability, of course, from his legal training, a prepared mind capable of administrative organization that he had developed until he'd become indispensable to the Berlin headquarters, taken into confidences, and sharing discussions and information far beyond what his rank justified. Gesler never betrayed a confidence or allowed an indiscretion. Which meant he was admitted to more confidences and further indiscretions.

Gunther Gesler became a man to be trusted. Reliable. And being reliable meant there was no danger in his knowing, from the moment of their creation when things started to go wrong, the escape organizations and routes, the establishment in Switzerland of the bank accounts from the looted treasuries and vaults, the pathways to South America safety—Paraguay and Uruguay and Argentina—through the Vatican and Spain.

Knowing about them from their creation had given Gesler the chance to plan his future. He'd planned it well, just as he had planned his career in the SS. Gesler hadn't wanted any faraway existence in a country where he didn't speak the language or know the customs, any more, he was sure, then Giselda did. Never, despite the opportunities in those halcyon days, was Gesler unfaithful to his wife or fail to consider her feelings. It had been better for them both to remain in a Germany they knew and loved. And where, despite the dangers, Gesler had known it was possible to remain. Gesler had known because he was the organizer, the man who dealt with the paperwork and the records. As early as 1944 Gesler officially became anonymous in the files of bureaucratically obsessed Nazi Germany.

Gesler was surprised, even now, at the panic in those last few months from men unable to believe the failed promise of the Thousand-Year Reich.

He'd gambled on their need for an administrator, a reliable, trustworthy man prepared to take the risk of remaining; guessed they'd regard him as brave in staying at all. And in their gut-churning gratitude be prepared to pay any price to ensure that their financial future at least remained secure.

Gesler had attracted a high price for that gratitude, a millionaire income that meant his lawyer's practice on Bonn's Rheingasse could have remained the front for which it was originally intended. That it had flourished to provide a matching income with that of his past was due to Gesler's constant ambition.

It remained, however, an ambition always tempered with the proper care. There'd been scares with witch hunts sufficient in the past, and Gesler, the diligent administrator, was determined that no one for whose safety he was responsible would become a victim. Because if they were detected, then it was likely that he would be, too.

It took time for the real identity of Fritz Lang to emerge publicly from the inquiries into the Zurich airport assassination and make clear the reason for the disappearance about which the man had warned, by the unexplained delivery of documents from the Bank of Switzerland in Geneva.

When Lang was identified as the victim, Gesler's first reaction was to destroy the files, because they were precisely the sort of incriminating documentation that should have been incinerated. But he hadn't. He'd locked them securely in a safe-deposit box, with the other things that might be useful, recognizing them as the potential blackmail material for his former colleagues that Lang had clearly intended them to be, even though the thought of approaching a Russian was an anathema to Gesler.

The recommendation about danger had to come from Gesler, as the coordinator, to those for whom he was responsible. On the day that Lang was publicly identified as an assassination victim, Gesler went to the Deutsche Bank and sat tensed in the anonymous cubicle, studying again the information in the yellowing dossiers.

It had been a useful exercise, because it had given Gesler the opportunity to think, to rationalize the danger. It had to be the Jews, because only they would bother or have any reason. But the gap between the Zurich bombing and the confirmation of Lang's identity was too long.

If their cell had been uncovered, then some other attack would have been mounted during the time it had taken for Lang's identity to become known. That had been Gesler's logical conclusion: the only cool, sensible reasoning. So his recommendation to the others had been to do nothing, apart from showing the caution to which they were accustomed anyway. Gesler had been convinced it was the right decision.

Until today's message from Conrad Schmidt that revealed what a ridiculous, careless fool the man had been, breaking all the rules, straying outside their close-knit cell, and endangering them all!

More had run than had stayed after the war. Conrad Schmidt was among the ones who had fled, to settle in the New York suburb of Queens. As part of the same cell, it was understandable that Schmidt and Lang had met, during one of Lang's visits to New York. But not that Lang should have introduced Klaus Reinhart. Or that, since that introduction, Conrad Schmidt and Klaus Reinhart had met, every Wednesday of every week, for coffee and cake and chess and reminiscence. Gesler sat back in his chair, looking out at the sullen, rain-threatening German sky and damned nostalgic old men who played chess and talked of the good old days. And then he returned to the message he held loosely in his lap, Schmidt's confession of what he had been doing for so many years, and an expression of his concern that inexplicably Reinhart had stopping keeping the regular Wednesday appointments.

By itself, Reinhart's absence wouldn't have been significant: of concern, even. But he'd been closely involved with Lang. Who was now dead. Which made it different.

If the Jews had picked up Lang in Panama and then Reinhart in New York, they would have traced and identified Conrad Schmidt. All the connections and communications between Gesler and Schmidt were carefully indirect, with one chance in a hundred of the chain being discovered. But Gesler had to be careful about one chance in a hundred. But not panic, like those who had panicked years ago. It looked bad—as if he'd made a mistake in not being more positive over the Lang murder—but there could still be an acceptible explanation.

It was necessary to find out what it was, of course. Gesler looked back to Schmidt's letter, considering the man's suggestion. To check Reinhart's apartment, after taking every precaution to ensure it was not under observation, was obvious. Reinhart could be ill, as Schmidt said. And if it were something more sinister, then he'd already concluded that Schmidt would be exposed anyway.

Gesler hesitated a further hour, trying without success to think of a safer alternative, before deciding that Schmidt had to make the approach. He'd impose a time limit for Schmidt's response. If it wasn't met, he'd conclude that Schmidt had been seized as well and send out the warnings, hoping he hadn't delayed too long.

Gesler took an hour drafting his reply, which was to be routed through subsidiary addresses in Madrid and Paris to conceal its origin. Three times he stressed the need for caution, criticizing Schmidt for the lax carelessness he had shown for too long and insisting that the man should not consider approaching Reinhart's home without at least a week's observation, to make sure it was not under surveillance.

Satisfied at last, he looked again through the window, realizing that the rain had started without his being aware of it. If they'd been discovered, a lot of important people could be affected, Gesler knew. One more important than any other.

Himself.

Conrad Schmidt decided he had it made; made in spades. Schmidt frequently thought in dated movie clichés because the movies had been his nervous introduction to America. In the early days in New York, when he'd been constantly frightened of discovery, he'd spent most of his time in movie houses, imagining protection in the darkness. Not that he needed it anymore; he didn't need anything anymore.

As he told himself every day, he had it made. Nice, obedient wife who didn't know anything about his past; nice, obedient kids he'd made damn sure didn't fool around with drugs or any shit like that. Nice house. Nice neighbors. Nice life. Made in spades.

Pity Klaus hadn't been able to adjust so easily. Dumb son of a bitch spent all his time daydreaming of what it had been like before and jerking off in some three-buck-a-trick whorehouse instead of doing what he should have done. What Schmidt had done. Become a good American.

Schmidt knew he was a good American. He paid his taxes and was a fan of the Yankees and voted Republican. He'd supported the war in Vietnam and the Cambodian incursion, although it was popular to oppose them. Goddamn Commies. He knew first hand all about them, because he'd been in the siege of Stalingrad and seen it for himself, although of course he never said so during the Friday-night poker-game arguments with the other drivers. He'd actually suggested during some of their meetings that Klaus come and play. Offered to teach him in advance, so he wouldn't feel uncomfortable. He hadn't accepted, of course. Just not able to adjust.

Schmidt wasn't worried about Klaus's sudden absence. He'd reported it, because those were the rules, and Schmidt obeyed the rules. The rules ensured the monthly hidden pension that helped with the good life. But he knew there would be a simple-enough explanation. Klaus had been badly injured, after all. And he never looked good, not for years, always coughing and wheezing and taking medication for something or the other.

It was a bastard, having to come this far down Franklin Delano Roosevelt Drive. He usually turned high, in the sixties, to cross town, but today he was going to leave the cab and go to Klaus's place on foot. He'd followed the instructions for a week, sometimes cruising by more than a dozen times in one day, actually carrying fares a lot of the time, and was convinced Klaus's place wasn't under any sort of surveillance.

Goddamn pain in the ass, the whole business.

He got out of the traffic jam at last, the flag turned off, and eased into an empty place at the cab stand near the Midtown Tunnel. He nodded and waved to some of the guys he knew, taking their rest break, and walked two blocks before picking up the crosstown bus.

Satisfied that there was still no observation, Schmidt still approached Klaus's place cautiously, making the final check before pushing through the street door and climbing the darkened stairway.

It was a long time since he'd been to Klaus's apartment. Shitty place: neglected, like Klaus was. As he began to climb the stairs, Schmidt decided it had been a mistake to get involved with the man. All they ever talked about was the good old days, and old days were just that: old and best forgotten. Goddamned playacting, strutting about in black uniforms with death's-head emblems and *sieg-heil*ing like a lot of jerks. Maybe he'd taper the meetings off. Not completely, because he knew Klaus was lonely and there had been comradeship once. But not every week, month in and month out. Another boring pain in the ass.

Schmidt knocked at Reinhart's door, head pressed against the paneling for the sound of movement inside. On the floor below someone was playing a Glenn Miller record. Schmidt smiled, recognizing it; he liked Glenn Miller. He knocked again and sighed. Maybe Klaus was really ill; unconscious even. Schmidt felt a stir of indecision about what actually to do.

The instructions from Bonn had been quite explicit. And he'd spent a goddamn week cruising up and down the street. Schmidt had come prepared, just in case. He eased the pick into the top lock first, fumbling the catch back. The second one was easier, although just before it gave the picklock slipped, skinning his knuckles.

"Shit," he said softly.

He edged the door open and called, "Klaus?"

The explosion of Reinhart's booby trap took away the entire front of the building and ruptured the beams, so that it caved in upon itself. Eight people were killed, including three in the florist's shop.

Schmidt took the full force of the blast, together with the darts with which Reinhart had surrounded his bomb. There was not enough left to identify him.

Things did survive, of course.

A Bakelite pressing of Glenn Miller's 'In the Mood' was found unscratched and intact.

So, too, was all the Nazi memorabilia that Klaus Reinhart had preserved so long and so lovingly in the wooden box in its mattress concealment.

6

Peter Berman, who was a bad driver but consistently denied it, shuddered the Volkswagen to an uncertain halt at the entrance to Langley and produced his identification. The guard, whose name was Hank Burlitski and who bowled with Berman every Thursday, examined the documents intently and compared the photographs, as if they were strangers.

"Thank you, sir," said Burlitski.

Berman nodded and jerked the car forward into the CIA complex. Fucking theatricals, he thought. He parked the car carelessly, across two spaces, and approached the main building, pausing as he usually did to look at the rigid statue of Nathan Hale, whom the British hanged as a spy during the War of Independence. Beneath the statue was the legend of Hale's last words as he mounted the gallows: "I only regret that I have but one life to lose for my country."

More fucking theatricals, thought Berman, moving into the building. He clipped into his lapel his identification button, with its serrated surround showing the color designations of his security clearance, and strode down the central corridor aware of the examination of internal security staff who knew him almost as well as Burlitski did. It was difficult to imagine that he'd once taken all this seriously—that he'd thought Hale's supposed last words stirring and patriotic, and even imagined himself saying the same thing, trapped in some inescapable situation. Berman emerged on the fifth floor, grunting at the thought. He *was* trapped in an inescapable situation: sentenced to life imprisonment with the title of analyst and with about as much future as the stone figure trying to look impressive in the forecourt. His office—fittingly—

was at the far end of the floor, a minimum-size desk and a minimum-size chair and a minimum-size cabinet with no security clearance, all enclosed in a closetlike space. His section was the smallest, entrusted with analyzing what little information the insular FBI felt it was necessary to pass on about the country's internal security. The suburbs of Washington enjoy imposing names, like Crystal City and Pentagon City. Within Langley, Berman's section was known as Tomb City and its occupants the Zombies.

Berman sat heavily. Before he could take off his jacket the messenger appeared at the door with his daily allocation of files. Berman finished taking off the jacket before signing for them; against the delivery would be recorded the time they were left with him, showing that he was twenty-five minutes late. But that would have already been recorded by Burlitski, the Thursday-evening bowling friend. Just as it had the day before and the day before that and the day before that. Fuck them, thought Berman; fuck them all.

Uninterestedly he opened the top FBI dossier, noting immediately that it was designated closed after a successful investigation and passed on merely for entry into the CIA files, because of the minimal foreign application.

And that's where it would have gone, within minutes, if Berman had not been involved with the attempt to scare Fritz Lang into confirming his Soviet contacts.

The failure of the Lang operation had cost Berman everything. It had become a phobia with him, to be constantly examined and reexamined in an effort to discover where the mistakes had happened and—less now but once a daily ambition—where the recovery might be made.

He knew not just the date but the time of Lang's birth. He knew about his schooling and his architect's apprenticeship and the date he joined the Nazi Party and the dates of his promotions and of his marriage and his mistresses.

And Berman knew of the man's associates, every officer and camp guard and soldier with whom Lang had traceably been involved. And so he knew about Klaus Reinhart, whose file lay before him now, complete with photographs of a shattered New York apartment house and pictures of Nazi memorabilia and the brief autopsy report, supposing what had been found were the remains of the fugitive Nazi.

Berman looked up at the movement at the doorway.

"There's been some complaints about the way you've parked," said the security officer. "You're across two spaces."

Berman frowned, irritated at the interruption, hurrying the keys from his pocket and offering them to the man. "You do it," he said. "I'm busy."

It was an idyllic day, one of the good ones. Hartman took a car and they drove leisurely into the countryside, toward Melk. Consciously trying to rebuild what he feared might have been damaged by his reaction to Rebecca's confession, Hartman planned it like the outings when their relationship first began, when they had driven into the countryside looking for the green bushes hanging outside the farmhouses, advertising the new wine. He remembered two of the farms, and stopped and managed to buy some that still remained. For lunch, continuing the nostalgia, he took her to the inn where they'd had their first meal, years before. He was pleased Rebecca remembered. She thanked him for the thought. It was a good choice. The mushrooms were picked from the overlooking hillside and the veal was perfect.

"I'm sorry for how I've behaved," he said.

"I've told you I understand."

"I think it's going to be all right," he said. "I really do."

"I hope so, my darling."

"I know it might sound odd, but I believe Karpov. I believe he thinks of me as a friend. It's been weeks now without contact."

Rebecca sipped her wine and said, "He frightens me."

"How?"

"I'm just not sure about him. How can he be a friend? He controls both of us, like a master controls his pets."

"He's a friend," insisted Hartman. "I know he is." "I'd like to believe it," she said.

Hartman felt into his pocket, bringing out the ring she had returned and offering it to her. "Will you wear it again?" he asked. "Please."

Rebecca trapped her lip between her teeth, pulling on it.

"I'm sure," he said. "That was the condition—that I was sure."

"I know," she said quietly.

"I prefer your apartment," he said. Leaving the one in which he lived, the one he'd pointlessly prepared and furnished for Gerda, would be cutting himself off from another part of his old life. He wanted to reduce everything from the past as much as possible. Which was not being disloyal to the memory of Gerda. He'd love her always and would never forget what she had done. But constricted and difficult though it might be, Hartman had the opportunity for a new life. And he wanted it so very much.

"All right," Rebecca accepted. She held out her hand and allowed Hartman to put the ring back upon her finger.

"I'm so happy," he said, making it sound like a discovery. "So very happy."

7

Ivan Migal moved restlessly around the room, impatient for the arrival from Vienna of Oleg Karpov. He was feeling more than impatient. He was nervous, worryingly nervous. Migal had a shortcoming in his career, and recognized it as a problem. He'd always been a headquarter man, politician as much as intelligence operative. So he needed an ally. Someone with the necessary operational experience, because what he was planning would definitely be an operation. But not an ordinary one. It would be unofficial, from Moscow. Because it had to be. So he needed someone he could trust—trust absolutely—because of the things the man would have to know, and to whom he could make the favors big enough to guarantee discretion. Karpov? A magnificent professional, certainly; few people with more responsibility. But someone to whom he could entrust his life? Migal wasn't sure.

If not Karpov, who then? Migal had always shunned intimate associations within the organization as part of his inherent caution; a friend today could be purged tomorrow, taking his immediate circle with him in disgrace. Not even Alena. His wife loved him and was loyal—he thought—but for the same reason he'd never sought friends within the KGB, he had never involved his wife in any aspect of his work. Even if he had, the crisis he now appeared to be facing would have been too sensitive to discuss with her.

The buzzer sounded, warning Migal of Karpov's arrival downstairs from Sheremetyevo Airport. Migal straightened the pince-nez he suspected made him the butt of jokes around the building and tightened the knot of his tie against the hard collar, seating himself positively behind the desk. He was still undecided about Karpov, but for the moment there had to be no indication of the apprehension he felt.

Karpov entered the room, appearing, as he normally did, at once to occupy it. Frequently Migal wondered how Karpov behaved when he wasn't subserviently subdued, as he was now.

"Comrade General," said Karpov, with the accustomed formality.

"Comrade Colonel," parroted Migal. Karpov's suit was outrageously loud, predominantly yellow checks, and the topcoat he discarded on a side couch was an elaborate affair with a cowled shoulder design and slits instead of proper arms.

"I'm worried about New York," opened Migal. The customary caution decreed that other people always had to lead.

"I've only read newspaper reports," said Karpov. He hoped this wasn't going to be another damned wasted visit, like so many before. He supposed he would have to visit his wife, but the last occasion had been a disaster. It was obvious that she had a lover and that his unexpected return had been inconvenient. He'd tried to show he appreciated the inconvenience of his intrusion, but she'd misunderstood and they had rowed, as they always had, even when they were together. Maybe it would be better not to bother this time. Hugo was lucky with Rebecca, he thought again.

"I've had it investigated as much as possible, through our bureau at the United Nations."

"And what's their conclusion?"

Migal frowned, realizing that it was Karpov who was leading, not him. "That it was Reinhart who died in the explosion."

"Then surely there's no problem?" asked Karpov. It *was* going to be a wasted journey.

''I'm not so sure,'' said Migal. How could he properly explain what he wanted from the other man without disclosing the link between Lang and Reinhart?

''We *knew* the CIA was on to Hartman, before he did,'' Karpov reminded his superior. ''I sent a cable recommending his abandonment.''

''I'm aware of the CIA observation and the recommendation,'' said Migal. ''Aren't the discovery of a Nazi who abused his wife and the identity substitution all a little bit too contrived?''

''I don't understand,'' said Karpov, who did but wanted the suggestion to come from the other man.

Migal looked down at his desk, to cover the expression of annoyance at being continually outmaneuvered by Karpov. ''What if he's gone over?'' he asked.

''Then it's exactly that: too contrived,'' argued Karpov. ''If the Americans were doubling Hugo, the last thing they would do is flood people into Vienna, where we could hardly fail to notice them. And then stage the discovery of Reinhart. What would be the point?''

''To confuse us, of course,'' said Migal. He was making a weak argument, he accepted.

''Why bother?'' asked Karpov. ''If they'd turned him, then all they'd have to do is to let him carry on as if nothing had happened. Why create something so involved as what happened in New York?''

''I think we should be careful,'' said Migal, recognizing the continued hollowness.

''We always are,'' insisted Karpov. He paused and then said, ''And there's another argument against turning Hugo. He's freelance—independent. He's only involved in the assignments we give him, and they are always constructed so that we could disown him. We've always been able to do that.''

''Nothing he said during the debriefing made you suspicious?'' persisted Migal.

"Nothing," said Karpov at once.

"What does the woman say?"

"She believes him too. Absolutely. And she'd know."

"What if she's in love with him, like you think he is with her? And that she's told him who she really is?"

Karpov shook his head, a positive movement. "She wouldn't do that. I asked her outright, and she laughed at the idea. She knows she can't afford to fall in love, not if she wants to keep her husband alive."

Migal lowered his head again, reminded of Boris Gusadarov's minimal existence. Rebecca's husband might become important to his own survival, just as Karpov might. He was still undecided about Karpov. But at least he could do something about the man in prison.

"Gusadarov."

The man looked up at the summons, campwise to its importance. Decisions were announced by name. All other communication was limited to prison numbers.

"Come."

Gusadarov inched backward from the coal seam to the main shaft, where he could stand, and then followed the guard at the required distance of five paces. The mine was full of day workers but no one looked at him: the call could be for correction, and in the camps a person's misfortune was his alone. The humidity was high in the frozen tundra of Kolyma, and Gusadarov was wet with sweat; he felt it begin to chill as they approached ground level. There was a wash house at the entrance, normally reserved for the underground guards. The man who'd fetched him stopped there and nodded toward it. "Get cleaned up."

So he was going to the administration building.

Knowing his clothes would be safe and not stolen, which would have happened if he'd left them unattended in the barracks shower area, Gusadarov confidently stripped outside the cubicle, removing first the quilted jacket, then the two undershirts he'd acquired during his imprisonment, and finally the reinforced paper that had originally been a cement sack but in the permanent subzero temperature of a camp beyond the Arctic Circle formed his next-to-the-body protection, not just under his shirt but wrapped around his legs as well. He'd used it over a long period, the sweat drying, then soaking the paper, then drying again, so that it was shaped to his body, like some papier-mâché armor. Gusadarov looked idly at the sores that the paper caused; no worse, he decided.

There was no soap. Gusadarov scrubbed harder than usual at his hands and face and neck, the parts that would show, because with obscene illogicality there was a regulation about cleanliness, and he could be liable for punishment. After drying himself on the linen cloth that was regarded as a towel, he tried to shake some of the coal dust from his clothes before putting them back on. After so long, he was oblivious to the body smell with which they were permeated. Because it was important, he'd learned mentally to calculate time: he emerged after exactly the three minutes allowed for showering.

There were two gates—both guarded—between the compound in which he had been working and the administration building, and at each there was an identification check.

Camp construction was formalized, and Gusadarov had been through so many that he recognized the route to the reallocation section. Its administrator seemed to be expecting him, which was unusual, calling him straight into the office. Gusadarov stood in the prescribed stance, hands clasped before him, head respectfully lowered.

"You're being moved out of the Arctic to the south," said the man, who enjoyed humiliating already humiliated men. "Potma."

Gusadarov had served time in the Mordavian complex

and knew it was warmer there. He bequeathed the cement-sack paper to the man on the bunk below. It was a gift incalculable in terms of money.

New York offended Peter Berman, the man who showered more than once a day. The cannibalized cars on the roads from the airport offended him, and the canyon-cracked pavements offended him, and the uncollected garbage stacked against the apartment buildings offended him. Just one big garbage dump, he thought; little wonder that people wanted to live thousands of feet up in the sky, where they couldn't look down to see what was at their feet.

He presented his CIA identity to the precinct sergeant with a confidence he didn't feel, stomach moving against the possibility of the man's invoking proper procedure and insisting that the inquiry be relayed through the FBI.

"All wrapped up," declared the sergeant positively.

"Just a query," said Berman dismissively. He'd made the trip from Washington on his day off, without any authority.

The sergeant consulted an incidents book, then a duty roster, and said, "You're in luck."

The detectives' squad room had long ago been painted green. Now it was a stained vault of a place, telephone numbers and graffiti inscribed on the walls, an empty prisoners' cage in one corner, and heel-chipped, overflowing desks arranged in two haphazard lines. Doors to both the lieutenant's and captain's offices were open, showing them to be empty. So was the main room, practically. One detective sat fixedly before a typewriter, picking out a report with one finger. Another sat near a window, absentmindedly creating a chain from paper clips and gazing out at the gap-toothed skyline. The man to whom Berman was directed was located against the inner wall, without a window view. The name on his identity tag said Murphy; he wore a Jewish yarmulke.

Again Berman felt the knot of nervousness as he produced his CIA documentation, but it was accepted without challenge. The detective shifted an overflow of papers from an interview chair alongside his desk and said, "Know the problem of working on this side of town?"

Berman sat down, shaking his head. "What?" he asked.

Murphy offered the bread he was eating. "Bagels!" he said. "Can't get a decent bagel for at least eight blocks. Gotta bring them from home if you want a decent bagel."

"I wouldn't know," said Berman. "I live in Washington." Thank God, he thought.

"Sure," said the other man. "What can I do for you?"

Berman produced the FBI report on the explosion at Reinhart's apartment. Murphy frowned down at it, then smiled. "Goddamned Nazi," he said. "Made quite a piece in the papers. Got my name in the *New York Times* and the *News*. Even a picture in *Newsday*."

"The FBI report was very brief," said Berman. "I wondered if there was a little more detail."

"Like what?" asked Murphy.

"There doesn't seem a lot of identification," pointed out Berman.

The detective laughed, putting aside the half-eaten bagel. "Believe me, fella, there wasn't a *lot* to identify. The son of a bitch was spread out over the wall like paint."

"So how was he identified?"

"By his apartment, of course," said Murphy. "Lot of Nazi crap, stuff like that. Wanna see the pictures?"

"In a moment," said Berman. "What about teeth?"

"Teeth?" frowned the man.

"Weren't any teeth recovered?"

Murphy felt down into a drawer of his desk like a child dipping into a cookie jar, emerging triumphantly with a carbon copy of his report. Newspaper clippings were stapled to it. The man flicked through for several seconds and then said, "Sure there were teeth. Pictures even. Wanna see the pictures?"

"I'd like more than just to see them," said Berman. "I'd like the actual teeth."

Murphy looked alertly across his cluttered desk. "Hey" he said. "There's nothing wrong with this, is there? I'm up for a commendation."

"Nothing wrong at all," soothed Berman. Taking a chance, he added; "I'll see Washington supports the commendation."

8

Hartman expected the summons from the minute there were reports of an explosion in the apartment of Klaus Reinhart and would have become even more worried than he was if he hadn't known from Rebecca that the delay was caused by Karpov's recall to Moscow. From Rebecca, Hartman knew at once of Karpov's return to Vienna. The postcard was delivered to his apartment the following day. It was fortunate he hadn't already moved, thought Hartman. He used the public-telephone bank in the foyer of the Sacher to go through the convoluted contact procedure, looking idly around and trying to detect the heavily breasted receptionist of whom Karpov boasted. There were two who appeared to qualify, and Hartman wondered which of them it was who got Russian caviar and American jazz as well as other things. It took thirty minutes for Hartman to be given the address on Dorotheergasse. He nodded in recognition: the old part of the city, the warren which Karpov liked because of all the entries and exits. Hartman was glad it wasn't somewhere like the Prater again.

It was a small building, overhwelmed and oppressed by those on either side, and because it was the only thought in his mind, Hartman was reminded of the stunted apartment house of Klaus Reinhart in New York. The explosion and the identification had been briefly reported in the Austrian newspapers, too briefly for Hartman's peace of mind. Immediately after the war it had been different: column-long accounts of every former Nazi ever detained. Now there were only ever a few paragraphs.

Karpov's greeting was as effusive as always, a shoulder-crushing hug that remained to haul Hartman into the apartment. Not as fully furnished as the one on Shüttelstrasse, but the stereo equipment was installed.

''How are you, Hugo? How are you?'' The Russian squeezed his arm, as if testing his weight. The odor of Gaulloise cigarettes hung about him.

''Fine,'' said Hartman uncertainly.

Karpov stood back, holding him at arm's length. ''Sure you're looking after yourself?''

''Well enough,'' said the Austrian.

Karpov punched him playfully in the arm. ''That sounds like self-pity, Hugo. I've warned you about self-pity.''

Hartman shrugged, uninterested in answering. ''What about New York?'' he asked.

Karpov grinned, recognizing the other man's anxiety. ''That's why I wanted to see you,'' he said.

There was a whisky bottle on the table, the cap already consigned to the wastebasket. Karpov poured two tumblers and handed one to Hartman. The Austrian accepted it but didn't drink.

''Please tell me,'' he said, not caring that it was a plea.

''Building was virtually demolished,'' said Karpov. ''Whoever it was in the apartment was obliterated . . .'' Karpov paused for effect. ''But the authorities have positively decided it was Reinhart.'' The Russian smiled at the obvious relief from the other man. ''There's no problem, Hugo. You're still officially dead.''

Hartman sat heavily in one of Karpov's overstuffed leather chairs, finally drinking. ''Thank you,'' he said.

''We'd have reason for worrying too,'' he said honestly. ''Even if the likelihood of there being any connection was so slim.'' He raised his glass and drank. ''Twelve-year-old Scotch,'' he said proudly. ''Damned good stuff.'' At least that was what it had been advertised as being, in the duty-free area at Schiphol Airport on his return from Moscow. The visit had unsettled him. Psychology had been part of his training, and Karpov couldn't lose the impression that there had been an undisclosed reason for Migal's wanting to see him. And he had seen his wife, against his better judgment, and they'd argued like hell. Maybe he should do something about that unreal situation.

"It's still good to know," said Hartman. The Russians had always treated him well. Karpov, at least. He had a lot for which to be grateful. He had Rebecca and he had money and he had in Karpov a man who sincerely seemed to be his friend. And he had at least got rid of one demanding employer because there was no way the Americans could believe him anything other than dead.

"Moscow considers you did well with what happened in New York," exaggerated Karpov. "I was asked to tell you that." He hadn't been, but Karpov decided Hartman needed encouragement. Migal hadn't said anything, but then he never did. Karpov wondered if Migal had ever done anything indiscreet in his entire life. Prissy old bastard probably blushed at his own farts in the lavatory, frightened they were being recorded.

"I'm glad," said Hartman.

"We can't risk the Americans' getting suspicious again, though."

"Fewer assignments?" It was an instinctive hope, but with it came an awareness. He couldn't seek complete retirement, not anymore. If he stopped working, they'd withdraw Rebecca.

"Only those that won't be risky," promised Karpov. "And certainly not in America."

Hartman's relief was mixed with another feeling: he'd never completely abandoned the thought that he might, very carefully and surreptitiously, making a pilgrimage one day to Gerda's grave.

"America might be dangerous," he agreed.

Karpov laughed, a bellowing sound. "You wanted retirement Hugo, and now you've got the next-best thing. Call it semiretirement."

The Russian filled both of their glasses and said, "It's a good life, Hugo. I keep telling you to enjoy it."

"I'm going to," said Hartman, almost fervently. "I've waited a long time, but now I'm going to."

Migal was a good chess-player. Not of Grand Master or even Master caliber but sufficiently competent to compete against them at the Academy sometimes and not be ashamed of his performance.

So what level of game was he confronting now? Grand Master? Master? Or what?

There'd been some moves for him to recognize. From the observations in Zurich, Migal knew it was a CIA operation: at least eight known CIA agents had later been positively identified from the photographs. The ploy had been to make Lang run, obviously to see whom else he would expose by contact. And because Lang had gone immediately to the embassy in Mexico City, enabling Migal to chart his timing, the Russian knew that Lang had not exposed anyone, apart from this traceable stop at the Soviet Embassy. About which the Americans had done nothing. So the move with Lang had been a luring one, a pawn moved toward a knight or bishop. Just like the bomb explosion in New York. What else could it be, the Americans staging the killing of Klaus Reinhart as a direct copy of the way he'd assassinated Fritz Lang? Migal felt a jump of satisfaction at the way the board was presenting itself. What else? Hugo Hartman. He didn't kow how the Austrian was being played, but there had to be an association, something that the inadequately briefed Karpov had failed to recognize. Was Hartman a pawn or a king? The method of play would have to answer that.

Migal went to his favorite position, the window overlooking the square. It was an overcast day and there were no definite shadows, but he knew precisely the spot that marked the line he wanted to cross. *Would* cross. Migal recognized that he had already made some improperly thought-out moves. Killing Lang was the most obvious. Delaying the approach to Karpov—someone so intimately involved that he had to know fully what was happening—another. But the game was far from lost. There was a conference table against the far wall of Migal's office, far larger than the desk, and because of the volume of material everything had been assembled there. Migal turned away from the view, going to it.

His game plan could work, Migal decided. Properly, cleverly handled, it could bring every knight and bishop and queen and king into play. And expose them all.

Migal decided that Karpov would be his knight.

Hugo Hartman would be a pawn, of course. But then he always had been. Pawns were disposable.

Conrad Schmidt became a soon-forgotten statistic in the New York police files, never connected with the explosion and designated instead one of the 5,000 a year in the city who, for whatever personal reasons, suddenly decide to abandon a settled, happy life and desert their families.

His wife was devastated. It was to take a year before she accepted that a husband whom she thought loved her had no intention of returning.

As an act of charity, the company allowed his son to take over the cab.

9

Gunther Gesler considered himself an objective man. And objectively, the only conclusion was that he and the group for which he was responsible were endangered. And had been, probably, from his misinterpretation of the Lang assassination. Gesler recognized, objectively still, that subconsciously he'd tried to prevent the daily fear from becoming a reality: that the constant self-warning not to panic had, in fact, been a refusal to face the obvious. With that acceptance came the apprehension he'd always managed to curb, the numbed sickness and the irrational few hours of staring around, imagining danger from everyone he encountered. The control of which he was so sure and so proud—the courage that had enabled him to remain all these years in Germany and live so successfully—was a long time coming. And even when he thought he had achieved it, there were times, in the first few days, when he knew it was slipping away and had to snatch out for it again, like someone grabbing for a fragile leaf in a strong wind.

The activity maintained Gesler's stability, the long-established and practiced procedure to be put into operation just for this, the moment they'd all prayed would never come.

There were twenty people living abroad for whom Gesler was responsible: seven in Spain, six in Paraguay, five in Argentina, Lang in Panama, and Schmidt in New York. To the eighteen overseas whom he considered still possibly in danger, Gesler dispatched the warnings the day after Schmidt failed to respond within his given time limit.

There was an untraceable cutout system, the warnings routed first to Paris, then to London, and finally, for those in the Spanish-speaking Latin American countries, to

Madrid. It didn't appear a warning, as such, just an inquiry in an apparently duplicated letter that their name on the mailing list of Barcelona publishing house would be deleted unless there were contrary instructions that the recipient still wished to continue receiving details of their publications. In the case of Schmidt—which Gesler feared no longer appropriate anyway—the warning had been finally sent from New York itself and referred to the man's subscription to *Sports Illustrated*.

Within Germany eight remained, and here the warnings were even better guarded than those dispatched abroad.

Practically all Nazi funds are deposited in the professionally anonymous and unbreakable banking associations of Switzerland. Gesler's was channeled through the Swiss Banking Corporation, but the corporation was merely an unwitting conduit, not the deposit holder. The actual funds were guarded in an equally anonymous and untraceable series of numbered accounts in neighboring Liechtenstein, the master account protected like the queen bee in a hive by linked drones of subsidiary holdings, from any one of six by which Switzerland was funded, once a month, for the regular payments. Gesler utilized the Liechtenstein supply accounts at random, without any predictable pattern, and every month transferred two to alternative numbers. It meant that if the Swiss corporation were traced and even penetrated—which had never successfully happened, in more than thirty-five years—then the likelihood of the supply account being traced with it was halved; and if it were, then that account ceased to exist within two months, an impossible time in which to infiltrate a banking system as geared to anonymity as Liechtenstein's.

As a customer of over thirty years' standing, there had been dozens of occasions when Gesler had received genuine communications from the Swiss Banking Corporation, which had enabled him to create perfect forgeries of their letterheads and style of letter-writing.

On the same day as he sent out the warnings to those he was trying to protect overseas, Gesler wrote to the eight Nazis remaining in Germany. The eight letters were identical: their account appeared to be overdrawn, and the writer would appreciate early contact with the client to discuss any possible embarrassment. Only in the reference numbers of the letters were there any differences, and then they were slight. Each number began with the first two figures of the recipient's own numbered account, to prove that the letters were genuinely from Gesler, the only man to possess then. Those figures were followed by three more—one, three, and two—to establish the timing of the suggested meeting: Wednesday—the third day—of the first week following the receipt of the letter, at two o'clock in the afternoon. The location had been established years before.

The method of response was similarly guarded. Letters were sent care of general delivery to the corporation for forwarding to Liechstenstein, and from there to Gesler, promising early contact but repeating the reference numbers to confirm that the meeting and timing were understood.

By the Monday of the designated week there had been three replies, and no more were received on Tuesday. Which meant that five had taken the agreed and understood alternative to any meeting and run immediately. They had every right to the decision, reflected Gesler sadly; he wondered if they'd made provisions or were fleeing blindly. By running, they'd cut themselves off from any further financial assistance. Another accepted part of the protection now being put into operation was that, the day before the meeting, the Swiss account would be closed forever. Another would be opened and authorized to function only when Gesler was satisfied the danger was over.

Should he have run, like them? Gesler put the question

to himself on the Tuesday night, armagnac in a crystal bowl, staring around at the genuine antiques in the living room of his four-story townhouse in Bonn's Berliner Freiheit. He seemed to have misjudged the problems, first with Lang, now with Reinhart and Schmidt. And as airlocked and secure as the precautions for the meeting were, there was always the possibility that he would be walking into a trap—the controller of the group and therefore the person for whom whoever they were remained content to wait.

Gesler sighed, swirling the liqueur around the glass. Giselda only knew that he'd been in the administration section of the SS, not that he had been so closely involved for three years in the transportation programs for the concentration camps. Neither did Hans nor Ilse, the children of whom he was so proud he'd always avoided any direct answer when the inevitable questions were asked, talking vaguely of a clerk's role in the army. It was unthinkable to desert them. Just as it was unthinkable to ask or even expect them to flee, without warning, giving up comfortable, secure lives and families of their own, rather than risk exposure by association and become a fugitive with him. As unthinkable as it had been thirty-five years ago. He'd been right then not to run. And he wouldn't run now. Not until he knew the full extent of the danger and recognized there wasn't any other alternative.

Gesler looked up at his wife's entry into the room. The maid followed with the coffee tray.

"Will you want anything else?" Giselda asked.

Gesler shook his head, watching as his wife dismissed the servants for the evening and thinking how beautiful she still was he'd defy anybody to put her age at anything more than fifty, and he knew she was frequently taken for younger than that.

He accepted the coffee and sat opposite her.

"You look tired," she said.

"I've been working hard," he replied, unhappy that the strain was showing.

"I don't really know why you do," she said.

"I'm going to Munich tomorrow," he announced.

"Munich!"

"Yes," said Gesler.

"Why didn't you say so before?"

"It's nothing important. There didn't seen any need to mention it earlier."

"You work too hard," she repeated in protest.

"Only for the day," he said.

"It'll still be a long one."

"I've done it a hundred times." Gesler was pleased by her concern, feeling a warmth of love toward her. He didn't think he could abanon her, whatever happened.

"What time will you be back?"

"I'm going to try for the early evening plane, so it should be around eight."

"The cook was planning pork for dinner."

"That will be fine."

"What time shall I say?"

"Nine, in case there's any delay."

There had been problems after Giselda's hysterectomy and they no longer slept in the same bedroom, so he didn't disturb her when he got up for the first available flight to Munich. Gesler was always depressed upon coming back to the city where it had all begun, allowing himself his only nostalgia. Munich now was brash and gaudy and loud, rhinestones instead of the real jewel. He'd preferred it as it had been before, colonnaded and impressive, a stirring place of uniformed street marches and fire-torch processions and banners fluttering at the head of precision-stepping columns stretching back as far as the eye could see.

Gesler forced the reflections away perhaps, he thought as the taxi took him back into the old, original part of the city, it was not so strange that men of his age preferred to live permanently in the past.

Never, during any previous postwar visit, had Gesler been to the Hofbräuhaus, the absolute place of memories, the cathedrallike beerhall where the Führer had actually formed the party.

He entered hesitantly, as if for the first time in his life. Unchanged, he decided. Not completely, because that would have been ridiculous, but still recognizable as the place in which he'd sat entranced, listening to the recruiters' promises for the future, felt himself part of something new and strong and exciting. He walked past the souvenir stalls at the entrance, frowning with displeasure at the gimmickry for sale, into the enormous cavern. The stage was as he remembered. And the interior, the line upon line of communal benches and tables. It would be interesting to come at night, to hear the songs that were sung now. He stopped himself at the thought; no, it wouldn't. The songs wouldn't be the same. Nor the camaraderie. Only the shell remained, nothing more.

The designated table was already partially occupied, but he sat at the far end with several spaces separating him from anyone else. Only three, he remembered. Who would they be? Would he recognize them after so long? They may have had surgery. It had never been necessary for him, because he'd been one of the faceless ones.

But there were others who hadn't been: others for whom he'd remained paymaster and whose activities he knew, activities that would have got them named and photographed on every wanted poster ever printed by the damned Jews.

Gesler ordered schnapps rather than the tourist stein of beer, staring around. There were a lot of tourists, bandoliered with cameras and maps and guidebooks, gawking and photographing and pretending they could envisage what it had been like. Fools, all of them. No one could imagine what it had been like, no one who hadn't been here and lived through it. Gesler felt a sudden burst of anger. It was a mistake to let the place become this, an amusement arcade. It should have been preserved for what it was: a monument to Germany's history, a history of which the country should be proud.

Gesler stirred at the arrival of a man in the chair facing him, nodding permission to the polite inquiry that the place was vacant. A stranger, he decided at once. Damn! They wouldn't be able to talk after the identification with someone so close. The man looked interestedly about, then ordered a stein. Damned tourist, like all the rest.

"The weather is mild for this time of the year in Bavaria," the man said.

Gesler tensed. The ritual had to begin with an innocuous remark about the weather, one in which he had to reply in a specified way. "I've known it milder," he said. He allowed a pause and then added the necessary words. "Although not frequently."

"I'm not a frequent visitor," said the man.

The lines were mannered and prepared now, apparently inconsequential small talk to anyone who overheard, but important to those involved. Who was he? wondered Gesler, looking at the strange face. "Nor am I," said Gesler. Then, stipulating the first and last digits of the meeting time, he added, "Not more than once or twice. Yourself?"

"Seven or eight," said the man.

Schroeder! Seventy-eight were the last two figures of the numbered account of Otto Schroeder, the numbered account which only Gesler possessed, apart from the man himself.

"Hello, Otto," he said.

"You haven't changed, Gunther," said the man. "Still as fat. Affluent-looking, too."

"You have," said Gesler. He felt a strange unreality,

meeting Schroeder after so long. Once they had been quite close, spending weekends together in the mountains with their wives.

The other man instinctively brought his hand to his face. "I thought it wise," he said.

"It would have been," Gesler accepted. Schroeder had been a lieutenant in the transportation division, Poland first, then Hungary, actually briefing the Arrow Cross Hungarian fascists in Budapest in 1944 when Adolf Eichmann had tried to clear it of Jews before the Russian advance. There would have been many people who survived who knew what Otto Schroeder looked like. He'd been a brave man to stay behind.

"How's Giselda?" asked Schroeder.

"Very well," said Gesler. "Emmy?"

"Troubled by arthritis, but not too badly." The waitress came and Schroeder ordered more beer. "So Im the first," he said.

"There will only be four of us."

The surgery seemed to have stiffened Schroeder's face, making it easy for the man to remain expressionless. "Do you know what it is? What happened?"

Before Gesler could reply there was fresh movement at the table. This time, despite all the years, Gesler recognized Rude Becher. The man had been in the same department, a major at the end, liaison with Eichmann's special extermination division. Becher seemed to have changed remarkably little, still stoop-shouldered, tall, and thin, cadaverous almost. Like Gesler, he failed to recognize Schroeder and went dutifully through the recognition procedure. They would have done it anyway; the rules had been established and they would have been followed. Gesler was reintroducing Schroeder when Martin Luntz arrived. The man had been ultimately responsible for organizing transportation timetables: he arrived precisely on time, at two o'clock. His plastic surgery was only partial, and Gesler thought he could have identified him, despite the repeated ritual.

Now that they had finally assembled, there seemed a strange embarrassment between them, like school reunion of students who had grown apart and no longer had anything in common. The hesitation remained until after they had all been served. Impulsively Gesler stretched around the table, shaking hands with them all. It slightly reduced the reserve.

"There will be no more?" asked Luntz.

"No," said Gesler.

"So it's as bad as that," said Becher. He looked around the huge beerkeller, as if imagining immediate danger.

"I don't know how bad it is," confessed Gesler. Succinctly he gave the other three men a concise, lawyerly account of what had happened and why he'd felt it necessary to send the warnings.

"There must be a connection," agreed Becher.

"How could they have got on to Lang in the first place?" queried Schroeder.

"How have they found any of us, over the years?" asked Luntz.

"What's happened has happened," said Gesler, with customary objectivity. "We've got to plan ahead, not look back." He turned first to Schroeder, then to the other two. "We're still ahead of them. We can survive if we stay calm. If we think and plan."

"How can you be sure?" demanded Schroeder. The surgery made him appear younger than he must have been.

"Recognition," said Gesler. "I'm the only one who knew all the account numbers—the only one who could make the recognition."

"If they'd broken Schmidt, he could have told them everything except the numbers," said Schroeder. Now it was he who turned around. "We could be sitting here surrounded by a hundred men, for God's sake!"

Gesler shook his head. "The Hofbräuhaus was for the people like us, the ones who stayed. Those who ran, like Lang and Schmidt and all the rest, never had an assembly arrangement. And none of them knew about this."

Luntz and Becher discernibly relaxed, but Schroeder asked, 'How many stayed behind?'

"Nine, including myself."

"What if the link isn't Schmidt through Reinhart to Lang?" Schroeder persisted. "What if the whole thing began from one of the five who aren't here today?"

"You're not thinking properly," said Gesler patiently. "If it had started from one of the others who remained here in Germany, then it is here where the attacks would have started. Only I knew the places and the identities of those who went abroad." Gesler looked around at the uncertain faces. "Could it?" he demanded. "Which of you knows a foreign country or a town in a country where any of our colleagues settled?"

Luntz gave a relieved smile. Becher said, "So we're safe!"

"If I thought we were safe, I wouldn't have sent out the messages," said Gesler.

"What the hell do you mean, then?" demanded Schroeder. He spoke louder than he had intended, bringing his beer mug down heavily against the long table. The group at the other end turning enquiringly and a girl in the group laughed.

"I mean," said Gesler steadily, "that we shouldn't panic." He paused. "Or make noise to attract the attention of others."

"Sorry," mumbled Schroeder.

It gave Gesler a feeling of power to realize he was still guiding these men; each was looking to him, seeking reassurance. It was a time to impose leadership, just as the Führer had imposed his leadership in this very place. Gesler was immediately uncomfortable at the reflection, recognizing the impudence in associating himself even in thought with someone so superior.

"I've protected each of you for over three decades," he reminded the other men. "The risk in coming here today was mine, as the coordinator, more than yours. Automatically, whatever happened in New York can't lead to us. But we've got to accept the possibility of it having happened, from some cause we can't guess at. But that's all it is, at this stage: a possibility. A possibility we've got to accept and decide how to confront."

"I think you've exaggerated it," complained Luntz petulantly. "For God's sake, man, I was at the point of running! I even considered it, after I got here to Munich today. You make it sound like something of no concern."

"Then you've misunderstood," said Gesler.

"You're right to have called the meeting," said Becher quietly. "It could be dangerous, and we've got to plan against it."

Luntz snorted, going to each of them. "What can we do!" he demanded. "Look at us: old men, every one of us. Who can we fight? What have we to fight with?"

"There's money," said Gesler. "A lot of money."

"Not necessary," said Schroeder positively.

For the first time since the encounter began, Gesler felt the control slip away from him. He sipped his schnapps, wanting the question to come from one of the other two. It was Becher who asked it.

"It didn't end in 1945," replied Schroeder. "There are some who still embrace the old ideas—the true ideas."

"Who?" demanded Becher.

"My son," replied Schroeder. "A son I've brought up properly. And many of his friends feel the same way."

Gesler knew of the existence of the neo-Nazi organizations but had never risked any association with them.

"Enough to confront force with force?" asked Becher hopefully.

"Enough," assured Schroeder. "Trained and waiting. In fact, they've been waiting a long time."

Gesler gestured for more drinks, to celebrate. "We'll need to keep in daily contact," he said. "We all know the importance of planning. If an attack comes, I want to be ready to meet it. Ready to teach the bastards the sort of lesson we were stopped from doing in 1945."

Because it came through a circuitous, undetectable route, it took four weeks for the letter to reach Karpov from Moscow. But it was dated, so the Russian knew Irena had written it within a week of his last visit, when they had their worst argument ever. As upset as she had been, Irena would not have forgotten the regulations governing such personal requests. Karpov sighed in anticipation. All his correspondence was monitored and censored, so they would already be aware of her request for him to return. Karpov knew he could refuse; that Migal and the others at Dzerzhinsky Square would expect him to. To hell with them, he thought. The bastards had been responsible for breaking up his marriage, so let them be inconvenienced. And what inconvenience could there be? There wasn't any current operation for which he was responsible.

The quickness of Migal's agreement to his application still surprised Karpov.

10

In their enthusiasm they had wanted to stage the demonstration at Funf-Seen-Land but Gesler, to whom the others had automatically conceded command, decided that it was too close to Munich, with the possibility of their being seen by tourists. Instead he chose the Alps, still close enough to drive to from Munich, but with more space in which they could lose themselves. They traveled separately, a week after the Hofbräuhaus encounter, Gesler moving the rented car carefully through Oberammergau and then on to Garmisch-Partenkirchen, thinking how beautiful it was. Another shrine, he thought, picking up the signpost to Berchtesgaden. He'd never been there, of course, when the Führer was in residence but he'd known others who had. It had been a fortress, certainly, but all the stories about excessive luxury were lies. Life had been simple there. A few close, sincere friends, the dogs he loved, home movies for their easy enjoyment. It would have been wonderful to have been an intimate part of it, reflected Gesler. To have known first hand what it was like.

It was late afternoon when Gesler arrived at the town and located the inn at which he had agreed to meet the others. Luntz and Becher were already there, and Schroeder arrived within twenty minutes. Gesler selected the alcove, overlooking the town and the twin-spired abbey. He was aware of how flushed Schroeder was when he joined them.

"They're all here," said Schroeder. "They're very excited."

So was Schroeder, realized Gesler. "How many?" he asked.

"Thirty," said Schroeder.

"Thirty!" It was Becher who spoke. "In Munich you said there were enough to confront force with force!"

"What they lack in numbers, they make up for in dedication and training," assured Schroeder. "I've seen them exercising. They're good."

"They'll need to be," said Becher, unconvinced.

Gesler felt a vague discomfort at keeping from the other three the correspondence from lang, enclosing the blackmail material and identifying Ivan Migal as a man who could be approached for help. It was not conscous deceit, he told himself. He'd only ever considered the Russian as an absolute last resort, practically a move of desperation to prevent what he wanted to avoid above all else: the need to run. If it became as bad as that, then of course he'd share the escape route with the others. It was his duty, and he'd always obeyed his duty. He looked steadily around the table, wondering what he owed these people after so many years of worrying and arranging their financial security. Wasn't it they who owed him?

"There might not be the need," reminded Luntz. "There's been nothing for some time."

"The moves against Reinhart and Schmidt weren't immediate after Lang's death," said Becher realistically.

They ate early, with traveling still to do the following day. The conversation was stilted and different. After the following day's demonstration, Becher and Luntz planned to go on to Kehlstein, actually to visit the Eagle's Nest, but Gesler declined the invitation to join them. The Hofbräuhuas had been an obscene travesty, a sideshow for ogling visitors. Kehlstein would be worse, he decided. It was better for it to remain as it did in his imagination, rather than for him to witness the mockery it had undoubtedly become.

They left at six the following morning, knowing from Schroeder that his son and companions had traveled ahead the previous night, to camp and to isolate a spot from which they were sure of being unobserved. Mist still shrouded Rossfeld-Höhenringstrasse toward Rossfeld Mountain, and very quickly after they left Berchtesgaden the snow became visible on the high reaches, pocketed at first in hollows and crannies, and then spreading out to form deeper and longer stretches.

The designated stopping point was three hundred kilometers beyond the toll station. When they approached, Gesler saw it was marked by a rest area, where the vehicles could be parked unobtrusively.

They fell into step behind Schroeder, setting out initially as if to climb the mountain more directly but then, fortunately, branching sideways, where the going was easier. Gesler aware of his age, felt his chest tighten from the altitude and the exertion. From their white-breathed panting and the unsteadiness with which they were scrambling ahead of him, Gesler knew the others were suffering as much as he was.

The first demonstration was impressive.

They were old men, physically unfit and already strained, but Gesler would have hoped one of them might have got some indication of the ambush. But there was none. One moment the group was struggling along the path, the next it was surrounded by a six-man squad who appeared simply to materialized from among the trees. They wore combat fatigues, and their webbing, helmets, and rifles seemed standard. Schroeder turned back from his lead position, smiling proudly.

The younger men formed into an escort party, taking them from the recognized track deep into the bordering pinewoods. It was obvious that, out of consideration, they marched more slowly than they would normally have done. It was fifteen minutes before they came to a clearing, and here again, although Gesler now expected it, he acknowledged the skill with which the others had concealed themselves. There was a hesitancy about the group that formed in front of them, an obvious admiration for men who had actually taken part in an era of which they were in awe.

"My son, Kurt," introduced Schroeder.

A tight-bodied, blond-haired man jerked stiffly forward and stood equally stiffly to attention. Gesler was unsure whether he was expected to salute or shake hands. He did neither, merely nodding his head in greeting. The man made an answering head movement and then stepped back among his men.

The command was sharp, so unexpected that Gesler was conscious of Luntz jumping in surprise beside him. The men split into two groups, wrapping designating war-game ribbons of red and blue around their arms, and then separating, moving easily into the woods on opposite sides of the clearing.

"Come," said Schroeder, a party to the maneuvers.

Gesler had imagined it an isolated clearing, but after twenty-five yards through the densely packed trees an even wider area ballooned out. Near a far corner was the skeletal, decayed frame of what once must have been a forester's hut. It was extremely quiet and peaceful, the only sound the occasional quiver call of a mountain bird.

Confirming Gesler's conviction that Schroeder had orchestrated the exhibition, the smooth-faced man suddenly put a whistle to his lips and sounded a shrill signal.

At once the apparently deserted hut became animated, the group who had donned the red armbands rising from places of concealment in and around it. As quickly as they had appeared, they vanished again, and Gesler realized it was the maneuver of which they were most proud: their ability to assimilate undetected into the countryside.

"Come," said Schroeder, leading the way farther up the incline on which they were standing to another construction. Gesler looked at it curiously and then realized it was something like a bird hide, a structure of logs half split and then made into a barrier behind which they could conceal themselves and observe the activities in the hollowed plain below them.

The attack was as sudden as everything else, and once again it was the nervous Luntz who quivered at the sudden explosion of noise. Gesler recognized that it was well staged, an apparent feint on two sides by minimal groups pouring in concentrated firepower while the real attack appeared to come from the third quarter. That proved to be the ultimate feint when the defenders turned to confront it and exposed their rear to the initial assault. Toward the end, when two stray bullets struck their barrier, Becher exclaimed, "Dear God, they're using real ammunition!"

The final assault was hand to hand, and again there was no holding back in their determination to impress the watchers on the hill. Gesler saw blood spurt from the shoulder of one man who failed to dodge a knife slash, and everywhere below him men gouged and writhed in hand-to-hand combat.

The war game continued for thirty minutes before Schroeder stepped from behind the hide and blew his whistle, signaling the end. The precision was gone from the men upon whom Gesler descended. They were either slumped, shoulders bowed, over the ground on which they had been fighting when Schroeder called a halt or actually collapsed onto it, panting to recover.

When he saw how close the old men were, Kurt Schroeder snapped an unheard command and the men regrouped, showing surprising recovery. As he stood before them, Gesler saw that the man he'd seen stabbed had staunched the blood flow with some sort of compressed dressing and that another man was cradling an obviously broken arm. Most of them appeared bruised or bleeding around the face, but surprisingly no one seemed to have been hit by the live ammunition.

Once more Kurt Schroeder put himself forward, appearing despite his fatigue even more rigid-backed than before. Gesler's awareness of what response was expected came suddenly. He thrust out his arm and said, *"Sieg heil!"*

Schroeder's son maintained his control, answering the salute with an echoing *"Sieg heil,"* but from the assembled men behind there was a discernible relaxation at the thought of approval. There was a moment of further hesitation, and then Gesler extended his hand and said, "Well done! Very well done!"

"Thank you, sir," said Kurt Schroeder.

He stepped back and shouted the dismissal. Around Gesler the younger group in the clearing began to disassemble.

"I told you they were good," said Schroeder proudly.

"They were magnificent," said Luntz.

"It's years since I've seen anything so impressive," said Becher in support.

Schroeder looked to Gesler, determined on a unanimous opinion.

"Very good," said Gesler. Games, he thought. Grown-up games, with real bullets and real knives and real blows, but just rehearsed games, men dividing into teams and designating themselves the attacked and the attackers by the color of the bands around their arms. In reality it wasn't like that. He didn't live in a forester's hut, where the clothes of his protectors would merge unseen into the trees. He lived in the middle of a city, where men really had to know how to hide and where the attackers, if they came, wouldn't wear colored armbands to identify themselves before they struck. Dear God, he thought, I hope I don't have to approach the Russians.

The line through the Mordavian prison complex from Potma up to Barashevo is not marked on any Soviet railway map because it serves only the labor camps and is entirely KGB-controlled. The camps follow the line, like some obscene frieze: camp then cemetery; cemetery, then camp. Gusadarov considered himself a commuter on the line and didn't crowd to the cattle-car slats like the rest of the prisoners, uninterested in the view. He stood sufficiently back from the door when the train halted to avoid the jostling and clubbing of the guards at their initial exit, inserting himself unobtrusively into the disembarkation line. The assembly was formalized and Gusadarov maneuvered himself well, remaining in the middle and best-hidden part of the group.

"Gusadarov!"

He stirred at the summons, frightened by it: he'd become accustomed to the protection of being considered a madman, someone to be avoided. He moved forward, head properly lowered but with his eyes straining up, trying to see the danger from the identifying group who faced him.

There were five men, two of them designated colonels. A guard alongside jerked out, clipping Gusadarov's chin so that his face was forced up to confront them. He was startled momentarily, then realized it was only for comparison with a photograph that one of the senior officers was holding.

"Yes," said one. "It's him."

"I think he should be medically examined," said the other colonel.

"Yes," said the first again.

11

Karpov gazed from the car windows at the huge fortress of the Kremlin and thought the red-glass stars topping the towers looked pitiful, a desperate attempt at gaiety in a land where nobody was gay. The vehicle skirted Red Square with its mechanically strutting soldiers, then passed the dutiful line wending its way into Lenin's tomb. At the corner of the Alexander Gardens, Karpov saw the first vodka stall, with its predictable knot of drunks trying to amass sufficient kopeks for the first communal drink of the day. Traffic congestion forced his car to halt a few yards away. They were staring around them sullenly, bundled in rags, unshaven and dirt-matted. An ordered existence of despair, thought Karpov: daytime around the vodka stalls and night in the sobering-up stations to which the collection vans took them to prevent their freezing to death in the subzero temperatures on the pavements. Poor bastards, he thought; poor, miserable bastards. Impulsively he wound down the window and tossed some rubles toward them. There was a moment of stilled surprise, and then they came forward as a mob, clutching and snatching at the money, fighting each other for it. They were still grappling, two prostrate and wrestling on the ground, when the jam cleared and his car moved forward again.

The car entered Ulitza Razina and Karpov wondered why the driver had come to the apartment by such a circuitous route. Maybe the man wanted to remind him of Russia's greatness.

The meeting and even the timing had been agreed, in the messages to and from Vienna, but Karpov was still surprised to find Irena waiting for him in the apartment. She'd laid a table in greeting. Vodka and some sort of red wine and some fish, he saw.

"Hello," said Karpov. He was unused to embarrassment but supposed that was the feeling. She wore a dress that appeared new and her hair was rigidly in place, as if she were trying to impress him. Illogically, he found himself comparing her to Rebecca. Irena looked shabby and gauche, he thought. But then Rebecca had acquired money and sophistication after so long in Vienna. Karpov was surprised at his thinking of her, in such circumstances.

"Thank you for coming," she said. "I wouldn't have asked for a meeting if I hadn't considered it important."

"I know," he said. He felt very sorry for her.

She realized he was still wearing a coat and hurried forward to take it from him. It occurred to neither of them to embrace. Carefully she put the coat on the hanger and hung it behind the door through which he'd entered.

"I've prepared some food," said Irena, seeming to share his embarrassment. "I thought you'd be hungry after the trip."

Karpov wasn't, but he said, "Thank you. That would be very nice."

He put the minimum amount of fish on his plate and nodded to the vodka, unwilling to trust the wine: he thought Russian wine was like cats' piss. She poured a drink for herself and Karpov frowned. Surely she didn't drink? But then how did he know, after so long? Karpov decided he knew the reason she wasn't already exacerbating a row and decided to help her. He hadn't helped much in the past.

"I wouldn't have asked to see you if it wasn't important," she repeated. She seemed to have difficulty looking at him.

"It wasn't a problem," assured Karpov. He was still surprised at Migal's easy agreement.

"I've always been very careful about your job. I know how much it means to you."

He had been overwhelmingly ambitious, to the detriment of everything else, conceded Karpov. "I've always been grateful," he said, trying to find a way to make it easier. Her glass was already half empty.

"You've been away fifteen years now," she said. "Almost sixteen. I don't suppose we've spent a total of more than four or five months together in all that time."

"I know it hasn't been a good life for you," said Karpov. "I'm sorry."

"It isn't a proper marriage, is it?" she said. "Not a proper marriage at all."

"No," he admitted.

"I've stood it for a long time, thinking what you did was important . . . that it was right for me to come second."

"Do you love him very much?" asked Karpov.

Her head jerked up and Karpov saw she was blushing. She'd always blushed, from the time he'd first known her as a girl of eighteen. Which was a long time ago. He felt a great fondness toward the woman. Not love—he didn't think he'd ever felt that, because he wasn't sure he knew what it was—but an affection, the sort of feeling of one good friend for another, a friend he would always try to help. It was unfortunate there had been so much animosity toward the end.

"He's a doctor, at the hospital," said Irena. "And, yes, I think I love him very much. Very much indeed."

"The divorce will be very easy," promised Karpov. "I can arrange it, even quicker than it's normally possible."

Irena's face twitched and for a moment Karpov thought she was going to cry. She covered the difficulty by pouring herself another drink. "I didn't think it was going to be like this at all," she said, her voice thick. "I didn't know what to expect, but I didn't think it was going to be like this, after so much arguing. Thank you."

"Is he married?"

She shook her head. "We're going to try for children. I'd like a baby, very much."

Karpov looked around the apartment, and she saw the look.

"It won't matter," she said. "I know I'll lose this. But he's a consultant; he's got a nonsharing apartment. It's not quite as nice as here, but it's adequate."

Poor darling, thought Karpov. "That's good," he said.

Irene stood abruptly and came to him, kissing him first on the cheek and then fully, on the lips. "I do love you," she said. She made a waving motion with her hands, as if she were irritated at herself. "Not *love*, not like that," she went on. "The friendly sort of love. I'm sorry we rowed so much. It was my guilt, I suppose. My fault."

"I love you too," said Karpov. He was glad they were going to be friends after all. That was what he'd really wanted, he thought.

"I don't suppose it would be right to invite you to the wedding?"

"I might not be able to get back."

"Thank you again for making it so easy."

"I hope you'll be very happy," said Karpov.

"I know I will be. He's a fine man, with a job and a home."

Karpov looked at his watch, remembering the appointment with Migal. "I have to go," he said.

She stood, helping him into his coat. "Will I see you again?"

"I'll probably apply for the divorce by proxy," said Karpov.

"Take care, then."

"I will."

"Do you know something I've never properly realized until now?"

"What?"

"What a good man you are."

Only the chairman and his immediate subordinates are allowed to enter the KGB headquarters through the main entrance, dominated by the bas-relief of Karl Marx. Karpov entered the building through a side door, away from the main square, standing patiently while his identification and appointment were confirmed. He wondered if the drunks back at the vodka stall would already be anesthetized. Karpov accepted his timed-entry permission and fixed the badge into his lapel, setting off easily behind the guide showing him to Migal's office, the route to which he already knew.

The head of the European Division was standing at the window of his office, looking out over Dzerzhinsky Square, when Karpov entered. Pale though it was, Karpov saw that the spring sunshine marked perfectly the outline of the building. They went through greetings as formalized as the downstairs entry, and then Karpov seated himself comfortably across the desk from the other man, wondering if this encounter was going to be as pointless as so many that had preceded it. He preferred the usual, distanced briefings.

"I hope you've solved whatever the personal problem was," said Migal referring to the compassionate application Karpov had filed to return to Moscow. Because such information was important, he knew about the woman's affair with the doctor.

"Irena and I are getting a divorce," said Karpov. It was something he would have had to report officially anyway.

"I'm sorry," said Migal automatically.

"It was inevitable, in the circumstances. I'm surprised she has been as patient as she has."

"You're a loyal officer," praised Migal. "Very loyal." At the point of commitment, he was still reluctant.

"Thank you," said Karpov.

"Perhaps for too long unrecognized."

Karpov became curious. "I try to do my duty," he said.

It sounded facile, but he couldn't think of anything else.

"I am shortly due for promotion," announced Migal. He was over the edge, he realized. There was no going back now.

"My congratulations," said Karpov. He wondered if the new section head would be better or worse. He hoped it was someone with operational experience, who understood some of the difficulties. Sometimes Migal had been over-demanding in his ignorance.

"Initially it will be a directorate," continued the older man. "But I do not intend it to stop there."

What was the point of this? wondered Karpov, his curiosity increasing. "I wish you every success," he said. That wasn't any better than the remark about duty, but it was the best he could manage until he figured out the point the other man was trying to make.

Abruptly, Migal changed the conversation. He said, "I've a job for Hartman."

I could have been told through normal channels, thought Karpov. But the compassionate return to Moscow made the personal briefing understandable. "What?" he asked. Hugo couldn't complain; he'd had a long rest.

"I want to expose some Nazis," declared Migal. He had intended it to sound like a normal announcement, but it came out too hurriedly.

Karpov stared in surprise at the man across the desk. "What for?" he asked.

Migal hesitated at the final admission, hands gripped tightly together beneath the desk, so Karpov couldn't see his emotion. "To prevent an embarrassment to this service," he said. "A service to which we are both dedicated."

"I don't understand."

Migal still tried to avoid a direct explanation, talking instead of Stalin's prisoner-repatriation scheme and of Beria's intentions to use it to his own advantage but how, in the event, no disclosure was made.

"I still don't see the connection between what happened all that time ago and now," persisted Karpov.

Migal swallowed heavily. Then he said awkwardly, "Some members of the service were forced to take part in that repatriation and imprisonment program, against loyal Soviet soldiers. . . ." He groped to a halt and then added, "Members still in the service."

Karpov sat back, beginning to comprehend. "Which members?" he asked.

"I had no choice," blurted Migal, in final admission.

But *he* did, Karpov realized. And it was one he had to make immediately, because if he let this discussion continue, then he was implicated by association. Which meant he had to make a move now—today. But how? He didn't even know his way around this labyrinthine building. He didn't know Migal's immediate superior in the directorate or how to gain unhindered entry into his office. And it would have to be unhindered. Migal might not have any operational experience, but he'd survived the intrigue of Dzerzhinsky Square longer than anyone Karpov knew. Migal would learn within an hour what he was trying to do. This place was Migal's jungle, not his.

"And afterward, one sort of blackmail became another," continued Migal, as if he were recounting a memory.

"Who?"

"Lang," said Migal. Now that the dam had been breached, Migal felt something approaching relief in confession, able after so many years to talk about it. The square outside had grown dark by the time Migal had finished.

"I still don't think Hugo was involved," said Karpov, referring to the link with Reinhart. "I still think it was a coincidence. Bizarre, perhaps. But a coincidence."

"Maybe," said Migal. "Maybe not." He began to

relax. He'd expected suspicion, even hostility from Karpov. Instead of which the man was remaining utterly professional, interested only in the operation.

"If Hugo *were* doubling," conceded Karpov. "Then he'd make immediate contact with Washington, the moment he's given the assignment."

"Yes," said Migal. "Which is where the woman becomes important. Brief her thoroughly. Indicate her husband might get his freedom if she proves it's true."

"Will he?" said Karpov. It would be good to bring Rebecca some happiness; she'd worked hard for a long time. She must love her husband very much.

Migal shrugged. "That's a decision to be reached at the time," he evaded.

"What happens if I'm right—that he's loyal?"

"The most current information is on three Nazis in Frankfurt. Get the confirmation of their existence from Hartman, and then we'll see if we can do what the Americans were trying to: make someone come out of the woodwork."

"All right," accepted Karpov.

"Do we have assets in Germany, who would warn us if the Americans became interested?"

"Maybe," said Karpov. Erich Dollfuss was his agent, not one controlled through Moscow. Until he'd had time properly to assimilate all that had happened that afternoon, Karpov decided to keep him that way.

Having apparently shown weakness in confession, Migal decided he had to indicate his strength. The older Russian said, "I control every means of communication between you and Moscow."

"Yes," accepted Karpov, recognizing the threat.

"You could, of course, break cover and report to any overseas embassy."

Karpov said nothing.

"Does your wife want to marry her doctor?"

"That's her hope," said Karpov. How long had Irena been spied upon, he wondered.

"It would be nice for her to be happy."

"Yes."

"Both with my promotion to a directorship and with what follows, I'll need a deputy," said Migal, changing direction and presenting the reward. "A man whom I know I can thrust . . . upon whose loyalty I can rely."

"Here in Moscow?" queried Karpov.

"In Moscow," confirmed Migal. He made a cornucopia with his hand. "Where all the power is, at the very center of things. One of the elite. An apartment of your choice, a dacha in the hills and at Sochi or whatever other resort you choose. Anything you want."

Karpov had always supposed that he would have to return from the West one day. This would certainly be the fitting echelon at which to do it.

Because the Klaus Reinhart file had been properly assigned to him, Berman needed no superior authorization to get the other Nazi records from the CIA retrieval system. The Agency is run on a 'need-to-know' basis, requests going to specialized departments without any explanation for requiring the information and almost always without reference to names. There was no surprise, therefore, when Berman sent the unidentified dental debris from the New York explosion together with the unidentified dental records of Klaus Reinhart from the CIA archives to the Medical and Technical Division for comparison.

It was an easy job for a dental surgeon. The report was returned to Berman in one day. They didn't match, judged the expert.

12

Hartman sat at the table in Karpov's apartment, staring down at the photographs and waiting for the sensation, the chilling fear that always gripped him at the reminder. And felt nothing. There was nothing frightening in these fading, torn-edged pictures of stern-faced men, stiff and proud in their uniforms. Rather, they appeared almost comical, as if they were dressed for some part in a performance or charade. Old men, Hartman thought; old, weary, tired men. Like him. Was that why there wasn't the fear? Or had he lost it, after so long? Perhaps it was because he didn't personally know any of them, hadn't suffered at their hands. Thousands had, though; millions maybe. He couldn't hate them by proxy, any more than he could feel frightened of them.

Karpov emerged from the kitchen, caviar dish held delicately in his huge hands like some precious object. The bread and aquavit were already there.

"Brought this back with my own fair hands," said Karpov, setting the dish carefully on the table. He nodded toward the files. "Arrogant lot of bastards, weren't they?"

"Arrogant?"

"Staying in Germany, after what they did."

"Yes," remembered Hartman. "They were always arrogant."

Karpov put a record onto his elaborate stereo equipment, operating the arm that lowered the needle with the delicacy with which he'd brought in the beluga. He straightened from the machine but remained by it, waiting for the first chords. "Brubeck," he said to Hartman. "Isn't he marvelous?"

"I don't understand the music," apologized the Austrian.

"Don't know what you're missing," said Karpov, returning to the table. He gestured, inviting Hartman to eat, and said, "Pretty comprehensive files, eh?"

"Very good," admitted Hartman, remembering the thin envelopes and narrow-ruled exercise books with which they had tried to work at the bureau immediately after the Holocaust. The three dossiers before him were each at least an inch thick, sightings and tracings carefully annotated and recorded in chronological order.

"Just those who stayed in Germany?" queried Hartman, anxious not to misunderstand the instructions.

"Just Germany," agreed Karpov. "It's only Germany and the NATO alliance we want to upset."

"Who's my Control?" said Hartman. "Which embassy?"

Karpov spooned caviar onto his bread, then sucked it noisily into his mouth, swilling back some aquavit before he'd emptied his mouth. "No embassy," he said. "This time you'll work through me."

Hartman frowned. "That hasn't happened before."

"An operation hasn't been this close to home before."

"I would have still expected a cutout."

"That's the way Moscow wants it," said Karpov. Poor, manipulated bastard, he thought. Even if Hugo were a double, which he didn't think he was, Karpov still liked the man. Perhaps he was getting too soft for the job, thought Karpov.

Was Karpov as ebullient as always? wondered Hartman. Certainly he appeared so, with the familiar ritual of caviar and aquavit, but today Hartman had the impression that the attitude was forced. He said, "I just identify them to you? Then someone else takes over?"

The Russian nodded, a globule of caviar wobbling on his chin. "Just pinpoint them, Hugo, just like New York."

Hartman helped himself for the first time to the food

and spoke looking down at his plate. "Why?"

Karpov smiled at the question. Hartman was damned good. He said, "Europe is becoming too unified. There's a need to raise old specters . . . open old wounds. It might have happened a long time ago, but there's nothing like the reminder of Nazism and how a lot of them still remain in positions of power in Germany to bring all the fears back."

Hartman gestured toward the dossiers. "Have you looked at them?" he asked.

"Of course," said Karpov. He brought a napkin to his mouth but missed the debris on his chin. The caviar shivered precariously.

"Don't you think they look comical?"

Karpov snorted at the suggestion. "Comical! They're fucking killers, all of them!"

"I think they look absurd," said Hartman. "Comical and absurd."

"They won't look absurd in a courtroom," insisted the Russian.

"Courtroom?" asked Hartman uncertainly. "Hasn't the German statute of limitations run out?"

Karpov smiled, glad he had maneuvered the conversation away from Hartman's suspicions. "In Germany, maybe," he said. "But not in Israel. That's what we intend doing, leaking the information to the Israelis once we've positively established their identities."

Hartman stared across the table at the other man. "Another Eichmann trial?"

"Just that," said Karpov. "But much more besides." He sat back expansively, hands linked over his ample stomach. "By exposing the Nazis, we create discord in Europe. By bringing in the Israelis, we ensure they've got to make some move. And by making that move and staging show trials, we prove thoughout the Middle East, where we're trying to increase our influence, and the world beyond that the Jews are a vindictive race who can't forget.'' Karpov smiled at the other man. ''Brilliant conception, isn't it?'' he said. It really sounded like a good political polemic, thought Karpov, satisfied.

''I suppose so,'' said Hartman. He'd spent his life in cesspools, he decided suddenly; a series of cesspools, one after another.

Karpov raised his glass toward the other man. ''To a great operation, Hugo,'' he toasted.

Hartman didn't respond. ''Sixty thousand,'' he said. ''Dollars.''

Karpov laughed. ''Always professional, Hugo,'' he said.

''I try to be,'' he said. There was always a satisfaction in making them pay.

''Sixty thousand it is,'' agreed the Russian.

At last Hartman replied to the toast. ''To a great operation,'' he said.

FBI liaison was regarded as the final backwater, the route to the retirement party and the insincere speeches and ''For He's a Jolly Good Fellow'' sung out of tune by men who think the man getting the clock and maybe the Agency medal is a prick to have allowed himself to be shuffled there anyway. Henry Willard was just ten months away from such a moment, already with the farm at Leesburg and the hint that he was going to get the Distinguished Service Award.

''So it isn't Klaus Reinhart,'' he said, putting aside Berman's report and the accompanying photographs and records.

''Definitely not,'' said Berman.

''It's FBI business,'' said Willard. ''Not ours. Throw it back to them.''

''Reinhart was at the same camp as Lang,'' said Berman. ''It's in the report.''

"I've read it," said Willard tightly.

"Lang was our operation."

"Which went wrong," said Willard accusingly. "That wasn't in the report, but I checked."

"That wasn't my fault."

"The inquiry board decided otherwise."

"Lang was important," said Berman, controlling his desperation. "We can't tell the FBI of the link between him and Reinhart. As far as they're concerned, it's a closed case. The police in New York are all getting commendations. If I throw it back, nothing will happen."

It was a bastard, decided Willard; either way he could lose out. "You're an analyst now," he said. "You're not operational any more."

"No one else knows the Lang file like me. Or Reinhart's, now."

"It couldn't be my decision," said Willard, seeing the way out. "I'd have to make a recommendation."

"That's all I'm asking," said Berman. "Just a chance."

Berman was an awkward bastard, a man with a grievance, decided Willard. And he couldn't afford awkward bastards. "I'll see what I can do to get you a transfer," he promised.

Erich Dollfuss physically conceded his homosexuality during his second year at the university, conducting an undiscovered and unsuspected affair with a classmate until their graduation. He had never, however, been able to lose the shame. The hurried marriage within two years, to prove that he was normally heterosexual, proved instead his incompatability with the wife he chose. He tried to control what his upbringing convinced him was an abnormality, only occasionally succumbing to the temptation and then always using the clubs that existed, so that he would not become encumbered with any difficult, lasting relationship.

The Russians, like every other intelligence service, regard sex as a classical entrapment device. In places such as divided Germany, which they consider important, they monitor the sex parlors and brothels, and frequently have the unsuspecting prostitutes, both male and female, on the payroll.

Dollfuss was caught by Karpov in a house he used specifically for its discretion, in Bonn's Am Hofgarten.

Dollfuss was physically sick when he saw the photographs, and for several days considered suicide and then realized he was not brave enough.

The first betrayal of documents he was called upon to provide was simple, as it always is, because for the victim the first time is always the most difficult, and it is necessary to build up confidence. Photographs were taken again, of course, making Dollfuss further dependent upon them. It took almost two years for his attitude to change from one of fear to one practically of enjoyment. The demands were never excessive, but the payment was always generous, enabling him to have a car more expensive than he could have afforded on his pay from the West German Federal Intelligence Service. It provided, too, for increasingly frequent visits to more luxurious establishments, where he could relax in the way that he properly enjoyed.

Of course, there was always the slight bubble of apprehension whenever he received a direct request. But it was only momentary when he decoded Karpov's demand for any information about unusual American activities in the country. It was an easy assignment with which to comply, as they usually were.

13

From the master files Hartman created smaller fact sheets, containing only the essential information he might require when he reached Frankfurt. He arrived on the afternoon flight and took a medium-priced room in the medium-priced Ketterer Hotel, the unobtrusiveness an automatic reaction.

Inside the room he carefully locked and tested the door, and then removed the notes he had made before leaving Vienna. In the order in which the Russians wanted them traced, the list was Major Hans Leitner, Lieutenant Otto Schroeder and Major Rudolph Diels. All SS—Leitner with an operational unit, Schroeder prison transportation, and Diels administration.

According to the Soviet documentation, Leitner had adopted the name Baur and until two years earlier ran a resturant at the corner of the Bahnhofplatz, called the Ress. Always do the most obvious, thought Hartman, remembering a lesson learned early. There was a telephone directory in the room, and within minutes Hartman had located a number for the Ress. He carefully noted it, and then moved on through the directory, taking longer to find the number of the association of restaurateurs and innkeepers, and the name of their trade journal.

Hartman left the hotel to continue the checks, wanting no traceable connection to himself through telephone calls. He changed money into coins at a bank two blocks up the Marienstrasse and from a phone booth telephoned the restaurant association. It took the minimum of explanation to gain access to the secretary. His name was Katz, Hartman lied. He ran a German restaurant on New York's Third Avenue and two years earlier had made the acquaintance of Hans Baur at a convention in America and promised to look him up if he ever visited Frankfurt. But unfortunately he'd lost the address of Baur's restaurant. The secretary was delighted to help. There was the rustle of a records book and back to Hartman came the name and number of the restaurant he already had.

Hartman emerged from the booth, sighing. If it were all as simple as this, it was going to be the easiest job he'd ever undertaken; the Russians were ridiculous sometimes, in their precautions. One of their own people could as easily have made the same basic checks without any possibility of discovery.

He walked to the journal office, knowing it was only two streets away, explaining this time that he was trying to locate a photograph of himself taken during the annual dinner of the Frankfurt restaurateurs. He was left alone in their archives and within an hour had located two sets of photographs, one of which named a man as Hans Baur in the caption. It took only another fifteen minutes for him to buy prints of the photographs. Before seven, he was back at the Ketterer.

The only part of the original Soviet files that Hartman had brought with him were the photographs. He polished his eyeglasses and then used a magnifying glass to compare the wartime personnel file picture of Major Hans Leitner with that of a man called Hans Baur, sitting back expansively with a cigar in his hand at a social function just four months earlier. There had been no attempt at plastic surgery. Leitner's face had lost the tightness of youth, but it was unquestionably the same—fatter, slump-jowled, but the same.

Hartman clipped the matching photographs together and replaced them in the folder, smiling contentedly at the day's work. He took a diabetic pill and considered telephoning Rebecca, actually looking toward the telephone before changing his mind. He would have to place the call through the hotel switchboard, which would mean a record, a link to him in Vienna. Hartman accepted he was probably being overcautious but overcaution had kept him alive for many years. And he wanted to go on living.

He walked two blocks from the hotel before picking up a taxi and dismissed that three streets away from the Bahnhofplatz. He worked out the location of the Ress from the street number and entered the road from the farthest end, so there would be a long approach toward it. The Reichsbahn was an unexpected advantage. He entered the hotel and found the bar which overlooked that part of the street in which the Ress was located. He took a schnapps and sat for thirty minutes, watching the restaurant run by the former Nazi. It appeared an old, well-established place, fronted with heavy wood, a lot of vine entangled with the facade. Alert to everything, Hartman decided it was exclusive and expensive. There was a doorman to park the cars, predominantly Mercedes or BMW's. The women were cocktail-dressed, the men lounge-suited, with no open-necked, blue-jean casualness.

Hartman paid and crossed the Bahnhofplatz, moving automatically into the shadows of the bordering building. The Ress was exactly the sort of restaurant that Hartman had guessed it would be. Beyond the chandeliered foyer there was a subdued cocktail bar, raised higher than the main floor of the restaurant. Examining it more closely, Hartman saw that above the main area was a half-balcony. Somehow the vines had been continued into the building to festoon the trellis of the protecting rail. At the far end, a string quartet in evening dress played quietly: Strauss, Hartman thought, although he wasn't sure from so far away. He apologized for not having made a reservation and the headwaiter apologized back, asking if he would mind waiting in the cocktail area. Hartman said not at all: the point of the visit was to spend as long as possible, to identify Hans Leitner.

Hartman ordered another schnapps, and accepted the

menu and the wine list, making the pretense of studying them while looking instead around the restaurant. It was extensively staffed, with captains as well as waiters, but no one resembled the man whose picture he had studied an hour earlier.

His table came after thirty minutes and, aware of the two schnapps he had already drunk, Hartman took only a half-bottle of wine with the meal. In the better light, Hartman suddenly realized that there were hardly any young people in the place; the clientele was all predominantly middle-aged or older. He recognized the Ress for what it was: a meeting spot for those with memories, somewhere in which they could feel comfortable with the past. How many of these expensively suited men would rather be wearing a uniform? he wondered.

He ate slowly, prolonging his stay as long as possible, taking a desert he didn't want and then coffee, which he didn't need either. Hartman concluded that Hans Leitner, now Hans Baur, was not in the restaurant. He had isolated each member of the staff, even someone who appeared to be the manager and who was not wearing evening dress, and none resembled the man for whom he was looking. After the uninterrupted successes of the day, Hartman felt disappointed. He'd hoped to establish the identity positively in a single day. He pushed aside the thought as illogical. He'd done surprisingly well, and it was ridiculous to consider this a setback.

As he paid, Hartman became aware of the headwaiter and the lounge-suited manager entering and leaving a room off the foyer, marked private. Could Leitner be a restaurateur who didn't mix with his customers? Unlikely, thought Hartman, emerging on to the Bahnhofplatz and shaking his head against the doorman's offer of a taxi. Unlikely, but something that had to be checked if possible.

He used a public telephone booth again, feeling a

security in its anonymous protection. He identified himself to the person who answered at the Ress as a wine salesman with a ten o'clock appointment the following day with Herr Baur, checking to see if the meeting was still convenient. There was a hesitation at the other end, and then a different voice came onto the telephone.

"Who is this, please?"

Hartman recognized the voice of the headwaiter who had apologized for making him wait.

"Herr Rieber," said Hartman. "I have a meeting with Herr Baur, to discuss some wine."

"I purchase the wine," said the man.

Damn, thought Hartman. "The arrangement was made with my head office in Cologne," he said. "I don't know any of the details. I was just asked to come down and give the tasting."

"I can see you at ten o'clock," said the headwaiter.

"I'm specifically supposed to be seeing Herr Baur," insisted Hartman.

"Herr Baur isn't available."

"I'm in Hesse for several days," said Hartman. "We could rearrange the meeting."

"Herr Baur isn't going to be available for several days."

"I really don't know what to do," said Hartman, feigning confusion. "I'd better check back with Cologne. Thank you."

"Who are . . ." began the man, but Hartman replaced the receiver before the question was completed. It had been professionally automatic to attempt an absolute identification, but unnecessary: he had enough. It was time to move on. Otto Schroeder was next on the list.

The headwaiter replaced the telephone, hesitated for a moment, and then crossed the main body of the restaurant and climbed the balcony stairway. At the top, completely concealed by the elaborate interior decoration, sat a young man who had occupied the table throughout the evening. Kurt Schroeder had eaten only cold meats, mostly ham, and drunk mineral water. He was a lean, exercise-fit young man, the jacket of whose immaculate suit had back pleats and a half-belt, giving it the suggestion of a uniform. The bruise he'd received during the demonstration exercise was fading.

He listened without interruption while the waiter recounted the telephone call, asked questions more for confirmation than for further information, and then followed the man back down the stairs, across the restaurant, and into the office.

"It could be nothing," said Otto Schroeder, when his son telephoned.

"I thought you should know," said the younger man.

"Of course. The name was Rieber?"

"From a wine firm in Cologne. The man here asked for the name of the company, but the phone was hung up."

"It's easily checked," said Otto Schroeder.

"My people are watchng your house," said his son.

"I know."

"I just wanted to reassure you: you're quite safe."

"I know I am," said the old man.

Scurvy is the most endemic of all the diseases in the camps. The traditional treatment is to make the prisoners brew a potion of pine needles and the leaves of the dwarf willow, to provide the deficient vitamin C. Those unable to avoid drinking it or spitting it out usually vomit from their stomachs what little food had been provided that day.

Two days after his admission to Potma, Gusadarov was summoned early from his barracks by the guard captain and a soldier, given a fresh lemon, and told to eat it. He stared down at the fruit, at first unable to recognize it, then, knowing he had to obey, bit into it, wincing at the sharpness. He consumed it, peel and all, staring warily at the men who had given it to him. They knew from his record that he wasn't a toady: trustee material. Or an informant. Or homosexual. So what did they want? Someone killed? But they didn't need surrogate killers.

"From now on, you're to have one lemon a day," said the guard captain. "And you're to eat separately." He nodded toward a room at the rear of the storage hut into which they'd brought Gusadarov, then smiled, knowing from the special treatment that the man was someone to be treated differently from now on. Disgraced men could rise again, and it was wise to take out insurance. "It'll be good food," said the officer encouragingly. "Our rations."

"Why?" asked Gusadarov.

"Orders," said the man.

"From whom?"

The man shrugged. "Orders," he repeated. "Tomorrow you're to see a doctor." There was another smile. "A proper doctor," he said. "One with a degree."

The acid of the lemon made him feel sick, but Gusadarov swallowed against the nausea. He didn't know what was happening and didn't care: survival had always meant that he snatched and grabbed at anything, and he was going to seize and keep hold of this for as long as he was able.

"Thank you," he said, remembering the regulation governing gratitude.

•

14

Hartman made the initial journey quickly, wanting only to orientate himself, driving from the modern, rebuilt part of the city and crossing the Main River by the Flosser Bridge and then easing through the gradually narrowing streets until he got to the old quarter, in Sachsenhausen, where the Soviet information said Otto Schroeder lived. He found Kolb Strasse easily, driving past the spacious house for which he was looking and continuing on down until he came to a loop in the river. He parked on the Schaumainkai, went into a café, and took his coffee at a window seat, looking out at the barges and boats hurrying up and down the waterway. Would any belong to Schroeder? The Russian file had described the man as a senior but still working partner in an import-export business. Probably too slow, decided the Austrian. Frankfurt had been reconstructed since its wartime destruction as a monument to modern commercialism, and that decreed air links and rail links and road links.

Hartman was retracing his route within half an hour, wanting a space in the designated parking area before commuting workers took them all. He slowed at one, then rejected it, isolating a place farther back and on the opposite side of the road from Schroeder's house. He was still within range for the photograph he wanted, but with less likelihood of his observation being noticed.

He parked the inconspicuous Volkswagen aong the other inconspicuous Volkswagens and slumped down in his seat, considering and then deciding against the protection of the newspapers he had brought from the hotel. Maybe later, but unnecessary at the moment.

From his vehicle Hartman gazed out at Schroeder's house, deciding that it was a survivor of the wartime bombing, an original nineteenth-century building—the sort of solid, imposing place that the original burghers had built to prove their importance and which were still occupied for the same reason. There was a high wall, in the center of which were imposing double gates. From what he could see beyond, the building must run to four or maybe five stories. There were a lot of trees, so Hartman guessed the grounds must be extensive.

The camera, with its telephoto lens, was concealed beneath the newspaper. Hartman checked that the pavement was clear, front and rear, moved the paper aside, and took it up. He focused on the gates, adjusted the range, and put it out of sight again.

How long had it been since he'd sat in another rented car like this in another part of the world, watching the building housing another old Nazi? Only months, he realized; so much seemed to have happened since. Maybe he needed a rest. The idea caught him and he smiled at it. Why not? He'd rationalized their refusal to let him retire; he knew that it was unthinkable now, because it would mean losing Rebecca. But they could take a holiday together. A really long vacation—a month or even longer, if they felt like it. The South of France perhaps. A villa in the hills, away from the coastline and its frenetic tourists. Or somewhere else, if Rebecca wanted. Hartman was excited by the idea. He recognized that the attraction lay in its simple normality. Normal people planned holidays, collected brochures, and discussed the advantages of one resort against another. and so could they. Briefly he and Rebecca could fantasize that they were normal people.

Hartman stirred at a movement down the road, relaxing at the arrival of the mailman. Customarily cautious, Hartman checked the road again and pulled the camera up to confirm his focusing. The image was sharp and perfect. Hartman laid the camera aside and looked at his watch. Eight forty-five. There was no indication from the Russian information of Schroeder's departure time. Perhaps he didn't go to his office regularly. The man could be a working partner on a part-time basis. Hartman frowned at the doubt. He was unwilling to maintain observation as open as this for an entire day. He stared down the road, seeking an inn or a hotel from which he could mount a secondary surveillance, and saw only the entrances to other houses; the restaurants and cafés were all farther down, among the shops on Schweitzer Strasse. He sat back, trying to curb the uncertainty: difficulties had to be confronted when they arose, not before.

One uncertainty fed another. Identifying Leitner had been too easy, he thought again; a simple, mechanical operation. But wasn't that what he'd asked for and been promised by Karpov—simple, safe jobs? So Karpov, his friend, was keeping his promise. Hartman's mind stayed on Karpov. *Had* his ebullience during the briefing been forced? Hartman snorted at his doubts. He'd always found it too easy to create monsters from shadows. He stared down the winding street, and then swiveled to look directly behind and not through the rear-view mirror. The only shadows were being created by the pale morning sun, but Hartman couldn't lose the feeling that somewhere there was a monster.

He was so engrossed in his reflections that, when it happened, it almost caught him by surprise. He hadn't anticipated that the chauffeured car would come from somewhere other than the house itself. Initially he was only vaguely aware of the limousine that passed him. Then the brake lights flared and he saw it was drawing up outside the Schroeder house. It was obviously a carefully timed arrival. As the vehicle halted, the gates were opening to emit the old man.

Hartman had the camera up, the image magnified, recognizing at once from the smoothness of the fact that there had been plastic surgery. He was a tall man, erect and thin, and he moved with aloofness, an attitude of command. Hartman managed two exposures before the chauffeur opened the rear doors and stood back for the man to enter. Instead of doing so immediately, the man looked across at the line of parked cars. Hartman jerked the camera down and lowered himself in the seat, frightened of detection.

Then he realized the attention wasn't upon him. The car they were looking at pulled out from the line of parked vehicles about ten spaces in front of him, sluing across the road to bring itself behind the limousine. Hartman took two more shots, almost automatically, then watched, frowning. Another young man got out of the second car, speaking across its hood to the group outside Schroeder's house. After a few moments they got into their respective vehicles and moved off in convoy, toward the query where Hartman had drunk his coffee.

Hartman had intended to follow, but now he didn't. Instead he remained in the car, head forward, thinking about what had happened. Even though he still needed proof, Hartman had little doubt that the shiny-faced man was Otto Schroeder, a wanted Nazi. But it was inconceivable that for more than three decades the man had been so terrified of detection that he'd surrounded himself with such protection. Hartman, the professional, paused at the word. And if he had been that frightened, then the protection would have been good. What Hartman had just witnessed was amateur, youngsters with pulled-in stomachs and tight shirts, posing the part. A professional group could have immobilized them before they realized what was happening and done whatever they liked to the man they were supposed to be protecting.

It had to be what had happened to Lang and the New York explosion. They'd been panicked by them, imagining some sort of concentrated operation. With that conclusion came several other thoughts. It was fortunate that

Schroeder's bodyguards weren't been professional; had they been, then he wouldn't have remained undetected. So where was his professionalism? Why hadn't he isolated them? The parking area had filled around him, with the beginning of the working day, but apart from the cars immediately adjacent to his, he hadn't checked each one to ensure that its occupants emerged. Careless, thought Hartman critically, very careless. *The* fault from which he couldn't afford to suffer.

He started the Volkswagen at last, moving out and driving back toward the river loop. There was no pause as he passed Schroeder's office, with the limousine and the second car positioned outside. Hartman was recrossing the Main River when another awareness came. Instinctively he braked, causing a blare of protest from the car behind, before reaccelerating back into the traffic stream.

Dear God, where was his reasoning! Because he'd been so close, so intimately involved, he'd automatically assumed that the clumsy protection he'd just witnessed was connected with Lang and Reinhart. Which maybe it was. But Lang had been a CIA operation. What he was now involved in had been initiated by the Russians.

Hartman felt a clutch of apprehension deep in his stomach. Peter Berman had sat dazed and deafened and bewildered in the CIA office of the American Embassy in Paris, unable to understand by whom or why Lang had been killed. And now Moscow had deputed him to trace Nazis on whom they appeared to have files so extensive that his involvement was practically unnecessary—Nazis who had hurried around them amateur bodyguards within months of Lang's being identified as the victim of the Zurich explosion.

The lines were being crossed for the first time in his operational life. Sometimes people strangled in crossed lines.

Karpov handed Rebecca the monthly letter that was always routed through him from her husband and said, "I'm sorry it's later than usual."

"There's nothing wrong?"

Karpov shook his head in reassurance, marveling yet again at her love for a man she hadn't seen in fifteen years. She really was a remarkably attractive woman. "He's been moved," he said. "To Potma. It'll be better there."

"I'm glad," said the woman. She sat before Karpov apprehensively, knees tight together, hands nervously in her lap. "He went there first, to Potma," she remembered.

Karpov was aware of her nervousness and saddened by it. He didn't want her to be afraid of him; he wanted her to regard him as a friend, as Hugo did. "I know," he said. He went on: "When I was in Moscow, there was some discussion about your husband. Things are being made better for him."

Rebecca looked at him curiously, the unopened letter moving between her fingers. "How much better?"

"Potma, instead of the Arctic Circle, to start with."

She was immediately aware of the qualification. "Is there a chance of his being released?"

Karpov hesitated, recalling how Migal had avoided an answer to the same question. "It could happen," he said.

Rebecca looked down to the letter her husband had written. Of all the possibilities, she had never considered a release. Which she recognized as absurd. Dear God, she thought, what would happen if he were freed? "That would be wonderful," she said.

Karpov decided her lack of reaction was understandable. The excitement would come later. He wanted to feel out for her hand in reassurance, but didn't. She might misunderstand.

"Have you heard from Hugo?" he asked.

She looked up. "I thought he was working directly through you."

"He is," agreed Karpov. "I thought he might have called."

"No," she said.

"There have been no messages for him?"

Rebecca immediately understood the question. "He's loyal," she said. "I've already told you."

"Yes," agreed Karpov. "You have."

"He wants to move in with me," she announced. "I've said it would be all right." She hesitated, then added, "It would be a further guarantee for you."

Karpov considered the suggestion and said, "Yes, it would, wouldn't it?"

"So there's no objection?"

Hugo *was* a lucky man, Karpov thought enviously. "No, no objection."

Rebecca opened her handbag, put her husband's letter inside, and took out another envelope. "My letter to Boris."

"I'll see he gets it."

"Thank you," said Rebecca politely.

"I don't enjoy this," said Karpov, with a suddenness that surprised her. "I never have. I wish I could make things easier for you."

Rebecca didn't know how to respond. "That's kind of you," she said finally.

"And I don't enjoy the absolute deceit with Hugo, either."

"Neither do I," she said. At once of the indiscretion, she said, "But it's necessary."

"Yes," said the other Russian, with a sadness that seemed genuine. "It's necessary."

There was a silence between them. Then Karpov said, "You won't relax with Hugo, will you? What happened in New York was very strange."

He *had* been trying to catch her out, decided Rebecca. "No," she promised. "I won't relax."

Otto Schroeder had talked everything over with his son in the library of the Kolb Strasse mansion. When there was nothing more to say, he telephoned Gesler in Bonn. The lawyer had his son and daughter to dinner, along with their families, so there was a delay while he switched the call to his study. When the reconnection was made, Gesler asked worriedly, "What is it?"

Schroeder told him of the call to the restaurant by a man purporting to represent a Cologne wine firm and then said, "Kurt and his people have checked everyone. No one has a salesman named Rieber. Or had a salesman in Frankfurt that day."

"I assumed Hans fled when he got the warning," said Gesler, the alarm obvious in his voice. "Have they got him?"

"I don't think so," said Shroeder. "He had loyal people around him. People he could trust and who have been working with us. He wouldn't say where he was going—just that he'd make contact when he was sure everything was all right. But we're sure he's safe."

"The phony approach would indicate that, I suppose," said Gesler. He looked around the wood-paneled room, with its leather-backed books and its heavy, leather furniture. He thought of the dinner party along the corridor, of his beautiful wife and pretty, gowned daughter and handsome, evening-dressed son; of the white linen and the crystal and the vintage wines on the long table. And physically shuddered. Don't say he had to run; dear God, please let there be some explanation.

"Are you there?" came Schroeder's voice.

"I was thinking," said the lawyer.

"Kurt wants to come to Bonn, to take over your protection."

Through his fear, Gesler recognized the open ambition, the boy's need to get next to the man he believed to be in command. "All right," he accepted. "What about you?"

"I'm adequately protected."

Gesler thought back to the playacting in the mountain woods and said, "Be careful, Otto. I don't like this. Be very careful."

"We'll be all right," said Schroeder.

Giselda looked up in immediate concern when Gesler reentered the dining room. "Gunther!" she said. "What is it!"

"Nothing," said the lawyer shortly.

"You look as if you've seen a ghost."

He had, thought Gesler; too many ghosts. "Problems have come up on something I've been working on for a long time," he said vaguely.

"Mother's right," said Hans. "It's ridiculous to work as hard as you do."

"Sometimes I have to," said Gesler. Why couldn't they stop their prattling, so that he could think!

"You should take a holiday," said Ilse, joining forces against him.

South America? wondered Gesler. Or Russia? He didn't want either.

15

Only Schroeder had been confident enough to retain his own name. Rudolph Diels had become Heinz Hiedler, proprietor of an exclusive jewelry shop on Rossmarkt, at the advantageous end near the pedestrian mall. It was advantageous to Hartman, too; it meant there was a crowd in which he could lose himself. But in which, he accepted, other people could lose themselves.

He made the first reconnaissance the same day as his observation upon Schroeder, immediately after depositing the photographs for development, arriving in midafternoon. All the surrounding shops were open, but Diels's was locked, the tight-mesh metal antiburglar screen padlocked across the front. Hartman let himself move with the flow of people, only once actually passing in front of the shop but never losing sight of it, watching not just for any sign of its being belatedly opened but also for anyone maintaining any observation, as he was.

He picked them out after fifteen minutes. He wandered leisurely up the connecting road onto Bleichstrasse and then completed the circuit by joining the pedestrian section again to see if he were right. It took forty-five minutes, but when he got back they were still in the café. There were three of them: young, like those outside of Schroeder's house that morning, empty beer glasses before them, hardly talking to each other but gazing around in constant, unguarded attention toward the shuttered shop. Hartman turned away, confident they would never identify him in their amateurism but unwilling to risk the barest chance.

Hartman walked confidently onto Berliner Strasse, knowing there would be a public telephone. As he moved into the booth, he reflected how mundane and ordinary his method of work was: clerks gnawing pencil ends and shop assistants pounding cash-register keys read spy books on their commuter trains and fantasized about paraphernalia, never dreaming of the basic reality. And the basic reality was that ninety percent of all spying activities were more boring than those of any clerk or shop assistant.

Hartman swapped his ordinary eyeglasses for those he needed for reading, especially fine print, and located the listing under Heinz Hiedler, smiling at his unexpected luck: a conscientious businessman, Diels had his private as well as his business address and number recorded. Hartman dialed the shuttered shop first, staring idly in the direction of the river while the telephone purred unanswered. Finally he hung up and tried the home number. Again there was no reply.

There could be a hundred reasons for the lack of response, Hartman accepted. But Diels's absence had too much of a pattern about it, linked with that of Leitner, for there to be a normal explanation.

Maybe the confirmation wouldn't be as absolute as that of the other two men, the standard the Russians normally accepted. But since his belated awareness that Moscow was involving itself in something that had connections with a CIA operation, Hartman found it increasingly difficult to believe he was engaged in a normal operation.

He hadn't managed to escape from anything, Hartman decided. Rather, he had sunk more deeply into the swamp. Until his attempted escape, the operations had been relatively clear, directed at least toward one objective, under the control of one service.

About this one, he wasn't sure. Not sure at all.

William Davidson belched noisily from indigestion, staring down at the recommendation. Reluctantly, after every effort to salvage something, he had accepted defeat. Accepted too, his being shunted aside. And, like Willard, who made frequent pocket-calculator computations about the size of his pension and benefits, Davidson didn't like recurring problems. He wanted them resolved, with no danger to himself, never to arise again. That's the way he'd always handled problems.

He hadn't intended Peter Berman to rise again—hadn't intended anything except that the man should disappear, never to remind him of the one operation that Davidson had sincerely believed would get him off the retirement shuttle on which he was now an accepted passenger.

And now this had come up.

Unquestionably there was cause for further investigation into the New York explosion, from the unarguable forensic proof that it hadn't been Klaus Reinhart who died. And unquestionably they couldn't share with the FBI the connection with Fritz Lang. The obvious answer would be to refuse the request from the analysts' division, keep Berman permanently atrophied, and give the inquiry to someone completely new.

But there was a danger there.

Davidson accepted that he had made mistakes in the original operation. Mistakes that some up-at-dawn, jogging asshole might discover and which might screw him even more than he was already screwed.

"Son of a bitch!" he said aloud.

He discovered a congealed remnant of either breakfast or lunch on his tie and scraped absentmindedly at it with his fingernail. It was a balance, he decided. Berman, who wanted to prove himself and get back operational, against a newcomer, who might be equally anxious to do a Superman routine.

The devil he knew, determined Davidson. Berman's transfer could be made to seem the magnanimous act of a section head not letting one mistake damn a man's career. But if things started to go wrong, then that mistake could be evoked at once, to stop further problems before they became major ones. If he had to dump Berman again, then, Davidson recognized, he could be accused of an error of judgment. But he calculated that as an acceptable risk.

It took Davidson a long time to draft his reply, because he knew some protection had to be prepared now. As well as a copy to the analysts' section, Davidson sent a carbon to the Deputy Director of Operations, so that the inference could be created (for any later inquiry) that the decision had been sanctioned by a superior anyway.

16

Hartman was up early the following day, waiting at the vehicle-licensing department when it opened and ready with the story of having had his parked car damaged by a hit-and-run vehicle whose number a passerby had recorded and left beneath his windshield wiper. He completed the application form with a false name and address, and within an hour had obtained the registration details of the car providing the protection for Schroeder's limousine. It was owned by Dieter Kleist, with an address near the zoo. Hartman walked from one administration building to another, obtained the voting register, and checked the listed address. There were only two names recorded. Apart from Dieter Kleist, there was a woman, Eva Kleist. She was described as a widow.

The photographs were ready at the time promised and Hartman returned to the Ketterer. He took the customary precautions to secure his room and then laid out the pictures for comparison with those provided by the Russians. Hartman recognized the ears at once. He looked up, frowning. Hadn't that been one of the pointers toward Lang as well? They spent money on plastic surgery, but they always overlooked the fact that ears, to a trained observer, could be as identifiable as fingerprints.

The official German photograph of Otto Schroeder showed a man with protruding, long-lobed ears. The upright figure he'd photographed the previous day, at the rear of a gleaming Mercedes, had identical protruding, long-lobed ears. There was a second picture, showing Schroeder full length and, Hartman used the calibrated photographic measure he always carried to calculate the height. One meter ninety, he decided. The Nazi personnel sheet showed Otto Schroeder to be 1.90 meters tall.

Hartman computed his timing carefully. He did not want to make the report in time for the telephone company to act before he got into position. He agreed easily to the service department's apology that they would not be able to look into a fault at the shop of Heinz Hiedler until the following day.

Hartman was on the Zeil mall before nine, far away but able to see the still-shuttered shop. The three men were at the sidewalk table they had occupied the previous day; one even wore the same shirt. Amateurs, thought Hartman again. Because of the distance he was from them, they were completely unaware of the photographs he took.

Hartman moved gradually toward them, finally selecting a table at the same café but one against the wall, from which he had a perfect view of Diels's shop and of the men he was sure were appointed watchers. He asked for a newspaper as well as for coffee, using the *Frankfurter Zeitung* as a barrier between himself and the youths. He was convinced they weren't good enough, but Hartman again wasn't taking any chances.

With German efficiency, the telephone repair van came onto Fahrgasse at ten o'clock. Hartman laid the newspaper aside and watched as the overalled man, leaning against the weight of his toolbox, walked into the pedestrian area and then went onto Rossmarkt. Hartman thought he could sense the man's surprise at the shutters.

By now Hartman had no need of confirmation, but it came from the three men as soon as the telephone engineer paused outside of Rudolph Diels's shop. They were moving as the man tried the door and then rapped against it, trying to attract attention from inside. The engineer turned at the challenge from the approaching men. Hartman was too far away to hear the conversation, but he didn't need to. There was a demand for identification, which the engineer provided, and an arm-waving conversation. Then one of the three detached himself and came back into the café, going straight to the telephone at the rear. Hartman guessed he could have positioned himself to hear what was said, but he didn't bother, it had to be a check with the telephone authorities that a problem had been reported.

Before the man emerged, Hartman signaled for his bill, paid, and walked quietly off in the opposite direction, taking himself away from the confrontation.

He had been careful to amass sufficient coins to telephone Rebecca in Vienna from a street booth, feeling a warmth move through him at the sound of her voice.

"I'm catching the evening flight," he said.

"So it's gone well?"

"Well enough," he said.

She detected the doubt. "You don't seem sure."

"I'm not," he said. "Not completely."

Peter Berman stretched to ease the cramp in his shoulders, got up, and walked to the window, staring out over the trees in the direction of the unseen Potomac. He'd studied everything about Klaus Reinhart and everything about Fritz Lang until he could practically recite the goddamn reports verbatim. But he still couldn't get any clue linking the unidentified man who had died in the New York explosion. He didn't doubt the Russians had killed Lang. And Reinhart had been Lang's immediate subordinate. Had it been a Russian who'd died, trying to gain entry into Reinhart's apartment? A possibility, reflected Berman. Whatever, he knew it *wasn't* Reinhart. Which meant the former Nazi had to be around somewhere, obviously running because of what had happened.

Berman brightened at the thought. There'd probably be some flak from the FBI, who had the file contentedly marked 'closed,' but that didn't matter a damn. He'd put out an all-stations alert for Klaus Reinhart. It would show action, and Berman realized how important it was to indicate that: he might be designated operational again. But he was frighteningly aware just how much of a trial it was, a trial on a very short leash. He couldn't afford to get it wrong again.

17

Hartman accepted that he hadn't kept his side of the bargain with Rebecca. After Zurich they'd promised each other complete honesty, but he'd held back, leaving her with the suspicion of his involvement with the Americans but not confirming it. So it was time to share the burden. He made the confession haltingly, intent upon her face, not bothering with the excuse (with which he'd always tried to reassure himself) about mitigating his guilt if ever he were detected. He set out his involvement with the CIA from the beginning, here in immediate postwar Vienna, itimizing the operations for which he'd worked for the Americans until Lang.

"And now this," he finished. "Doing for Moscow what I did for Washington. It's too close."

Rebecca's face twisted, as if she were in physical pain. Was it just to trick Hugo into something they already suspected? "Oh, my God," she said. "Oh, God."

"There isn't one," said Hartman bitterly.

Her effort at control was obvious. She took his hand reassuringly. "They're not sure," she said. "Karpov asked me again, but they're not sure." She hesitated, then said, "If they were, they'd have killed you. That's their way."

"Maybe not."

"Why *did* the Americans want Lang to run?"

"I was never told," said Hartman. "I just had positively to identify him. And then frighten him."

"And why did the Americans come here looking for you?"

Hartman shook his head. "I don't know that either."

"It doesn't make sense," she protested.

"Nothing does," said Hartman.

She took his hand again, pulling at him so that he

moved along the couch they were sitting on in her apartment. She reached up and cradled his head against her shoulder and said, "I'm scared, darling. I'm very scared for you."

"So am I," said Hartman honestly.

Hartman was intent upon Karpov's face, knowing that it was ridiculous to expect a visible reaction from someone as professional as the Russian, but trying just the same.

"Excellent," said Karpov. "As always. Moscow will be pleased."

The message from Erich Dollfuss earlier that day had said there was no indication of any sudden American interest in Germany. And there surely would have been if Hartman had made contact. Karpov was glad at the proof that he had been right about the Austrian. He'd miss Hugo when he got back to Moscow. He looked around the apartment. There was a lot he'd miss.

"It's hardly difficult," said Hartman. "Someone out of training school could do what I'm doing."

"I promised you something easy," reminded Karpov.

"Is it easy?" demanded Hartman pointedly.

Karpov gestured to the other man's report on Frankfurt. "You're not getting nervous about watchers as amateur as these, are you? They're young boys, flexing their muscles." He splashed whisky into Hartman's glass. "Drink up and stop worrying."

"It doesn't feel right," said Hartman, ignoring the drink.

"Other people will be taking the risk," assured Karpov. "We've gone beyond the rough stuff, you and I."

When the antibiotic pills and powder failed to clear up the sores, the camp doctor gave Gusadarov injections daily for a fortnight. At the end, only one remained, an abscessed ulcer on his left calf. They finally operated, and then allowed him to remain for more than a week in the prison infirmary, in a real bed with real sheets and proper blankets, which were thick and had warmth in them. Gusadarov was so used to straw mattresses on slated barracks shelves that for the first two nights he remained sleepless, unable to adjust. He found it difficult to adjust to the food as well. Twice a week there was meat, which was fresh. So were the vegetables. Every day he was given the promised lemon, and he ate it all, stomach moving against the unaccustomed richness, mouth clamped shut against any sickness that would cause him to lose the nourishment.

He was still in the hospital when Rebecca's letter came. He read it hurriedly, rushing it as he rushed the food. He held tightly to the paper her hands had held, his mouth moving to form the words, trying to imagine her as she wrote them. He was in a small side ward by himself, but if there had been other patients it wouldn't have mattered; when he got to Rebecca's concluding paragraph, Gusadarov read it aloud, repeating the words over and over, trying to believe that Rebecca had also spoken them when she'd written them.

"I love you," recited Gusadarov.

18

The Executive Action Department—also known as Department V—of the First Chief Directorate is a secret division actually within the KGB itself. Men employed in it are killers. Five men formed the squad to assassinate Otto Schroeder. Four traveled separately to Frankfurt, through disguised transit stops in Tokyo, London, Paris, and Madrid, to assemble as a group at the Frankfurter Hof on Kaiserplatz after a further forty-eight-hour check, following their arrival, to ensure they remained undetected. The fifth traveled by road through East Germany, acting as courier with the mechanics of the operations.

The men already in Frankfurt regarded Hartman's report as nothing more than a preliminary ground plan. For four days they monitored Schroeder's daily movements, creating a pattern of the man's habits.

On the fifth, Friday, they extended their surveillance by following Schroeder's limousine from the old man's house, after he had been dropped off for the evening. Each of the squad had his own rented vehicle so that, at timed intervals, the car immediately behind could pull off at a side street or intersection and avoid any possibility of detection. Schroeder's driver lived in a high-rise development off Habsbergeralle, comparatively close to Schroeder's home, and two Russians were still in position behind the limousine when it stopped. One halted; the other continued on.

They were all back at the Frankfurter Hof by seven in the evening.

''Twenty minutes,'' said the man who had stopped.

''I agree,'' said the second, who had driven on.

''We'll allow twenty-five, to be safe,'' said Mikhail Frolov, who was in command.

"Why this way?" demanded the fourth man.

"Specific orders," said Frolov.

"It'll be an obvious killing."

"It has to be, apparently."

The courier arrived at breakfast the following day. The now-complete group drove west in two cars, into the open countryside beyond Höchst, to dismantle and check the devices and ensure there were no mechanical faults. There weren't, so they were back in Frankfurt by late afternoon. They ate at the Gumpelmann, taking the waiter's recommendation and having the *rippchen*.

Because Sunday was a nonworking day for Schroeder, they spent it sightseeing, taking a pleasure boat out on the river. In the afternoon Frolov and one of the others bought dolls dressed in national costumes for their children. Frolov's daughter had an extensive collection, from his visits abroad.

Only one of them made the initial, unstopping reconnaissance of the Habsburgerallee area at eleven, the rest of the group accepting without argument his recommendation that they wait another hour for the area to become quiet.

The bombs were digitally controlled, capable of being set to explode months in advance, if necessary. For the Schroeder killing, they were fitted with magnetic clamps. It took two of the Russians less than a minute to secure one device beneath the rear fender and the other inside the front wheel arch on the passenger's side while the driver of their car stopped momentarily outside the chauffeur's apartment, apparently to check a doubtful front light.

Otto Schroeder was a man of strict habit, which necessitated his driver being the same. The man permitted himself thirty minutes for the journey to Kolb Strasse, as he did every day. There were no unexpected traffic delays and so, as he also did practically every day, he was able to stop briefly on the Tiergarten for a coffee and to buy cigarettes.

He arrived outside Schroeder's house precisely at nine-thirty, just as the old man was emerging from his gates. The regular pattern was interrupted, as it had been for almost a month now, by the younger men pulling from the parking area to escort the limousine to the office. So it was nine-forty before Schroeder actually got into the rear of the vehicle. The detonations occurred a minute after the car had set off toward Schweitzer Strasse. Schroeder's car was actually broken in half, and the bomb at the rear caused the gas tank to explode. Schroeder's body, surprisingly, was thrown clear but the chauffeur was incinerated. So, too, were the two guarding youths in the following car.

The day of the killing had been set out, like everything else, in Migal's scheme. As soon as he received confirmation from Frankfurt that it had been successful, the Russian initiated the second stage. For years the KGB had cultivated journalists on the Axel Springer newspaper group, particularly for their anti-Nazi bias, so it was there that Migal had leaked—through cutout journalists in Berlin—the details about Otto Schroeder's past. Stories got into most newspapers throughout Germany three days after the explosion. Migal had them airfreighted to him from Germany, spreading them out over the wide conference table in his office and nodding in satisfaction at the display. Two had actually included the Zurich death of Fritz Lang and referred to the similarity in the methods—which was precisely why Migal had insisted that Schroeder be killed by a bomb explosion.

As a matter of courtesy—and to avoid clashing independent inquiries—the CIA office on Bonn's Mehlemer Avenue was notified of Peter Berman's arrival in Germany, but the advisory cable made it clear that he was working entirely alone. Berman knew that Davidson was taking out further insurance, but he didn't care. He wanted to work alone because he wanted to crack this alone. Entirely alone, without any other greedy bastard grabbing the credit.

He asked only one favor from the Bonn embassy: an introduction to the police and security services as someone who should be given help. The request was made to the Germans after consultations with Langley.

Because liaison was the position he had occupied so successfully for the previous eight years, the request was channeled between the German intelligence service and the police by Erich Dollfuss.

19

The most difficult part for Gunther Gesler was to continue as if everything were normal: to visit his office every day, and every day go through at least the minimal business necessary with clients, and above all, every day, to keep his terror from Giselda.

Inexplicably to Gesler, the killing of Otto Schroeder became a *cause célèbre* within Germany. Newspapers, television, and then magazines maintained continuous coverage, and inevitably questions were asked in the Bundestag by MP's aware of the advantages of anti-Nazi publicity. When the matter reached parliamentary level, Israel officially denied any involvement, a contention few—least of all Gesler—believed.

There had been initial, terrified contact with Luntz and Becher—clipped, hopeless telephone conversations with none of them knowing what to do. And then Luntz ran. He left a letter of apology and explanation for his wife, who had known nothing of his wartime activities. The woman, imagining she was doing the best thing to protect someone she loved, took it to the police, who made it public. And the publicity was resuscitated.

When he came to make his escape plans, Gesler realized, frighteningly and sickeningly, just how stupidly ill-prepared he was. It was simplicity itself to initiate the Swiss account for five million marks from the Liechtenstein holdings. But, having established it, Gesler recognized that he didn't know how to continue the finance chain. So unthinkable had flight always been that he knew nothing about Buenos Aires or Montevideo or Rio de Janeiro or Concepcion, or which one was preferable to another. And safer.

Like a man trying to find a winning horse by sticking a

pin in the racing form, Gesler warned the Swiss bank to expect instructions for future funding from Rio de Janeiro. It would be a starting point, he rationalized. If he didn't like Brazil, he could move on, amending the authorization as he went.

Alone in his office, with the door locked and all calls held, Gesler closed his eyes and brought both hands to his mouth, conscious of how near he was to a breakdown. Frightened though he was—fear actually shaking through him—he still didn't want to run. He didn't want the bowel-opening immigration checks at airports; packing from hotel to hotel before people began to wonder who he was; haggling for a place finally to live, never knowing when he would have to move on yet again.

Was that why he had gone to the safe-deposit vault to look over the wartime records? Not entirely, he conceded. From his vest pocket he took the tiny medical containers that until two hours before had occupied the secret bank box, next to the documents. He knew the containers were airtight; so the cyanide should have survived all these years. Uncertainly, he lifted them in front of his face, sniffing. If there'd been a leak, there should be a discernible smell of almonds. Another way, he thought, as unacceptable as running. Hadn't he been a practicing Catholic all his life. Hurriedly he put the poison back into his pocket.

Although he had tried to avoid the cameras, Kurt Schroeder had been photographed at his father's funeral supporting his crippled mother, so Gesler ordered that the boy should not return to Bonn but leave the attempted protection to others he had seen perform in the mountains. When he entered the garage beneath his office that evening, he saw the boy talking to two others who, since Schroeder's death, had maintained a permanent watch on the vehicle.

"What the hell are you doing here?" demanded the lawyer.

"Don't worry," said Schroeder. "No one could have kept up with me. I went to Paris first, then Munich. I was very careful." He paused and then—showing the logic denied Gesler by his nervousness—Schroeder added, "And if it's as bad as we think it is, they'll know about you already, without having to follow me."

Gesler bit his lip, able only to nod.

"I'll drive you," offered the young man.

"All right," said Gesler wearily. What did it matter? What did anything matter? He felt bowed with fatigue.

One of the others checked the garage exit and then signaled, and Schroeder took the Mercedes carefully up the ramp and out into the street. At once more of Schroeder's group pulled away from the curb in a BMW, forming a convoy.

"Did you see the pictures of the funeral?" asked Schroeder.

"Yes" said Gesler. "And the television."

"A circus," said Schroeder. "An absolute fucking circus."

Gesler could see Schroeder's hands white against the wheel, gripped in anger. "Yes" he agreed. "It was."

"I'm going to avenge my father," Schroeder announced, his voice quiet despite his anger. "I'm not letting them succeed in making him out as some kind of monster."

Dear God, thought Gesler, another performance. "I understand how you feel," he said.

"He wasn't a monster," insisted Schroeder, as if Gesler needed convincing. "He was a loyal German."

"A good man," agreed Gesler.

"Do you know where Herr Luntz has gone?"

"No," said Gesler. "I don't expect him to contact me, either. It wouldn't be sensible, would it?"

"My people went with him as far as the airport," said Schroeder. "He took the Madrid plane."

"He'll have gone on by now," said Gesler. Poor, harassed bastard, he thought.

"We've got ten people watching Herr Becher, around the clock," reported Schroeder. "He's quite safe."

Like your father was safe, thought Gesler. He closed his eyes against the naiveté but at once reopened them, staring around the familiar streets as if he were seeing them for the first time. He intended to buy an airline ticket for the Saturday flight. So there were only another two days. Only another two days to impress upon his memory the buildings and the streets he took for granted, to stare across the Rhine in the direction of Königswinter and the matted forests, and remember the visits there with Giselda. Dear Giselda! She was going to be so frightened, so bewildered by it all. And she'd never been truly well since the operation.

"Thank you for all you're doing," he said.

Schroeder looked quickly sideways. "It's an hour, sir," he said.

Giselda was waiting for him in the smaller of the two drawing rooms of the Berliner Freiheit house, the frame of the newly started cushion tapestry in her lap. Gesler started across the room toward the bottles before he remembered, turning to kiss her lightly on the cheek, as he did every night.

"Do you want anything?" he asked from the table where the drinks were set out.

"No, thank you."

He came back toward her, thinking how frail she looked, as well as beautiful. He nodded to the needlework and asked, "What's it going to be?"

"A forest scene," she said. "There's a stag in it."

She'd never finished it by Saturday, thought Gesler. "It'll be pretty."

"How was your day?"

Gesler hesitated, realizing he could hardly recall any of

he work part of it, at least. "All right," he said. g special."

He went back to the drinks. She said from behind, "That's the second, in less than ten minutes."

He turned to look at her. "So what?" he said. He hadn't meant to sound rude, but he knew he had.

"What is it, Gunther?"

"What's what?"

"Don't be silly," she said. "I want to know."

"There's nothing to know."

She put her tapestry aside and said, "I wondered if you'd suggest our going to Herr Schroeder's funeral. There used to be good times with him and Emmy, don't you remember?"

"I didn't think it was a good idea," he said.

"I didn't know, until all the publicity, what it was he did in the war."

"He obeyed his orders," said Gesler tightly. "We all did." How many times had that defense been used? he wondered.

"Have you got any reason to be worried?" she demanded.

"Why should I have?" he said, again more sharply than he intended.

"I don't know," she said evenly. "That's why I asked."

If he wanted her to come with him to Brazil—and he did, because the thought of running alone was something he couldn't contemplate—then now was the moment to tell her. To let her know, as gently as possible, that everything they'd known for the past thirty-five years was over and that they were going to abandon it, just as they were going to abandon Hans and Ilse. Gesler felt the sweep of dizziness and closed his eyes against the sensation, swaying.

She started up from the couch, and he felt her hand against his arm. "What is it, darling? Please tell me what it is."

He opened his eyes, gulping too quickly at his drink, so that his breath caught and he coughed.

"I don't want you to suffer," he said.

"Why should I?" asked the woman, further confused.

Gesler felt a professional annoyance at the awkward way he was expressing himself. "Stupid things are happening," he said. "Mistakes are being made."

"Mistakes?"

"People are being publicly blamed for things in the war . . . things they had no control over." She was his wife, for God's sake! Why couldn't he be honest with her?

"Could you be blamed for something that happened in the war?"

He shook his head. "I didn't do anything wrong," he said. "Just orders."

He saw her face close against him and said, "Not personally. I didn't do anything personally."

"Thank you for telling me," she said stiffly.

Gesler took the containers from his pocket and said, "I want you to know about these . . . in case anything happens to me." He saw her frown and repeated hurriedly, "I don't want you to suffer."

She took one of the boxes, lips moving slightly as she read the instructions, and then gazed up at him, openmouthed in shock. "Oh, no, Gunther. We couldn't do that. No!"

There was an alternative, the one he'd always considered the last resort. So why had he gone through the charade of settingup the money conduit and confirming the flight times to Rio de Janeiro and now this—producing the cyanide pills like wartime medals? Playacting, he thought angrily. As facile as war games on a mountain hillside.

"No" he said. "There's another way."

Giselda straightened firmly in front of him, someone coming to a decision. "I love you," she said.

"I love you too," said Gesler.

Normally Karpov preferred instrumental jazz to vocal, but tonight he was playing Billy Eckstine and Sarah Vaughan on the duet album, which he supposed wasn't proper jazz at all. *Passing Strangers* was one of his favorite tracks. He sat, eyes closed, savoring the lyrics, unable completely to clear his mind of the information that had come from Erich Dollfuss in Bonn.

Did Peter Berman's arrival confirm Migal's suspicion that Hugo was a double? Maybe. But then again, maybe not. There had been three weeks from the beginning of the Frankfurt assignment. And another fortnight before the killing. If Hugo had been working with the Americans, then logically he would have involved them before—not after—Schroeder was killed. And if he continued the speculation logically, then it was the assassination that had brought the CIA man to Germany.

Passing Strangers finished, and Karpov turned down the volume. He didn't think that would be Migal's conclusion: Migal needed very little to make up his mind. Which wasn't the only problem. Karpov had affirmed Hugo's loyalty on several occasions, and the signal from Dollfuss could indicate that he was wrong. It wouldn't look good, so near to promised promotion, to have been wrong.

Three couples agreed to Hartman's asking price for his apartment. The most obvious solution would have been to sell it to the first who had seen it. But the third couple had been young and nervously uncertain, clearly getting the money from her parents, because on several occasions Hartman had seen the boy defer to her when the price was discussed. He decided to sell it to them, because he was reminded of himself and Gerda, all those years ago.

When the negotiations began, their lawyer said there was no hurry to close, because they hadn't yet married. But Hartman prepared to leave anyway, seeing no need to prolong his departure now that the decision had been made. There would be very little to move, because Rebecca's apartment was already furnished. Just his clothes, he supposed. And a few personal belongings. There was the wedding photograph of him and Gerda. Some pictures of David when the boy had been young, and then more, of David's marriage to Ruth. But little else. Hartman's was not the sort of life to gain possessions.

Hartman packed everything carefully, wrapping each individual item in tissue paper before putting it into the box. He left until last a picture of Gerda, before their arrest. He could clearly identify the Vienna opera house in the background. Although he couldn't remember, it must have been a breezy day, because her hair was blowing to one side and her hand was half raised, trying to control it. So beautiful, he thought; so very beautiful.

He stood up from the box, because his legs were cramped, still looking down at the picture. He wanted another, he decided abruptly. It would be an irritating request, he guessed, but they made constant impositions upon him. He'd ask Karpov to arrange for a photograph of Gerda's grave. It was an old man's nostalgia, he recognized. But so what? Rebecca would understand. He wondered if she had a picture of her husband.

20

The approach provided the confirmation Migal needed, because it came along the same conduit that the Russian had established to pay Fritz Lang. And who else would know the details, other than whoever held the duplicate of Lang's information? For the first time in months Migal stood looking out over the jagged, shadowed outline of the square without the gnawing, persistent apprehension. He'd taken risks—appalling risks—but he'd done it. He'd made some unknown Nazi frightened enough to make contact. Almost at once, Migal's satisfaction faltered. This was only the beginning; there was still a long way to go. With the possibility of disaster every step of that way. Migal recognized he was going to be very dependent upon Karpov—more than he'd envisaged when he first conceived the idea. Could he avoid going at all? Migal snatched at the question, aware that he was considering the most appalling risk of all—leaving Moscow and crossing into the West—to control everything on the ground. He supposed Karpov could do it alone, with Hartman as the tethered goat. But there would be an uncertainty: the possibility of whoever it was trying to withhold something, and of Karpov having to liaise and then wait for an answer before proceeding. Which meant more delay. More possibility of disaster. There'd been too much delay. Migal wanted it ended, completely, without any loose ends and any more tattered, unexorcised ghosts appearing from the past.

So he'd go across. It would mean endangering everything, but then he had everything to lose. And so far it had gone as he had planned. And it would continue going his way, providing he didn't lose his nerve.

He routed his response back through the same bank

channel, accepting the meeting, and then considered what he could do in advance.

He guessed the location would be somewhere in Germany, but that was not certain. Karpov had to be brought back for the final briefing. He was fortunate to have Karpov as a friend.

"You did what?" Henry Patterson's voice was almost unnaturally soft but it emphasized rather than disguised the Operations Director's fury.

"All we had when I sent him was some small disparity over teeth," said Davidson desperately.

"Disparity over teeth!" echoed the Western Europe Director, Gerard Jefferson. "Jesus Christ, man, we should have been involved from the beginning!"

It was the first time Davidson had been on the sixth floor at Langley since the meeting months before at which it had been decided to shelve the Lang operation. As soon as they began to review the assassination in Frankfurt of Otto Schroeder, and Davidson admitted sending Berman, he'd realized he was in trouble.

"Why?" demanded Patterson. "Why Berman? The inquiry found him guilty of the first foul-up, and when the possibility arises of pulling some of the chestnuts out of the fire, you reassign him operational and risk the whole thing fouling up again."

"He was already briefed," tried Davidson. "How could I know there'd be a tie-in with the Schroeder assassination? That took days to emerge."

"Schroeder was a Nazi and you knew that from the beginning," said Jefferson. "That should have been enough."

"I sent you a memorandum, setting out what I'd done."

Jefferson came forward in his chair, waving the single sheet of paper. "Don't try and pull that with me," he said. "That's an ass-covering memo and we both know it. There should have been consultation between us."

"Shall I pull Berman out?" asked Davidson.

Jefferson deferred to the Director of Operations, and for several moments Patterson sat gazing across the desk without replying. Then he said, "No. He's there and he's liaising with the Germans, so let him stay." The man paused, ignoring the bewilderment that showed on Davidson's face. He went on, "But I want a backup team in there by tomorrow, enough men to lift up every paving stone and look behind every tree in Germany. I thought we'd lost our chance with Lang, but now it seems we haven't. And I'm sure as hell not going to lose it again."

"All right," said Davidson.

"And another thing . . ."

Davidson looked up.

"You go, too," ordered Patterson. "And this time make sure you get it right. If you don't, I'll want your retirement."

With half-pension and no chance of getting work with any of the front companies the Agency maintained for ex-employees, realized Davidson. They were bastards—all of them bastards.

Erich Dollfuss was made nervous by the instructions from Karpov. Until now the demands had been comparatively easy. All he'd had to do was relay the information that came past his desk, which involved little more than copying or photographing reports. But now he had been told to make contact with the American and actively involve himself with the man. There was sufficient excuse, because the Schroeder dossier was an extensive one and the orders from his own service were to liaise.

But Dollfuss was still nervous.

21

Karpov studied the message that had come through Switzerland and then nodded across the desk to Migal. He said, "I agree, it could only have come from whoever has the Lang material."

"Maybe more than we've seen already."

"Perhaps," agreed Karpov. "But I don't see what we'lll achieve by getting it back. He'll surely keep copies, just as Lang kept copies."

"This time it'll be balanced. The moment whoever it is identifies himself, then the risk of his exposure balances ours."

Karpov nodded again, aware that Migal was referring to the wartime Nazi cooperation as the service's, rather than his own. "So whatever you get back doesn't matter."

"If there's a prisoner shipment that Lang didn't include in the material he left at the embassy in Mexico, it will. But it's the identity that I'm primarily interested in. The meeting in Bonn has been established. So our man stayed. He stayed, and he's got as much to lose as we have." The Russian stopped. Then he added, "And more: there'll be murder, as well."

"Murder?"

"What do you think will be terrifying them all?"

Karpov considered the question and said, "Discovery, I suppose."

Migal shook his head. "Being killed," he insisted. "That's why I ordered Schroeder bombed, so that it would match what happened to Lang and then to Reinhart. I wanted whoever it is to recognize the pattern and to imagine it was all a series of killings, carefully planned."

"Why?" asked Karpov.

"I'm not paying in money this time. Paying in money is always a mistake."

"What, then?"

"The identity of who's pursuing them."

"But that's . . ." started Karpov, but Migal talked across him. "Hugo Hartman," he completed. "A Jew who once worked for a bureau tracing war criminals and who has every reason for leading a terror campaign against people who once terrorized him."

"They'll kill him," said Karpov quietly.

"Which is the murder I've already talked about—a murder of which we'll have evidence and with which we can blackmail them. This time I'm determined to get everything back, even the copies." Migal smiled, a rare expression. "What do you think?"

"Very clever," conceded Karpov.

"Yes," said Migal, without conceit. "It is, isn't it? And there's more."

"More?"

"I'm crossing into Germany."

"You!"

"I know it's unprecedented, but that's what I intend to do. I want to be actually there, on the spot, to ensure that everything goes exactly as I've planned." Migal stopped, unsure of the wisdom of the admission. Then he said, "There have been too many already."

"It's dangerous," said Karpov.

"Of course it's dangerous, but it's the only way. . . ." Again there was a pause. "Which is why I'll be relying so much on you."

"Of course I'll do everything I can," said Karpov.

"I'll want you to negotiate," announced Migal.

"Me! Negotiate!"

"There can't be anyone else, can there? Nobody else knows."

"No," said Karpov desperately. "It would be madness!

And it's directly against every operational procedure. There should be a chain of cutouts, with no provable links to us. We'll need dozens of people."

"Just us," said Migal with quiet insistence. Deciding the pressure was necessary, he said, "You're implicated now, Oleg. Involved, just like me. We can do it together."

Bastard, thought Karpov. Migal couldn't think in any terms except those of blackmail.

"How?" he asked.

Migal passed across the instructions that had been routed to him through Switzerland, waiting patiently while Karpov read them. After fifteen minutes Karpov looked up and said, "This is kid's stuff!"

"That's what Hartman's report from Frankfurt said they were—kids playacting," reminded Migal. "There'll be no danger."

"There's more danger from amateurs than from professionals," said Karpov.

"Just us," repeated Migal.

"They want a meeting in three days," said Karpov, looking back to the paper he still held. "I'll start tomorrow." There wasn't much he could do without the sort of backup the operation demanded and which Migal was refusing, but he'd try to ensure as much protection as possible.

"Through Vienna?"

"Yes."

"Warn Hartman you'll want him again soon. We'll need to provide some evidence, to make the exchange seem genuine. Hugo will have to go Nazi-hunting again." He gave one of his rare smiles. "And this time we'll record it."

Because the Schroeder file was so voluminous, Dollfuss had arranged for an adjoining office to be made available. It was late in the afternoon before Berman reappeared through the linking door.

"That was very complete. Thank you," said the American.

"We were asked to cooperate," said Dollfuss. He thought Berman was an extremely pleasant man, polite and without any of the brashness usually associated with Americans. Attractive, too, although that was only a passing thought; Dollfuss never allowed his private life to intrude into his working environment, despite the obvious indications that within the building in which they now sat there were others who felt as he did. Because the recording was to be unofficial and without the knowledge of his superiors, Dollfuss rigged the equipment himself: a pocket mike taped beneath the outside lip of the desk against which he'd placed a chair for Berman, and the tape button inside his top drawer. He made the pretense of replacing some papers in the drawer, activating the machine as he did so. He hoped to God the thing worked. And that Berman didn't get suspicious.

"The investigations seem to have come to a halt," said Berman.

Dollfuss nodded. "It looked promising, at first. Then suddenly it all dried up."

"What about the Israelis?"

"There have been private assurances from their service that they're not involved. They'd lie, of course, if they felt it necessary," said Dollfuss. He hesitated, remembering Karpov's instructions. "In which are you most interested?" he asked. "The death of Fritz Lang or that of Otto Schroeder?"

"Both, if there is a definite link."

"Is there?" pressed Dollfuss. "I'd like any liaison to go both ways, you understand."

Berman paused, wondering how far he could go. With Davidson and God knows how many others flying in that evening, Langley had obviously decided he couldn't handle it alone. Maybe the whole damned thing would be taken away from him, unless he could show some practical results. So he had more to gain than to lose by being frank with this slight, mild-mannered German. And they were in the same business and interested in the same thing, after all. "What do you know of Klaus Reinhart?" he said.

Dollfuss looked to the Schroeder dossier, as if the answer might be there, frowning. Then he looked up and said, "Nothing."

Berman recounted the New York explosion and the connection with Lang, and then his discovery from the dental examination.

"So there have been assassinations of three Nazis?"

"*Attempted*," qualified Berman. "Whoever died in New York wasn't Klaus Reinhart."

"That's what brought you here."

"Yes," said Berman. "There was an obvious chance of a connection."

"There still might be," said Dollfuss.

Berman indicated the record of the German investigation. "Not from that," he said.

"Schroeder's son has disappeared," offered Dollfuss. "And there's some evidence that he was part of some neo-Nazi organization. There are quite a few. Stupid young fools."

"It could be that he's scared, after the death of his father," said Berman.

"There's an alert out for him."

"What about the other man who vanished, Luntz?"

"Traced him as far as Madrid, but then lost him. The Spanish authorities aren't very helpful about ex-Nazis. There's still a lot of sympathy."

"More of my people are arriving tonight," said Berman. It was the man's job to know anyway, and they might need further help.

"How many?"

"I'm not sure."

This was information for his official as well as unofficial paymasters, Dollfuss realized. "Why?" he demanded.

Berman stopped, knowing he had gone too far. "Something that happened a long time ago might have some benefit now," he said.

"Something involving Nazis?"

"Yes," said Berman.

"Benefits to whom, America or Germany?"

"Maybe both," said Berman. "Don't worry; it won't be embarrassing."

"Publicly disclosed assassinations of old Nazis like Schroeder and Lang are always embarrassing," pointed out Dollfuss. "The memory makes our European partners uneasy."

"It needn't, not this time."

"I don't understand," said Dollfuss.

"I can't go any further than that," said Berman. "You must understand."

"And you must understand that you're on German territory seeking German assistance," said Dollfuss forcefully. "This meeting is supposed to be one of cooperation."

At the moment this man was his only contact, and Berman knew it would be a mistake to antagonize him. "Something that happened a long time ago might be relevant, and the assassinations of Schroeder, Reinhart, and Lang might be relevant," said the American awkwardly. "But the effects won't be here in Germany."

"Where, then?" asked Dollfuss. He was surprised at having achieved such control over the discussion.

"You have my word, as soon as I discover more, I'll share the information with you," promised Berman, seeking an escape. "At the moment we're working on hearsay, without any concrete evidence."

"On hearsay you fly a whole group of people something

like four or five thousand miles?'' queried Dollfuss.

''If it becomes fact, then the operation will be worth while,'' said Berman.

He had something to report, decided Berman. He wondered if it would be sufficient.

He had something to report, decided Dollfuss. He wondered if it would be sufficient.

Gunther Gesler wanted to be absolutely secure, so he took the Russian response to the Deutsche Bank and withdrew the safe-deposit box containing Lang's material, to entitle him to a cubicle in the vault. With the attendant he went through the performance of opening the box with their matching keys, but after the man left made no attempt to life the lid. Instead he looked down at the brief, three-line message that had arrived that morning from Switzerland. He'd made his commitment, and an unknown man named Ivan Migal had made his. And within four days. Considering the delay in relaying through Switzerland, that was practically by return mail. Gesler decided the Russian was worried; maybe as worried as he was himself. He looked at the unlocked but still closed box, wondering just how much protection the material afforded. He hoped that it was more than that of Kurt Schroeder and his posturing friends: he'd discovered them fooling around in the office garage that afternoon, relegating the whole thing to a joke.

Gesler opened the box at last, to put in Migal's message from Moscow, then pressed the call button for the attendant to come and complete the locking with him.

22

Boris Gusadarov was issued with another uniform for his release from the camp infirmary, a new one that didn't have anyone else's smell on it. The boots were new, too, of better design, the sides stiff protective canvas and not the felt that became waterlogged in the winter snow and grew so cumbersome that they had to be dragged across the ground, too heavy to lift. When he put the trousers on, he was confused by the momentary discomfort, and then realized they had provided the size of the suit in which he had been admitted and that he'd put on weight, so that the waistband was tight around his stomach. From the hospital building he was escorted not back to the brick-making huts, which he'd considered a favored assignment because it was under cover, but to the reselection offices of the main administration building.

He stood properly polite before the officer, head bent, cap held between both hands in front of him.

"Doctor's report says you're fully recovered."

"Yes, sir." Were they going to take him away from the brick kilns? There was protection and warmth in the kilns in the winter. It was better working there, even in the warmer months.

The man looked up. "Feeling all right?"

Gusadarov held back from answering immediately, unaccustomed to such solicitude and trying for an answer to retain his old job. "Better than I was," he said.

The man went back to his prison file. "You used to be an engineer?"

Did he? thought Gusadarov. It was so long ago it was hard to remember. But yes, he had been an engineer. A tractor factory in Vinnitsa, trying to build first-rate machinery with third-rate supplies to provide absurd wheat quotas imposed by the foreigners in Moscow. "Yes," he said at last. "I used to be an engineer."

"Know about figures, then?"

Gusadarov made the longest pause of all at this question, trying to understand its significance. What had figures got to do with making bricks or digging coal or cutting timber or mining gold? Was it a trick? Were the food and the hospital treatment and the new clothes some bizarre trap? But for what? He couldn't hold the thoughts and keep them separate, so one doubt overlapped another until his mind fogged.

"Aren't you used to figures?"

Gusadarov jumped at the man's insistence, at once conscious of a mistake at making an officer repeat himself. "Yes," he said hurriedly. "Yes, I'm very used to figures." He hadn't been, he realized. There had originally been blueprints and drawings, with measurements and calibrations he was supposed to follow and insist upon. But all the manufacturing machinery had been obsolete, with a huge variance in all he tolerances, so in the end they'd usually built every vehicle as they went along.

"We need a clerk," announced the officer. "Here in the administration building."

Gusadarov gripped his hand together behind the concealment of his cap, trying to create some physical pain he could concentrate on, to stop his mind slipping into absolute confusion. It was unthinkable—to be transferred into administration! Only the trustees got that, the cowed toadies. And then not like this; only after years of offering information and black-market money and often their bodies.

"You start at once," said the officer.

"Yes, sir."

It was only a short walk to a large, open room in which men were seated at three rows of tables, six deep. He was signed over to the guard in charge of the room. The man gestured to an empty desk to the let, and Gusadarov dutifully went to it and sat down. No one looked at him. There were pencils, pens, an inkwell, and a ruler in a small trough at the top of the desk, and a soiled blotter directly in front of him. Gusadarov wondered whether to open the drawers and decided against it; no one ever did anything without a positive order.

The guard who had signed for him approached with an expandable document case, like the bellows in an accordion that Gusadarov's father used to play, and put it heavily in front of him.

"We want an output graph," instructed the guard. "The figures for the camp's production for last year and this year are filed here. We need a comparison."

Gusadarov nodded, not knowing what to say.

"Graph paper in the desk," said the man.

Gusadarov found the paper in the top left-hand drawer and set it out carefully in front of him. From the document case he extracted the figures, realizing that they were filed against the separate divisions of the camp's activities. Because it was the section in which he had previously worked, and it fit in alphabetical order, Gusadarov first set out the figures for brick production.

He sat hunched, staring down at them until they merged and blurred before his eyes. The sickness formed, deep in his stomach, and he sat with his hands beneath the desk lid, so the guard wouldn't see the nervousness shaking through him.

Gusadarov didn't have the slightest idea how to do it.

By the time Davidson reached the embassy from the Königshof Hotel, Berman had established a communication system matching the one they had set up in Berne months before for the arrival of Lang, and signaled Langley fully about his meeting with Erich Dollfuss. Davidson's face reddened when he saw the length of the telex. He read it, his color deepening, and then said, "You knew I was coming.

You should have waited until I got here."

So you could take the credit, thought Berman: asshole. He said, "I thought it had become impotant, because of the buildup. And that I'd better not waste time."

Davidson regarded this skeptically but didn't challenge the other man. "Spain's a lead," he said. "We'd better alert Madrid."

"I've already done so," said Berman, offering the second signal sheet. "I sent a duplicate to Washington as well, so that everyone would know what everyone else was doing."

"You've been very efficient," said Davidson sarcastically.

"Shouldn't I, after last time?" Berman decided he had nothing to lose by not deferring to Davidson. His being here meant that Davidson was fighting for his existence, just as much as he was for his. And this time Berman didn't intend being the one to go under.

"So we've got the cooperation of the Germans and we know the extent of their investigation," said Davidson, seeking a weakness. "What about our own inquiries?"

"I've only been in Bonn for three days," said Berman. "And in Germany less than a week."

Davidson smiled, imagining he'd found the crack. "So the answer's nothing," he said. "Apart from picking up what other people have done?"

"No," said Berman. "From Langley I brought the names and all the information available about every Nazi ever associated with Fritz Lang and Klaus Reinhart and Otto Schroeder. I was having the Agency bureau here check back as far as 1945, to see if there was any record of their having stayed on in Germany or gone underground. And I'm putting out tracers on that organization Schroeder's son belonged to." He stopped, conscious of Davidson's annoyance and pleased at it. "Now that you've brought in extra people, we should be able to do it a great deal quicker," he said. "I've also asked for the Mossad's help in Israel. I've asked them to check through the Nazi-hunting bureau set up after the war, promising them liaison if we find anything."

"I suppose you've told Langley all this?"

"Oh, yes," agreed Berman. "After what happened last time, I think it's important they know from the start who does things and who doesn't, don't you? I wouldn't want you held responsible for any more mistakes I make."

"It won't happen," said Davidson. "Believe me, it won't happen."

"I don't intend it to," said Berman, turning the other man's expression. "Believe me, I don't intend it to."

"What is it?" demanded Rebecca, the moment Hartman entered her apartment from his meeting with Karpov.

"More Nazis," he said.

"Where?"

"Cologne."

"They'll be more nervous after the Schroeder killing," said the woman.

"Yes," said Hartman. "The German authorities might be more active, too."

"When?"

"Not immediately. I'm not to go until I'm told."

"Why not right away?"

"I don't know."

"How much did you ask for?"

"Seventy-five thousand dollars," said Hartman. "I said it would be more dangerous than Frankfurt."

"He didn't argue?"

"No," said Hartman. "He never does."

"When do you think your apartment sale will be completed?"

"Maybe two months."

"I'm looking forward to your moving in, darling," said Rebecca. She hadn't told him of the conversation with Karpov about loyalty. She didn't want Hugo any more nervous than he already was.

"So am I," he said sincerely.

23

There had been other occasions when he was assigning Hugo a particularly dangerous or difficult operation, that Karpov had found difficulty in retaining his natural exuberance. But today had been the most difficult of all. He was killing the man, Karpov thought, as surely as if he were firing the bullet or wielding the knife or whatever it was they would use. It was an absurd reflection for him to have—dangerous even, for what he was supposed to be. Hugo Hartman was a freelance operative. And freelance operatives were always disposable. That was precisely *why* they were used. But Karpov had never thought of Hugo as a disposable freelance operative. They could never be friends, because professionalism didn't permit such relationships becoming friendships, but if it had been possible, Karpov realized he would liked to have had the other man as a friend.

He'd meant what he said, months ago, to Migal about bravery. How did any of them know how they'd behave in the sort of camps in which Hugo was imprisoned. He'd shit himself, Karpov thought objectively, if he ever thought he was going to be sent to Siberia. So he didn't think Hugo was a coward. Or even weak. He thought he was a kind, abused man who was probably the best agent he'd ever run. Or would run in the future.

Karpov stood up abruptly from the table at which he'd prepared the Austrian for Cologne. If he were to have any future, he had to put aside his sentimentality and remember what he was, a professional intelligence officer. More than that: a professional intelligence officer shortly to gain promotion that would give him power and prestige and respect in a country from which he'd been away far too long. He wondered if his marriage to Irena could have been saved if all this had happened two or three years earlier. Another sentimental thought, he realized, irritated at himself. It hadn't happened earlier, and divorce was inevitable now.

Karpov went to his stereo equipment and clipped the cassette into its socket. The recording was inferior, but the installation was sophisticated enough to amplify it. Even so, Karpov missed several words the first time he played it through, so he rewound and listened to it a second time, and then, to be sure, a third. Not just the words but the nuances were important.

Dollfuss had done well, concluded Karpov; better than he would have expected. But he still hadn't managed to take the discussion beyond the initial sparring. Karpov frowned at the qualification: initial sparring was to gauge your opponent's advantages and weaknesses. So what advantages and weaknesses were evident in this scratchy recording?

The fact that the Americans were building up was the major information. But he still didn't know why. Adept at utilizing his machine against the count register, Karpov wound forward until he'd almost exhausted the tape and came in almost exactly at the point he wanted.

At the moment, we're working on hearsay without any concrete evidence. The American accent, basic Midwest with overtones of an Eastern education, echoed around the Viennese apartment.

True or false? If it were true, then any suspicion about Hugo was resolved. But would Berman have gone as far as to reveal his source? As well as the tape, Dollfuss had made out a report, saying he believed the American had been completely open. But to have disclosed the origin of any information flew in the face of any training manual of any intelligence agency in the world.

Karpov played the tape through again in its entirety. All the reports from New York indicated that the authorities believed Reinhart had died in the explosion, which made the later CIA attention to forensic dentistry intriguing. It wouldn't have been necessary if the CIA had turned Hartman and helped in providing Reinhart for the supposed suicide. They'd have known anyway it wasn't Reinhart.

The only purpose would have been some sort of public announcement, to maintain the interest briefly caused by the New York bombing. But there hadn't *been* any announcement; the publicity had lasted a week, maybe a little longer, and then died. Karpov snapped the cassette out of the machine, hefting it in his hand. He was trying too hard with too little. For each argument in favor of Hugo's loyalty, there was usually a contrary one.

He began walking toward where he intended hiding the tape and then halted abruptly, caught by a thought. If this operation were successful—and it had to be, because his safety was involved—then Karpov knew he would be going back to Moscow. And if Hugo were killed, then Rebecca would be returned as well. The satisfaction went as quickly as it came. Rebecca would be returning to her husband, he remembered.

Karpov continued on across the room. With apparent carelessness—but in fact with great precision—he concealed the tape among the dozens of other recordings in his jazz collection, putting it in a box labeling it a performance of Charlie Parker in Birdland.

He checked his watch against the time of the Bonn flight and turned to the correspondence that had arrived as Hugo was leaving. Karpov exercised great care with his communication to and from Moscow, aware that its interception and then monitoring was the most likely way of his being arrested by the Austrian counterintelligence service. Never, at any time since his establishment in Vienna, had there been any contact between him and the Soviet Embassy.

But he used them, untraceably, for pickups because he

never personally collected anything from the dead-letter drops set up around the Austrian capital. That was always done by an accredited Russian who could claim diplomatic immunity in the event of detection. And the packages were never addressed for final delivery to him at the same location in any succeeding week. His response to Moscow always listed as many addresses as there were weeks in the following month. And the addresses to which the packages had to be sent always had to accord with the number of their week. The drops were numbered correspondingly, which enabled Karpov to observe the pickup by the Soviet diplomat and ensure that at no time—either there or during his subsequent journey to the post office for onward mailing—was the man under surveillance.

If that happened, Karpov would have at once abandoned the address and gone into hiding until he was satisfied it was safe to reemerge or that he had to make his way across the border into Czechoslovakia and from there to Russia. It was a time-consuming procedure but one that he didn't mind, because it ensured his safety. Safety was something of paramount importance to Karpov.

The pickup the previous evening had been from a newly established cache beneath a small bridge over the trickle of the Wein River, and from his observation Karpov knew there had been no surveillance. Like a child at Christmastime, Karpov decided on the larger of the two packages.

Stiff cardboard had been taped around the package, to prevent it bending during the journey from New York, and Karpov needed scissors to cut it away and extract the photographs of Gerda Hartman's grave he had requested. There were two, one a general shot showing its neatness compared to the surrounding burial plots, and then another taken very close, so that the inscription could be read. The first lines read:

Gerda Hartman,
Deeply loved wife of Hugo and their son, David

Beneath had been added a slightly newer inscription. It read:

Hugo Hartman
Sadly missed by their son, David

Here were Hugo's loyalty, Karpov recognized at once. He supposed there would have to be a final test, to be sure, and that would have to wait until he returned from Bonn. But Russian didn't have any doubts now. Somehow he wished there had been. It would have made setting Hartman up to be killed far easier.

"You haven't started."

"No," mumbled Gusadarov.

"Why not?"

Gusadarov squinted nervously up at the guard, knowing that every one of the inexplicable privileges could be taken away. "I didn't want to make any mistakes," he said. "I thought it best to assimilate all the figures completely, for every division, before I started to draw."

For several moments the guard seemed doubtful at the logic. Then he nodded. "I want to see something right after the dinner break," he warned.

Gusadarov stood at the bell and dutifully formed the line from the room.

"Draw anything," said a voice behind him.

"What?" Gusadarov's lips hardly moved; years ago he'd perfected the way of undetectable prison talk.

"Draw anything," the man behind advised. "The figures are shit anyway, made up to make it appear the quotas are being exceeded. All you've got to do is ensure that the line for this year's production is bigger than that of the previous one.''

''That's very good,'' said the guard, when Gusadarov offered his completed graph four hours later. ''You can obviously handle figures.''

''Thank you,'' said Gusadarov.

24

When he got to Bonn, Karpov employed every precaution and used every device he had been taught and upon which he had improved over the years. Because he needed to. Migal regarded him as operational, and so he was. But not at this level. Not down in the street. He'd been beyond that for years; he controlled others who took risks like this. He hoped to Christ he hadn't forgotten anything.

He used the Steigenberger Hotel, not only because he knew it was good but because he knew from Dollfuss that the Americans were headquartered at the Königshof, which he otherwise might have used. On the morning of the intended identification he set off along Am Bundeskanzlerplatz at the slow, meandering pace of an unhurried tourist. Only near the corner did he increase his stride, unexpectedly, so anyone following would have been caught off guard. He walked faster after turning the bend and sat at the nearest sidewalk table when he reached the café he had already chosen, during his earlier reconnaissance. The quick arrival of the waiter was an added advantage, because the way the man stood to take his order completely concealed Karpov from anyone hurriedly turning the corner in pursuit. No one did.

Remembering the requirements of the identification procedure he had to go through, Karpov asked for matches as well as coffee. When they were delivered, he wrote the figures 2-13-80 inside the cover and closed it again. No one except himself and the man for whom it was intended would draw any significance from the date of Lang's assassination. Still kid's stuff, he thought, irritated.

Karpov lingered over his coffee, intent on the faces around him, and timed the settling of the bill with the approach of a taxi, so that his entry was practically simultaneous. He asked for the Rheinland Hotel, his money ready when the vehicle pulled up parallel to the river. He went in the main entrance, left immediately by one to the side, and stopped a second taxi at the approach to the Rhine bridge. He gave the Colmantstrasse address of the main museum and only changed it when he satisfied himself there was no following vehicle. He arrived on Bonngasse fifteen minutes before the rendezvous with Dollfuss, patiently joining the small line to enter Beethoven's birthplace.

Karpov was by the composer's piano when Dollfuss made the contact, and the Russian moved away from the crush of people, going nearer the narrow window.

"Was the information about the American helpful?" asked Dollfuss at once.

"Extremely so," said Karpov. He thought the other man's cologne sickly.

"They've all arrived now."

"What are they doing?"

"General inquiries, as far as I understand. Our people keep bumping into them."

"Have they promised cooperation?"

"Of course," said Dollfuss. "They would, wouldn't they?"

"Are you sure there's no specific investigation, concentrating on any one man?"

"No," said Dollfuss honestly. "I'm not sure."

"Would any request for records come through you?" asked Karpov.

"Yes," said Dollfuss.

"How long would it normally take you to respond to a request, if one were made?"

Dollfuss pulled down the corners of his mouth in an uncertain expression. "Not more than twenty-four hours; thirty-six at the outside," he said. "Most of the archival material is on microfiche."

"If there is one, I want to know immediately."

Dollfuss shifted, uncomfortable at the increasing demands being made upon him. "How can you be told immediately?"

"There's to be daily contact between us."

"Daily!" Dollfuss' alarm flared.

"This is a particular operation," said Karpov, seeing the need for reassurance. Apparent consideration would produce better results now than open pressure. That could come if Dollfuss raised serious objections.

"Over what period?"

"I don't know yet," said Karpov. "Maybe only a day or two," he lied easily. He looked around the cramped room and said, "We'd better move on."

Side by side the two men rejoined the line passing the piano. Karpov frowned at the exhibited ear trumpet used by the composer and said, "Amazing, isn't it, that such wonderful music could have been created by someone who was deaf."

"Where?" demanded Dollfuss, uninterested in small talk.

"Are you known at the Schlosspark?"

"No."

"The Eden?"

"I've been there a few times."

"What about the Bristol?"

"Not often."

"Succeeding days, starting tomorrow," instructed Karpov. "The bar of the Schlosspark first, then the Eden, then the Bristol."

"What time?"

"Six, every evening."

"We could be conspicuous, establishing a regular pattern," protested the German.

"No, we won't," insisted Karpov. "Only approach me if there's a reason. If there isn't, don't bother with any recognition. And I'll only approach you if I need to. At the Bristol, three days from now, we *will* meet, to arrange other places. We won't repeat any twice."

They funneled down the stairway toward the street and Karpov said, "You were paid five thousand marks for the information about the American."

"Yes," agreed Dollfuss.

"For this you'll get seventy-five hundred," promised Karpov. He paused, then added, "A day."

For the first time since the encounter began, Dollfuss' face lightened. "Thank you," he said.

"You're going to earn it," insisted Karpov.

Karpov arrived at the Alter Zoll precisely at noon, pausing to gaze up at the huge fortress overlooking the river before setting out on the recognition procedure stipulated in the message that had reached Migal in Moscow. It was practically choreographed, like some ballet sequence, Karpov thought; except only he was being made to dance. He remained on the required bench for the required number of minutes, stopped for the specified time overlooking the Rhine from one of the wall buttresses, and found the trash bin against the lamppost. As he passed, he threw the marked matchbook away. They were too quick in trying to retrieve it, and Karpov isolated them at the next identification halt, near the signpost advertising steamer trips on the Rhine. Young, smooth-faced men, casual in jeans and leather vests, but neat. Karpov showed no sign of his check, continuing on. The sort of people Hartman had described, he remembered.

There were two more specified halts along the promenade toward the Bundeshaus. After the second, Karpov sat on another unnecessary bench, staring at the parliament buildings in which the questions had been asked that had maintained public interest in the killings of the Nazis. It was a grand, imposing building, he thought; but then the Germans had always excelled in impressive architecture.

Karpov looked away, back down the promenade. The men who had gone to the bin had disappeared, naturally, and Karpov did not try to identify any other watchers from the crowd that thronged the walkway. They weren't important. He felt a sudden burst of irritation at having blatantly to identify himself to these amateurs. It was an insult to his professionalism. Just like the whole bloody operation.

To his left the Rhine was silver in the sun. Busybody ferryboats hurried among the barges, aloof, like swans among ducklings. The tight-packed forests were black against the hills of the far bank, and because the heat haze was so strong, it was difficult for Karpov to distinguish the Eifel Mountains he knew were there. He rose, after the allotted time, to retrace his steps.

It *was* a dance, he decided, recalling his earlier reflection. He was performing like a puppet for two different sets of masters, jerked and pulled in one direction by a frightened Migal, and in another by some unknown frightened German—all for an audience of fools.

For what? Power, he accepted. Prestige, too, within a closed, insular circle. Somewhere out on the river a vessel hooted, and he looked toward it. It was very beautiful, Karpov thought. As Vienna was beautiful and Paris was beautiful and Rome was beautiful. All cities that he could visit and enjoy. All beautiful.

The realization was so sudden that Karpov faltered, putting out his hand to the bordering wall for support. His control was so superb that the hesitation was only momentary, the apparently automatic reaction of a man who feared missing his footing. But it wasn't the danger of missing his footing that caused Karpov to stumble. It was the awareness—the shocked, abrupt awareness—that it was freedom he didn't want to miss. He didn't want to return to the claustrophobia of the Soviet Union. Ever.

The information that Berman requested from the Israeli authorities arrived in the diplomatic pouch, via Washington. Because of its volume, it was stacked in piles beyond the strictly controlled CIA section, in a basement room of the American Embassy on Mehlemer Avenue in Bad Godesburg.

Five men were already attempting to create some order in the files when Davidson and Berman entered the room.

"It could take months to check them all," said Berman.

"Then, if it's necessary, it'll take months," said Davidson.

"Any sort of priority?" asked one of the sorters.

Davidson shook his head. "They're all priority," he said unhelpfully.

"We could make a computer listing of the names, together with those we've got in the Langley archives. And then do a comparison run against those in the German records," suggested Berman. "It might cut down the time. Some of these could be dead. Or in jail."

Davidson jabbed his toe against one of the stacks of files, irritated that the idea hadn't occurred to him first. "It's worth trying," he said.

"Who is he?" demanded Kurt Schroeder, who minutes before had handed Gesler the identifying matchbox from the trash bin.

"I don't know his name," said Gesler. "Somebody who can help."

"I don't understand."

"You don't need to," said the older German curtly.

"If I'm to protect you properly, I should know everything," insisted the younger man.

"We don't know what you're trying to protect me from," said Gesler. "Or who."

"Will he?"

25

Karpov walked completely around the public vestibule of the Bundeshaus, wanting to be sure, and then obeyed the next set of instructions to join the tour of the third guide, a sharp-featured, autocratic woman who seemed to dislike her function. She strode ahead of them, giving her commentary in a clipped, mechanical voice, and Karpov felt sorry for the visitors who genuinely wanted to make the tour, which he didn't. He remained at the rear of the group, not bothering to listen to the historical account of the transfer from Berlin, waiting for the contact.

It came on the second floor, as they were trailing along a corridor toward the visitors' gallery of the debating chamber. Karpov saw the man farther ahead, apparently studying a guidebook, and recognized him from the previous day as one of those who had retrieved the matchbook from the bin. As the group passed, the man joined it alongside Karpov and said, "I think you are expecting me."

"Am I?" asked Karpov.

Kurt Schroeder opened his closed hand, and Karpov saw the dated matchbook. "Yes," said Karpov. "I am expecting you."

"You're to come with me."

"Where?"

"Just come." The German was excellent, decided Schroeder, but there was an accent. He couldn't determine what it was.

Karpov walked uncomfortably beside the younger man, all his instincts screaming protest. They emerged from the main door of the government building, leading out onto the promenade. Karpov had expected them to go toward the road, but instead the younger man continued on, parallel to the river, and the Russian realized they were heading toward one of the pleasure steamers. They got in line at the booth and the German bought tickets.

"We go across," said Schroeder.

"All right," said Karpov.

"Inside," ordered the German.

"No," refused Karpov. "We stay outside." He didn't want to get trapped in any confined space.

Schroeder stiffened at the challenge, then relaxed. "All right," he said. "Outside."

The ferry pulled away, and Karpov stood looking back at the city's outline forming behind him, like one of those stand-up pictures in children's books. Very beautiful, he thought again. He was aware of the German studying him intently and wondered if there were anyone else on the boat photographing him. It was crowded with tourists, all with cameras, so any precaution was difficult. He took what he could, remaining with his back to the people, staring out over the river.

"Do you like Bonn?" asked the German.

"Yes."

"I think it is one of the better cities in Germany, don't you?"

The younger man was trying to discover how well he knew the country, Karpov recognized. "Perhaps," he said unhelpfully.

"You had a long journey?" Schroeder decided the accent wasn't from any Latin language.

"No," said Karpov. The far bank was forming more clearly now, jutting jetties and wooden hills beyond.

"Königswinter is very popular at this time of the year," offered Schroeder, trying to encourage the conversation. He was determined to identify the accent.

Karpov looked away, not replying.

The ferry nudged into its mooring, to pick up more passengers, and Karpov filed into the disembarkation line behind his guide. They went side by side along the jetty, and the man indicated a parked Mercedes. "Not far now," he said.

Schroeder opened the front passenger door, but Karpov pointedly ignored it, sitting instead in the rear, where he had a full view of the other man.

"You have no need to be nervous," said Schroeder when he got behind the wheel.

"I'm glad," said Karpov, unconvinced.

"We've been very careful." Perhaps the accent was Polish, he thought.

The car began almost at once to climb through the lower hills of the mountains. Just after they crossed the bridge over a narrow stream, the man pulled off the main road onto a smaller highway, and then turned again onto a track. After five minutes the vehicle stopped. From the odometer, which he'd monitored since they started, Karpov knew it was precisely eighteen kilometers from the ferry dock. It was automatic for him to make such checks.

He followed the other man along a pathway, and then stopped at the clearing that suddenly opened ahead of them.

"We're here," announced Schroeder.

Karpov decided that the forest meeting was melodramatic but also practical; it meant there was no way he could identify whoever it was he was going to meet by a city address or by following him after the encounter. He was isolated, without transport, so any pursuit would be impossible. Gunther Gesler arrived five minutes later, coming from behind along the same path, and Karpov guessed the man had waited until he was sure they hadn't been followed from the ferry. Gesler looked first to Schroeder.

"We'll talk alone," he announced.

The younger German looked uncertain and then moved away, to the far side of the clearing.

To the Russian, Gesler said, "You are Ivan Migal?"

"Of course not," said Karpov. He was looking fixedly at the other man, wanting to impress every feature upon his memory, in case it ever came to studying the old photographs in the Moscow archives. The face was full but naturally creased, so there hadn't been any surgery. No identifying marks. The man walked normally, so there was no injury that might have been noted in the records. Well barbered. The suit was expensive, and the ring on his left hand was inset with a diamond. Successful, then.

"I think I have something he might want," said Gesler.

"Yes."

"You're empowered to negotiate?"

"Fully," assured Karpov.

"I know the position that Migal holds. And therefore what you must be."

"Yes," said Karpov.

"You've got unlimited facilities?"

"What is it you want?"

"Protection," said Gesler. "Complete protection."

Karpov gestured toward the younger German on the other side of the clearing. "What about him and his friends?"

"Three of us have been killed," said the German. "I want more than him and his friends."

"We can give you protection," promised Karpov.

"And I want to know who it is," said Gesler. "It will provide proof of your efficiency."

So Migal had correctly guessed the demands, thought Karpov. It really hadn't been difficult, he supposed. "That too," he agreed. "But we'd need an exchange."

"Of course," said Gesler.

"The complete records."

"You'll get everything," promised Gesler.

Liar, thought Karpov. Brief though the meeting had been, Karpov decided the other man wasn't a fool.

"We'll need to have other meetings," said Karpov. "I'll need a way to make contact."

"You're surely more expert than I."

"An advertisement in the *Bonner Rundschau*," said Karpov. "It will say: 'French student, wishing to improve German, seeks summer exchange.' "

"French student, wishing to improve German, seeks summer exchange," parroted Gesler.

"The following day we'll meet at the cathedral."

"Where?"

"Outside, in the cloister colonnade."

"All right," agreed Gesler.

"*We* will meet," insisted Karpov. "No more intermediaries."

"If anything happens to me, the material automatically becomes public," said Gesler.

"I understand," said Karpov. "I've promised protection."

"You go back first," insisted Gesler, nodding toward the path.

"All right," said Karpov. It was the first mistake the man had made. But then he wasn't a professional.

Gesler called to the other German, and this time Karpov led the way down the path. The second Mercedes, a blue vehicle, was parked neatly alongside the one in which Karpov had been driven from the ferry. Karpov got into the first car, leaning back against the upholstery. It had gone well, he decided.

It was late afternoon before Gesler and Schroeder got back to the office in Bonn.

"It was a good meeting?" queried the younger German.

"I think so," said the lawyer. "Thank you for what you did."

"He's not German?"

"No," agreed Gesler.

"What, then?"

"I've told you, somone who can help."

"I don't think we can go on, unless we trust each other completely," said Schroeder, imagining a threat of withdrawal would be the ultimate weapon.

"Please yourself," said Gesler easily. It was a good feeling to know that he didn't need these amateurs any more.

Dollfuss protested at the demand but Karpov insisted it wouldn't arouse any suspicion, and so finally the German made a telephone call from the hotel booth to the registration department. It took only five minutes.

"It was a blue Mercedes, 1979."

"Yes," said Karpov.

"It's registered in the name of a man named Gunther Gesler. Address is Berliner Freiheit, here in Bonn."

"If the Americans make any inquiry about him, I want to know at once," insisted Karpov.

"Why is he important?" asked Dollfuss.

"Because of a mistake, a long time ago."

26

There is a lot of cover on busy trains and in busier railway terminals. Which was why, after receiving Karpov's mailed orders to resume the Nazi hunt, Hartman traveled by rail to Cologne, twice breaking and then resuming his journey, quite satisfied when he finally arrived that he did so alone. He emerged from the futuristic glass-walled station to confront the immediate contrast of the ancient cathedral alongside, laced with its filigree of flying buttresses and ornate stonework. He paused momentarily, deciding that the old was definitely preferable to the new.

He knew the city and how close the terminal was to where Magnusstrasse looped in to join Friesenstrasse, so he decided to walk. He turned away from the river, automatically using window reflections to ensure he remained alone. There was a lot more Soviet material on Rude Becher than there had been on the three he'd traced in Frankfurt, and Hartman supposed it was because the wartime major had been liaison officer with Eichmann's special unit when the Russians overran Budapest in 1944; a large number of German records had been captured in the speed of the Russian advance. Those records wouldn't have contained Becher's new identity, Ernst Strauss, of course. So the Russians must have invested considerable time and effort in maintaining their records. Then why had they apparently stopped, making it necessary for him to become involved?

Hartman knew that intelligence services were corseted by bureaucracy and frequently did inexplicable, illogical things, but he couldn't lose his doubts about this. Any more than he could lose his doubts about Karpov. Hartman was convinced, from his meeting three days earlier in Vienna, that the Russian's attitude was forced now. And that was as illogical as everything else. Because Karpov's demeanor was not one of suspicion, as Hartman had feared, but almost one of embarrassment. And what did Karpov have to be embarrassed about in his dealings with him? Circles within circles, thought Hartman.

At the junction with Tunisstrasse, Hartman crossed to the far side of the street, wanting to approach the antique shop identified in the Russian information with the maximum view. He isolated the premises at the intersection and realized he would have to cross again to confirm they were no longer occupied.

Becher's shop was more on the smaller Friesenstrasse. Hartman stayed to the right and on the opposite side of the road. There were advertising signs of three different realtors, offering the place either for sale or rent. Both windows were empty, but the paintwork appeared comparatively new. Hartman continued on without a pause, wondering if he would have the same luck with the profession Becher had chosen that he had had in Frankfurt with Hans Leitner.

He used the directory from a street telephone to get the address of the local antiques association. Because of his need to eat regularly, he lunched before making the approach. It was virtually the same that had been so successful in Frankfurt: he identified himself as a dealer who had encountered Herr Strauss in New York's Parke-Bernet Galleries and had arrived in Cologne to discover the address he had been given no longer occupied. It took five minutes for Hartman to get the new location near the Severin Bridge.

It was late afternoon when Hartman made his approach, and he got his confirmation immediately. Becher's clumsy protectors were in two cars, one immediately outside the shop, the other at the corner of Follerstrasse. St. Severin's Church gave Hartman all the protection he needed. He settled easily in the wall's shadow, waiting. Would Becher be assassinated, like Schroeder? Probably. The reaction to Schroeder's killing had been incredible, which seemed to be the objective that Karpov had outlined. Hartman supposed he should feel some moral revulsion at his involvement in a murder. But he didn't. And it wasn't because he knew the history of these men—that they were responsible for the deaths and torture of thousands. He felt nothing, because the capacity for such emotion had been drained away, years before. The irony—that emotionally he had been prepared to do what he was doing by the sort of men whom he was now identifying—was almost obscene.

When Becher emerged, the security was much greater than it had been for Schroeder, which Hartman guessed was *because* of Schroeder. Shortly before five, the men in the car directly outside of Becher's shop went into the building, and two more cars moved around as backup. Becher emerged surrounded by the group, so that it was difficult to see him. It was only possible because of his height. Hartman managed two photographs but didn't bother further; it wasn't necessary. It was automatic to record the car numbers, and by noon the following day the Austrian had the registration details of their owners. The previous night the convoy had gone south, along Bayenstrasse, and Hartman was pointing that way in a rented car when the convoy passed him. He allowed three cars to separate him before following, along a route he recognized as being around the perimeter of the old walled area of the city. Becher's house was a large, walled building just beyond the Volksgarten. Unlike Schroeder in Frankfurt, Becher was driven through the gates, which closed immediately behind. The other two cars took up positions on either side of the gatehouse. As he continued on, to loop back into the city, Hartman wondered if they got as bored as he sometimes did, just sitting and waiting and watching. But this time he hadn't been bored. This time it had been as simple as Karpov kept promising, and if he hurried he could catch a late flight back to Vienna.

The contracts should be completed very soon now, so there was no reason why he shouldn't move in with Rebecca. Would it be easy, living with her? Hartman confronted the question, surprised at it. He'd never lived with anybody, he realized—not properly. The time he spent with Gerda before their arrest hadn't been properly living together. Nor had it been afterward, when they were released. Certainly he'd remained in Rebecca's apartment and she in his, sometimes for several days, but again that hadn't been normal. Hartman telephoned her from the airport, after confirming his flight, excited by the obvious pleasure in her voice at the thought of his returning. Of course it would be easy to live with her.

Oleg Karpov was a long way from the telephone booths, completely concealed by the luggage lockers, but still able clearly to see Hartman when he emerged and at once joined the line leading into the departure terminal.

There should have been photographs other than those he had taken, showing the American at work, Karpov decided. Movies, too. For two days he had watched and recorded a consummate professional operating at a standard the training schools tried to achieve but rarely succeeded in doing. Realistically Karpov accepted that if he hadn't briefed the man—given him the addresses and known where he would be and what he would be doing—it would have been impossible for his own surveillance to have remained undetected. But it had. He had the photographs of Hugo that were necessary to exchange for the information Gunther Gesler possessed.

What about the other photograph, showing that Klaus Reinhart was in Gerda's grave? Karpov had avoided it during the Cologne briefing, because he thought it might interfere with Hugo's performance. But he'd just witnessed that. So there was really no reason why he shouldn't confront the man with it. Damn positive proof, thought

Karpov. And damn Migal, for demanding it. Karpov didn't want any further evidence of Hugo's loyalty. Or any further pain for a man who had suffered enough. An explanation would be easy enough: he'd say the request was regarded as frivolous and unimportant.

Karpov confirmed his own return to Vienna on the last plane. He considered waiting in the bar until Hugo's departure and then deciding against it. He didn't want to drink. He didn't want to go back to Russia. And he didn't want to set Hugo up like this.

Mikhail Frolov led the assassination squad, as before. And as before, they were extremely careful. The orders were again for an explosion, so they concentrated initially on the cars, before abandoning a repetition of the Schroeder killing as impractical. The alternative involved being seen, which was normally unthinkable, but on this occasion Frolov knew there was no possibility of any witness coming forward to provide a description. Although Cologne is the largest city in the Rhineland, Frolov remained cautious, making the thirty-five-mile journey to Düsseldorf to buy a genuine ormulu Louis XVI clock rather than risk Becher discovering through colleagues the purchase in his own town. It took a day, when he returned to Cologne, for him and his team to prepare it, so it was Thursday before Frolov drove down Severinstrasse and entered Becher's shop with the unwrapped piece beneath his arm. An assistant made the initial examination and then summoned Becher from his office at the rear. Frolov said he recognized that an immediate decision would be difficult and that he appreciated the antique dealer would like to subject the clock to a proper examination before considering a purchase. He was prepared to accept a receipt, to guard his ownership, and return the following day for a fuller discussion.

At the door, receipt in hand, Frolov paused to satisfy

himself that Becher was still examining the clock. Outside, he turned right. The direction provided the signal to the man on Follerstrasse, who waited until his squad leader was fifty yards away from the building and therefore safe. Then he dialed the number of Becher's shop.

The bomb was triggered by the electrical impulse of the telephone. A passerby as well as three assistants were killed with Becher in the blast.

On the way to the airport, one of Frolov's squad asked, "How much did that clock cost?"

"It was genuine," said Frolov. "I wanted him greedy, not suspicious. I paid a hundred thousand marks."

"What a waste!" said the first man.

The initial lesson had been the important one. Within days Gusadarov realized that the figures were never checked, his graphs and compilations never analysed. Only one thing mattered: making the figures show that production for the current year was an improvement over the last. So it should have been easy. But Gusadarov didn't find it so. It wasn't—directly—the figures. Or what he was required to do with them. There is a simplicity to animal survival. Food is snatched and stolen and hoarded. Possessions—like an animal's territory—are protected and guarded and fought for, to the death if necessary. Because, if they're not, it means you die.

Gusadarov had adjusted to that; had known always how to behave and what to do. But what was happening now confused him. He didn't know how to conform on this middle level. He knew he had to, to remain on it and avoid going back down again. If only he could think clearly! If only his mind would hold a thought and link it to another and continue in some logical sequence. But it wouldn't. His mind was as jumbled as the mess of figures he had to compute. And as meaningless.

27

Ivan Migal crossed into the West by the required dog's-leg, changing his identity according to his false documentation in Paris, backtracking to Amsterdam, and from there flying directly to Bonn. He traveled in a turmoil of uncertainty, far worse than anything he'd anticipated. In Moscow or in any of the satellite capitals—anywhere in the East, in fact—he traveled cossetted, with officials to arrange his transportation and his itinerary and his accommodation. Now he was quite alone, unprotected and unadvised. He didn't know how to look after himself on a journey the whole purpose of which was to look after himself! He imagined every polite official inquiry a challenge, every policeman his pursuer. He was confused by customs formalities that were normally waived, bewildered by airport indicator boards he'd never before had to consult.

At the Steigenberger he made a mistake filling in the first registration card and actually pulled away from the porter when the man approached to carry his cases. He nodded, not understanding the purpose, when the man went through the charade of showing him the advantages of the room, and only when the porter remained pointedly silent did he belatedly fumble for a tip. He followed the porter to the door, bolting it behind the man, and then further secured it with a safety chain.

It was a large room, a minisuite. What had once been bedchambers in some of the official buildings in Moscow had rooms as luxuriously appointed as this, but they had been built by the Romanovs or their courtiers. No hotel Migal had ever stayed in was furnished in such style. Like a blind man suddenly recovering his sight, Migal made a slow tour, reaching out in the bathroom to feel the unaccustomed thickness of the towels, putting on and then immediately turning off the enormous television in the sitting room, and testing the brocaded bed in the bedroom annex.

Back in the main room he saw a small closet he hadn't noticed before, and when he opened it smiled gratefully at the bar. He read the paying instructions, lifted the flap, and poured both miniature bottles of vodka into a single glass, needing the drink. Halfway through it, he decided to unpack. He did so slowly, examining the clothes he was not used to and then examining his reflection in his own clothes in the mirror inside the wardrobe. The angle made it possible for him to see the door and its securing chain. He turned, crossing to it and needlessly testing, to make sure it was in place. For the first time since leaving Moscow, Migal felt safe inside this locked and chained room.

He finished the drink and realized he would need room service for more vodka, so he decided not to bother. He tried the television again, jabbing his way through the selector buttons, and decided not to bother with that, either. He returned to the bathroom and cleaned his teeth, peering closely into the mirror and becoming aware for the first time how waxen and sallow his skin was.

When the knock came, Migal jumped at it, not moving to respond. It came again, more insistent. He moved to the door and said, 'Yes?'

"It's me."

Migal was suffused with relief at the recognition of Karpov's voice. He hesitated for several more seconds, wanting to compose himself, then released the chain and finally the lock.

Karpov could recognize fear, because it was an advantage he had been trained to use, and he recognized it in Migal as soon as he entered the suite. The men smelled of it, like a positive odor, his apprehension obvious in every gesture and movement.

"Sorry about the room," apologized Karpov. "By the time I tried to make a reservation, there were only these smaller suites left."

"It's fine," said Migal.

"No problems?" inquired Karpov.

"None," said Migal. I hope, he thought. He gestured towards the attaché case that Karpov carried and said, "Show me what there is on Hartman."

Karpov unlocked the bag and offered the photographs he had taken in Cologne. They weren't perfect, because of Hartman's instinctive and automatic use of concealment, but there was a photograph clearly identifying him near the empty shop on Friesenstrasse and another, camera in hand, photographing Becher outside his second premises. Becher was visible, despite the protection around him, in the second shot.

"Good," said Migal enthusiastically. "Very good. You've got the personnel records as well?"

"Everything," said Karpov. "What about Gunther Gesler?"

"Definite identification of membership in the SS, but nothing apart from that."

"Nothing?" persisted Karpov.

"He's been a careful man. We know a lot about him since the war, so you'll have enough."

"Becher's killing has brought everything almost to the point of hysteria," said Karpov.

"Gesler will be terrified," agreed Migal. "Just as I want him to be. Have you placed the advertisement?"

Karpov nodded. "So the meeting should be tomorrow. But I'm not going to turn up," he said. "It'll increase his fear if I'm not at the cathedral."

Migal frowned. "Where, then?"

"I'll be waiting for him at his home, when he gets back. It'll show how vulnerable he is—and how good we are."

"That's clever," said Migal. He'd been wise in choosing

Karpov. He thought they were going to make a good partnership. He asked, ''Can we trust him?''

''Of course not,'' said Karpov at once, surprised at the naiveté. ''Certainly he'll be frightened, but the likelihood is that it will make him make copies of what he holds.''

''Of course you're right,'' accepted Migal uncomfortably. In sudden admission, he said, ''I'll be glad when it's all over.''

''So will I,'' said Karpov.

28

Gunther Gesler sat hunched in the back of the car, knowing a fear he'd never experienced before, uncaring that it was obvious to the Schroeder boy at the wheel, or that it had been to the others who had been at the cathedral to protect him. What they thought didn't matter. What mattered was the failure of the Russian to make the meeting. For the countless time Gesler took the newspaper clipping from his pocket, mouthing the words of the advertisement, rocking back and forth as if he were in physical pain. It *was* the signal; he knew it was the signal. And he'd done exactly what they'd arranged: gone to the cathedral and lingered outside, among the columns. Then, when there had been no contact and the nervousness had started, he'd walked completely around them. And a second time, more quickly. Finally there had been the hurried entry into the building itself, searching for the face. Why hadn't he been there! He wouldn't be treated like this, Gesler determined, in his fear-driven desperation. *Couldn't* be treated like this. Because he had the means to make a man called Ivan Migal suffer.

And he would suffer. Dear God, how he would suffer. Since Becher's death there appeared no other subject in any newspaper or on any television channel but the war. So now he'd give them something really to make headlines! Not all at once, he decided. A file at a time, one revelation about the Soviet participation following on to another. *If he could*. The qualification intruded into his mind and Gesler whimpered, aloud, so that Kurt Schroeder looked around inquiringly. Who or what was going to keep him safe, if it wasn't the Russians? Otto Schroeder was dead and Becher was dead, so the young idiot in front and his posturing friends weren't going to do it. Why hadn't they turned up at the cathedral; dear God, why hadn't they turned up?

Gesler's house in Berliner Freiheit had an electronically controlled garage opening which could be activated from the car, and since the Becher assassination he had insisted that Schroeder take him straight into the basement and ensure that the doors were closed behind them.

Schroeder took the Mercedes in too fast, so that the the underside scraped the curb edge. Gesler waited until the younger man had pressed the switch to lower the doors behind them before getting from the car.

"No one showed up," said Schroeder.

"No," said Gesler, leading the way to the door into the house. Another demand, since Becher, was that Schroeder accompany him right into the safety of his home.

"Can I still please myself about whether I stay or not?"

Arrogant bastard, thought Gesler. "I'm sorry," he said.

They began ascending the stairs. Schroeder asked, "So who was he?"

"Someone I thought might help. But didn't," said Gesler. He certainly didn't intend admitting liaison with the Russians now.

Gesler jumped, surprised to see Giselda in the hallway, when they emerged from the garage stairway. There hadn't been any further discussion between them following the Becher killing.

Gesler was moving forward to kiss her, clinging to some sort of normality, when she said, "There's a man waiting for you in the study. He said he had an appointment."

Gesler halted, as if he'd encountered some invisible barrier. When he tried to speak, no words came. It was Schroeder who asked the question. "How many?"

"Just one," said the woman.

The younger man went by Gesler, hesitated at the door, and then thrust it open, swinging it wide. Karpov was at the bookcase, a volume in his hand. He looked beyond

Schroeder to the still speechless Gesler and said, "I always found Goethe difficult. Mann, too. Perhaps I just don't understand German literature."

With a supreme effort of will, Gesler forced himself into the room, remembering to close the door to keep Giselda free of any involvement.

"Bastard!" he said, all the fear of the previous hours emerging in his anger. "You bastard!"

"Is that the way to talk to friends?" said Karpov. The German's attitude was precisely what he wanted it to be. He adjusted his—to arrogance—to keep the man off balance.

"We made an arrangement," said Gesler. "You didn't keep it."

"Oh, but I did," said Karpov. "I promised you protection, which you've got. And I promised to discover who was pursuing you, and I've got that too." He gestured around the room. "And coming here and showing that we could discover your identity was done as a further proof of our efficiency."

Gesler found difficulty in speaking again, confronted by everything Karpov had said. Then the important fact registered and he said, "You know who it is!"

Karpov looked pointedly at Schroeder. "Does he stay?" he said.

Recovered now, Gesler looked around to the younger German and then back to Karpov. "Yes," he said. "He stays." Minimal though it was, Schroeder provided some protection, and Gesler was still unsure about the Russian.

"It's a Jewish operation," announced Karpov.

"I *knew* it," said Gesler, slapping one hand into the palm of the other. "I knew it."

"Yids," said Schroeder, from just inside the door. "Always it's the damned Yids."

From an inside pocket Karpov took the picture of Hartman in turn photographing Becher in Cologne. "This was taken a week before Rude Becher's killing,'' he said. ''The man's name is Hugo Hartman. Since the war he's worked for a Jewish identification bureau in Vienna.''

He offered the photograph toward the two men but retained his grip upon it, so that they both had to come forward to see it. It was Schroeder who spoke. ''I know him,'' he said.

''What?'' asked Karpov, genuinely surprised.

''Frankfurt,'' said the younger German, his voice distant. ''I saw him in the Ress the night of the phony telephone call. I sat on a balcony and watched him eat a meal. . . .'' There was a pause and then he said, ''He killed my father. He was the bastard who killed my father!''

He tried to snatch out for the photograph, but Karpov pulled it away, putting it back into his pocket. To Gesler he said, ''There's more—more photographs and a file of information.''

Schroeder looked between the two men and asked, ''What is it?''

''Be quiet,'' ordered Gesler, fully recovered now. To Karpov he said, ''When?''

''Tomorrow night,'' said Karpov. ''Here, because it's secure. Say seven.''

Gesler nodded. ''Will it be you?''

Karpov shook his head. ''Someone else.''

''Migal?''

''The two of us.''

''No,'' said Gesler at once, regarding the man who had frightened him. ''Just one.''

Karpov did not respond at once to the refusal. Then he looked toward Schroeder and said, ''Then he's excluded.'' To Gesler he said, ''Just the two of you, one to one.''

''All right,'' agreed Gesler at once.

''It's important that the files be complete.''

''They will be,'' promised Gesler.

"We still have to be sure."

"Of course." It was going to be all right, decided Gesler. He'd almost cracked, coming to the very edge of the panic for which he'd criticized others so often. But he hadn't gone *over* the edge. Now it was going to be all right. Everything was going to be all right.

"Russian!" Schroeder's face had whitened during Gesler's explanation, and now the man erupted in fury. "You're working with the Communists! Have you forgotten who almost brought this country to its knees between the wars—the people against whom my father and millions like him took to the streets, to save Germany? The Communists, with their crazy demand for revolution."

Gesler was unmoved by the tirade. He'd told Schroeder because there was no alternative, and—sure now of Soviet cooperation—he was unconcerned by the man's reaction. "Don't twist history to suit your own arguments," he said quietly.

"What do you mean?"

"Certainly we had to cleanse our own streets," he agreed. "And we did it. But when it was politically sensible, we made a pact with Moscow."

"It didn't last," argued Schroeder defiantly.

"Again because it wasn't politically expedient for it to do so," said Gesler.

Schroeder smiled, an uncertain expression. "You mean you're planning something?"

"Yes," said Gesler. "I'm planning something." He had a lot of photocopying to do before seven the following evening.

"You shouldn't have agreed to my exclusion tomorrow," said Schroeder.

"Only from the meeting," qualified Gesler. "I want the outside of this house as secure as your people can make it."

"I want him," said Schroeder in sudden vehemence. "I want the bastard who traced my father, who traced Becher. I want to kill him myself."

"Of course," agreed Gesler.

They established the same pattern as before, and Erich Dollfuss was waiting in the bar of the Eden when Karpov entered. As the Russian approached he saw Dollfuss' face twist at apprehension of positive contact, and hoped the German was going to be strong enough. They moved to a booth. Karpov was aware of the other man's quick agreement to a second drink, even though the one he had was still half full.

"You all right?" he asked.

"The pressure is too much," insisted Dollfuss. "Since the second killing, everyone is running around in circles. Did you know there's an emergency debate scheduled in the Bundestag for Wednesday?"

"No," admitted Karpov.

" 'Specially convened to reassure the rest of Europe,' " quoted Dollfuss. He swallowed, glancing away from Karpov's direct look. "I don't want to go on," he said.

"You've got to," said Karpov quietly.

Dollfuss' face quivered again. "Let me alone! Please let me alone!"

"You're being well paid."

"Damn the money."

The time had gone for kindness and consideration, Karpov realized. Now it had to be pressure. "Do you want to lose your job?" he asked.

"No," said Dollfuss shortly.

"In disgrace?"

"Stop it. Please stop it!"

"Humiliate your family . . . your wife?"

Dumbly Dollfuss shook his head.

"Then don't go weak on me," said Karpov. "Don't think you can stop, not yet."

"What do you want?" asked the German sullenly.

"Any inquiries about Gunther Gesler?"

Dollfuss shook his head. "None."

"Good," said Karpov. He didn't enjoy bullying this man, any more than he enjoyed pressuring Hugo. Not that there was any comparison.

They talked for a further fifteen minutes. At the end, Karpov said, "It's all going to be fine, believe me. Everything will work."

Dollfuss didn't speak at once. Then, still uncertain, he said, "You're sure?"

"Absolutely," assured the Russian. "You have nothing to worry about."

Dollfuss was the weak link, he decided. It was unfortunate he didn't have any other choice. Someone like Hugo, for instance.

Peter Berman expeced the outburst. The pressure had gone far beyond the almost continuous stream of cable traffic from Langley to telephone calls. During the last one, it was clear from what he'd overheard from their end of the conversation that there had been talk of Davidson returning personally to provide an explanation.

"So what the hell's happening?" demanded the section head. "There's practically a fucking war going on out there in the streets, and we don't even know who's fighting who."

"We're coming up with a lot of names," offered Berman, indicating the distillation of their computer analysis; there was a stack of folders, and he knew it was going to take weeks to investigate them all.

"What about the right names?" demanded Davidson. "Why didn't we know about Becher? There was a link between him and Schroeder. We should have got that."

"Three men are concentrating on that," said Berman. "By tonight we should have a complete dossier on everyone who ever had any contact with either Schroeder or Becher."

Neither of them was aware of the telephone until one of the other CIA men working on the analysis called out, "Peter!"

Berman turned to the man.

"Call for you," he said. "Someone named Dollfuss."

29

Migal ate nothing all day. After twice calling for the miniature bar to be restocked with vodka, Karpov ordered a full bottle from room service. By five in the afternoon it was half empty. The fear Migal imagined he had kept from the other Russian permeated the room in which they'd sat, throughout the day, rehearsing and planning the meeting.

"I don't want to go alone," blurted Migal.

"That was the deal."

"You shouldn't have agreed."

"You'll hardly be alone," said Karpov. "In the house, maybe. But I'll be directly outside."

"He didn't show you anything he had?"

"What would have been the point of asking?" said Karpov. "We know he's got *something*. Only you can establish its importance. That's why you're here at all."

Migal shifted at the logic, looking toward the bottle and deciding against it.

"We should go," said Karpov.

"It's still early," protested Migal.

"I want to be early," said Karpov. "You never go straight to a meeting."

Migal shifted again, irritated at the reminder of professionalism. "Directly outside?"

"Of course."

Karpov allowed for the evening rush hour, and they approached Berliner Freiheit thirty minutes before the appointed time.

"There!" said Karpov, indicating a parked car in a side street forty yards before Gesler's house. "And there!"

Migal twitched at the indentification of the first and then the second vehicle. "Who?" he asked.

"Louts," said Karpov dismissively. "It was predictable."

He took the car past Gesler's house without slowing, taking the turns that brought them fully around the block. Karpov isolated three men on foot and two more cars.

"Gesler's surrounded the damned house!" said Migal.

"Yes," agreed Karpov. "That's why I wanted to be early."

"So you can come in with me?" The relief was evident in Migal's voice.

"Not at once," said Karpov. "We use it."

"How?"

"For the moment, the protection you need is from the outside, not in with Gesler. I stay outside to see what these young fools might do."

"Anything could happen to me in there! The house will be full of them."

"Which is why I stay outside," insisted Karpov. "Because you go in with nothing. Only when you're satisfied with what he's got, and only when we ensure that all these people are doing is watching, does Gesler get his material."

They were approaching the house.

"It's dangerous," said Migal desperately.

"It's always been dangerous," said Karpov. He reached across the car and said, "Give me the Hartman stuff."

Migal sat unmoving.

"You've got to go in," said Karpov. "You've always known you've got to go in."

Migal put the file on the tunnel shelf between them. "Be ready," he said.

"I will be."

Migal went up the short pathway, climbed the steps, and stood uncertainly in front of the door. He looked back but couldn't see Karpov in the parked and darkened car. At last he stabbed out for the bell. The door was opened immediately by Gesler. The two men stood looking at each other. Then Gesler said, "Come in." Migal followed the German into the study, looking nervously about him. The house appeared deserted.

"You've got something for me," demanded Gesler at once. He was striving for the control he'd always had, wanting to dominate the meeting.

Migal shook his head, trying to match the forcefulness. "You've been told what I've got—seen photographs. I want to know what you have."

Gesler and Schroeder had worked until almost five that afternoon, copying the material withdrawn from the safe-deposit vault. The originals were in a desk drawer. The duplicates, secure until they could be returned to the bank, lay in a floor safe concealed beneath the hinged bookshelf where the German now stood. Despite this double protection, Gesler still resisted, showing a lawyer's reluctance to immediate concessions. "A simultaneous exchange?" he suggested.

Migal discerned the slight weakening, realizing how fortunate he had been to have Karpov with him for the last-minute planning. "No," he said. "The arrangement was that we meet alone. I kept it. Your people are surrounding this house."

Gesler's face tightened at the exposure. It showed how much more expert these people were than those upon whom he'd had to rely. "Just a precaution," he said.

He was winning, Migal decided. "That's why I want to see your material," he said. "Just a precaution."

In a legal contest there is a time to oppose and a time to concede, to gain another advantage. Gesler knew he had nothing to lose by showing the other man what he wanted; by surrendering it completely, in fact. He wanted what the Russian had. And the safeguards it provided. He went to the desk, took out the bundle, and offered it to the other man.

Migal exposed his anxiety by the eagerness with which he snatched for it. On the front of each file was the stamp of the Nazi emblem, and on all but two the second insignia—that of the SS. Migal hunched over them like a connoisseur with his favorite collection: for more than thirty years he'd lived with these, knowing the form in which they were assembled, recognizing the place-names and the bureaucratic clichés and the pedantic German phraseology. He'd been right, Migal knew at once. He'd taken risks of which he'd never believed himself capable and driven his nerves to the point of near collapse, but he'd been right! There were twenty files, all documentating an exchange in which he'd been involved and identified. Fifteen had the gloss of a copying machine, and he knew every one as an operation from which his name had been erased in the Moscow records. But it hadn't been erased from these, which would have been just as disastrous. But that wasn't all. In addition to the incriminating copies, there were five originals, old and soiled, the folder edges furred and torn—five that he hadn't known existed and for which, somewhere in Russia, there would be confirming documentation.

Migal felt a sweep of faintness at the thought of how lucky he'd been. He was going to cross the division in Dzerzhinsky Square, take Karpov with him in perpetual gratitude, and spend the rest of his life secure!

As if aware of the Russian's thoughts, Gesler said, "They could have been extremely embarrassing."

It was the moment to show his strength, decided Migal. To show that he wouldn't be open to blackmail anymore. "You've made copies," he said.

Gesler's head jerked, as if he were pulling back from some physical blow. "No!" he said.

"Don't be ridiculous," said Migal. "You'd have been a fool not to." He wasn't nervous anymore; for the first time in months there wasn't the hollowness in his stomach, the feeling that something was gnawing at him. "You know what I did," he went on. "And you can identify me from your copies. Just as I can identify you. Expose you, as the others have been exposed."

"No, wait. . ." started Gesler, but Migal, who had been ashamed of his own fear and saw it in the other man, said, "No, you wait. You wait and you listen. You'll get the file you were promised, in exchange for these. And you'll get the protection; nothing's going to happen to you. But don't you ever forget what it is now. It's equal dependence. I never want to hear from you or about you again. Any more than you do from me. Agreed?"

This wasn't how it was supposed to have been, thought Gesler. He'd been the one with the evidence, the facts that gave him the power to convict. But it was all being taken away from him!

"If anything ever happened to me, everything would be released," he said, trying to reduce the other man's supremacy. He'd have to establish the system the following day.

"I've told you, nothing will," insisted Migal. The evidence of their killing Hartman would make him absolutely inviolate.

"I want the file," said Gesler.

The first shot was fired at that moment, but neither heard it. They both heard the next, though, because it was nearer, and suddenly there was a stutter of small-arms and automatic fire.

"What the hell. . .!" said Gesler.

"Let me out!" screamed Migal.

The German thrust by him to the door, and Migal ran after him, holding the files against his chest like a shipwrecked man clutching a piece of driftwood. He couldn't think about what was happening; didn't want to. All he wanted to do was escape. He collided with Gesler at a hall window, and before he could focus he heard the German say, "Police! There was uniforms out there." Gesler wheeled on the Russian. "Protection!" he shouted. "You promised me protection!"

From outside came amplified shouts, and then searchlights burst on, blinding them, so that they shied away from the glass. Over the sound of shooting came a louder explosion, a heavy crump of noise, and at once the now brightly lit garden began to fill with smoke.

"Gas!" said Gesler. "They're gassing us."

He turned helplessly to Migal. "What shall we do?" he demanded.

Migal stared back, equally helpless. "I don't know," he said.

Gesler ran farther along the corridor, toward the back of the house, thrusting into the kitchen and then opening a rear door. At once the gagging smell of tear gas swirled into the room and he slammed it again, choking.

"Another door," said Migal, desperately "There must be another door." He still clung to the files, ignoring the immediate itch in his eyes.

"Garage," coughed Gesler. "Basement stairs."

They reached the top when the grenade exploded against the outside of the garage doors, opening them, and the blast threw the Russian and the German back against the kitchen exit.

Both men were back in the study when the police burst in, Gesler half-crouched in an automatic reaction of trying finally to hide beneath the desk.

"Holy Mother of God!" said Davidson, who came in directly behind.

Migal still stood with the folders tight against his body, as if they were the final shield.

Kurt Schroeder lay huddled beneath some shrubbery, not knowing where he was, only that it was parkland and it was dark and that it was somewhere to hide. He wanted so much to hide. The breath howled into him when he breathed, scorching his throat from the effects of the gas. His nose and eyes were running, and the sobs wracked through him. But, because of the chemicals he'd inhaled. He'd been confused by the attack, totally surprised by it. And frightened—desperately, shakingly frightened. No one would have seen him run, because the chaos had been absolute, but that's what he'd done. Fled blindly from garden to garden and then, just as blindly, out onto a road far beyond the blocks that had been set up. And still he hadn't stopped running, not until now, when he'd seen the sudden total blackness of the park and thrown himself down into it. He lay with his arms tight around his body, holding himself as he might have held someone else in attempted reassurance. He'd failed them. He'd failed his comrades and he'd failed his father and he'd failed Gesler, whom he vowed to protect from any attack. Coward, he thought; he was a frightened, runaway coward.

All the gas was gone now, but he sobbed on, into the already damp earth.

Gusadarov sat tensed at his bench, pretending to work on the next set of figures, but actually gazing up under his lowered eyebrows to see the clerks' officer checking the analysis he'd just submitted. He'd already forgotten what he'd done. Just that it wasn't right. He knew what he'd do if there were a challenge. He could be at the desk in seconds. There'd be an advantage in surprise. It would only take a few moments, once he got his hands around the man's throat. Rationality came slowly, like a noise gradually becoming louder. What was he thinking of, attacking a guard! No one ever attacked guards; no one who wanted to live, anyway. Insanity, to think like that. Gusadarov looked away from the man, down to another batch of incomprehensible figures. Shouldn't let his mind drift like that. It hadn't, in the past. Should try to think more of the focus for his survival. Think more of Rebecca.

30

Once the seizure was made, there was initial uncertainty whether any official charge could be brought against either Gesler or Migal. It was Berman who showed the way—and made sure Washington knew it was his idea—by checking Migal's false documentation, proving with CIA photographs the man's true identity, and providing the grounds for an accusation of illegal entry into Germany. It enabled a charge against Gesler of aiding and abetting, before the Germans who had been protecting him made statements trying to minimize their involvement. That was sufficient for six additional charges, all involving the organization, financing, and administration of an illegal paramilitary group.

The West German government immediately saw a way out of the intense embarrassment caused by the earlier Nazi assassinations and issued orders to the counter-espionage service—whom the CIA had persuaded to organize the swoop in the first place—to cooperate fully with the American agency.

That would anyway have involved publication of the wartime records with which Migal had been arrested. But Moscow's reaction made it easier: the Russians issued a formal denial of involvement.

Through the German service, the CIA released their archival photographs, together with several of the Russian after his arrest, one actually in Gesler's study when Migal was still holding the incriminating files. And then they provided the files—not all at once, because they properly recognized that the effect would be drowned in a welter of evidence—but gradually over a period of days. The compilation showed matching care. When—in addition to Gesler and Migal—their names appeared, details were released on Fritz Lang and Klaus Reinhart and Otto Schroeder and Rude Becher.

The publicity was unprecendented and worldwide. It was afterward calculated that in the first fortnight there was no newspaper or journal in any media-oriented country outside the Eastern bloc in which there was not substantial coverage. At the end of the second week, the West German government demanded an official explanation from Moscow. Who made another mistake. There was no formal response. Instead, the Russians requested Migal's repatriation to the Soviet Union, arguing that he was covered by diplomatic immunity. Bonn immediately rejected the demand as risible, repeating the precise wording of the official charge that made it so and adding that Migal was not in any case an accredited diplomat in the country.

A special squad of police had to form an arm-linked corridor for Giselda Gesler to get through the horde of grappling, shouting journalists to visit her husband in prison on the Wednesday of the third week. The chaos of her arrival was the explanation at the later inquiry for normal visitor precautions having been relaxed. That night Gunther Gesler killed himself in his cell with the cyanide his wife passed to him. When the police went to Berliner Freiheit the following day, they found Giselda Gesler dead in bed, contorted in final agony by the same poison.

Gesler, the trained lawyer, had refused any response to every question during the periods of interrogation. He declined also to make any statement. So, too, did Migal. Unusually, the entire West German Cabinet convened to hear the federal prosecutor's opinion before making the political decision that the criminal case be brought on the evidence available.

It was a short hearing, completed in two hours. Migal refused to plead or acknowledge the court, which entered a formal not-guilty plea on his behalf. Ironically, the

Russian request for Migal's return provided the evidence of his real identity, so the hearing was almost entirely devoted to scientific evidence of photographic comparisons and proof that the documentation found on the man was forged. Disregarding all legal rules, the verdict had been decided at that same Cabinet meeting addressed by the federal prosecutor. At the conclusion of the hearing, the carefully briefed court dutifully ordered that Ivan Mikhailovich Migal, whom they found guilty of illegal entry into West Germany from the Soviet Union, should be repatriated immediately to his country of origin.

He was flown out from Frankfurt that afternoon. The last pictures of Migal published in the Western press showed him walking cowed, head bent, to an Aeroflot plane, flanked by three unidentified members of the crew. Photographers hoped he might turn at the top of the steps for one final look at the West, and several shouted, trying to attract his curiosity. But Migal entered without once looking back.

There was an open fireplace in the Dorotheergasse house, so that was the safehouse Karpov used. He prepared it professionally, lining the grate with foil that he could later remove. He burned first the photographs he'd taken of Hartman's Cologne observation of Rude Becher and then, after raking his fingers through the ashes and creating a dust which fell through onto the foil, the documentation about the Austrian that had been prepared to accompany them, had it been necessary to carry through the exchange with Gunther Gesler. He raked that, too, making more dust. He squatted back, finally staring down at the picture by which he knew that Klaus Reinhart was in the same grave as Gerda Hartman.

It could only cause agony, he decided. And Hugo had known enough of that. He held the match against the photograph's edge, watching it blacken under the flames until it became too hot to hold. When he'd made that into dust, he tested the foil to make sure it hadn't overheated, and then carried the debris into the bathroom and flushed it down the toilet. He had to do it twice, because after the first time there were still black remnants lingering in the bowl.

So Hugo was safe; as safe as he would ever be. And so was he. Karpov smiled, injecting the same qualification: as safe as he would ever be. But from Moscow, at least. There would have been recall before now, if he'd made any misjudgment. Probably forceful recall.

His awareness, after his realization that he didn't want to go back to Russia, that Migal would not have kept any documentation convinced Karpov the risk was worth taking. He supposed it was the passage of time, comparatively short though it had been, but it was strange how easy it had all been.

When he'd decided to betray Migal and so stay in the West, Karpov had tried to evolve all sorts of convoluted schemes, with escapes and halts in case they went wrong. But in the end it had been simplicity itself.

Erich Dollfuss would never understand why he had been told to lead the Americans to Berliner Freiheit, but Dollfuss' understanding wasn't important. And Migal wouldn't ever know how it happened.

It might have been more difficult, Karpov supposed, if the watching Germans whose presence he had anyway intended inventing hadn't been so obviously in position. But then again, maybe not. Migal had been scared—stinking scared. And had a lot of vodka. Not drunk; certainly not drunk. But sufficient to impair the sort of considered, balanced judgment that might have made him suspicious.

Karpov discarded the reflection, returning to the main room to await Hartman's arrival. A lot of things might have gone wrong, but they hadn't. It had all worked perfectly. He'd rid himself of a superior he'd never really liked, and he was going to live happily ever after in the West, just like in the fairy tales.

He responded at once to the Austrian's knock, embraced him warmly, made the drinks, and boomed, "How are you, Hugo? How're things?"

Hartman examined the Russian curiously. The bonhomie had been forced for weeks, yet today, when the man had every reason for uncertainty, he seemed exactly like his old self. Ignoring the other man's question, Hartman asked, "Aren't there any problems over Germany?"

Karpov shook his head, "I was always careful to distance you," he said easily.

"I still find it difficult to believe that Migal himself would come across."

"He had to, didn't he?" said the Russian. "Who else could have done it?"

"It was still a desperate thing to do."

"He was a desperate man."

"Did you know he was personally involving himself?"

"No," lied Karpov. "The instructions came from Moscow and so presumably from him, but I took them at their face value—that it was an exercise to upset NATO."

"It's a disaster for Russia," said Hartman.

"Absolutely," agreed Karpov. He added, "I'm glad we're out of it."

"Have you any idea what's going on?"

"Not a clue," said Karpov. Sincerely he said, "There are a lot of advantages in being away from the center of things."

Hartman sipped his drink and said, "I was wondering if there had been any response to what I asked you?"

"The photographs of the grave?"

Hartman nodded.

Karpov spread his hands apologetically. "I tried, Hugo; believe me, I tried. It would have been difficult enough, without what's just happened. It was rejected out of hand as a frivolous request."

"It was hardly frivolous," said Hartman.

"That was their description," he said. "Not mine. I'm sorry, Hugo. Really I am."

Hartman shrugged, not really surprised. He'd expected the rejection, after all.

"When are you moving in with Rebecca?"

"Probably a fortnight."

"You're a lucky man, having a woman like her," said Karpov sincerely.

"I know," said Hartman.

That night Karpov followed the carefully established routine of watching the Soviet diplomat collect from his letter drop and mail the communication on, quite unobserved, to the stipulated address. That week it was the apartment with a view of the Prater. Karpov was waiting for the delivery. There was only one instruction: his recall to Moscow.

Peter Berman realistically expected the sixth floor. On that first night of celebration drunkenness in Bonn, he'd fantasized that they might actually make the Director's sanctum on the seventh, but he'd sobered up in the morning. But not this: never in any wild hope, drunk or sober, had he expected this. The car took the road to cross the Potomac by the Memorial Bridge and Berman glanced across at Davidson, knowing but not caring that his grin would look inane. Davidson's trousers and shirt were crisp and freshly pressed. Like Berman, he traveled with his jacket off, so that it wouldn't be creased when they got there.

"You know we're fireproof after this, don't you?" said Davidson.

"Yes," said Berman.

"Asbestos-lined, flash-resistant, one hundred percent fireproof," said Davidson.

Berman realized the older man was an excited as he was. "I've been told I can choose what I like," he said.

"What's it going to be?" asked Davidson.

"Paris, I think," said Berman. "I really liked it there." He'd take up rowing again, on the Seine. It was a long time since he'd done any exercise.

"So we'll be working together," said Davidson, whose promotion to Deputy Director of Operations had been confirmed that morning.

"Yes," said Berman.

Unexpectedly the older man extended his hand across the car. "No hard feelings?"

Berman accepted the gesture. "No hard feelings," he said.

The car was radio-equipped, so the Secret Service escort were waiting when they entered the White House through the East Gate. The two men walked side by side through the corridor lined with portraits of former First Ladies. After they had passed the small drawing room that acts as the receiving area for official occasions, Berman stared out to his left at the barbered trees and shrubs. Their escort was changed just before the Oval Office.

"He's expecting you," said the second man.

There was no delay. As they entered the room, the President stood from behind his desk and crossed toward them, hand outstretched. Remembering precedence and their newly established relationship, Berman deferred to Davidson.

"I wanted to thank you personally," said the President. "Unofficially, of course."

"Thank you, Mr. President," said Davidson.

"It was a superb operation," said the man. "Superlatively conducted."

"Thank you, Mr. President," recited Berman.

"I want you to know I've made Langley very aware of how I feel about this; how grateful I am to both of you," said the politician.

"Fireproof," exulted Davidson in the limousine taking them back to Langley. "Absolutely fucking fireproof."

31

There was a subservience about the way Oleg Karpov entered the room, but it was a proper demeanor, reflecting the respect due to the men already there and not fear of them. And he wasn't frightened—apprehensive, but not frightened. Because they didn't have anything. There might be suspicion; even doubt. But that's all. If there had been more, his recall would have been by strangers suddenly appearing at his doorway to form the escort. And it wouldn't have been this, an inquiry. It would have been an official trial.

There were three men at the table facing him. Aleksai Tsinev was the chairman, befitting his function as head of the First Chief Directorate. His deputy, Sergei Kiktev, was on the left. Vladimir Krivoshev, to the right, completed the inquiry board.

Tsinev indicated a chair set immediately before them and Karpov lowered himself into it. He looked around the room, conscious for the first time that there were no windows. From the corridors along which he'd been guided, Karpov guessed it would be at the rear of the building, overlooking the Lubyanka prison. Had Migal ended there? he wondered.

"This is an inquiry into the affair in West Germany," announced Tsinev.

Karpov was unsure whether he was expected to respond. Let them lead, he decided: that had always been a characteristic of Migal's, and Migal had survived a long time in these surroundings.

After waiting several moments, Tsinev continued, "An inquiry—a trial—has already been held into the part played in that affair by Ivan Mikhailovich Migal. During the course of those proceedings, certain allegations were made."

While it was important not to respond prematurely, it was equally important not to antagonize these men by appearing obtuse. "And you believe I might be able to help?" Karpov asked. He chose the words carefully, wanting them to appear the reaction of an unafraid man.

"Yes," said Kiktev.

"I shall, of course, be delighted to assist in any way I can," said Karpov. His confidence was registering with them; he was sure of it.

"During the course of his trial, Migal stated you were actively involved in the planning of the operation," said Tsinev.

"I was," said Karpov at once. The reply completely confused them, and Karpov realized they didn't know that a good liar tells the truth as often as possible.

The three men looked among themselves. Then Krivoshev said, "You admit taking part!"

"No," said Karpov.

"You're not making sense," protested Tsinev, his attitude hardening at the thought of another prosecution.

"Some weeks ago I received instructions from Comrade General Migal to return here to Moscow," said Karpov. It was the first admission to make, because there would be records of his arrival, his transportation from the airport, and then the ridiculous charade of passes and escorts from the ground floor.

"For what purpose?" asked Krivoshev.

The archives would have a record system, Karpov knew. "I was shown a number of files," he said. "Files on wartime Nazis. Comrade Migal told me to establish an operation to trace the whereabouts of some whom his information said had remained in Germany. I was not told where that information came from."

"What names were there?" demanded Kiktev.

"Initially Hans Leitner, Otto Schroeder, and Rudolph Diels," said Karpov.

"Initially?" echoed Kiktev.

Damn, thought Karpov, he'd been put into the position of having to offer information, rather than supply it. He saw an escape. "Yes," he said.' 'I was told to have these men traced in Frankfurt, where they were supposed to be living."

"Were the names Lang and Reinhart mentioned?" said Tsinev.

Karpov hesitated momentarily. There was no danger in an admission. "Yes," he said.

"In what context?" pursued Kiktev, who'd seen his earlier query avoided.

"In that they were Nazis," said Karpov. "Comrade Migal told me he had decided to mount an operation to find and expose other Nazis in Europe, to create discord there between West Germany and the rest of her partners."

"He said what!" demanded Tsinev.

"That he wanted to create uncertainty in Europe."

"What about his wartime association with these people, Lang particularly?" asked Krivoshev.

Karpov smiled apologetically. "He said absolutely nothing about that. Had that been discussed, it would have been my duty to acquaint someone in higher authority."

"Yes," said Tsinev. "It would have been your duty." He hesitated. "What did you do?"

Another fact that could be checked, recognized Karpov. "For many years now, we have had in Austria, under my supervision, a particularly outstanding freelance agent named Hugo Hartman. He's a Jew, a victim of the concentration camps. He was an ideal operative. I sent him to Frankfurt, and he located Schroeder."

"What about the other two?" asked Krivoshev.

"They appeared to have lived there until recently but to have disappeared. The inference had to be that it was in fear, because of what had happened to Lang and Reinhart."

"So you set up Schroeder's killing?" asked Kiktev.

It was a clumsy attempt, easily avoided, but Karpov isolated Kiktev as the most dangerous person on the panel. "Oh, no," he said. "Those weren't my instructions. Hartman prepared a report, and I forwarded that report here to Moscow." Where there would be a provable record of its arrival, just as there would be a provable record of the dispatch of the assassination team under Migal's authorization. It was impossible to be certain, but Karpov didn't think he'd made a single mistake so far.

"Did you know Schroeder was to be killed?" asked Tsinev.

"No," said Karpov. "The first indication I had was from newspaper and television reports."

"So you have no idea why it was done?" asked Krivoshev.

Karpov paused, as if he were trying to supply the answer, and then said, "No, none at all."

"What about frightening other Nazis?" pressed the suspicious Kiktev.

Karpov smiled, apologetic again. "It's a possibility, I suppose. Just as I suppose there could be a dozen other possibilities. I don't know the facts, so I really can't provide an opinion."

"Then what happened?" Tsinev went on.

More facts, remembered Karpov. "I was recalled again to Moscow," he said.

"For what purpose?"

"To continue the operation of identifying Nazis."

"During your operational career, have you been recalled to Moscow every time you were briefed on an operation?" asked Kiktev.

"No," said Karpov. "On the initial occasion, when the

Nazi operation was raised by Comrade Migal, I was here for personal, compassionate reasons, which made such a briefing understandable.'' They would know from the files about the divorce application and his request to return.

''What about the second visit concerning Nazis?'' pressed Kiktev.

''It was unusual,'' said Karpov, allowing the safe concession. ''I would have expected to have been briefed through the normal communication channels, without the need to return here.''

''Was there ever any discussion about Gunther Gesler?'' pursued Krivoshev.

''Never,'' said Karpov. Sure of himself, he added, ''His name was never in any of the files I saw.''

Kiktev inquired, ''You have an extensive system of cells organized not just in Austria but in Germany as well?''

''Yes, I do,'' agreed Karpov.

''Did you employ any of them during this operation?'' pressed the man.

Clever question, conceded Karpov. ''No, none,'' he said.

''Why not?'' asked Kiktev, overstepping himself.

This time Karpov's pause appeared one of embarrassment for a superior. Then he said, ''This was an operational activity,'' as if reminding the man. ''Standard instructions are that, whenever possible, such activity is conducted by an asset from a bordering country, to lessen the chances of arrest through earlier indentification and surveillance.''

''Quite so,'' said Kiktev. He was flushed.

''Was anything said during this subsequent meeting about the liquidation of Schroeder being the work of Soviet operatives?''

''Not directly,'' said Karpov. ''It had to be the obvious inference, since his death followed immediately upon my operative identifying the man in Frankfurt."

"So you knew Becher was going to be killed?" asked the chairman.

"It was the obvious inference, again."

"What was the purpose of these killings?" asked Kiktev.

"There was no discussion between us about it, apart from the initial reason of fomenting dissent among the partners of NATO." Karpov hesitated and added, "There was a great deal of public interest in what happened to Schroeder. As an exercise, it seemed to be succeeding in its purpose."

"What about Bonn?" demanded Kiktev suddenly.

"I'm afraid I don't understand the question," said Karpov, refusing to be tricked into committing himself.

"You supervise Germany?" pursued Kiktev.

"Not all of it. I would expect there to be others of whom I am unaware."

Kiktev sighed, irritated at the avoidance. "Sufficient to be called upon for assistance if an operation were being established."

"I myself had been called, for Frankfurt and Cologne," said Karpov with deliberate awkwardness. Of the three, this man had to be confronted, despite Karpov's earlier reluctance to antagonize any of them.

"I asked about Bonn," said Kiktev.

Karpov cleared his face, in apparent understanding. "I was not involved in Bonn," he said. This was the moment of his greatest danger, the moment when some proof might be produced like a rabbit from a conjuror's hat and damn him to a lifetime's imprisonment or worse. For an hour he had parried every thrust, admitting things for which he knew there was independent evidence. This was the only thing he was uncertain about. Karpov knew that, for his part, his presence in the West German capital was unrecorded and untraceable. Only Dollfuss could confirm it, and Dollfuss was unknown in any Soviet file. The gamble was that Migal hadn't kept any record. It wasn't a desperate gamble—the man's anxiety had been to destroy records, not keep them—but it was still a gamble. And if he won this, then he'd won everything. Because everything else they knew he'd confirmed for them with perfectly acceptable explanations.

Karpov sat, waiting for the challenge—some damning piece of evidence he'd forgotten or overlooked that would be sufficient to get him taken from this room directly to the cells God knows how many feet below.

"You believe Migal made the journey entirely alone, without any support or protection?" asked Tsinev.

Karpov felt the beginning of satisfaction, but he was still cautious. "I don't know *what* to believe," he said. "I have no evidence on which to base a belief. He did not make it with *my* support or protection. . . ." He permitted just the right amount of pause and then added, "But, as I have said, I would not expect to be the only man operating assets within Germany."

It was from Kiktev, whom he'd feared as an opponent, that the confirmation finally came. "We've already investigated them," he said.

Karpov controlled any reaction from reaching his face. The reason for the delay in his being summoned, he realized: the bastards had been trying to gather evidence against him. But he'd beaten them! They'd tried to get evidence and failed, and they'd tried to trick him and failed. Christ, how glad he was that he didn't have to exist in an environment like this, twitching at shadows and peering down toilet bowls to look for hidden cameras. He wondered how they kept their sanity. Perhaps they didn't. Perhaps they were all mad. It was important that the three men didn't appreciate the significance to him of what Kiktev had said.

"Then if they didn't support him and I didn't support

him, the only inference is that he did go alone," he said.

"Don't you find that inconceivable?" asked Tsinev.

"Yes," said Karpov. "Utterly inconceivable." Karpov had the impression that he had climbed a long ascent and was now descending the other side, where the going was easier. In front of him, the three men drew back. A head-bent, inaudible conversation lasted for several minutes before they pulled apart again.

"You will understand that the most searching inquiry has been made into every aspect of this matter," said Tsinev.

"Yes, I would understand that," said Karpov.

"During which time we have had the occasion and opportunity to examine every one of our European operatives," said Kiktev.

"It would need to be complete," said Karpov. He'd started uphill again, he thought worriedly. And this time he didn't recognize the route.

"You have had a very long and successful operational career," said Krivoshev. "An exemplary one."

"I'm gratified . . ." started Karpov uncertainly, but Tsinev cut across him. "I am delighted to inform you officially, Comrade Karpov, that you are being appointed Director of the European Division, to replace the disgraced Migal."

The three men stood and advanced toward him, smiling and extending their hands.

"Congratulations," said Krivoshev.

"You must be very happy," said Kiktev.

"Very happy," agreed Karpov. It wasn't easy for him to speak.

Kurt Schroeder had frequently fantastized about being a fugitive, hunted by the authorities, like so many of the great ones had been in the 1920s. That's why—secretly, because he was ashamed to admit it to anyone, even his father, who might have understood—he'd established the money caches and planned escape routes. The money had been invaluable after the assault at Berliner Freiheit, but the escape routes had proved more difficult. From the newspapers and television he knew within a day how many of his friends had been seized. Then the incredible publicity had gone on, like some obscene, unstoppable parade, secret after secret. They'd been loyal though, his friends—more loyal than he'd been to them in his cowardice. His name had been mentioned, but in connection with his father, not with the organization in which he'd been so active. And there hadn't been any photographs; not any that caused him any difficulty, at least. He still knew they'd be looking for him, of course. So he couldn't be sure of the borders of those carefully drawn maps over which he'd spent so many hours.

He drove south, too hurriedly at first, but then charting his route, ignoring the instinct to try faraway, hidden villages where a strange face—even one that hadn't appeared on any wanted posters—might arouse curiosity. Instead, he chose the large, anonymous towns, Stuttgart first, because he'd thought of trying to cross into Switzerland, His courage failed on his way to the border, so he spent a week at Ulm.

Munich was a place in which to hide, too, but it was as much for a pilgrimage, as well. It was in Munich, hunched in a cheap room, without hot water or proper heating—the sort of room that the Führer had occupied in his struggling days Schroeder convinced himself—that he fully confronted what had happened. And sought reassurance. It was an understandable mistake. He'd only been under fire once —proper fire, not the rehearsed rubbish they played in the mountains. So the fear had been understandable. Everyone was frightened the first time; afterward as well. Wasn't that what bravery was, managing to control fear?

He knew he could control it if it happened again. But it wouldn't happen again, not like that.

There had to be something, Schroeder decided: some way he could restore his self-respect and show to himself, because there wasn't anybody else, that he wasn't a coward. That he'd just made a mistake the first time.

When the idea came, he laughed at it, out of excitement. No one else would know, if he were successful. But *he* would. And that's what mattered to Kurt Schroeder. Restoring his faith in himself.

The border crossing was the first test. He chose the protection of a busy one, as he had with cities, continuing eastward to Salzburg. He was very frightened, at the checkpoint, wet-faced with perspiration, his stomach in tumult. But he didn't run. He remained in the line and wiped his face before the moment of examination and was waved through without the slightest question. Not a coward, he told himself as he accelerated away from the border post. He'd prove to himself he was not a coward.

How difficult would the rest be? he wondered.

32

The departure formalities from Vienna could have been boring, a wearying necessity to avoid there being any suspicion about his sudden disappearance. But Karpov didn't find them so. Instead of boredom there was nostalgia, a near-aching regret that, after so long, it was all over.

The first day after his return from Moscow, when he was terminating the house on Dorotheergasse—actually standing in the main room, comparing his list against that of the vendor's inventory and agreeing to the final settlement figures—the insane idea had come to him to defect. It was momentary, because he couldn't allow it to be any more. Because the idea *was* insane. Defectors were always hunted and killed, whenever possible, as an example to others who might consider doing the same. In his case, Karpov knew the search would be more intense than normal, despite whatever protection the Americans or the British promised. By running, he would be associated with the disaster of Migal. So the need for an example would be greater than ever.

He had no alternative. He had to go back. Back to the office overlooking Dzerzhinsky Square with the view that Migal always appeared to find so interesting. Back to bureaucracy and political maneuvering and considering each word before he spoke back to some barren, ill-equipped apartment and telephones that didn't work. Back to restaurants where food he didn't want took three hours to be served anyway. Back where he didn't want to be.

Karpov, who was a natural optimist, shrugged his huge shoulders as if he were physically trying to slough off the depression. He was prejudging things. It had been sixteen years since he'd actually lived in the Soviet Union. He hadn't been impressed during his recall visits, but things had to have improved in sixteen years.

His recollections were those of a lowly office; he'd only been a captain when he'd been posted to the West. He was a general now, in control of a huge department within the service, and with power for exceeding the titular rank. He wondered if it would take him as long to adjust to that power as it would to Moscow.

He'd used it, like an experiment, before he returned this time and had been impressed by the response. Perhaps the power would compensate for whatever else he lost.

The apartment on Schüttelstrasse had always been Karpov's favorite, and so it was the one he kept until last, for the final disengagement from Vienna. He spent the morning packing the stereo equipment for its circuitous return to Moscow, and then the jazz collection, padding each album against the other and then padding the case itself. Would his power extend to having agents maintain the collection for him? It would be another experiment. But not immediately. It was something that could attract criticism, so he'd have to be careful. Karpov sighed, aware that he was already adopting the attitudes.

During their meetings, Karpov had never shown Rebecca the hospitality he extended to Hugo. He'd tried, early in the association, soon after her arrival from Moscow, but the gesture appeared to embarrass her. But he'd made preparations today, because today was different. There was caviar and smoked salmon. And, because he'd heard Hugo talk of their visits there, he'd had the receptionist from the Sacher bring some Sacher torte. As he set it out, Karpov realized there was another farewell to pay. He'd been unsure of what Rebbeca drank, so he'd allowed a selection: vodka, schnapps, and red and white whine. And champagne, of course. There would be the need for champagne. He realized he wanted to impress her.

Her knock came precisely at the arranged time, and she entered the apartment with the uncertainty she had always shown at their meetings. He wished she weren't so apprehensive. Almost at once the uncertainty became curiosity. She looked from the packing cases to the prepared table and back to the cases again, finally coming to Karpov.

"You're closing the apartment down?"

"Yes," said Karpov. He did't want to rush; power was better if it was protracted.

"I see," she said.

Karpov gestured to the table and asked, "Would you like something?"

Conscious of the effort he had made, the woman said, "Maybe a little salmon."

She moved to help herself, but Karpov insisted serving her.

"Wine?" he asked. "Or something else?"

"Wine," she said. "White."

She accepted the glass and the plate, and sat in the chair as she always did, stiffly on the edge, with her knees tightly together. She didn't try to eat or drink.

"You think this place has become dangerous?" she asked.

Karpov poured himself schnapps, took some caviar, and said, "No. There's no danger."

"Why, then?"

"I've been recalled."

"Recalled!" As bad as it had been, she and Hugo had managed to establish some sort of relationship with Karpov. Certainly the man had appeared considerate to Hugo. Now they'd have to start all over again with whoever replaced him.

"Whoever comes after me can set up his own establishments; it's always safer."

"Of course," she said. "Who is it to be?"

"I haven't decided yet," said Karpov.

For a moment the significance of what he said didn't register with the woman. Then she said, "*You* haven't decided!''

Karpov smiled. ''I've been appointed Director of the European Division.''

Rebecca stared at the man, trying to decide what that would mean to her and Hugo. Remembering her manners, she said, ''Congratulations.''

''Thank you,'' said Karpov. He refilled his glass, pausing to turn the champagne in the bucket, and said, ''My going will mean changes for you.''

''Yes,'' she said. ''I'd already thought of that.''

''My position is one of great responsibility now,'' he said. ''Authority, too.''

''Yes,'' she said. ''I suppose it is.''

''And I've decided to use it.''

Rebecca sipped the wine, looking at him over the rim of her glass. ''Use it?'' she asked.

''I'm going to let Hugo do what he wants most,'' announced Karpov. ''I'm going to let him retire.''

''Retire!''

''Germany was his last job. He's earned the right to quit.'' Karpov went to uncork the champagne. Half-turned from her, he said, ''So you'll be going home. I've ordered Boris' release. He's already free.''

The cork exploded from the wine, so that he looked toward it and missed the anguish that seared her face. By the time he filled two glasses and turned back to her, she was composed again.

''Excited?'' he demanded.

''I don't know what to say,'' replied the woman honestly. It had been difficult to respond at all; her throat seemed blocked and her whole body felt weighted.

Karpov raised his glass to her and said, ''You've done a great deal. You've earned the rest, like Hugo has earned his.'' He hesitated, then said, ''I've always told you I didn't enjoy the pressure upon you. But you didn't believe me, did you?''

"I didn't know what to believe," said the woman. "When are you going to tell Hugo?"

"Tonight," said the Russian.

"He was moving in, next week," said Rebecca.

Karpov looked at her curiously. "You always said you didn't love him."

"I don't," said Rebecca hurriedly. "But it would be impossible for me not to have some feeling for the man." She had to be careful—desperately careful—to say nothing that would take away from Hugo the one chance he had.

"You'll want to get back to Russia as soon as possible," said Karpov.

"Yes," said Rebecca emptily. "Yes, I will."

"We'll arrange the sale of the shop on your behalf," said Karpov. He smiled and said, "I'm afraid you won't be allowed to keep the profit."

"Thank you," said Rebecca, pressed down by bewilderment. "For disposing of it for me, I mean."

"Transferring the lease of the apartment to Hugo will be easy if he wants it. It's fortunate, in the event, that he's moving in."

"Yes," she said. "I suppose it is."

"Here's to the future," said Karpov, raising his glass. He'd maintain contact when they were together in Moscow. Only as friends, of course. What else could there be? She was returning to her husband.

"The future," she Rebecca. The wine seemed to burn when she drank.

It was a trick, Gusadarov knew. Everything was a trick. The food was a trick, and the special treatment was a trick, and the hospital was a trick, and the job where they knew he cheated was a trick. But they hadn't caught him. Whatever it was they had expected him to do, it hadn't worked. Which had to be the reason for this, the biggest trick of all: traveling in a train with seats instead of slatted cattle trucks with a hole in the middle of the floor to piss through. But he'd beat them. He wouldn't do anything and he wouldn't say anything. He couldn't be trapped if he said and did nothing. Camp law, to say and do nothing; the way to avoid attention and survive.

"We're here," said the escort.

Gusadarov followed the man into the vault of Kazan Station, staring intently around him. A lot of people: assembly camp, then. So where were the guards? There were a few people in uniforms, but they weren't prison regulation. And there weren't enough, either. Could be a break, with supervision as poor as this. Maybe that was the trick: maybe they were going to stage a prison escape and try to involve him, to provide a reason for punishment. He pulled up close to the escort, determined to ignore any sudden rush.

The pavement and the streets outside bewildered the man even further. There were more people and fewer guards, and there was traffic: cars and buses and trucks. It had been years since Gusadarov had seen so many vehicles, and the movement and noise frightened him. There was a car waiting. Gusadarov obediently got in when he was told to. He had only been in Moscow for a month before his arrest, and he recognized none of the streets along which they drove. His only impression was of size and speed and noise, and he wished he were back in camp. He understood camp—knew how to behave and stay alive. Everything here confused him.

He got out of the car when he was told to and followed the man up the stairs into a tall building, without any wire around it or bars at the windows or guards in the corridors. The escort opened a door and stood back, gesturing Gusadarov into the apartment. The man entered tentatively, head twitching from side to side in his nervousness.

"Quite an apartment, eh?" said the escort from behind.

Gusadarov turned to him. Cautiously he nodded. They couldn't prove anything from a nod.

The man held out his hand and Gusadarov stared down at it. "Here's the key. You've got to sign for it."

Gusadarov had his crabbed signature half finished before he remembered the trap and he completed it badly, so that it was almost illegible. It wasn't a good defense, but he could always try to say it wasn't his signature.

"I don't know how it happened. Or why," said the man at the door. "But you're a lucky bastard."

Gusadarov looked around the empty apartment. After a long time, he cautiously explored further, finding the bedroom and then the bathroom and then the kitchen annex. He returned finally to the main room, staring about him.

Gusadarov felt more imprisoned than he ever had in any of the camps. He squeezed his eyes shut, trying to concentrate, knowing that he had to beat them. He had to learn the rules; learn the rules, so that he didn't make any mistake. Had to think. That was it. Think. He chose a hard chair, one against the table, so that he wouldn't depress the cushions of the easier seats around the room. He'd seen men disciplined for things as stupid as that. But they wouldn't catch him. He was going to sit here and do nothing until someone came and told him what the rules were. They couldn't trick him if he followed the rules.

33

Having got what he wanted most—the freedom for which he'd killed—Hartman felt no excitement. Instead, irrationally, his emotion was anger, because he feared what it would mean to them. Just as irrationally, he was directing it at Rebecca, because there was no one else. And that was pointless because she refused to argue with him.

"You should have warned me!"

"I wanted to think."

"You ran away," he said.

She wanted to. It seemed the obvious answer when she left Karpov's apartment and wandered the streets of the city, her mind blocked by what had happened. And still seemed so. She wanted to run, as Hugo had suggested all those months ago in Zurich. To run and hide with him, doing anything and going anywhere, to ensure they stayed together. But she knew she wouldn't: that she couldn't. Somewhere in Russia—Moscow, she supposed, maybe back in Vinnitsa—was a man she'd once loved and who had once been her husband. And who would be sent back to a hell worse than any he had so far endured if she defected. Maybe even killed. So she couldn't run. Any more than she could remain in Vienna. To save a man she didn't love, Rebecca recognized, she had to abandon one she did.

"It all happened so suddenly, unexpectedly," said Rebecca. "It was best you didn't have any warning anyway. Your reaction had to be right."

"He called it the final proof of his friendship," remembered Hartman.

"He was clearly your friend," she said.

"What about you?"

Rebecca knew she would have to lie. Not just for his feelings. For her own, as well. She couldn't face a confrontation, to see his pain when she told him what she was going to do. "I've got to go back, but not for good," she said.

"What do you mean, not for good?"

Rebecca had rehearsed the story during her aimless walking in the streets. And in the streets it had appeared acceptable. Now she wasn't sure.

"I told Karpov I wanted to stay here in Vienna," she said. Rebecca told the life looking directly at Hartman, willing him to believe her.

"Stay here!"

"I said I would go back to Moscow to divorce Boris, and then I wanted to be allowed back here."

"You told him that I knew who you really were!"

"Of course not. Just that I wanted to stay with you—that I could make an excuse for going away for a few weeks, to make it possible."

"And he agreed?"

"He said he'd do all he could to help."

"So you could still be refused?"

She shook her head, coming to the point of her story, which she hoped would make it appear truthful. "I just couldn't disappear; just walk away from the business. It would create too much suspicion. They'll have to let me back."

"Maybe just to close it down."

"Karpov proved himself a friend to you," she reminded him.

"Why didn't he say anything to me about it?" seized Hartman.

"How could he?" she said, glad of his confusion. "You're not supposed to know about me, are you?"

Hartman looked at her, the doubt obvious. It ***hadn't*** sounded convincing, Rebecca thought desperately. It had sounded exactly what it was: a hastily thought-out lie by someone who was so bewildered she had hardly been able to find her way home.

"You're not going to leave me, are you?" he asked, in direct challenge.

"No, darling," she said. "I'm not going to leave you." How long would he hate her, when he discovered the truth? Probably forever. Rebecca felt hollowed and numbed by what was happening. She'd go immediately. Tomorrow. She wouldn't be able to sustain the deceit. Imagining the hatred would be bad enough; she didn't want to see it in his eyes.

Rebecca knew he was unsure, by the way they made love that night. Just as she realized she was probably confirming his doubts by the way she responded, pulling and snatching at him, wanting to fill her body with his and clinging to him after they both stopped, exhausted, never wanting the sky to lighten into day, the day that would mean she had to go. They both pretended to sleep, each knowing the other was pretending. Rebecca got up first, locking herself in the bathroom and staring at her reflection in the mirror, unsure how much longer she could continue before the tears came.

She was worried about crying. He'd be certain, if she began to cry. Trying to erect a barrier, Rebecca consciously attempted to remember the man she was returning to, the man with whom she would be spending the rest of her life. And realized—horrified—that she couldn't. She had a recollection of their wedding, which had been happy and where they had had a wonderful party, with dancing and singing, and where Boris had got too drunk to make love to her on their wedding night. It had remained a secret joke between them. She recalled his growing interest and then participation in the dissident movement, which had frightened her. But she couldn't remember *him*. She knew his hair was very black and that he was tall and very strong, strong enough to lift her easily off her feet and hold her before him to kiss her. But she couldn't remember his mannerisms or the tone of his voice or the things he liked and disliked, like clothes and food. It would come back, she tried to reassure herself; very quickly come back.

Rebecca made breakfast, which they both had difficulty in eating, just as they had difficulty with conversation.

"How long?" he asked.

"I don't know," she replied. "There'll be formalities."

"Weeks, then?"

"Probably." Oh, my darling! she thought.

"No reason why I shouldn't move in, though?"

"No," she agreed. "None at all." He'd know—for certain—when they approached him to transfer the lease.

"Will you be able to get a message to me, when you're coming back?"

"I don't know," she said. "It might not be easy. I'll try."

"I'll be here," he said. Attempting a lightness that failed, he said, "I'm retired now—all the time in the world. And nowhere to go, not until you're with me."

"Eat regularly," she said.

"Of course."

"And don't forget the pills. Sometimes you're careless about the pills."

"I won't forget."

"And not too much wine. You shouldn't drink as much as you do."

"I'll be careful."

"I don't want you to come to the airport with me," she announced suddenly.

"Why not?"

"I just don't."

He hesitated. Then he said, "All right."

There were a lot of clothes—jewelry too—and Rebecca knew she should pack carefully, because this was her last day in the West and her last opportunity to take such things with her. Instead, she packed with complete lack of interest, unable to remember the moment she closed the suitcase what dresses and suits it contained, and what brooches and necklaces she had included.

"Don't be away too long," he said.

"I won't," she promised.

The intercom from street level burred, signaling the arrival of the car to take her to the airport.

"I love you," he said. "I love you very much."

"I love you too," she said. "Too much."

She walked from the apartment and down the curving stairway without once looking back to the man who stood in the doorway.

Kurt Schroeder's intention had been to get a rented room, imagining it would provide anonymity, but then he realized what would happen afterward, and that he would be more easily identified and described by a landlady who saw him daily, so he chose instead a small hotel on Mariahilfer Strasse. The ease of the border crossing had bolstered his confidence. There were moments, during the first day, when he felt lightheaded, but he was careful to control it, discerning the nearness of hysteria. That would come later, when he'd proved himself. Not now.

He was uncertain how to begin. All his training had been in combat and military exercises, not in finding people. But he'd do it. He *had* to do it. He had to show he wasn't a coward.

34

The insertion of the key into the lock was extremely quiet, but Gusadarov knew how to detect such sounds and what they meant, so he was on his feet, hands clasped openly before him his head bent respectfully, when Rebecca entered. The old rules until he learned the new ones. They wouldn't catch him with a stupid trick like trying to enter quietly. Idiots.

Rebecca paused just beyond the threshhold, the door still open behind her, the single suitcase loosely held in her hand. She supposed the man to be some official, waiting to talk to her about Boris. Why was he behaving so peculiarly? She said, "Hello?"

Why didn't they tell him the rules! That was the system, the way it had been, in every camp in which he'd been imprisoned. Always the rules, to be learned immediately and then obeyed. Desperately he sought safety, and then felt the sweep of relief when the way came to him. Raising his head slightly, so there would be no mistake, he said, "Seven three nine nine two zero four."

"Boris?" said the woman. She closed the door and put the case on the floor carefully, as if it contained something that might break, all the while gazing at the cowed man in front of her. No, it couldn't be Boris! Closer now, she saw a bent, hunched man, white-haired, with gnarled hands, engulfed in a suit too large for him. This wasn't Boris: difficult though it had been for her in Vienna, she was sure this wasn't Boris. He'd been tall and strong, and never bent his head to anyone. Wasn't that why he'd gone to Moscow, because he didn't bend to anyone? Impossible for it to be Boris. "Who are you?" she asked.

Easy answer, Gusadarov realized gratefully. "Seven three nine nine two zero four," he repeated dutifully.

Would they feed him if he passed the test? He'd used the toilet, carefully wiping and then examining the bowl after he'd flushed it, but that was all. He hadn't risked lying down on the bed or looking into any of the cupboards to see if there was food. He was very hungry and very tired; more hungry than tired.

Rebecca clutched out for the wall, needing its support. She hadn't known what to expect; not really. Thinner, obviously, because of what he'd been through; possibly sick. Coughing from some consumption, perhaps. But not this. This wasn't Boris Gusadarov, the Boris Gusadarov who'd been able to lift her up and hold her at arm's length. The Boris Gusadarov who'd clutched her hands, and told her to believe in him and in what he was going to do—create so much trouble that the Russians were going to have to let the Ukraine go back to those who had the right to rule the country.

"Boris?" she asked again. "Boris, is it you?"

The man shifted his feet very slightly, getting again the impression of being imprisoned more securely than he had been before. Almost at once there was another feeling. He was filled with anger, the rage he'd felt when the guard had so dangerously checked his figures. The hands held before him as regulations required tightened as he clutched for control. If only he could ask what they wanted him to do! But that was against the rules. Never speak until you're spoken to. The primary rule.

Rebecca came farther into the room, to stand in front of him, her head forward to stare at him. Nothing was the same. The hair wasn't the same, and the blank, avoiding eyes weren't the same. Nor the face, chiseled now into some indefinable hardness. And he seemed smaller than she remembered, as if he were physically worn away. She reached out toward him, aware from her closeness that it had been a long time since he'd bathed. At the last moment, at the very point of touching him, she hesitated, thinking she would not be able to do it. But she did, with effort, putting both her hands on his shoulders. She was conscious of the sharp boniness of his body beneath the cloth and of his flinching when she touched him.

"Boris," she said. "Boris, it's me. 'It's me, Rebecca."

He didn't look up, not completely; it wasn't permitted, to look directly at the guards. But he knew how, just as he knew how to hold a conversation with other prisoners without his lips moving discernibly. He looked at her with his head still lowered, not holding her gaze but repeating it sufficiently to be able to study the face and the body, and be sure. Another trick! Another obscene, filthy attempt to trap him into God knows that. This wasn't Rebecca. They were fools, idiots, if they imagined they could get him as easily as this. More than anything else, he knew what Rebecca looked like. She'd been the focus, his talisman, every day of every week of every year. And every day he'd pictured her in his mind, remembering the lustrous darkness of her hair and the slimness of her body and the roundness of her breasts. This wasn't Rebecca. This woman was old, middle-aged, overdressed, wearing rings and bracelets to make herself seem beautiful. Rebecca wasn't middle-aged. She was young and fresh and lovely —so lovely. Didn't need anything to make herself beautiful either, not like this wman. It was necessary to respond to authority. "Seven three nine nine two zero four," he repeated dully.

Rebecca took her hands from him, squeezing her eyes tightly togehter as if to shut out what had happened. She'd nurse him, she decided; it was her duty to nurse him. But that's what it would be: a nurse and a patient. She felt nothing for this stranger before her except absolute and utter pity. Would it change when he got better, when he came to realize who she was and that he was free? An unanswerable question. And a pointless one. First he had to *get* better. Realizing from his behavior that there would be only one way to get him to react, Rebecca stood back, hardened her voice and said, "Bath!"

Gusadarov turned at once, as much to conceal his satisfaction as to obey instantly. He'd beaten them! They'd tried to trick him and he'd beaten them, and this was the admission—the reversal to orders and commands. He carefully left the door fully open, as was required, and equally carefully folded the clothes as he took them off. She confused him by coming past him in the small bathroom and running the water, but he decided to ignore it, knowing that they were still trying. He stood before the woman, as unaware as he was unashamed of his nakedness, waiting for the order to get into the bath.

Rebecca stared at the man whose body she had once known and enjoyed, and the pity ached through her. The skin was unnaturally white, unexposed to any air or sunlight for years, and there were a lot of scars, some of them apparently new, particularly the one on his leg which she could see had been professionally stitched in some operation. There were other marks, a black-spotted pigmentation, which she guessed came from some work he had to do in a mine. The muscularity surprised her, although she supposed it shouldn't. Although bent, his body was hard and firm from the unremitting work regimen. His sex was flacid between his legs, small, like that of a child. Rebecca decided it was a fitting analogy: he'd become a child, with the body of a man.

Recognizing his need, she told him to get in, considered bathing him, and then decided against it. Not because she couldn't bring herself to touch him, she thought; because it would be wrong, confusing him even further. While he washed himself, Rebecca explored the apartment, wincing at the comparison to what she had known in Vienna. It was particularly bare in the living room, and she halted there, gazing around and wondering what she would be able to do to improve it. The unanswered thought linked to another: to how she and Hugo had furnished his apartment, and how they had always discussed and considered improvements to her own. What would he be doing now? she wondered. She actually raised her watch to calculate the time difference and then abruptly dropped her arm to her side. It was over. Finished. Thinking about Hugo was as pointless as speculating whether she would ever come to have any feeling for the man who was legally her husband.

There was some canned food in the kitchen and she found some bread, already with the beginning of mold forming on it. She scraped it off and prepared a meal of canned meat and potatoes. She supposed she would have to go shopping the following day. Where? she wondered. And how? Rebecca gripped the table edge against despair, fully realizing for the first time that she had never been to Moscow before and didn't know where or how to shop here.

She'd need to contact Karpov the following day. Not about the shopping—that was ridiculous. But at least about the requirements for it. Boris was clearly incapable of work. And she couldn't, if she had to care for him. She'd been part of the service, so perhaps she qualified for a pension. She didn't know how they could live if she didn't qualify.

She became curious about Boris' absence and found him in the bathroom awaiting permission to leave. She ordered him into the kitchen, noting as he moved by her that he had cleaned the bath and perfectly folded the towels.

She sat opposite him at the table, unable to eat, watching with disbelief the way he did, making only token use of the knife and fork but more often thrusting the food into his mouth with his fingers, filling it until it was so full that pieces dropped from his lips when he tried to chew. There was a constant sound when he ate, animal grunts of satisfaction. He devoured all the meat and all the potatoes, and when she took the plates away and she saw him sneak a piece of bread into the pocket of his jacket she pretended not to notice.

There was no detergent, so she stacked the dishes, intending to get some the following day. She led Gusadarov back into the stark sitting room, seated him on the couch, and sat opposite, determined to break through the barrier.

"Boris," she said.

Gusadarov moved, uncomfortable. Against regulations to sit when addressed by authority. But she'd told him to. Typical sort of entrapment.

"It's over, Boris. You're not in prison anymore. You're free. They've set you free and we're back together again." She paused, then said, "Together forever."

Only orders; that's all he had to respond to. Orders.

Rebecca looked helplessly about her, not knowing what to do. She wasn't a nurse; didn't have any training. And that's what he needed. Proper, trained help. Hesitatingly, unsure if it would work, she began to talk about Vinnitsa and how they'd met, brought together by their parents, at first not liking each other. She talked of their walks in the forest and how irritated he used to get at the shoddy machinery in the factory. Of the wedding and the room they'd shared in his parents' home, embarrassed by their noises at night. Throughout it all he sat dull-eyed and totally unresponsive. Seeking the key to let herself into his private world, she spoke finally about his nationalism, the secret meetings, and the cells they tried to form against discovery. Still he remained unmoving, showing no reaction.

They'd never attempted an interrogation like this before, Gusadarov realized. He'd never suspected they knew so much; everything, in fact. Not everything. She'd mentioned the cells and the secret meetings, but she hadn't named the others. He knew now what they wanted. Why there had been the privileges and the food and this special prison with all its comforts. They wanted the names and the identities of everyone who'd worked with him. Tried to get it before, a long time ago, by beating him. He hadn't given it then, and he wouldn't give it now, when they were trying kindness instead of cruelty. The beatings would come, of course, when they realized this approach wasn't working. Already things were being denied him. He'd been allowed a lemon recently, for as long as he could remember. But she hadn't given him a lemon.

Rebecca felt crushed by fatigue and hopelessness: fatigue at having flown in one day to Moscow in a roundabout route from Vienna, and hopelessness at the thought of having to spend the rest of her life with a man she didn't know and who didn't know her. Didn't know anything, in fact. She ordered him to bed and snickered—more from hysteria than amusement—at the realization that from habit he intended sleeping in the clothing he wore. She made him undress and then, conscious of his need, allowed the clothing to be laid beside him on the bed, where he could guard it. It covered that part of the bed she supposed she should occupy but which she had no intention of doing. Obediently he lay with his eyes closed. Soon his breathing became heavier, but she knew he wasn't asleep: in a series of apparently natural shifts and turns he managed to get his arm fully across the clothing he wanted to protect.

She left at last, watching from the darkness of the adjoining room. He was extremely careful, moving so slowly that she missed the beginning, but she saw him sneak the hoarded bread from his pocket and force it into his mouth. Then he pulled the clothing into the bed with him, so that he could actually lie on it to prevent its being stolen.

Rebecca went finally to the hard couch and stretched out along it. She'd managed to hold them back in Vienna and to hold them back here in Moscow, until now. But she couldn't hold back anymore. The tears gushed from her uncontrollably. She turned her head into one of the seat cushions, trying to muffle the sobs that shook through her, and then she stopped bothering, because it didn't matter. Nothing mattered.

From the bedroom, Gusadarov heard the sounds, unsure at first what they were. Then he realized. She was laughing at him.

Rebecca set out intending Gusadarov to accompany her, but as soon as she reached the street she became aware of his terror and realized how it would worsen when they reached their destination, if he recognized it. So she took him back to the apartment, knowing he accepted it as his prison and would feel safer there.

She discerned a reluctance from people of whom she asked for directions to Dzerzhinsky Square. When she finally found it and stood looking up at the massive, joined-together building, she was confronted by her naiveté in expecting to reach Karpov. But there *was* no one else. Karpov was the only person to whom she could go for help. From whom she could expect help. Would he be as willing to provide it here as he had been in Vienna?

Rebecca tried to enter through the main door, unaware that no civilian is permitted through that entrance and that anyway an approved pass must first be obtained from the citizens' office farther along the square. She went to the indicated building, patiently waited in line, and when she reached the KGB clerk who asked her business replied unsuspectingly what guaranteed her attention.

She identified Oleg Karpov by name and position, two things that were officially state secrets within the Soviet Union. She was immediately arrested. She didn't appreciate at first what was happening, not until the uniformed men entered from behind and seized her by the arms, half-lifting her from the chair. Then the sickness formed, so that she actually belched her fear. Irrationally, the social rudeness embarrassed her. She tried to snatch for her handbag but the clerk seized it first.

Rebecca was escorted deeper into the building and then along what she imagined was a linking corridor. It was a long way, which gave her time to think. She had to think —and do it quickly and get it right. On the other side of Moscow there was a catatonic man dependent upon her release for his survival. And it wasn't just his survival. There was her own, as well.

The interrogation cell was a bare box of a room, just a table and two chairs, the only light coming from a wire-protected bulb recessed into the ceiling. She was put into the chair facing the door, the escorts positioning themselves on either side. It was almost thirty minutes before it opened to admit a slightly built, bespectacled man. He wore a lounge suit, with pens and pencils clipped into the top pocket, and in one hand carried a folder. In the other was her handbag. Momentarily he stood behind the chair, looking down at her, and then seated himself and opened the folder. Her Austrian passport was clipped inside. It was a mannered, rehearsed approach.

"So you are Austrian?" he began officiously.

She had something to fight with, Rebecca knew. Not much, but something. And that's what she had to do: fight. If she let herself be intimidated by this petty official, she'd probably be locked up in some detention cell until Boris died from neglect. She was glad of the man's prepared attitude.

"No," she said.

He blinked up at her, comparing the photographs. "This is an Austrian passport. And this is your photograph."

"Yes," she said. It was important constantly to confuse him.

"You have committed an offense against the

state . . ." he started, seeking protection in officialdom, but Rebecca said, "You are talking nonsense."

The man imperceptibly moved his head, conscious of the two guards witnessing the contemptuous treatment. No one, no matter how brave, behaved like this in the Lubyanka. "You will explain yourself," he said.

"You have insufficient security clearance to hear anything I want to say," replied Rebecca. She was unsure how much longer she could keep it up. The sickness was still there, worse than in the first moments in the outer office.

The man unclipped the passport, looked down at it, and tried again. "Your name is . . ."

Rebecca snatched across, her quickness surprising both the interrogator and the two uniformed men who were supposed to prevent by their very presence anything like this happening. Before the one to the right of the door began moving forward, Rebecca turned the pages, identifying her entry into the Soviet Union. She thrust it into the man's hand and said, "Look at the visa!"

She thought briefly that the questioner was going to hit her, and knew that if he did she would probably collapse and lose everything. "Look at it, I said," she repeated. Dear God, if there is one, don't let my voice break to show my fear, she thought.

He did look, and Rebecca commanded, "And at the accompanying stamp."

The man came back to her, blushing, and she realized that he'd missed the KGB authorization during his examination of her handbag's contents. "I must know why you made the approach that you did," said the man. "That is strictly against procedure."

He failed to conceal the plea in his voice. Rebecca said, "I've already told you that you have insufficient clearance to know anything. You will communicate with Comrade General Oleg Karpov, Director of the European Division of the Komitet Gosudarstvennoy Bezopasnosti." She stopped, looking pointedly at the watch they had not taken from her, and said, "I've already been delayed an hour."

"But—"

"One thing," said Rebecca. Now that he was running, she couldn't afford to let the man stop. "Tell Comrade General Karpov one thing, just a word. Say 'Hugo.' " Irony upon irony, she thought; she was using the name of the man who loved to save the life of one she didn't. But one who needed her more, she supposed. She sat back, a finality in the movement, ending the discussion. The balance was as delicate as when she'd thought he might strike her; the slightest tilt, and she would have lost. He stared across the table at Rebecca, and she stared back across the table at him. Rebecca thought it was like a child's game, except that the stakes were much greater; infinitely greater. She strained to keep her face impassive, to avoid even swallowing. When the hesitation had gone on longer than she could calculate, she looked again at her watch, striving to make the gesture appear casual, and said, "An hour and ten minutes."

And he broke. The man jerked from the table, said, "Stay here"—as if she had any choice—in a futile attempt to retain his control, and strode from the room. For the first time Rebecca appreciated how much she wanted a bathroom. She'd have to control it, until it became absolutely desperate.

It was an hour before the man with the regimented pens returned. The moment he entered the room, Rebecca guessed that she had won. The confirmation came immediately. The man said, "Please, you will come this way." He seemed to remember her handbag. He offered it to her and said, "Nothing has been taken."

"I hope nothing has," she said, unwilling to relax even now. Walking made the need for a toilet even more urgent. This time the route wasn't so protracted. They came almost immediately to elevators, and the upward snatch did nothing to relieve Rebecca's discomfort. She lost count of the number of floors they ascended, but as soon as the doors opened she was pased over to another escort. Then, after going the entire length of one corridor and turning into a second, she was entrusted to a second guard.

Karpov was waiting at the end of the passageway, his face clearing as he saw her.

Her control went as he closed the door. "Thank God it's you," she said. She bit her mouth closed, frightened of crying. She'd done enough of that last night.

"You've caused a hell of a flap," said Karpov. "There'll be an inquiry."

"I'm sorry," she said. Rebecca hadn't expected to see Karpov in uniform. Colorful though the scarlets and khakis were, he still seemed subdued.

"It doesn't matter," he said. "I'll turn it to my advantage—say it was an exercise I initiated, to test the security and common sense at ground level." It was surprising how automatically the necessities of survival were coming to him. As surprising as how pleased he was to see her.

"I'm still sorry. I couldn't think of anyone else."

"Which was my fault. I should have anticipated your need."

"There *is* a need," insisted Rebecca. It didn't take long to explain. Only minutes to outline the problem of money, but longer to talk about her husband's mental state.

Karpov listened, head bent, staring down at his desk, occasionally moving his head in some aimless pattern across the blotter. When she finished he said, "The money is easily solved. Of course you deserve a pension. Arrangements are already being processed." He had intended using the announcement as a reason for making contact with her again; he should have anticipated the need for immediate spending money.

"What about Boris?" she asked. In Vienna she'd never trusted this man, Rebecca realized. But if he hadn't wanted to be her friend, he wouldn't have seen her today. As intriguing as her approach might have been, he could still have avoided direct contact and whatever difficulties the later inquiry might cause him, by deputing some subordinate.

"You can't help him by yourself?"

"I don't think I know how," she said honestly.

"I'll arrange something," he promised.

"Quickly?" she pressed, disclosing her anxiety.

"Yes," he said. "Quickly." Then he said, "I'm sorry, I didn't know how he would be."

"How could you?"

"It still wasn't how I intended it to be."

An awkward silence came between them. Then Karpov asked, "How's the apartment?"

She hesitated fractionally too long and he said, "I'm sorry about that, too. Nothing compares very well to Vienna, does it?"

Not knowing what to say, Rebecca shook her head. Would he have heard from Hugo?

Karpov scribbled on a jotting pad and said, "Here, you'd better have this."

Rebecca looked down at the paper, then asked, "What is it?"

"My number here. And at home," said Karpov. "It's restricted, so I'd like you to memorize it." He smiled and said, "I don't think today's method of contact would work more than once." It was just to help her husband, Karpov told himself; that was all.

Rebecca realized that Karpov was taking risks, for no good reason.

"Here," said Karpov. He took money from his pocket and offered it to her. "Until I establish the pension," he said. "You'll need money for a week or two."

Rebecca paused and said, "I'll repay you."

"Of course," said Karpov easily. "Anything else you want?"

It would be dangerous to ask about Hugo. Instead, shyly, she said, "Do you have a toilet?"

He stood, bellowing with familiar laughter, gesturing her through a side door which led to a complete bathroom. When she emerged, Karpov said, "Don't worry. I'll look after everything."

"Thank you," she said.

Wanting to convince her of his sincerity, Karpov said, "I'll make sure Boris gets better."

The remark was like a dropped glass at a quiet moment of a party. "Yes," she said. "He must get better."

Hartman moved into Rebecca's apartment a week after she left Vienna. Because he was lonely and wanted people to talk to, and because the couple reminded him of himself and Gerda all those years ago, he bought champagne and personally welcomed them to the one they had bought from him. But it didn't really work, because they were strangers and embarrassed by the gesture.

Hartman hadn't intended to remain long in any case, because he didn't want to be away when Rebecca telephoned to say she was coming back. He knew she was coming back, that she wouldn't abandon him. He hoped she'd hurry. He was utterly alone without her. They were going to have a wonderful life together—absolutely wonderful.

Because of the champagne, Hartman drank nothing when he got to Rebecca's. He took the prescribed pills and prepared the meal his illness required. He'd made the commitment before and then let things lapse, but this time he wasn't going to; he was going to do everything the doctor advised, because he was determined to have as long as possible with Rebecca. He wished so much that she would telephone.

Klaus Schroeder hadn't realized it was such a common name. Or that it would be so difficult to check. Early on he actually thought, in sudden fear, that his memory was faulty, but it was only a temporary doubt. He couldn't forget anything as important as that. It was all he'd thought about for weeks.

35

In the back of the ambulance Rebecca felt out instinctively for his hand. He allowed her to take it but made no response. His skin felt hard and calloused, and she wasn't sure he could feel her fingers at all. Rebecca had been worried when they came for him; there had been a brief moment of wild-eyed reaction, and she'd feared he was going to fight against them. But then he seemed to recognize the uniform—or maybe it was just that the hospital attendants were wearing uniforms—and he quieted down. Now he was like she'd known him ever since she entered the apartment, catatonic and obedient.

The institute on Kropotkinsky Street was a stark mausoleum of a place, the windows appearing too small for its size; closer, she saw they were all barred. Because of Karpov's authority, they entered through the front door. Inside two white-coated doctors were waiting. One took Gusadarov away for an initial medical examination while the second, who introduced himself as Dr. Aksenov, interviewed Rebecca.

''I have his records,'' said the doctor. ''I know about his imprisonment.''

''Is there anything about his being like this?''

Aksenov made a gesture of uncertainty. ''Indications of violence,'' he said. ''But that's not unusual in the circumstances in which he was kept. Has he shown any violence toward you?''

Rebecca shook her head. ''Absolute apathy,'' she said. ''I'm not sure at times that he's even aware I'm with him. Certainly I don't think he recognizes me as his wife.''

''What have you done to convince him?''

Rebecca frowned at the question. ''It's only been days,'' she reminded the psychiatrist. ''Days after a gap of sixteen years. What could I have done except tell him?''

''What about before?'' asked Aksenov. ''Before his arrest and imprisonment? Was there any history of mental illness?''

''None,'' insisted Rebecca.

''In his family?''

''No.''

The second doctor entered the room, and this time there was no introduction. ''He's perfectly fit,'' he announced, talking more to Akesenov than to Rebecca. He turned farther toward the woman. ''One of the paradoxes of our prison system is that survivors from it are often extremely fit. The body learns to function on less food, and there are no such things as tobacco and alcohol and sugar and other killers that the more fortunate of us are allowed.''

Rebecca nodded, without replying.

''It will take a long time,'' said Aksenov, rising.

''I'll wait,'' said Rebecca. That's all she had to do, forever. Just wait.

The two men left the room and turned right along a corridor. When they were beyond the hearing of the woman, Aksenov said, ''Well?''

''Institutionalized, very obviously,'' said the other psychiatrist.

''That's not irreversible,'' said Aksenov. ''Maybe she'll be lucky.''

Gusadarov saw them enter and rose obediently to attention. Aksenov stood in front of him to conduct the examination, and the second man went to a side table to take the notes.

''Name?'' demanded the psychiatrist.

''Seven three nine nine two zero four?'' responded Gusadarov at once. He wasn't worried: he knew the rules. They were authority and he was subservient. It was a relief, after the last few days.

''Name?'' repeated Aksenov.

"Gusadarov, Boris, number 7399204."

"How old are you, Boris?"

There was a momentary hesitation. "Fifty-one," he said.

"Where's your home?"

"Vinnitsa."

"So you're Georgian?"

"Ukrainian," came the immediate correction. "I am a Ukrainian."

"Where have you spent the last sixteen years?"

"Prison."

"Why?"

He had to be careful, Gusadarov knew. "Crimes against the state," he said.

"Sit down."

Gusadarov sat at once. Aksenov produced a box of shapes, in different colors, and instructed Gusadarov to arrange them into an acceptable design. As long ago as it had been, Gusadarov's engineering training helped, and he completed the task well within the alloted time and with an acceptable arrangement. The Rorschach test took longer, and he had difficulty with a word-association examination to which neither psychiatrist attached great importance, aware of how long the man had been kept from any sort of written material. They then made Gusadarov lie on a couch to carry out sensitivity tests to the soles of his feet and his elbows and knees, and finally took him through coordination reactions, making him perform tasks with his eyes closed.

"Good," said Aksenov, leading him back to the table. "Very good."

Gusadarov knew he'd done well. The writing had been difficult, but he'd had no problem with the rest.

"Are you a single man?" asked Aksenov.

"Married."

"What is your wife called?"

"Rebecca."

"A woman came here with you, in the ambulance?" said the psychiatrist.

Gusadarov shifted in his seat worriedly. They were baiting a trap, he knew; doing something to deceive him. "Yes," he said.

"Who is she?"

Easy to answer. "I do not know," he said.

"She is your wife," said Aksenov. "Your wife Rebecca."

More difficult, thought Gusadarov. He knew she wasn't, but the man in authority said she was, and authority was never challenged. "Yes," he said.

The two psychiatrists exchanged looks. "Do you know she is your wife?" persisted Aksenov.

"Yes," said Gusadarov.

"She tells me you haven't acknowledged her as such," said Aksenov. "Why haven't you acknowledged her, Boris Gusadarov?"

They'd got him! The bastards had maneuvered it so that, whatever he said, he was opposing them. And that meant punishment. Don't let it be back to the north, to the cold! Please not! He couldn't stand the cold. He'd even given away the sacking, so it would be worse this time. Please not the cold.

"Why?" insisted the man.

"Frightened." It wasn't a reply to the man's question but an admission of how he felt, and it was the wrong answer anyway. Gusadarov moved to speak, and then saw the doctor smile, so he stopped.

"You have nothing to be frightened of, Boris Gusadarov. Not anymore. You're not in prison now. You're free."

Gusadarov stared across the table at the white-coated man, uncertain whether any response was expected from him. It hadn't sounded like a question.

"Do you understand? You're free."

"Yes," replied Gusadarov automatically.

"Free with your wife. Free to establish a home again."

"Yes," said Gusadarov.

In the corridor returning to where Rebecca waited, Aksenov said, "Badly institutionalized."

"But treatable," said his assistant. "He picked up the question about Georgia and the Ukraine."

"I think so," said the older man. "A lot will depend on her."

Rebecca listened intently to the man, nodding when he queried if she understood. When he asked if she had any questions, she said, "He knows it's me now? He knows I'm Rebecca?"

"Yes," assured Aksenov. "But be gentle with him. He's conditioned himself for what he had to endure. It's not going to be easy for him to adjust."

"How long?"

Aksenov extended his hands in a helpless gesture. "With the mind, it's impossible to say."

"Months?"

"Certainly months. We'll arrange outpatient treatment here, but it'll certainly take a long time." The psychiatrist saw the woman grip the chair and smiled sympathetically. "But he'll get better," he said. "I'm sure he'll get better."

"What must I do?"

"Convince him," advised Aksenov. "Convince him that you're his wife."

"You said he knew!" she reminded the man.

"Still convince him," said the man. "He's been a long time away from any woman, apart from those in the women's section of the camps." Aksenov tapped the file. "And there's no indication of his ever having been involved."

The psychiatrist was offering her evidence of Boris'

fidelity, she realized. "Thank you," she said.

"It won't be easy," Aksenov warned.

"I understand."

"But we'll do what we can to help you."

The release surprised Gusadarov. He'd expected to remain in detention; be entrained for a transit camp, perhaps. But they led him out to the same vehicle that had brought him here, and then the woman got in with him. And he knew they hadn't given up—that they were still trying. He had to pretend he believed them, until he worked out what was happening.

Rebecca smiled at him and he smiled back. He was immediately conscious of her expression faltering.

"Boris?" she said.

"Yes?"

"You know it's me, don't you? You know it's Rebecca."

"Yes," he said. "You're Rebecca." They should have gone to the trouble of finding out what she really looked like if they'd properly intended to confuse him. They were so stupid, sometimes.

"It's all right now, darling. Everything is going to be all right."

"Yes," he said.

The previous day Karpov had arranged a pass and coupons to the commissary, so that night Rebecca prepared fresh beef and vegetables, cabbage as well as potatoes. She bought wine, too. As she set the table she offered the bottle and the corkscrew to him, but he looked at it without comprehension, so she opened it. He ate as he always did, jamming food into his mouth. Rebecca sat opposite him, trying to keep any expression from her face, unable finally to look directly at him. Again she found it impossible to eat, drinking only the wine. He saw her and copied, gulping at it noisily and leaving the glass streaked with the grease stains from his fingers. She offered him more, which he drank, and then made him go to the bathroom to wash.

After Rebecca cleared the table, she sat in the living room, looking across at the man she had to make a life with. . . . *a long time away from any woman . . . there's no indication of his ever having been involved*. The psychiatrist's assurance echoed in her mind. And then something else the man had said. *Convince him that you're his wife*. Dear God, she thought; oh, dear God. Rebecca drank more wine, and when the bottle was finished wished she'd bought the brandy that had been on display, too. Tomorrow. She'd definitely get some tomorrow. They remained, unspeaking, for two hours in the room. Then, sighing, she said, "Bed."

When he didn't move at once, she wondered if she would have to go through the performance of the prison number, but then he shifted, going dutifully ahead of her. He undressed with the same awareness of his body, and she allowed him to store his clothing beneath the pillow, where it would be safe. It left her side free, at least. Dear God, she thought again. On their wedding night, the wedding night when he'd failed through too much drink, she'd undressed outside the bedroom, too shy for him to see her body. She wanted to again, now, but didn't. She turned sideways, though, conscious of his eyes on her as she took her clothes off.

Naked, she forced herself to confront him fully. She said, "I'm your wife, Boris."

He was lying rigidly when she pulled back the bedclothes, legs stiff, arms tight beside his body. His sex lay between his legs, sleeping. Rebecca got carefully beside him. Their bodies didn't touch. She turned off the light and lay on her back, like him.

"Boris," she said after a long time. He was so still and breathing so shallowly that she was practically unaware of his presence in the bed.

He gave no response.

"Boris," she said again. "Love me."

There was still nothing from the man beside her. The psychiatrist had warned her that it wouldn't be easy, she remembered. Rebecca turned toward her husband, feeling out for him. His body twitched when she touched him. His stomach was hard as she moved her hand across it and then down, and at last he responded. She stopped, guessing that he was coming toward her, wanting to give him control the moment he felt able.

Gusadarov knew now! It had been obvious from the beginning, but he hadn't identified what the entrapment was. But now he knew. He'd seen it happen before, the first time at Irkutsk and then again at Taishet. Female guards from the women's section lifting their skirts and unbuttoning their blouses and opening their legs, leading the prisoners on, letting them start to fuck them before screaming rape. The punishment was standarized. The men had been whipped to death, strapped against a triangular rack in the center of the camp, with everyone assembled to witness what was happening.

But he'd defeat them. Even now he'd defeat them.

His hand touched her breast, and she lifted herself toward him to make it easy. Which was her mistake—because it told him how she was lying. He snatched upward, grabbing her throat first with just one hand, bringing the other around at once to complete the grip.

The attack was so abrupt and so unexpected that Rebecca was unable to scream—unable to do anything. Her breath was cut off completely by the strength of his grip and she felt his body pressing down, as if he were trying to crush her as well. There was shock, too, so that almost at once she felt the first sweep of dizziness.

She thrust out instinctively—desperately—without any intention other than getting the weight off her and the band around her throat loosened. The fact that they were in bed saved her. His attack brought them to the edge, and her fighting took them over, so that they rolled onto the floor entangled in the sheets. As he fell, Gusadarov's head struck the side table. Momentarily his hold relaxed, and Rebecca jerked herself free, wheezing the breath into her lungs. She was still dizzy and completely disoriented. As she rolled across the floor, her hand touched the knocked-over lamp. Her first inclination was to use it as a weapon. She never knew what made her turn it on instead. Or how the way to control him came to her.

Gusadarov was on all fours, more animallike than she had ever seen him, even in the way he swung his head toward her. A predator seeking prey.

"Gusadarov!" She intended it to be more of a shout and for there to be more authority, but her throat was badly bruised and the word screeched from her. "You're Gusadarov, 7399204!"

His body moved toward her, to attack.

"Tell me your number!" Her voice was stronger now, less hysterical.

A sound came from him, and she was unsure if it was a grunt or a whimper.

"Your number!" she demanded.

"Seven three nine nine two zero four," he said.

Faintness engulfed her, from relief this time, and she was glad she was crouched on the floor. She was suddenly embarrassed to be naked in front of him.

"Again!" she ordered.

"Seven three nine nine two zero four," he said. Then he fell forward, still entangled in the sheet, and began to sob.

This had to be the one, because there weren't any more. Kurt Schroeder had checked every record and every directory and investigated every listing, looking for the recognizable face. So this had to be the one. He pressed the bell and stood back, hand ready around the butt of the Luger, the safety catch already off.

He wanted to see the face again, just briefly, before he fired.

A man he'd never seen before—a young man, not the face he knew—answered the door, looking out curiously at Schroeder's bewildered reaction and the way he fumbled with something in his pocket.

Haltingly the German managed the question, and the man smiled. "No," he said. "We've just moved in."

36

Karpov had the meeting in the government apartment on Kutuzovsky Prospekt to which his new position entitled him. He considered it important to get away from the official atmosphere of Dzershinsky Square, but he conceded to himself that there was another reason. He wanted further to impress Rebecca.

The stereo equipment was installed and fully operational, through a transformer, and all the furniture was imported from Finland. He guessed the style would be too modern for someone who had acquired the knowledge and taste for antiques that Rebecca possessed, but compared to most Moscow apartments—as elevated as some occupied by privileged members of the government—he knew his was exceptional.

He'd considered hospitality and then decided against it; she'd never seem to enjoy it in Vienna, not even during the celebration of her pending return to Moscow, and what had happened provided little excuse or cause for enjoyment. He was going to have to be extremely careful, for everything to happen as he wanted it to.

Rebecca was prompt, as she'd always been. She looked around the apartment as she entered. Karpov said apologetically, "It's quite good, considering what's available."

"It's very nice," said the woman. She wore a medical collar and her voice was hoarse.

"How are you?" asked Karpov. He was in one of the lounge suits she remembered from Vienna, the one with the predominant yellow checks.

"Quite well," she said. 'Apparently there were some small bones broken in my neck, but they'll heal.'

"You were lucky," he said.

"Yes."

The government apartments on the Prospekt are within a compound, but by arranging the seating Karpov had managed to achieve a view where the protective fences weren't visible. He put her in a chair with the best view.

"What about Boris?" he asked. He decided she was still a very beautiful woman. Not flashy, like the women he'd gone with in Vienna and the rest of Europe. But that had been just sex. He wanted more than that now. He wanted to settle down and not have to return alone every evening to this stark, overmodern place.

She gestured, and Karpov thought how lost she looked.

"No one knows," she said. "Some talk of paranoia, others of schizophrenia. The fact is that none of them has any idea."

"It was a ridiculous mistake," he said angrily, wanting to boast to her. "I've ordered an inquiry."

"Please don't," she said.

"You could have died!"

"It was a mistake, that's all. They had no way of knowing, from one examination. I don't want any more suffering."

"If that's what you want."

"Yes," she said. "That's what I want." For the first time since she'd entered the apartment she became aware of his nervousness. She dismissed the thought at once. Karpov had no reason for nervousness. He was a powerful man now. Too powerful, in fact, to have demands made of him. Except that he appeared solicitous. And having her here, instead of to his office, indicated a willingness to be friendly.

"I'll cancel it, then."

"Thank you."

"Can I get you something?" asked Karpov, changing his mind. "A drink? I've got everything."

"No, thank you," she said. Would Hugo be keeping his promise to control his intake? She hoped so.

"How long will he have to be detained?" Karpov inquired.

Rebecca didn't reply at once. Then she said, in a voice quieter than that necessary because of her throat, "No one is positive about that, either. But it could be permanent. Having made one mistake, they're being very cautious against another. A very long time, certainly. Years. He'll always need care."

It would be wrong to approach her now, Karpov decided; for weeks, even. It would have to evolve naturally, for both of them. He'd arrange theater and restaurant visits—maybe take her to the dacha that had been made available to him in the hills outside Moscow, always ensuring at first that there were separate sleeping arrangements. He didn't want to frighten her away. "It hasn't worked out at all, has it?"

"No," she said. "Not at all."

"I tried to help," he said.

"I know," she said. "I'm grateful. No one could have known what might happen."

"And I'd still like to. Help, I mean." That wasn't rushing her; that was letting her know she had a friend, someone she could trust and rely on.

Rebecca looked up at the remark. He *was* powerful enough, she supposed. But it was unthinkable. "Thank you," she said.

"Anything," insisted Karpov.

"That's kind."

"Have you thought of what you're going to do?"

"Not properly." That wasn't strictly true; she'd thought about what she'd like to do.

"You needn't worry about the apartment or the pension or the commissary rights," he said.

"That's good of you."

"You've earned it, all of it."

For the first time Rebecca fully appreciated how alone

she was. She was in a city she didn't know, among people she didn't know—apart from this one man—in an apartment like the prison her pitiful, demented husband had thought it to be. Dear God, why hadn't she run when she'd had the chance! Any life would have been better than the one she would now have to endure.

Karpov saw that she was retreating into her misery. She hadn't understood the first time. "If there's anything I can do, you have only to ask," he repeated.

She looked up at him without focus at first, the concentration coming gradually. Why not? He could refuse. Punish her. Punish both of them. But they were both being punished, whatever happened.

"There is something," she said.

"Anything."

"I want to go back to Vienna," she said. "Back to Hugo."

"Hugo!"

She misinterpreted his surprise as outrage, hurrying forward a defense. "I didn't realize it in Vienna. But I do now. I know now that I love him. That I want to be with him."

When Karpov didn't respond, Rebecca felt her control going. "Please!" she moaned and began crying.

Hartman didn't doubt her. He knew Rebecca meant to come back, after divorcing her husband. But he knew, too, that there had to be permission. Karpov might have promised to help, but his wasn't the ultimate decision. There were other people superior to him who could veto his intention. The undisposed ownership of the shop didn't appear as valid a reason for her returning as it had during the confused emotion of her departure. It was a legal thing, and legal things could be handled by lawyers.

He telephoned the salon twice toward the end of the second week, talking to the manager who knew him and who said nothing about any unexpected or unexplained disposal of the shop. But the reassurance was only temporary, rarely lasting the full day. He couldn't imagine life without Rebecca. She *was* his life now. He didn't know what he would do if she didn't come back—couldn't even consider the possibility.

He stopped bothering to go out, in case she telephoned and he missed her call, then to shave, and finally to bathe. On the Friday of the third week he drank most of a bottle of wine without any food and forgot about the pills. There was a sugar reaction and he became physically ill, frightening himself. On Saturday he was still unwell, but by Sunday had recovered sufficiently to clean up the disorder into which he'd let Rebecca's apartment fall, and then bath and shave himself. There was no food in the apartment, so he decided that he would go out for dinner and eat properly. She'd know if he'd been neglecting himself. And he'd promised not to.

He made a reservation for the Three Hussars and was on the point of leaving when the telephone rang. In his hurry to pick it up, Hartman dropped it. It clattered against the table, and when he finally got it to his ear he still didn't recognize her voice.

"Where are you?" he asked.

"Amsterdam," said Rebecca. "There's a connection to Vienna in half an hour."

Hartman felt the table edge for support, weak in his relief. Almost at once the fear came. "For how long?"

"For good, darling," said the woman. "He *was* a friend."

"But . . ."

"Not now," she stopped him. "They're calling the flight."

"I'll meet you."

"I want you to."

Hartman couldn't move immediately when he replaced

the telephone. He remained holding the table, eyes misted, and then finally wept openly, uncaring because nobody could see him. So long, he thought; he'd waited so long for this. And now it had happened, exactly as he had prayed it would. Maybe he'd been wrong in thinking there wasn't a God.

Hartman straightened, breaking the mood, and hurriedly wiped his eyes. Everything had to be right for her. He checked the airport to confirm the time of the incoming flight from Amsterdam and then telephoned the restaurant, postponing his reservation and increasing it to two. Nervously—as nervous as he had been all those months ago in Zurich—he went through the apartment again, making sure that there was no trace of his stupid collapse and that everything was as clean as she would expect it to be.

After an hour he stood surveying the apartment, wondering what else to do. Flowers! There weren't any flowers, and she always had flowers in every room.

He hurried down the curving stairway into the vestibule and then out into the street, momentarily unsure. Then he remembered the shop near St. Stephen's. It was closed, but Hartman could see the owner still inside, clearing the displays, so he rattled the handle until the man answered irritably. He calmed his annoyance at once by the size of his order. He only stopped when it was obvious he wouldn't be able to carry any more, stumping from the shop with his arms enclosing irises and gladioli and lillies and roses. It was difficult for him to see, and twice he collided with other pedestrians, smiling and laughing his apologies in his excitement.

It was dusk by the time he got back to Rebecca's apartment and completely dark inside the vestibule. With both arms full, he couldn't press the timed light easily, having to thrust against the button several times before it went in far enough to trigger the illumination.

Kurt Schroeder had been ready to do so, if Hartman hadn't bothered. He was determined not to miss. The German had followed the directions of the helpful new owner of Hartman's apartment and watched for days for Hartman to emerge and provide the confirmation he needed, because it was important that there not be any mistake. He'd actually begun to fear that Hartman had moved on again. When the Austrian had hurried out thirty minutes earlier, Schroeder had been unable completely to bite back the mew of anticipation. He imagined he'd have to do it in the street, which he hadn't intended, because he was determined to see the man's face just before it happened. Then Schroeder realized from his observation of the purchase of flowers that the old man meant to return.

Hartman was on the first step when the shout came, tinged with hysteria.

"Jew!"

Hartman turned, his euphoria still momentarily greater than his bewilderment.

"You killed my father!"

Then Hartman saw the gun, held by someone he'd never seen before in his life. The flower bundle sagged, and Schroeder said, "Yes, you're the one."

"No—" said Hartman, actually starting down the stairs and going toward the younger man.

Schroeder jerked back apprehensively, pulling at the trigger. The explosion was deafening, reverberating in the closed building. The bullet flew harmlessly wide, chipping stonework high above Hartman's head.

"No!" screamed Hartman a second time, and Schroeder giggled, excited by the other man's terror. Not a coward anymore, he thought. Schroeder grimaced in the concentration of taking better aim, and the gun roared again.

The bullet caught Hartman high in the shoulder, shattering his collarbone and sending him reeling backward against the stairway. Oddly, the pain of striking the stonework was greater than that of the wound. The flowers billowed upward but stayed linked together by their cord, falling back down over him like some brightly colored blanket. Hartman tried to push them away and clawed at the stairs, trying to pull himself up to the apartment to safety.

"Jew!" shouted Schroeder once more. He was close now, practically standing over Hartman, and this was the shot that killed him, penetrating his heart. He slumped back, still covered in the celebration blooms.

There had been a tailwind, so the flight from Amsterdam was ahead of time. At the moment Hartman died, Rebecca stepped from the aircraft, looking hopefully around the arrival terminal. She was early, she knew. She'd wait.